WHO KILLED THE DUVAL SISTERS?

Rain began to fall, droplets falling through the trees to the forest floor, the wind causing leaves to shiver. Nikki threw up the hood of her light jacket and kept walking. The questions that had been swirling in her mind propelled her onward. Why were the Duval girls taken from the theater? To kill them? Why bury them here at the Beaumont estate? What was the connection? Or was this place chosen randomly? Who would know about the secret hiding spot? Margaret Duval? Nurse to Beulah? Mother of the sisters who were killed? And why or how did Rose escape? Was that all part of the plan? *Whose* plan?

Who had access to the house? The Beaumonts? Baxter or Connie-Sue, his wife, or his son, Tyson? Margaret Duval who had once been the nurse here—mother of the victims? Or any of the Cravens? Wynn or Jasper or Bronco? They had access and their cabin had once belonged to the Beaumonts.

Or someone connected to the Marianne Inn? That old lodge kept coming up and the boat that she thought she'd seen beneath the drooping branches of the willow tree. Who was in that boat?

The rain kept falling ever faster, the path growing muddy, leaves dripping. Nikki feeling that she was getting closer to finding out the truth, but missing something vital, the link that brought it all together . . .

Books by Lisa Jackson

Published by Kensington Publishing Corp.

LISA JACKSON

THE THIRD GRAVE

ZEBRA BOOKS

Kensington Publishing Corp.

www.kensingtonbooks.com

ZEBRA BOOKS are published by

Kensington Publishing Corp.
119 West 40th Street
New York, NY 10018

All Kensington titles, imprints, and distributed lines are available at special quantity discounts for bulk purchases for sales promotion, premiums, fund-raising, educational, or institutional use.

Special book excerpts or customized printings can also be created to fit specific needs. For details, write or phone the office of the Kensington Sales Manager: Attn.: Sales Department. Kensington Publishing Corp., 119 West 40th Street, New York, NY 10018. Phone: 1-800-221-2647.

Zebra and the Z logo Reg. U.S. Pat. & TM Off.

First Kensington Books Hardcover Printing: July 2021
First Zebra Books Mass-Market Paperback Printing: August 2022

ISBN-13: 978-1-4201-4907-4
ISBN-13: 978-1-4967-2225-6 (ebook)

10 9 8 7 6 5 4 3 2 1

Printed in the United States of America

THE
THIRD
GRAVE

CHAPTER 1

Bronco Cravens was sweating bullets.

Not only because of the heat from an intense Georgia sun.

But from his own damned case of nerves.

He rubbed his fingers together in anticipation but didn't move, just searched the undergrowth through narrowed eyes one last time. He tuned in to the sounds of the lowland: the lap of water against the muddy banks, the whir of dragonfly wings as the narrow-bodied creatures darted along the shore and the tonal croak of a bullfrog hiding somewhere in the reeds.

The air was still and thick. Sultry enough to paste his shirt to his body.

His nerves were stretched thin, his blood running hot at the thought of what he was about to do. He searched the heavy undergrowth for any kind of movement and licked his already-chapped lips. Sunlight and shadow played through the Spanish moss–draped live oaks, but he saw no one, no flicker of movement, felt no eyes boring into his back.

Squinting, he tried to distinguish sunlight from shadow through these dense woods. The swollen river moved quickly in a soft rush, mosquitoes buzzing near his head, but he heard nothing out of the ordinary.

No sounds of footfalls or twigs snapping. No murmur of hushed voices or the crunch of tires on old gravel just over the rise. No whine of a distant siren.

No, it seemed, he was all alone.

Good.

No time to lose.

He patted his pockets, had the keys, his cell phone, a flashlight and his pistol, a Ruger LCP, a lightweight semi-automatic that was forever with him. All set. "Let's go," he hissed, glancing over his shoulder to his boat, where the dog he'd inherited sat at attention, ears cocked, waiting for a command. Fender had been a gift from Darla. The dog was a purebred bluetick heeler if the previous owner were to be believed. But that was before Darla had left suddenly, slamming the door behind her while screaming, "Don't you ever call me again, you fuckin' loser! And you can keep the damned dog."

He had. Kept the dog, that was. And yeah, he'd never phoned or texted again. Nor had she tried to contact him. Which was just fine.

Today, bringing the heeler along may have been a mistake. Sleek coat glistening in the sun, Fender leapt over the edge of the boat to land in the shallows and followed as Bronco took off, running, his boots sinking into the thick mud. Fleetingly Bronco remembered playing on the grounds as a child, fishing, catching snakes and bullfrogs, skipping stones across the pond, watching dragonflies skim the surface, their wings crackling, sunlight catching on their iridescent bodies. He'd run this path often as a kid, but it had been years since he'd taken out his father's fishing boat or stole some of his Camel Straights, or hid a six-pack in the old culvert. Back then, those had been the worst of his sins.

Now, of course, there were others.

More than he wanted to count.

Now the stakes were a damned sight higher than pissing off his old man and risking Jasper Cravens's considerable wrath. But he wouldn't dwell on that now, couldn't dare think about his run-ins with the law. Just the thought of prison, of being hauled back to a cement-walled cell, made his skin crawl. He couldn't go back there. Wouldn't.

And yet, here he was. Trespassing. Tempting fate. Intending to break into the Beaumont mansion, where his grandfather had once been caretaker and had sworn the old lady who had lived there had secreted a fortune. His blood ran hotter at the thought of it. Wynn Cravens had admitted he'd seen the rare gold and silver coins, some dating back to the Civil War, along with a cache of jewels and silver certificates and thousands of dollars that old Beulah Beaumont had secreted in the basement of the once-grand home. Beulah had been mad as a hatter, Gramps had claimed, but he'd sworn the valuables were there—viewed with his own eyes.

Bronco was about to find out.

And change his life.

He grinned at the thought.

No time to lose.

Sunlight was already beginning to fade.

Yesterday's hurricane, named Jules and a goddamned category five, had torn through this part of Georgia, leveling homes, splintering trees and flooding the city. Telephone and electric poles had been uprooted, the power was out for miles, and cell phone service patchy at best.

A disaster for most of the citizens of Savannah.

And a blessing for Bronco.

He crested a rise, a natural levee that had kept most of the flood waters surrounding the old home within the river's banks. From the corner of his eye, he caught a flash. Movement. His heart nearly stopped. But it was just his stupid dog taking off through the tall grass, startling two ducks. Wings flapping noisily, quacking loudly, they took flight.

Shit!

His heart leapt to his throat, but he heard no footsteps, or shouts, or sirens, or baying of hounds.

Good. Just keep moving.

Get in.

Find what you're looking for.

Get out.

No more than fifteen minutes.

Twenty, tops.

He saw the sagging fence with its rusted NO TRESPASSING sign dangling from the locked gate and vaulted over what was left of the mesh, then spied the house, built on a rise, surrounded by live oaks, the once-manicured lawn surrendering to brush. The whitewashed siding was now gray and dimpled, paint peeling, roof sagging and completely collapsed around one of four crumbling chimneys.

For half a beat, Bronco stared up at the house, its windows shuttered and boarded over, graffiti scrawled across the buckling sheets of plywood, the wide wraparound porch listing on rotted footings.

His grandfather's voice whispered to him: *Don't do it, son. Don't. This—what y'er contemplating—is a mistake, y'hear me? It'll only bring you trouble, the kind of trouble no man wants.* He set his jaw and ignored the warning. He'd waited long enough. Now, finally, the old man was dead. As if Wynn Cravens had heard his thoughts, his raspy voice came again: *Boy, you listen to me, now.*

Bronco didn't.

Y'er gonna get caught, Wynn Cravens cautioned from beyond the grave. *Sure as shootin'. And then what? Eh? Another five years in prison? Hell, maybe ten! Could be more. Don't do it, son.*

"Oh, shut up," Bronco growled under his breath. Something he would have never said to his big, strapping grandfather if the man were still alive. Of course he wasn't. Wynn Cravens had given up the ghost just two weeks earlier, his big heart stopping while the old guy was splitting wood.

With Wynn's passing, Bronco's fortune had changed.

This was his big chance, maybe his last chance, and Bronco was going to make the best of it. After all of the bad breaks in his life, finally something good was coming his way. He took the hurricane as an omen. A sign from God Himself.

Right now all of the cops and emergency workers were busy being heroes.

Which gave Bronco some time.

From the corner of his eye he caught a glimmer of

movement, a blur through the trees. Not the dog this time. Fender was right on his heels.

He felt his skin crawl. There had always been rumors of ghosts haunting the grounds, lost souls who'd found no escape from the tarnished history of the Beaumont family. Bronco, though he hated admitting it, couldn't help believing some of the old stories that had been whispered from one generation to the next. Even his grandfather, a brawny no-nonsense Welshman, had believed that tortured spirits moved through the stands of live oak and pine and had sworn on the family Bible that he'd seen the ghost of Nellie Beaumont, a seven-year-old girl who drowned in the river in the late 1990s. Bronco knew nothing more than that her death had devastated the family. Glimpses of the girl had always been reported the same: a waif in a dripping nightgown, dark ringlets surrounding a pale face, a doll clutched to her chest as she forever wandered along the edge of the water.

And the sightings hadn't stopped with Gramps. Bronco's father, too, a man of the cloth, had sworn he'd seen the ghost, though Bronco thought Jasper Cravens's glimpse of the apparition had been the result of his affection for rye whiskey rather than an actual viewing of a bedraggled spirit. And hadn't he once, while sneaking through these very woods, thought he'd caught sight of a pale, ghostlike figure darting through the underbrush?

He'd told himself the apparition had been a figment of his imagination, but now, the thought of any kind of wraith caused the hairs on the back of his arms to ripple to attention.

"A crock," Bronco reminded himself just as he spied a deer, a damned white-tailed doe, bounding through a copse of spindly pine.

He made his way toward the back of the house, through weeds and tall grass to the listing veranda that stretched across the rear of the house and offered a view of the terraced lawn and bend in the river. Quickly across the rotting floorboards, he walked to the side door, the one his grandfather and the rest of the staff had used. He slid the key from his pocket, sent up a prayer for good luck, then slipped the key into the lock. A twist of his wrist and . . . nothing. The key didn't budge.

"Shit."

He tried again, forcing the key a bit. Shoving it hard.

Once more the lock held firm.

"Goddamn it!" Just his luck. After waiting all this time, after planning and hoping and . . . this always happened to him! In an instant he saw his decades-long dream of wealth disintegrate into dust. Maybe he'd have to break through the old plywood covering the windows. But that would take too long, be too noisy.

"Fuck it." He wasn't going to give up. Not yet. Setting his jaw, he jammed the key in again, then suddenly stopped. This was all wrong.

He'd watched the old man do this a hundred times.

He remembered his grandfather babying the lock.

Bronco tried again but didn't force the key in hard, "gentled it," as Gramps used to say. *Like dealing with a hotheaded woman, son, you got to tread softly, touch her gentle-like.*

"Come on. Come on—"

Click!

The bolt gave way and the door creaked open.

He was in! Quickly, his heart hammering, his nerves strung tight, he stepped into a small vestibule with a narrow set of stairs running up and down and a door leading into the kitchen. He headed down the curved steps to find another door at another landing. Unlocked, it swung open easily to reveal yawning blackness and a horrid stench that seemed to waft upward in a cloud. Nearly gagging, he pulled a rag to cover his mouth from one pocket and a small flashlight from another. God, the smell of rot and decay was overpowering. He switched on the flashlight and descended the final flight to step into three or four inches of water, black and brackish and thick with sludge.

This better be worth it.

He skimmed the standing water with the beam of his flashlight and tried not to think of what creatures might nest down here—rats and gators and water moccasins or black widows hidden in dark places.

Don't go there. Don't think about what could be living down here. Concentrate, Cravens. Find the loot and get the hell out before you get caught.

Ducking beneath raw beams black with age, rusted hooks and nails protruding, he slogged through years of forgotten furniture, books, pictures, all ruined and decaying. The flashlight's beam skated over the water and mud, across broken-down chairs and crates stacked atop each other.

A spider web brushed his face and he felt a skittering of fear slide down his spine.

This place was getting to him. Too dark, too smelly, too . . .

Scritttcch.

He froze at the sound.

What the hell?

His heart went into overdrive, thudding wildly.

He whirled, swinging the beam of the flashlight past a

listing armoire to . . . oh, shit! A dark, disjointed figure stared back at him!

Bronco jumped backward, startled. Automatically he reached for his Ruger. Someone was down here! A weird apparition that, too, was staring at him while scrabbling for a weapon and pointing a beam of a high-powered flashlight at his face. Reacting, Bronco fired just as he realized his mistake.

Blam!

The dirty mirror shattered.

His own distorted image splintered into a hundred shards of glass that flew outward, glittering crazily in his flashlight's beam. "Shit!"

A rat squealed and scurried between several stacks of boxes.

Freaked, Bronco took aim at the rodent but stopped himself before pulling the trigger. The damned rat was the least of his problems. If anyone had heard the gun go off, they'd come and investigate. *Shit, shit, shit!*

"No way," he said under his breath. He just had to work faster.

Get in. Get out.

That was the plan.

Gramps had said there was some sort of hiding space at the southeast corner of the foundation, a deeper cache where he'd seen Beulah Beaumont hide her valuables.

So find it already.

Pushing aside a bike with flat tires propped against a post, he kept moving, still bent over as he stepped around a pile of empty bottles that had been stacked near the brick foundation. He ran the beam over ancient bricks stacked nearly four feet tall that made up the foundation.

Carefully, he eyed the mortar, searching for any cracks and—in a second he saw the seam. Partially hidden by an ancient armoire, he noticed a flaw in the design where the pattern of the bricks changed.

The old man hadn't lied.

With renewed effort, he held the flashlight in his teeth and shoved one shoulder against the armoire, shoving the heavy chest to one side, wedging it tight against a stack of stained boxes. Sure enough, the seam was the outline of a small door cut into the bricks.

He just had to figure out how to open it. He had no more keys, no crowbar, but as he shined his light over the seam in the bricks, he ran the tips of his fingers over the rough edges of the mortar.

No knob.

No pull.

No handle of any kind.

Damn.

There had to be a way.

More carefully he touched the edges of the seam again but . . . nothing. "Come on, come on," he muttered in frustration.

No one said it would be easy, but he could use an effin' break.

Thump, thump, thump, thump!

The noise thundered through the basement.

Bronco froze.

What the hell?

Oh, shit! Someone was running across the porch!

No!

Had he closed the outside door? Locked it behind him?

Hell, no!

Crap!

Why was anyone out here after the damned storm?

In one motion, he ducked, dimmed his flashlight and raised his gun, his eyes trained laser-sharp on the foot of the stairs, where only the faintest shaft of illumination was visible. Sweat drizzled into his eyes.

Could he really do it?

Kill a man? Or a woman? Or a damned kid?

Crap, crap, crap!

Heavy breathing, more thumping as whoever it was rounded that final landing.

Oh, Jesus. Someone heard the shot! That's what it was!

Bronco's finger tightened over the trigger.

In a blur of motion a shadow leaped from the final steps.

He fired—*Bang!*—and caught a glimpse of shiny fur as an animal yelped as if in pain, or scared and out of his mind.

No! His stupid dog! Jesus Christ, he'd just killed his damned dog!

The shot was still ringing in his ears but still, he heard a pitiful whine and scrambling paws. "Boy . . . here, boy."

The heeler was at his side in an instant, unhurt, just scared and shaking, brown eyes bulging. But no blood. Bronco checked with his flashlight, running the beam over the dog's mottled coat. "You idiot," Bronco muttered, but gave the shivering animal a quick scratch behind his ears. "I coulda killed . . . oh, hell . . ." There was no time for this. Now there had been two shots fired. No telling who might've heard them. One could have been dismissed, but two? Nope. No way. He had to work fast.

To the dog, he whispered, "You stay. You hear me? Don't move a muscle."

Fender whined, his tail tucked between his legs, his body trembling.

Shit!

Bronco couldn't worry about it. He had less time than ever. He had to find the release for the door. And fast.

He swept the light over the beams, searching for electrical wires that would lead him to a switch for the small brick portal, even though, if that were the case, if the catch on the door was electrically controlled, he was screwed. The power to the house had been shut off long ago.

Think, Bronco, think. This has to be simple. Something you're missing! What had Gramps said? Something about a combination?

He returned to the door, crouched beside it, ran the flashlight's beam over the dirty bricks once more.

From the corner of his eye he saw the dog nosing around again, but ignored him. Right now he had to concentrate. Crouching low, Bronco took a step backward, ran the flashlight over the door again and . . . he saw it. A chip on one of the lower bricks that was slightly different from the others. Smoother. A long shot, but he knelt in the muck, placed his finger in the small divot and waited for a click.

Nothing.

Yet . . . then he spied another, similar notch on the brick above. He touched it. Again, zilch.

Get in.

Get out.

Fender crept up to him. Curious. Nosing around.

Bronco ignored the dog and tried several times to open the latch. But nothing happened.

This had to be it. Right?

The dog whined, the hackles on the back of his neck bristling, but Bronco was deep in concentration before he noticed the third notch on a brick that abutted the other two.

Tentatively, sweat dripping from his nose, he placed a finger on the notch. Still nothing. Damn. Maybe he was way off base with this.

Fender, muscles tense, let out a low growl.

"Hush!" Bronco muttered. He couldn't be bothered with the dog right now. He rocked back on his heels holding the beam steady on the small door. No more notches. Just the three in those abutting bricks. That had to mean something. Had to. He chewed on his lip. What if he touched all three impressions at once? What were the chances?

Again the dog let out a warning growl, but Bronco paid no attention.

He leaned forward, placed his fingertips into the holes one at a time. Nothing budged. He tried again, this time touching all of the indentations simultaneously.

Over the low rumble of Fender's warning growl, he heard a soft, but distinct click.

His heart hammered. He licked his lips. But nothing moved. "Damn." This had to be it. Nervously, knowing he was on the brink, he tried again, then on inspiration, pushed on the rough bricks, rather than waiting for the door to magically open.

It gave!

Scraping loudly as he shoved on it, the door slid slowly inward. The scents of dust and dry rot sifted out.

He was in!

Bronco could have shouted for joy.

All the years of waiting!

As Bronco leaned forward, shining his light into the dry space beyond, the stupid mutt gave out an eerie whine. "Shut up," Bronco said, leaning forward. He peered into the dark, tight cavern, sweeping the beam of his flashlight over the interior, expecting to find a cache of unimaginable treasure.

But no.

No glittering gems or stacks of bills.

Instead . . .

What the hell?

What the bloody hell?

The flashlight's beam landed on a skull.

A human skull.

With empty black sockets where eyes had once been, the jaw open, teeth visible in an eerie grin of death, the fleshless face seemed to stare straight into the bottom of Bronco's soul.

He let out a scream before he saw the second skull, next to the first, smaller and just as long dead. The clothes on the bodies were tatters, blouses, one with a bra, shorts and sneakers. Bits of jewelry winking in the flashlight's glare.

Oh, fuck!

Kids!

Fuck! Fuck! Fuck!

Frantically, he scrambled backward, as if expecting the

skeletons to stand and start chasing him. He stood quickly, his head cracking painfully against a rough beam.

His knees buckled, but only for an instant.

Then he ran. Knocking over boxes and bins, banging his knee against a forgotten chest of drawers, Bronco Cravens ran as he'd never run before.

CHAPTER 2

"You buyin' this?" Detective Sylvie Morrisette asked from the passenger seat of Reed's Jeep. His partner for years, she was a small, compact woman made up of west Texas grit and muscle. Her platinum-colored hair was spiked, a tattoo of a snake's tail visible at her neckline and she didn't give a rat's ass about what anyone in the department, or anywhere else for that matter, thought about her. And right now she was irritated. Disbelieving, scratching her chin as she thought, her eyes laser-focused through the bug-spattered windshield.

"Buying what?" Reed asked, taking yet another detour out of Savannah. The hurricane had torn through the city, destroying buildings, smashing cars and uprooting hundred-year-old trees. Power poles had been mangled and leveled, parts of the town flooded, and every city

worker was working overtime to get the town's basic ser-
vices restored. Traffic was being diverted by road crews
from the city and power company. Many streets had been
cordoned off where trees and electrical wires had been
downed. Some roofs had been blown off, exposing the in-
teriors of damaged homes. Cars had been overturned or
stalled in the flood waters, sign posts twisted in the violent winds, most traffic lights dead. Traffic, what little
there was of it, was stalled and crawled through detoured
streets as the main arterial roads were being cleared.

"Buying what?" she repeated. "Sheesh, Reed. You
know what I mean. That some dick found a body in the
basement of the old Beaumont mansion," she said, her
weathered face screwing up in thought. "I mean, what the
hell? Who was out there?"

"Don't know. Yet."

"And they were just out there after a category five?
Right on the river? Makes no sense." She cracked her
window, allowed some air to rush in. "Whoever it was, he
was up to no good. Or jerking our damned chains!"

He wasn't about to argue that. Sylvie Morrisette was
in a mood, as in a bad mood. Detective Pierce Reed had
been her partner for enough years to recognize the signs.
Today she was fidgety and sharp-tongued, well, sharper
than usual, and she was popping Tums as if they were
going out of style. Morrisette had grown up in west
Texas, her drawl still evident, was prickly by nature and
had been married four times—bang, bang, bang, bang in
her twenties, though she quit tying the knot after her
fourth husband and father of her children had turned out
to be "a real prize, if you're into bullshit awards." Now,
her lips pursed, her eyes squinting through the windshield, she was definitely antsy.

"Jesus, Reed, could you drive any slower?" She shook out the last two tablets from the plastic bottle and tossed it onto the floor.

"You okay?" he asked.

"Fine. Just a little heartburn."

"A little?"

"Yeah! That's what I said. And why the hell are you drivin' like an old lady?"

Traffic was stacked in front of him. He sent her a questioning glance. Where the hell did she expect him to go?

"You could hit the lights and siren, y'know." She twisted her neck until it cracked, then fiddled with the air conditioning, then played with the automatic windows, something she did when she was nervous. "Shit, I could use a smoke right about now. I know, I know." She held up a palm. She'd given up cigarettes years before. "And if I dared come home with even a whiff of tobacco on me, Priscilla would have a shit-fit." She rolled her eyes. "My daughter has taken the position that she's the rule keeper at the house at seventeen. As if!" She let out a long-suffering sigh. "But it gets worse."

"It does?"

"Oh, yeah." Nodding, she said, "Get this: Toby wants to go live with his father. Like that's some sort of threat or something. I think it's because my brilliant ex promised the kid a car when he turns sixteen." She ran a hand through her spiky hair and let out a huff of disgust. "Like that would ever happen. As if Bart would want a thirteen-year-old cramping his style." Rolling her eyes, she said, "And his sister. Seventeen going on goddamned thirty! Do you know how many times a week I hear that Priscilla is 'almost eighteen'?" She made halfhearted finger quotes as Reed glanced at the GPS screen, searching for a faster way through the town. "Teenagers."

"We were all there once," he said.

"Oh, yeah. I was hell on wheels. Don't know how my mother survived," she admitted as Reed slowed to a stop, waiting for a member of a road crew to wave them around scattered debris—branches, limbs, and a shattered window pane, the aftermath of a live oak crashing down on a garage. Not only was the roof of the garage collapsed on the sedan inside, but a pickup that had been parked in the drive had been totaled. A photographer was taking pictures, while a heavyset worker in a hard hat, orange vest and a sour expression beneath the shadow of a beard waved them through.

"Some detour," Morrisette muttered ungraciously. "Seriously, this is the best they can do? One lane?"

"Give 'em a break, will ya? It'll get better."

"Let's hope. Or it will be midnight by the time we get out there."

"It's less than three miles."

"Exactly!"

Reed was waved through and picked up speed.

Morrisette said, "I just can't believe someone found bodies out there. In the basement of the old house? How likely is that? I mean, there aren't that many cellars out here, especially not on the flood plain."

"It's an old house."

"That's what I'm talkin' about! A basement? Maybe a root cellar . . . but a full-on basement? I dunno."

"Anyone talk to the Beaumonts?"

"Yeah, I expect they'll show up. The deputy who called

the son, Tyson, said he freaked out that bodies had been found on the place." She glanced at Reed. "Well, duh."

"Anything else?"

"The deputy said we'd be over to talk to them, but Tyson said he was gonna round up his old man, so I expect they'll show up."

"Good," Reed said. "Let's see what they have to say. Maybe they can shed some light."

"My thoughts exactly."

An anonymous caller had phoned in to 911 to report a body in the basement of the old Beaumont house. A male who refused to identify himself. Reed had listened to the call; the guy had been freaked out of his mind, his voice raspy and strained. "I-I mean, I saw. Oh, Jesus . . . there are bodies at the Beaumont estate . . . in the basement . . . oh, Holy Christ . . . two . . . maybe more, I don't know. Just . . . just fuckin' skeletons."

The operator had asked, "Sir, could you give me your name?"

"Didn't you hear me? For the love of God, they're *dead!*"

"Sir, please, if you could calm down and give me your name and address."

"I told you. At the fuckin' Beaumont estate out on Old Carriage Road. In the fuckin' basement."

"Sir—"

"They're girls! Didn't you hear me? Dead girls! In the fuckin' basement!"

And then he'd clicked off. Without giving his name or whereabouts or any information on how he'd come across the bodies and why he'd been on the grounds in the first place. But they had his number, and even as the first deputies had been dispatched to the scene, the department was working to ID the caller. Reed wanted to be first in line to talk to the guy, whoever the hell he was.

"Why wouldn't the guy who called emergency identify himself?"

"Because he doesn't want to be known, be a part of it."

"Maybe he's the killer?"

"If it's a homicide. But unlikely."

"What? You think it might be something else? Like kids playing and getting caught in the basement and dying?" she scoffed.

"We don't know yet."

"*You* don't know yet. My money's on murder." Folding her arms over her chest, she raised an eyebrow to stare at him. "What d'ya say? Five bucks?"

He wanted to counter with, *Fine, you're on.* But he couldn't. Because she was probably right. "No bet."

"Thought so. Anyway, I've got one of the newbies, Delacroix, trying to run down the phone call. Maybe we'll get lucky."

"Maybe," he said without any conviction as they slowed and eased around another utility truck, its amber lights flashing. "The call could have come in on a burner phone. No trace."

"Hell, Reed, let's not go there yet." She shot him a look that could cut through steel.

"Just sayin'."

"Well, don't. Okay? Would it kill you to try to think positive?"

"Like you?"

"Oh, fuck you," she said, but scared up the hint of a smile as he cut through a neighborhood going to seed,

took a side street and finally connected to the highway.
He hit the gas. When they rolled up to the gates of the old
Beaumont estate, they weren't the first. Three cop cars, a
cruiser and two SUVs, blocked the entrance.

A deputy for the Chatham County Sheriff's Department was posted at the rusted gate. Reed had met her several times. Tina Rounds, a tall, no-nonsense policewoman
with a dour expression, her springy black hair pulled
tightly away from her face, her hat square on her head.
She made them sign in and display their badges despite
knowing who they were. By "The Book" all the way.

The sun was hanging low in the sky, the air muggy despite the canopy of branches overhead. Together they
walked along a winding lane that had once been gravel
but now was two faint ruts separated by a band of grass
and weeds. A few birds twittered in the heavy, still air,
and a snake, shining like silver, twisted quickly out of
sight, slithering away through the knee-high grass.

Leaves and branches littered the lane, and a long,
rusted real-estate sign was wedged into a larger limb that
partially blocked their access. "You'd think if you owned
a place like this, you'd take care of it better," Morrisette
observed.

"Unless you just wanted to subdivide it into parcels."

"Humph." Around a final bend, the live oaks and
pines opened to a small rise where the old house stood. It
may have once been grand, but now it was waiting for a
bulldozer to put an end to its steady and imminent de-
cline. "Sad," she said as they walked to the front door,
which was securely locked, then made their way to the
back of the house and the open doorway, where Phil
Carter, another deputy for the county, was waiting. About

five-ten and trim, with blue eyes cut deep into his skull and the ravages from teenage acne still visible, he was a good cop who was known as "Crater," the nickname having been pinned on him by a bully of a football coach twenty years earlier.

They knew each other. No introductions necessary. "This way," he said, and they followed him past a bank of boarded-over French doors to a side entrance most likely used by delivery people and servants back in the day.

"What've you got?" Reed asked.

"Nothin' good," Crater said, the trace of a Georgia drawl evident. "Two bodies. Maybe more. Been there a while. Other than that, the place is clear. No one else inside."

"Forced entry?" Morrisette was eyeing the dingy doorjamb.

"Nope. Door wide open. But it hadn't been open for long. Wasn't wet inside. And that storm would've poured gallons inside." He led them down a narrow, curving staircase to a basement where Reed couldn't quite straighten without bumping his head on ancient beams. He sank into water and mud that had collected. Maybe the rain hadn't gotten into the stairwell above, but it sure as hell had seeped through windows or cracks in the foundation.

"Swell," Morrisette said as she sank into the mud. "Just . . . swell."

They sloshed past piles of discarded furniture, clothing and equipment to a spot on the far wall where an entrance led to a cavern of sorts, where a door, now open, had been cut into the brick foundation. "In there," he said, and shined the high-wattage beam into the musty, dark space, where the smell of old death lingered and two small corpses were visible.

Reed's stomach clenched.

The flesh on each body had long rotted away, the bones of small skeletons stark and white, tufts of blond hair still attached to each weirdly grinning skull, the clothes disintegrating but recognizable. One of the small frames was still covered by a dingy blouse and skirt, a bra visible beneath the tattered fabric, a chain encircling the neck bones, a locket resting on the sternum glinting in the flashlight's beam.

Reed fought nausea.

The smaller skeleton was clad in shorts with a belt and a faded blue T-shirt, along with tattered sneakers that appeared identical to those worn by the larger skeleton, a ring on one finger.

"Holy Mother of God," Morrisette whispered as she peered inside the crypt. "They're just girls. Priscilla had shoes almost like those. Keds. What the hell happened here?"

Reed didn't answer, just studied the crypt, his jaw tightening, his thoughts darkening. Had the girls died here? He didn't think so because of the positioning of the victims. They had been laid side by side, the bony fingers of the older girl's hand entwined with those of the smaller child.

"You don't think this was some kind of weird suicide pact, do you?" Morrisette was looking at the clasped hands.

"What? No." He couldn't imagine anyone would put themselves into this dark hole on purpose and slowly die of either lack of oxygen or starvation or madness.

"Or a game of, like, hide-and-seek gone bad? No one

found them and quit looking?" But even as she posed the thought, she was shaking her head. "Nah, course not. Someone killed these girls and put them in here. Placed their hands together. *Arranged* them just so. What kind of a sick jerk-wad would do that?"

Reed didn't know. Serial killers sometimes staged the positioning of their victims to throw off the police, or posed them to fulfill some kind of fantasy. But in this case, bodies locked away as they were for what appeared to be years, possibly decades, why would anyone go to the trouble?

Reed felt sick inside.

This tight, dank place was getting to him.

Yeah, he'd seen more than his share of death and mutilated bodies. Had witnessed firsthand how malevolent one person could be to another, but this . . .

Carter swung the beam of his flashlight to an empty space between the smaller victim and the wall of the crypt. "Look at that," the deputy said, shining the bright light over the small depression in the dirt floor of the crypt. "Don't that look like another spot for, y'know, another one?"

"Another body," Morrisette clarified. "You mean, like he wasn't finished or got interrupted?"

"Or used another spot," Carter suggested.

Reed's stomach clenched again. The deputy was right. The first two bodies were lying side by side, yes, but each nestled in a small, carved-out spot in the floor, their joined hands slightly elevated on the rim of dirt between them. Next to the smaller of the two another shallow indent was visible, just large enough for a third body.

"Holy crap," Morrisette whispered. She straightened

and ran a hand through her near-white hair. "Any other bodies?"

"Not that I saw. Been through the top two floors and looked through all the stuff down here. Found nothing. But I guess there could be more inside here. Y'know, buried beneath these. Stacked like sardines in a can. Or maybe there's another crypt here somewhere." He swept the beam over the interior of the tomb again. "Who's to say?"

Reed asked, "Crime scene team?"

"On their way," Carter said. "Same with the ME."

Reed eyed the mess in the basement. "Might need cadaver dogs."

"And a hazmat unit," Morrisette said. "C'mon. I've seen enough down here. Let's check the rest of the house." She was already heading for the stairs.

They took the narrow servants' steps to the top floor, intending to work their way down. The attic/maids' quarters was dark and dank, stuffed to the gills; some of the rooms were exposed to the elements as a portion of the roof had collapsed near the chimney. The sky was visible here, treetops swaying slightly, clouds skittering high overhead. Water from the recent storm pooled on the buckling floors and seeped under the stacked, already-moldering boxes, crates and baskets. What had been stored here—boxes of clothes, an old sewing kit and treadle machine, books and records—were long ruined and scattered by nesting squirrels or birds or whatever.

Morrisette said, "I'm surprised this whole house didn't come down with the hurricane. Can't be safe up here. Let's go."

The second floor had been stripped of most of the furniture, the remaining bedframes stacked against the walls of four massive bedrooms complete with fireplaces. A large, intricately tiled bathroom had been stripped of fixtures aside from a stained claw-foot tub, and the center ballroom was devoid of its chandelier, electrical wires exposed, a few crystals scattered and broken on the stained, intricately laid hardwood floor below. Layers of spider webs and insect carcasses clung to the windowsills while water from the floor above dripped from bowed ceilings.

"Nothin' here," Morrisette observed, frowning. "Hard to believe anyone would let this happen, y'know."

"Too expensive to keep up?"

"Too greedy to spend the time and money to keep it up, most likely. More money in sectioning it off, I guess," she said sourly.

On the main floor, dark because the windows had been boarded over with waterlogged plywood, they picked their way through the kitchen. Cabinets and appliances were either broken or missing, the dirty floor uneven, evidence of rodents visible on the loose tiles as the grout had crumbled away. Morrisette trained her flashlight on an overflowing garbage bag stuffed near the dumbwaiter, and a rat, fat and dark, scurried from the bag and through a hole in the woodwork, its thin tail snaking behind.

"Nice," Morrisette remarked, skimming the light behind a rusting, ancient stove. "Just peachy."

The dining room was mostly empty, though a broken-down piano missing keys had been shoved against a huge, blackened fireplace, its tiles cracked or fallen. In the parlor or main living area, the stained wallpaper peeled from the wall, exposing previous layers.

She shined her flashlight up the broad, curving staircase in the foyer, where balusters had splintered and several steps had rotted through.

"Looks clear," Morrisette said. "Like Crater said, no more bodies. No bad guys hiding in any closets. No squatters. Just squirrels in the attic and rats down here."

"And two dead bodies in the basement."

She nodded. "Let's hope we don't find any more."

Amen, he thought. Two was more than enough.

CHAPTER 3

Her abdomen was still flat as a board.

Her red-blond hair caught in a messy bun, Nikki Gillette turned slowly in front of the full-length mirror. She was wearing only her bra and panties as she surveyed her image. Still no hint of the baby growing within her and she was ten weeks pregnant. Ten weeks! After months of trying to conceive and two heartbreaking miscarriages within the first weeks of pregnancy, she finally was closing in on her second trimester. "You hang in there," she whispered to her unborn child, then pulled on a T-shirt and jeans that were, she had to admit, a little snug around the waist. But she didn't care. Not at all.

Bring on the ice cream.

Bring on the donuts.

Whatever the baby inside her wanted, she'd devour . . . well, within reason. She hurried downstairs and flopped onto the couch as her phone started to buzz. News alerts. She was, after all, still a reporter for the *Savannah Sentinel* and had to keep abreast of what was going on.

Probably something about Hurricane Jules, which had thankfully not destroyed the old historic part of Savannah, where she called home. She wasn't all that interested, until she noticed that police units had been dispatched to the old Beaumont estate.

Why?

The place had been abandoned for years. As she understood it, the current owner, a Beaumont heir, either Baxter Beaumont, now in his seventies, or his son, Tyson, had been trying to parcel it off and sell it, letting the old plantation house go to seed, but had been fighting with the historical society for years.

Interesting.

She did a quick sweep of the Internet but found nothing.

So the news was fresh.

Probably not a big deal.

Maybe squatters found on the property.

Or a poacher caught hunting in the off season.

Or . . .

She called the office of the newspaper, got hold of Millie Foxx, a recent hire who contributed to the online edition of the *Savannah Sentinel*, where Nikki still worked. In the past few years Nikki actually spent little time in the office and did most of her writing, editing and communicating from home, but luckily Millie, all of twenty-two and serious beyond her years, nearly camped out on the computers at the newspaper's offices.

"So what's up?" Nikki asked. "At the Beaumont estate."

"We're trying to run it down. I thought you'd know. Homicide's been called in."

"Someone was killed?"

"Unconfirmed. But looks like. I was about to call you. I figured you could maybe talk to Pierce."

"Hmm." Pierce Reed was Nikki's husband, but . . . "You know how he feels about that." Everyone at the *Sentinel* knew. Detective Reed had made his position clear about his wife *not* getting involved in police business, which was pretty damned difficult as Nikki not only worked at the paper but had three true-crime books under her belt. "I'll check, though."

"Do it," Millie said. "From the police band activity, I think something big's going on there and I thought you'd want a heads-up before Metzger gets interested."

Millie was right about that. More than right. Metzger was such a pain in the rear. "You got it," Nikki said. "In the meantime, can you keep checking to see if there's any more info coming from the police. Like who called in the report?"

"Hmm. Don't know. I'll see what I can find out."

"Good. Later." Nikki clicked off.

She smiled to herself as she grabbed her keys and slipped her cell phone into the back pocket of her jeans. A murder? At the Beaumont estate?

Perfect.

This was just the kind of story that was right up her alley. Even if her husband didn't think so and would be pissed as hell.

* * *

Reed and Morrisette looked through the few outbuildings that were still standing at the Beaumont estate but found nothing significant. An old John Deere tractor without wheels was rusting in a garage, and the stove in the smokehouse had weeds growing through it. And daylight was fading. With the sun setting steadily, they stepped into an old pump house, where evidence of an owl was visible, feathers and splashes of feces on an open beam, roost debris scattered on the floor.

"Guess the flood waters never made it here," Morrisette muttered. "What a mess." After a quick look around, they headed back to the house, where they noticed that the forensic team van had arrived, parked close to the back verandah. Investigators in boots and masks were hauling equipment inside.

Morrisette said, "I guess the party's really starting now," just as a vehicle from the Medical Examiner's Office rolled up and Reed felt his cell phone buzz in his pocket.

He retrieved the phone, saw his wife's name and number appear on the screen, and felt a twinge of worry. Nikki rarely called him while he was working. Unless it was important. Or, well, when she wanted something.

"It's Nikki. Give me a sec," he said.

Morrisette gave him a quick nod and started for the house as he clicked to the call. "Hey."

"Hi." Then right into it. "I heard that Homicide was called out to the Beaumont estate and thought you might be there."

Of course. She was already chasing down the story. He glanced at the house, where he spied Morrisette chatting up one of the deputies. "You heard right. And yeah, I'm out here."

"And—?"

"And we're investigating."

"A murder?"

"Unknown."

"Oh, Reed, come on," she prodded, and he was tempted, as always, to confide in her. "I already told you I know Homicide was called in and you're there," she pointed out. "Obviously someone is dead. Foul play suspected. So is it one body? Or more? Was it found in the house or on the grounds, and have you got an ID?"

"Whoa, whoa, whoa. Slow down." He imagined her already scouring the Internet on her phone while she was carrying on this conversation. Or maybe she was already heading to her car, ready to spring into action, probably to come out here. She was like a horse with a bit in its mouth at full gallop: dangerous and running headlong to who knew where. He held up a hand, though, of course, she couldn't see him, but he had to stop the madness before it took root. "You know I can't talk about a case."

"Too late. It's already news."

"Just let this one go for now. Okay?"

"I can't, Reed. You know that, so save your breath."

"Then call Abbey, she's the PIO."

"When I'm married to the lead detective. You are, aren't you? The lead?"

Oh, hell. She sounded excited, even breathless. "Look. Back off of this for now. There's nothing more to tell, and isn't this Metzger's beat anyway?" The minute he said the words, he wanted to call them back because bringing up Norm Metzger was like adding gasoline to an already-simmering fire. She and the crime reporter had always butted heads, and she'd made no bones about the fact that she wanted his job.

"Don't even go there," she warned.

Reed more than anyone knew it had always burned her that Norm was on the crime detail, despite the fact that she had three true-crime books under her belt.

"There's nothing I can tell you. Not yet. I just got here a while ago myself."

"Just give me something."

"Not yet."

"I want an exclusive on this, Reed."

"There's nothing—"

"Nothing you can talk about yet. Yeah, I know. I get it." Her frustration was palpable, even over the wireless connection. "But I don't care, I want an exclusive."

"You don't even know if there's anything to write about." He batted away a wasp and started walking to the house again. He was too busy to argue with her right now.

"I'm your wife."

"And that's why you need to leave this alone. Okay? Let it go. For the time being." But he knew she wouldn't. Couldn't. Hadn't her curiosity always superseded her brains? As smart as she was, she was even more inquisitive. Scarily so. To the point that she'd gotten herself into trouble—serious, life-threatening danger—on more than one occasion. And the thought of a murder mystery would be too exciting, too enticing for her to ignore. Nikki would want to be more than involved peripherally. She would want to see the crime scene herself. Explore the house. View the bodies if she could. She'd been itching for a new crime to write about. "Look, we'll talk when I get home, but in the meantime, call Abbey." He was already up the steps to the porch and paused for a second at the open door to the stairway.

"Don't try to placate me, Reed. You and I both know

that Abbey Marlow will tell me just the same as she'll tell anyone else," Nikki argued, and he didn't disagree. As the public information officer, Marlow knew the boundaries of speaking about an ongoing investigation; she wouldn't be swayed by any of Nikki's arguments. Abbey Marlow would treat his wife just as she would any reporter, and that had never sat well with Nikki. She repeated, "I said, I want an exclusive."

"You always do," he said, stepping inside.

"This time is different."

"Just leave this be, Nikki. For now. I'll talk to you when I get home. Sit tight. At least for a little while. Okay?"

When she didn't immediately respond, he was a little more forceful. "You got that? Nikki, stay home." He caught a glimpse of Morrisette half a flight down, at the turn in the staircase leading to the basement. "Look, I gotta go. I'll see you tonight." He cut the connection but had the gut feeling that she hadn't heard a word he said. Bullheaded didn't begin to describe his wife.

"Everything all right?" Morrisette asked, lifting an eyebrow as he reached her.

"Right as rain."

She sent him a disbelieving glance and headed downward. "Yeah, sure. And I'm a goddamned virgin."

"Just stay put. Okay? Nikki? You got that? Stay home."

"Fat chance," Nikki said as her husband's suggestion, no, his order, echoed through her brain. She punched the accelerator of her Honda CR-V, speeding past the city limits as she'd finally, with the help of a driving app, maneuvered through the tangled mess that was most of Savannah. Despite the heat, some water was still standing on the roads and there were potholes to dodge. Fortunately, most of the downed trees had been cut out of the way or pushed to the side, so she could make decent time.

Until just two hours ago, the storm had been the biggest news that had hit Savannah in a long while. All that had changed with whatever was going on at the Beaumont estate. Her mind teemed with possibilities. One person dead? Or multiples? Maybe a murder/suicide? A drug deal gone bad? Why way out at the abandoned plantation? Squatters? A lovers' quarrel? She didn't know and wouldn't until she got there or she collected more information off the Internet or from Millie. But she felt a sizzle of adrenaline in her bloodstream at the thought of what she might find, maybe something that was more than just a local story, possibly an idea for a new book. It had been two years since she'd submitted the Blondell O'Henry story, a year since *Mommy Most Deadly* had been published, and her agent was pushing her, but so far she hadn't been inspired, hadn't found the right mystery to investigate.

Until today.

She could feel it in her bones.

Don't get ahead of yourself. You don't even know what's going on.

But she knew.

Deep inside she knew.

This might be the story that could jump-start her career and she could kiss the *Sentinel* goodbye forever. Or maybe buy the paper. That thought had always circulated in the back of her mind. She'd be the boss! Her fingers curled more tightly over the steering wheel.

Just calm down. You've been here before.

It was true. Each time her latest book had been released there had been some press, a little buzz, and then the book had slowly died and she'd been back to fighting her way for a more interesting job at the *Savannah Sentinel*. But breaking into that good ol' boys club at the newspaper had proved tough. It was as if Norm Metzger had a lock on his job and his best bud, editor Tom Fink, just wouldn't let him go. Because, Nikki suspected, Norm was a man and whether he admitted it or not in this day and age, Tom Fink thought a man should work the crime beat. Same with Metzger, who had barely hidden his looks of disapproval and jealousy at her for actually being a published author. She'd overheard some of Metzger's remarks:

"Don't care if it's 'true' crime. Any way you cut it, it's pulp fiction . . . all it is . . ."

". . . thinks she can write like a man."

". . . just because her father was a judge . . ."

And the one that really stung?

". . . and she's got the inside track. Right? Her husband's a goddamned homicide detective. Hell, how do you compete with that?"

"Ugh." She rolled down her window and let the warm air inside. It was all so frustrating. She eased off the gas as she rounded a curve and came across a flatbed truck stacked high with bales of hay, bits of straw flying and swirling from the truck. Reed had suggested she quit to concentrate on her books, which would make sense considering the fact that she was pregnant, but she couldn't let the reporting gig go. She loved being a reporter, always on the edge of the news, ready to charge into any situation. There was an electricity to it that made her feel alive.

Still, she didn't have to think too far back to the whole Blondell O'Henry case to remember how her investigation had almost cost Reed his job.

Doubts assailed her. Of course they did. But damn it, she was going to do this. And he'd weather the storm. He always did.

But she wouldn't worry about that now and drove past sodden fields where cattle, sinking deep into mud, were trying to graze. Less than a mile later, the pastures gave way to Channing Vineyards. Acre upon acre of grapevines lined the road and wound upward on a small hill. Atop the knoll, a huge brick and white pillared home, a replica of Jefferson's domed Monticello, stood. Nikki barely noticed the house because her eyes caught a glint of silver just as a sleek sports car shot through the open wrought iron gate and she had to slam on her brakes.

Her Honda screeched, sliding a bit as the BMW convertible sped past, the driver in sunglasses, his blond hair flying, not a glance in her direction as he hit the gas and the engine roared.

"Hey!" she yelled as he flew by, but of course he didn't hear her. "Jerk-wad!"

Jacob Channing.

He was the owner of these vineyards, a man she'd met on more than one occasion and had even interviewed when his vineyard had hosted the mayor's last fundraiser. He'd smiled at her, that thousand-watt grin, his eyes narrowing. "I remember you. You're Andrew's little sister, right? A shame about him," he'd said, bringing up her older brother. "We went to school together, you know, before . . ."

He hadn't continued, but the remark had endeared him to her at the time.

Now, though, the fact that he'd nearly killed her changed her opinion.

Handsome, athletic and wealthy, and one of Savannah's most eligible bachelors, Jacob was a man as comfortable in black tie as he was dressed in hunting camouflage.

"Get a grip," she told herself, trying to control her anger, while her heart thudded, her pulse in the stratosphere. She had to focus.

Her heart still thudding, she tamped down her anger and kept driving, hoping beyond hope that she wouldn't run into Reed.

She sent up a quick prayer that she would be able to investigate before her husband found out, because, of course, he would.

And then all hell would break out.

Oh, well. It wasn't as if they hadn't been through all this before. She and Reed, they'd manage.

Right?

But now it's not just the two of you. Remember? She smiled and cast a quick glance into the rearview mirror. Her green eyes sparkled at the thought of her pregnancy. After suffering two heartbreaking miscarriages, she was now ten weeks pregnant, the furthest she'd ever carried a child, and she couldn't—wouldn't—do anything to hurt her chances of carrying this precious life to term.

So she'd be super careful.

But really, her kind of investigating didn't *have* to be physical.

But she caught a glimmer of indecision in her gaze and looked back to the road ahead. She was getting close to the lane leading to the old estate.

It's now or never.

* * *

Reed eyed the basement of the old Beaumont mansion from the bottom step. Now the place was crawling with cops. Photos were being snapped, measurements taken, the area swept for fingerprints and trace evidence, the bodies pulled from their resting place under the medical examiner's watchful eye. He and Morrisette moved between the crates, boxes and piles of junk, careful not to touch anything.

"Find anything else in there?" she asked one of the crime scene investigators as they made their way to the opening in the wall where the bodies had been discovered.

"Who is that? Morrisette? You're standing in my shot."

Morrisette and Reed backed up a step.

"Great. Now, could you give us a second?" Tanisha Seville, the videographer, was peering through the lens of her camera, focusing on the entrance to the crypt. "Damn." To an assistant standing near a huge lamp, "Any way you can get more light in here? All I've got are shadows. It's like a damned dungeon in there."

Reed agreed.

Morrisette said, "We're just checking to see if you discovered anything else."

"Well, check after we're done." Tanisha was known for not mincing words. Just like Morrisette, though they couldn't be more physically different. Whereas Morrisette was short and wiry, her skin lined from years growing up under a harsh Texas sun, Seville was tall and big-boned with smooth mocha-colored skin, springy black hair she didn't bother taming and eyes that flashed when she was irritated. Like now. Ignoring the detective, she leaned into her camera and slowly panned the area.

Carter caught Reed's eye.

"So far, only two bodies located."

"That's more than enough," Morrisette muttered.

"Let's hope it stays that way." Reed didn't want to see the body count going up, didn't want to think that this once-grand estate had become a dumping ground for a serial killer. But what about that empty depression in the crypt? Had a third victim escaped? Would they find more skeletons when they began to dig? What the hell had happened here in this dingy, forgotten cellar filled with years of discards now illuminated by the eerie glow of temporary lights?

They talked with a couple of the techs, found out nothing more and watched grimly as the skeletons were painstakingly withdrawn from their resting spaces.

"This is something you just can't unsee now, can ya?" Morrisette swept her gaze over the small bodies before they were bagged. "Gonna be with me for effin' ever. As long as I live. C'mon. Let's get outta here." She was already heading for the stairs.

Outside, the air was still heavy with the smell of the river, but they'd left the pervasive scent of rot in the basement, thank God. Reed noted it was late afternoon, not a breath of wind to stir the air, the heat oppressive. His phone buzzed in his pocket and he took the call from the department. "Reed."

"Yeah, it's Delacroix," a female voice stated, and he remembered the woman, a relatively new hire and junior detective. Auburn hair, medium build, serious beyond her years. "I've got a rundown on the phone number who called 911 about the bodies at the Beaumont estate. A guy by the name of Bruno Cravens."

Reed was familiar with the name. "Goes by Bronco," he said, remembering the small-time hustler who had been busted time and again for burglary, robbery, passing bad checks, that sort of thing. Always at the wrong place at the wrong time and up to no good. "We'll round him up and have a chat."

"You got his address?"

"Cabin on Settler's Road?"

"That's the one. Want me to check him out?" she offered, and Reed remembered she was a go-getter. Single, a little sassy and extremely gung ho.

"Nah, we're about done here anyway. Thanks." He hung up and was about to explain when Morrisette said, "I heard. Bronco Cravens again." She shook her head. "No surprise there. Just can't keep his nose clean." Her eyes narrowed and she followed the path of a bee flitting through the tangle of weeds. "Wonder what he was doing here?" She scrabbled in the pocket of her blouse, her fingers coming up empty. "Man, I could use a smoke," Morrisette admitted, scowling. "But if I did, man, oh, man, you can bet Priscilla would smell it on me and I'd never hear the end of it. Got a nose like a goddamned bloodhound and she's death on smoking. At least for now. And as far as cigarettes go." Morrisette's eyes slid away. "Can't say about anything else. Kids these days are into weed a lot younger than when I was in school. She's a good kid, but you just never know."

Priscilla was a handful, Reed thought. Morrisette's son, Toby, was a few years younger than his sister and to hear Morrisette tell it, already thinking he was an adult and "the man of the family." His mother disagreed. "In his dreams," she'd confided not long ago.

"Come on, let's get to it," she added. "You go south, I'll head north. Let's just get a feel for this place and hope we don't find any more bodies." Reed eyed the woods, tall and gloomy, and wondered if the whole damned estate was a dumping ground for corpses and if there was a serial killer on the loose. The victims discovered in the basement had been there for years, possibly decades, but what if there were more? Fresh ones?

Reed didn't like the turn of his thoughts. And there was Bronco. Why was he on the property? What was the connection?

As to the victims—yes, girls, he decided, his stomach churning at the thought. They'd been hidden in that hole in the wall a long time.

Who the hell were they?

CHAPTER 4

Nikki eased off the gas as she reached the gates of the Beaumont estate, then sped past. Before she was spotted. Of course the entrance was closed off, police vehicles blocking access except for the authorized vehicles from the department or the medical examiner or forensic team. And, she noted, Reed's Jeep was wedged between two sheriff's department SUVs. Deputies had been posted to prevent the public and the press from getting too close to the crime scene and keeping neighbors, the general public and lookie-loos from catching a glimpse of what was going on. Well, too bad. Fortunately, she knew this area like the back of her hand and so she rolled on past the main entrance. Around two curves she found a turn-out where the road was wider, a spot that fishermen used to park their cars before they hiked to the river.

She pulled in and parked, locked the car and started jogging along a familiar path through the forest. She came to a fork near a blackened stump and turned without hesitation to the right, doubling back toward the Beaumont estate. She'd come here as a kid along with her brothers and sister. Andrew, the oldest, leading the way, Kyle dogging at his heels, Lily and Nikki lagging behind as they'd followed the old deer trails through the sun-dappled forest. It had been long ago—so long—and now . . . she closed her mind to the past, didn't want to think of her shattered family. Andrew had died so long ago and his death had sent the family into a tailspin, Kyle rebelling and becoming distant, Lily set upon her own introspective path of bad decisions, and Nikki's own innocence destroyed. Her parents, never loving to begin with, had never been the same.

But she wouldn't go there. Not now. Not when she had to concentrate.

She kept running.

Twilight was fast approaching, the gloom settling under the canopy of branches overhead, the smell of the river thick in her nostrils. Roots and rocks made the ground uneven, and spider webs and limbs brushed her bare arms as she caught glimpses of the river through the trees. She was breathing hard as she spied the wire fence, the mesh disintegrating, a faded NO TRESPASSING sign hanging by a single strand as it warned that violators would be prosecuted.

"Too bad," she muttered, and slipped through a large gap in the mesh.

Speaking of prosecution and the law—what happens when Reed finds out you've been here? Not just trespassing, but nosing around his crime scene? Huh? What then?

Ignoring that nasty little voice in her head, she hesitated at the edge of the woods leading to the clearing beyond, where the tall grass met the river's edge and nestled in a copse of live oaks. The proud old house stood, crumbling now, on a small rise. As a child, Nikki and her family had attended parties here. Even then the old house had been starting to show its age, but now, nearly thirty years later, it had fallen into near ruin. As she peeked between the leaves of an overgrown crepe myrtle, she eyed the house and grounds now crawling with cops. So different from how it had been. In her mind's eye she remembered the parties Beulah Beaumont had hosted, here on these very grounds. Nikki had been little more than a toddler who, like the other children of guests, had been allowed to play and run down the terraced lawn and in the surrounding trees while the acrid smell of smoke from the barbecue mixed with sweet aromas of hummingbird cake and pecan pies wafting from the kitchen.

She remembered Beulah Beaumont, the matriarch, as a proud woman with flaming red hair piled high, blue eyes that narrowed suspiciously and thin lips that were forever drawn into a saccharine smile. Miss Beulah had smelled of some odious perfume meant to cover the scents of alcohol and cigarettes, though those acrid scents had always lingered. As Nikki's mother, Charlene, had once said, "Who does she think she's fooling? And that wig! Dear Lord!"

At the events, Beulah had never left the shade of the veranda but had sat in her wheelchair as if it were a throne, sipping from her tall glass of her own special Chatham Artillery punch. The boozy recipe included more than a little sugar and lemons, along with a concoction of whiskeys, rum and champagne "kissed with lemons and oranges," as Beulah herself had often drawled.

Even as a five-year-old, Nikki had made it a point of avoiding Beulah's watchful eyes; there was just something fraudulent in her seemingly gracious smile when she greeted the Gillette family and offered sweet tea or "something a little stronger."

But that was long ago. Before Beulah had passed and her stepson, Baxter, had inherited the house and surrounding acres.

Now, still hidden in the foliage surrounding the overgrown lawn, Nikki watched as a couple of deputies talked by the ME's van parked near the rear of the old house. Other cops came and went through a back side door, but she didn't spy Reed.

Good.

But was he still inside, or had he left in the time it had taken her to park her SUV and jog back through the forest? She slid her cell phone from her pocket, hit the camera app and zoomed in on the porch. Reed would really have a fit if he found out she was taking photos, but he was going to have one anyway.

She wanted to talk to some of the officers involved but couldn't chance it just yet. Not when Reed was probably still nearby. A mosquito buzzed near her ear and she slapped at it as she eyed the area and thought that if she skirted the house along the river, then cut into the old rose garden, she might be able to overhear a conversation or even get a peek inside the house.

The house sat on a point where the river turned nearly back on itself, the grassy bank overhanging a narrow rocky beach. Not great cover, but it would have to do.

She slid her phone back into her rear pocket, then eased from the cover of the undergrowth to crouch beneath the rim of grassland. Noiselessly she started circumventing the grounds and past the point and the remains of what had once been a dock and was now reduced to a few weathered boards and dark pilings nearly obscured in the swollen river. Debris moved swiftly downstream—branches, limbs, a bucket and a volleyball swirling by.

Nikki edged carefully beneath the overhang, her boots slipping on wet rocks. She had to slip through the reeds, but all the while she watched the house and wondered what had happened.

She couldn't fight the rush of adrenaline as she imagined finding out the facts to whatever story was evolving on this old plantation. Who had been killed? When? Why? She just didn't have enough information. Who had phoned in the crime to the police—who was that anonymous caller? She needed to get to the bottom of this story, or at least be the first to report it. Carefully she eased along the bank and hoped she didn't step into an alligator nest or come across any snakes or . . . *Stop it.* A tomboy in her youth and a daredevil in her teens, she didn't let too many things frighten her, so she wouldn't worry too much about the creatures she'd grown up with, and she moved as quickly as possible as darkness was encroaching, shadows fingering through the marshy bank.

She was starting to perspire and nearly crawling along the bank, the smell of earth and the river heavy in her nostrils, a slight breeze playing with the tendrils of her hair. She had always been athletic and agile, but she was making slow progress past the old dock, around the bend, relying on the scant overhang and impending darkness as cover. Here the river was deeper, the narrow bank and cat-tails giving way to dark depths, where, as youths, her brothers had dived and swum and boats could maneuver close to the shore.

It was tricky going, pebbles and rocks slick under her boots, and she braced herself by hanging on to any ex-posed root or weed on the underside of the shelf. She picked her way around a garden rake and a broken doll-house that had been carried away during the storm, inch-ing around the point, feeling a burn in her thighs from crab-walking. The thought crossed her mind that this might not have been the best idea she'd ever come up with, but she ignored it and kept moving, shifting her weight, trying not to turn her ankle on the slick pebbles and stones. By the time she'd rounded the point and was on the north side of the grounds, she was wet with sweat. But at least she was closer to the weed-choked rose gar-den and long lane that curved to the back of the house. Unfortunately, here the shoreline was nearly nonexistent, the overhanging shelf much lower, and ahead she saw in the gloaming that soon the land would level off, the shelf disappearing into a marshy lowland. There would be no hiding place.

So what then?

Expose herself?

Hope Reed had taken off?

Pretend that she'd gotten past the deputies at the front gate?

Take a chance that one of the cops would talk to her?

This would be the tricky part.

Biting her lip, she dared straighten a bit and peek over the ledge of the overhang, and her heart nearly stopped as she caught a glimpse of white-blond hair. Sylvie Morrisette was standing only a few yards away from the river, but fortunately she was turned back to face the house and didn't catch a glimpse of Nikki.

Crap!

Of all the people to be nearby. Reed's damned partner. Just what she did not need.

Nikki fought a surge of panic; after all, this was bound to happen. She just had to be careful because she didn't want to be found out until she could explain the situation to her husband first and convince him that she would be a help rather than a hindrance to the case!

So what now?

Keep moving!

Adrenaline pumping through her, she bent even lower and scrambled over the slick stones and mud. All the while she scoured the area for a spot to hide until Sylvie Morrisette was out of sight.

Where, where, where?

There had to be a hiding spot. Had to!

As the beach narrowed, she was barely able to place one foot in front of the other. Here the river deepened, rushing closer before turning again away from the house, and finally giving way to marshland on the far side of the garden.

Her legs were cramping and she was seriously second-guessing herself as the sun slid beneath the horizon.

She started to slip, caught her balance and then spied a willow tree leaning over the water not fifty yards ahead, near the next bend in the river. The tree's leafy branches draped over the water, some flexible limbs touching the river and being tugged by the current.

If she could just make it the short distance without

being seen, she could hide in the shelter behind the curtain of leaves. She started to move as she heard Morrisette's twangy voice.

"Yeah, nothin' so far. Still lookin'. Probably a wild-goose chase anyhoo, y'know. Hopefully there's nothin' more." Then a pause.

Oh, God. Morrisette was closer than Nikki had thought, just on the ledge above, and she was talking to someone . . . no, more likely speaking on the phone. To Reed?

Nikki held her breath.

Morrisette began to talk again. "Yeah, yeah. Good. Meet back at the house . . . yeah, I can't wait." A brittle laugh.

Straining to hear, Nikki leaned forward. She kept her balance by grabbing a wet, exposed root.

"It'll be interesting to hear what our pal Bronco has to say for himself."

Bronco?

"Wouldn't you know that lowlife would be the one to call it in. Even if he did it anonymously. Makes you wonder what else he knows, y'know. Maybe he can tell us why there looks like a third grave in that basement. Two bodies, three burial spots? I can't figure it. What the hell's that all about? Yeah . . . yeah, I know. I hope we don't find any others. What? Oh, yeah. Deputies are looking for our buddy as we speak, but it looks like Bronco's gone to ground, y'know? Not at home, not at work . . . Yeah, heard he was laid off from the construction company. . . . uh-huh, staking it out . . . What? Oh, the Red Knuckle. He's a regular there. Hangs out there every damned evening, the way I hear it. They probably have a stool with his name on it. . . . What? His home? . . . Yeah,

it's a cabin across the river from here, been in his family
for years, I think. . . . Yeah, yeah, me too. Can't wait to
hear what he has to say."

Nikki couldn't believe what she was hearing. Her
pulse jumped and her brain raced with the information.
The only person named Bronco that Nikki knew about
was Bronco Cravens, a two-bit con artist who had lived
in the area for years. Bronco had been trouble from the
get-go, the son of a preacher and yet always at odds with
the law. He'd even been to prison if she remembered correctly. Burglary or robbery or something? She couldn't
remember the exact charge, but she did know that he had
a connection to the place.

Bronco's grandfather had been the caretaker at the
Beaumont place for years. Nikki herself had seen Wynn
Cravens, his hair as white as an egret, working in the tool
shed or clipping roses in the garden more than once when
she and her family had visited the estate.

She chewed on that for a second, her mind spinning. A
third burial spot? In the basement? Two bodies, but three
graves? What was that all about?

And why had Bronco called the police anonymously?
No reason, unless he was guilty, right? Was he involved?
But surely not the killer—because he wouldn't have
called. Was he an accomplice who had second thoughts?
Or, unbeknownst to the killers, had he surreptitiously witnessed the murder being committed? And the police had
already figured out he'd been the caller?

"Okay." Morrisette's voice broke into the spool of her
thoughts. "Yeah, got it," she said, and seemed to end the
call.

Dozens of questions racing through her mind, Nikki

redoubled her efforts to get to her hiding spot. The tree was much closer now. Crouched over nearly double, she started moving again. If she could just cover the distance of twenty yards or so under the overhang of the bank, she might be okay. She would be able to—

She saw movement between the branches, the silver-green leaves a shifting veil and hiding something within.

She froze, her heart hammering as she squinted into the gathering darkness. Had she spied an animal . . . a muskrat or . . . a bobcat . . . maybe an alligator? No good options there.

And then she caught a glimpse of pale red. As the willow leaves shuddered, turning with the current, she spied the shadow of . . . a boat?

What?

She stopped suddenly, the fingers of one hand twined around a clump of weeds that had poked through the rocks, her throat tight. What the hell?

Why would a boat be moored beneath the tree after a storm the likes of which hadn't been seen in this part of the country in decades? She thought of a local fisherman braving the swollen river but immediately discarded the idea. More likely whoever had shown up was someone interested in what was going on at the Beaumont mansion, someone who had heard the news that bodies had been located, but a person who didn't want to be noticed by the cops.

Someone like her.

Another reporter?

Someone who had been held at bay at the main gate and had circumvented the police by boat?

For the briefest of seconds, the image of Norm Metzger with his neatly trimmed goatee and sneering disapproval flashed before her eyes. Wouldn't it be just like him . . . but no, he was too damned lazy.

Maybe some other reporter, or perhaps a nosy neighbor.

Or the boat could be abandoned, tied to the tree and moving with the current that flowed more swiftly here where the water was deeper.

That was more likely.

You don't know anyone's there. The boat could be empty. And it could have been there for days or weeks for that matter.

But would it have survived the hurricane?

And if she squinted, she could almost make out a shadowy figure inside, some white illegible wording near the stern.

Or was that all part of her imagination?

No matter what, she had to check it out and she needed the cover of the tree for a few more minutes. The evening was falling fast now, dark shadows creeping over the river's surface, the air thick with insects, but she could still be spotted. And that would be a disaster. The plain hard truth was, she didn't have much of a choice. Not unless she wanted to be found out by her husband's partner, which she definitely did not!

Hurriedly, she took a step.

Her boot slid.

She tried to right herself. Frantically scrabbled for something to hang on to, but no.

Too late!

Her other foot slipped.

No!

Oh, God—no!

Frantically she searched again for some kind of purchase.

Nothing!

A second later, she splashed into the deep water.

Gasping, Nikki caught a mouthful of water as the river converged over her and the current tugged her violently away from the shore. Automatically, she kicked, her feet weighted by her boots, air bubbles escaping from her lungs. She'd been in this river a hundred times as a kid, so she didn't panic, just swam upward, toward a dusky sky visible through the swirling water. Up, up from the depths to break the surface, twenty feet from the shore. Coughing and sputtering, she tried to tread water but was dragged farther downstream, along with branches and boards, bits of plastic, even a doll bobbing past, all churned up from the recent storm. She shoved a branch out of the way, saw that she was getting farther from the house.

Don't panic! You can do this! You're a strong swimmer. The shoreline isn't that far. Just swim, Nikki.

She saw the house; now, if she could just—from the corner of her eye she caught a glimpse of the edge of something big and round and black and—*Bam!*

An old tire slammed into her head. Pushed her under again. She gasped. Gulped more foul-tasting water. Blinked to stay conscious. Was pulled deeper into the murky depths. She tried to grab on to the slick rubber tire as it bounced, but it slipped away, floating far overhead as she sank.

Darkness tugged at the edge of her consciousness.

Her eyes closed.

The rush of the river seemed to disappear and she felt as if she were floating, being carried softly away.

Don't black out. Don't!

Her lungs were tight, starting to burn.

She wanted to let go. So badly . . .

Nikki, don't! Think of the baby! Think of Reed! Nikki, for God's sake, do NOT let go!

Her eyes flew open, still submerged far below the river's surface. She blinked and kicked. Forcing herself upward. Ignoring the fire in her lungs. Refusing to give in to the dizzying feeling of weightlessness.

Don't even go there!

With one strong kick she shot upward, one of her boots falling free. She broke through the surface and gasped, blinking, still being swept downstream. Toward the willow, where through drops on her lashes she saw a shadow, movement between the long tendrils of branches. Another streak of red, the side of the boat visible, white lettering she couldn't decipher from this distance. Whoever was in the boat was guiding it away. If she could let the river carry her downstream—

"Holy shit! Someone's in the water!" a woman yelled from the bank. The voice was sharp, edged in concern. *Morrisette. Reed's partner.*

Nikki's heart sank as she saw Morrisette rushing toward the bank as if she was planning to jump into the water. "No, no, I'm fine," Nikki tried to yell, but her voice was strangled and she was coughing, but she was okay.

Too late!

The detective launched herself, diving into the swiftly moving current.

No, no, no! This is no good.

From the back, more people began to shout.

"What the—?" A deep male voice.

"Is that Morrisette, what the fuck does she think she's

doing?" A different man was speaking, and she spied a deputy running to the shore. "Hey, we need some help here! Christ, there's another one in the water."

"She's going to drown!" A woman's voice this time as Morrisette appeared, bobbing up from beneath the surface. She flipped her short hair from her eyes and got a bead on Nikki. "You!" she sputtered, focusing as she started to swim closer. "For the love of God, what the hell are you doing here?"

There were more excited shouts from the bank. Deep Voice yelled to someone, "Get a rope! Or something."

"What's that gonna do?" the woman demanded.

"You got a better idea?" Deep Voice again. "Yeah, right! I didn't think so. Just get the fucking rope!"

And then, over it all, another almost-angry voice, "What the hell got into her?"

Reed! She'd recognize her husband's voice anywhere. She turned her head and spied him. "Nikki?" Reed yelled. "Nikki? Oh, Jesus. What—?" He was already sprinting toward the bank as if he, too, was going to dive in, just as Morrisette, spitting water and blinking, surfaced about twenty feet from her.

The detective's eyes were like lasers as they focused on Nikki. "Why am I not surprised?" She was trying to swim toward Nikki but fighting a losing battle with the swift river. "What the fuck do you think you're—? Oh, shit!"

From the corner of her eye Nikki caught sight of a small boat, unmoored and swirling wildly in the current. The same boat? Or another craft? She didn't have time to think. It spun crazily, heading straight toward her.

Her heart turned to ice and she started frantically swimming.

"Move!" Morrisette ordered, eyes round.

Upstream, Reed surfaced and he, too, saw the impending disaster.

The boat was spinning crazily, careening faster and faster, closer and closer.

"Nikki!" he yelled, his eyes round in horror. He was already swimming toward her. "Watch out!"

Nikki cut to one side and dove deep.

Too late!

Thud!

The side of the boat slammed into her shoulder. Hard.

Pain jarred her, radiated from her shoulder.

Her arm went slack.

Stunned, she nearly blacked out. Felt something break deep inside of her. The water—so much damned water—swirled and danced around while a dull, throbbing ache crawled up her neck.

Swim! an inner voice yelled at her and she blinked, then with one arm forced herself upward, making her legs kick, breaking the surface in time to see the boat—red and white in the gathering darkness—careening wildly toward Morrisette.

No!

"Watch out!" Reed's voice boomed from somewhere behind her.

Morrisette was already swimming toward shore, but she looked over her shoulder and—

Bam!

With a terrifying crack, the boat's prow rammed into the side of Morrisette's face.

Blood bloomed across Morrisette's forehead as she let out a sickening moan.

Morrisette didn't move.

No. Oh, God, no!

Despite the pain Nikki kicked hard. Using one arm, she fought the current and swam toward the motionless woman. "Morrisette!" she yelled frantically, gulping river water and choking as she swam. "Hang on!"

But it was no use.

Before Nikki could reach the unmoving woman, Morrisette sank like a stone.

CHAPTER 5

"What the hell were you thinking?" Reed demanded, raking stiff fingers through his hair. He was seething, his eyes dark with a deep, underlying worry, as he stood at the end of Nikki's hospital bed in the emergency room of St. Luke's Hospital.

The last two hours had been a blur—an ambulance ride after he'd dragged her from the river, doctors and nurses in the ER, checking her, hovering over her while Reed waited impatiently for her diagnosis. He'd been worried sick when he'd pulled her from the river, had been scared out of his mind that she might not survive, but now that he knew she was going to recover, that she hadn't lost the baby, his anger was rising. And he wasn't bothering to hide it. A bad sign.

She slid her gaze away from his. "I told you, I was working on the story."

"Not good enough, Nikki." To his credit, he paused, looked away, attempted to contain himself, but he was failing. "I asked you not to go to the crime scene," he said.

"There was no asking about it," she shot back, her own temper rising. "You ordered me."

"And you disobeyed."

"I don't remember the whole antiquated 'obey thy husband' in our wedding vows," she threw back, staring at him again. "That wasn't our deal, remember?" She wasn't about to put up with his attitude. She felt bad enough as it was. Guilt, ever sharp, needled into her heart.

"No . . . hey, don't play that game with me," he warned. "I 'ordered' you as a police officer. I 'asked you' as your husband." A vein started to throb near his temple. "And—big surprise—you ignored me."

"Sometimes the lines get a little foggy, y'know. Indistinct. Blurred between the cop and the spouse."

"Not this time," he argued, jabbing a finger at the floor. "This time I was talking to you like a detective who is in charge of a crime scene where a homicide had been discovered, a place specifically off-limits to the public and," he added before she could cut in, "the press. You know that, Nikki." He glared at her, then threw his hands into the air. "I don't know what I have to do to get through to you. And more importantly, you put yourself in danger. Not to mention the baby. And Detective Morrisette!"

Again she felt that painful prick of guilt.

He looked up to the tiled ceiling. "For the love of—What the hell were you thinking?"

"I told you, I was going after a story and . . . and . . ." She let out a long sigh. "Look, I'm sorry."

"Are you?" He shook his head, his hair gleaming under the dimmed lights of her room at St. Luke's.

"It's my job."

"Then quit. Okay? It's too dangerous. No. No, that's wrong. *You* make it too dangerous. *You, Nikki.* Not only for yourself, but for others." He was beside himself.

"But, Reed. I saw something," she said. "There was a boat under the willow tree."

"What?"

"I think someone was there who shouldn't be."

"You're right about that," he said, and she knew he was talking about her.

"Just listen—"

"No . . . I don't care if you saw a boat, or a yacht, or a damned submarine in the river, okay? It doesn't matter!" He was shaking his head, his emotions raw. She'd known that he'd been worried sick when he'd dragged her from the river, had heard his voice crack with fear. *"Nikki! Nikki, oh, Jesus, honey. Are you okay? Oh, please, God. Nikki!"* He'd been kneeling beside her in the tall grass and the mud and had looked over his shoulder frantically. *"I need an ambulance! Right now! For my wife! Can someone call an ambulance! Now!"*

But once they'd made it to the hospital and she'd been diagnosed with only a dislocated shoulder, her pregnancy still viable, his fears had morphed into a quiet, seething rage as he'd heard from a deputy that Morrisette was teetering between life and death, on the edge and in emergency surgery.

All because she'd tried to save Nikki.

"How is Sylvie?" She hated to ask, but had to.

"Who knows?" he snapped, then quickly gained control of himself. "Still in surgery. But as far as I know, alive."

She'd heard that Morrisette had suffered a broken jaw and not just a mild concussion but a serious brain injury requiring surgery.

Blowing out a sigh, he shook his head and stared at the ceiling tiles. "I don't . . . I don't really know. I mean, they're not saying she'll pull through."

"Not saying?" she repeated, sick inside. "But surely . . . I mean . . ." She couldn't, wouldn't think that Reed's tough-as-old-leather partner wouldn't make it.

"She's strong. A fighter. You know, she always says she's 'Texas strong,' whatever the hell that means. But . . . well, we just have to wait." He cast a look to his wife that was a little less caustic. "She took a bad blow."

"I know." Nikki cringed beneath the bedsheets and remembered the prow of the boat striking Morrisette with a horrid sharp crack. Blood had poured from Morrisette's head, staining the river as the detective had lost consciousness and turned ash gray. Reed had dragged Nikki from the river while a female deputy had gone in after Morrisette and hauled her out of the water to start CPR on the muddy bank in the ensuing pandemonium.

The ambulance Reed had demanded had arrived within minutes, the EMTs taking over from the deputy who had started CPR on Morrisette on the muddy bank of the river. Within seconds Reed's partner had been put on a stretcher and carried into the waiting vehicle. The second ambulance showed up seven minutes later. Reed had ridden with Nikki to the hospital and stayed with her during her examination in the ER. Her diagnosis was simple: a dislocated shoulder, the result of being rammed into by the unmoored boat lurching wildly in the swollen river. Thankfully, despite a feeling that something had broken while she'd been in the river, she hadn't miscarried.

At least not yet.

She touched her abdomen with her right hand, consoling herself with the new life still growing tenaciously inside her. That, at least, was a blessing.

She thought about Morrisette's phone call, the one Nikki had overheard while hiding beneath the rim of the bank. "So," she asked carefully, as she knew Reed wouldn't want to discuss his case. "Is it true that Bronco Cravens called in the homicide?"

"What?" Reed said, his eyebrows knitting. "How did . . . What did . . . How do you know about Bronco?"

"So it is true. How's he connected?" she asked, unable to stop the questions that had been plaguing her to keep from rolling off her tongue. "And what's with the empty grave? Two bodies, but three burial sites? Was one moved?"

"Oh, my God! Nikki—stop! Just . . . Stop!" He held up a hand, palm out, his expression one of utter disbelief that she would still be investigating. "You're in the damned hospital for crying out loud, so just—"

At that second there was a soft tap on the already half-open door and a uniformed cop, a woman Nikki didn't recognize, peeked in. "Detective?"

"I'll be right back," Reed said, then quickly stepped into the hallway, disappearing and leaving the door ajar before Nikki could ask the next question already forming on her lips. But he'd practically confirmed that Bronco had made the call. She strained her neck to peer through the crack in the door but couldn't see Reed or the cop, only the view of a curved desk of blond wood, where three nurses—two women and a man, all in blue scrubs— were huddled over monitors, the man speaking into a phone as he stared at a computer screen.

Nikki shifted on the bed to get a better view, or to find out if Reed was anywhere within sight, but a sharp pain in her left shoulder caused her to suck in her breath and reminded her that she was far from a hundred percent. Damn. For the next several weeks she would have to keep her arm immobile, which would slow her down. She'd also have to ice her shoulder and eventually start physical therapy. The only reason she hadn't been discharged yet was because of her pregnancy, considered high risk because of her previous miscarriages, and the ER doc wanted to talk with Nikki's OB/GYN.

The last thing she needed was to be laid up, but, she reminded herself, she was lucky. Yeah, she had to wear a sling to keep her arm immobile for a while, but other than that she was okay.

Unlike Morrisette.

"Hey, Detective!" a voice boomed down the corridor. Reed looked down a hallway and spied a tall, muscular man in khakis and a black tight-fitting T-shirt striding toward him. His blond hair was clipped so close to his skull that the beginning of male pattern baldness was visible and two days' worth of beard covered a tight, angry jaw. His eyes, laser blue, were focused on Reed as he skirted past an aide pushing an empty gurney toward a bank of elevators.

Tyson Beaumont, Reed guessed. And he looked as if he were fit to be tied.

A few steps behind him was a trim man in his late sixties or early seventies who looked as if he'd just stepped off the golf course in his Izod shirt and crisp plaid shorts. Reed supposed it was Baxter Beaumont, Tyson's father.

He braced himself.

"You!" Tyson charged, heading in Reed's direction, the older man following. "I've been looking for you!" He closed the gap between them. "I heard you're in charge!"

The elevator call button dinged, the doors parted, and the aide and gurney disappeared inside.

"What the hell is going on?" Tyson demanded as the elevator's doors closed. "I heard there was a body found on my property, maybe more than one. Is that right? Who are they, what happened?" His face was flushed, his eyes worried as another elevator opened and two nurses in scrubs hurried into the hallway as Baxter caught up.

"Baxter Beaumont," the older man said, jutting out his hand. He was tanned and fit, only his shock of silver hair and the crow's-feet at the corners of laser-blue eyes giving away his age. His handshake was firm, his teeth a brilliant flash of white. "You're Detective Reed?"

"Yes." Releasing the man's hand, Reed offered up his ID.

"Yeah, yeah, we know," Tyson said dismissively. "We've been looking for you. Or whoever is in charge. Went to the old house and were stopped by cops. Got the runaround, let me tell you." He was agitated, his lips twisting down. "Finally found out from a deputy that you were here. I—we"—he motioned with his hand to include his father—"we need to know what's going on." His blue eyes, so like his father's, narrowed on Reed. "Dead bodies? Really? In the old house?"

"Impossible," Baxter said. "That's unimaginable!" He

shook his head. "Two, right?" He scowled at Reed. "That's what they said on the news. Two bodies and you're looking for more."

"That's crazy!" Tyson ran a hand through the stubble over his skull.

The elevator dinged again and an orderly pushing a thirtyish woman in a wheelchair appeared. Her casted leg was propped in front of her and she was holding two vases of flowers. A man who appeared about the patient's age lagged behind and was struggling with a plastic bag, another vase and a bouquet of metallic Mylar balloons in a rainbow of colors that caught inside the elevator car before floating loftily behind.

"Let's find a spot where we can talk," Reed said, watching the trio make their way to the main doors. He figured he had a few minutes. Nikki was stable and Morrisette was still in surgery; there was nothing he could do for her. "There's a spot just around the corner." He led them around a corner, past the Information Desk and down a short distance to a windowed alcove with a view of the parking area near the main doors. A couple of chairs and a small love seat were arranged around a coffee table, where someone had left a half-empty paper coffee cup and an out-of-date *People* magazine.

"Sit," Reed suggested. Father and son took the chairs while Reed dropped onto the small couch across from them.

"Who are they?" Baxter asked. "The bodies. Who the hell are they?"

"Unknown at this time. We're working on that."

"How many?" Tyson asked. "As Dad said, the news reported that you found two, but that you were still looking."

"That's right. Two in the basement."

"Of the old house?" Baxter clarified. "Jesus God . . . I . . . I can't believe it. How long were they there?"

"Looks like years."

"Men?" Baxter asked, rubbing one hand over his bare knee as he sat. "Or . . . women?"

"Still figuring that out."

"You couldn't tell?" Tyson's mouth dropped open. "But—"

"He's saying they were decomposed beyond recognition," his father pointed out.

Tyson shot to his feet, stood, his back to the windows, his reflection watery behind him. "But they must've had something, their clothes or something to ID them, let you know if they were men or . . ."

"Unless they were naked." Baxter glared up at his son. "Just let the detective tell us."

"Fine." Tyson crossed his arms over his chest, stretching the fabric of his shirt. "What did you find, and what're we supposed to do about it?"

Reed was reticent to give out too much information until the police had decided which details they would keep to themselves, at least for now, information that only the killer would know. "Other than that there were two bodies located in the house and it looks as if they've been there years, there's not a lot I can tell you. We received an anonymous tip that they were there and we went to investigate, cordoned off the place, searched and confirmed, then kept searching."

"And someone got hurt. There were ambulances and you ended up here." He motioned to the surroundings.

"Right."

Tyson demanded, "Who? Another victim? This isn't making any sense!"

"An officer was injured while trying to help someone who'd fallen into the river. Look, I can't tell you any more than that," Reed said, his guts squeezing as he thought about Morrisette and Nikki and the baby. "There are privacy laws."

"Will they be okay?" Tyson asked.

"We're hoping."

"Oh, Lord." Baxter let out a long breath. "This isn't good," he said, "not at all. We're trying to sell the property, you know." He motioned to include his son. "And we've got a couple of interested parties, two different construction companies, or is it three?"

"Two for certain and a third, maybe." Tyson's jaw tightened. "After all these years and finally the zoning is going through. It looks like a deal might finally go through and now . . ." He ran a hand through his short hair.

"And now this," his father finished for him.

"Yes, and so we'll need a statement from you," Reed said, and spying a nurse, cell phone plastered to his ear, hurrying past, added, "Probably it would be best if you could come down to the station."

"What!" Baxter said. "A statement? Why? We certainly didn't have anything to do with what happened!" For a second he seemed panicked.

"Whoa, Dad. Slow down. We do own the property." Tyson placed a steadying hand on his father's forearm. "Of course the police are going to want to talk to us."

Reed nodded. "We just need a thorough list of anyone who had access to the house, who lived in the house or nearby, who takes care of the place, that sort of thing."

"And for that we need to go to the police department?" Baxter asked, his chin tightening.

Reed eyed the older man. "For privacy."

"Makes sense." Tyson was quick to agree as he stared
out the window, and Reed, following his gaze, spied a
news van roll into a parking lot near the emergency room.
"We don't need any bad publicity . . . or any more than
we already have. Detective Reed is just trying to do his
job and be discreet."

"Well, yes. We want that. We need discretion." Baxter,
too, eyed the news van as it took up two parking spots in
the lot. "We don't want to lose any potential deal." He
was nodding to himself. "It happened before. We ended
up losing a buyer on the property north of the house."

"We've lost a lot of deals."

"But that one stung, y'know." He turned his gaze to
Reed. "We had an interested investor from Chicago. Very
interested. A big developer. But then he got wind of what
had happened to Nell and . . . well, the deal fell through
and we had to sell locally. Lost nearly two hundred grand
on the deal." He was shaking his head, lost in thought.

Tyson was having none of it. "Bodies were found on
the property, Dad! What is it you're not getting about
that?"

"Nothing I can do about that," Baxter pointed out.

Tyson held up his hands, palms out, to Reed, then let
them drop. "Sorry. It's just that we don't want a lot of bad
publicity."

"Exactly my point." Baxter threw his son a disgusted
look.

Tyson explained, "The deal we're working on, it's
been a long time in the works and a hard decision for

Dad. We haven't sold off any of the estate since the Cravens bought the parcel on the other side of the river, and that was years ago. So, what we don't want is a media circus."

"I can't stop that," Reed said.

"We know. Well, I do anyway," he said, sending his father a sharp glance. "It's just . . . just when you're done with your investigation at the old house, if, you know, everyone could clear out."

"We will," Reed assured them. He thought of his wife, how she'd risked her damned life, as well as Morrisette's, all for a story. "I can't speak for the press, though. You'll have to deal with them."

"Great," Tyson muttered.

"Signs," Baxter chimed in. "More of those NO TRES-PASSING signs that tell them they'll be prosecuted if they set one foot on the property. And cameras! We'll get some of those little spy cameras—you can pick them up online these days and they're pretty cheap—so we catch the damned violators. That should do it. We'll threaten them all with legal action, that's what we'll do!" His eyes actually brightened at the prospect as a woman in her twenties, phone in hand, scanned the alcove, then found a seat not far away, across the hallway, very much in earshot. She half-lay in a chair, long legs over one arm, flip-flops dangling from her feet as she texted like mad.

Tyson watched her and said, "Maybe you're right. We should do this at the station. We can come up with a list of people who've been on the property that we know of, or people who were interested, but my guess is no one who was thinking about buying the place was stashing bodies there."

"Include workmen. People you hired."

"You were at the house today, right?" Tyson said as Reed nodded. "Then you already know we don't exactly have a crew maintaining the place."

"But you did have a caretaker?"

Baxter said, "Wynn. We had Wynn Cravens on the payroll for years. My mother hired him."

"That's right," Tyson said. "Wynn took care of the place while Beulah, that's my grandmother, lived in the house. Then, over time, you know, when we moved out of the place and eventually Grandma, we decided to sell off parcels and didn't really need him." Tyson slid his hands into his front pockets and rolled back on his heels. "Besides, he was getting older."

"Just passed on," Baxter said. "I read his obituary in the *Sentinel*."

"What about his son or grandson?"

Baxter shook his head. "Didn't deal much with Jasper. He wasn't around much, and the grandson . . . what was his name, Buster?"

"Bronco," Tyson supplied. "Well, really Bruno, but everyone called him Bronco."

"Oh, yeah, that's what it was," Baxter agreed.

"And a real loser." Tyson shrugged. "I was in school with him, he was a little younger, but he kind of faded into the woodwork, y'know. Wasn't a jock, or a brainiac, just . . . kind of was." He frowned, remembering. "We didn't hang out."

The woman in the nearby chair stood and stretched, then settled into the chair again, draped out over the cushions and once again started texting, just as a nurse pushing a rattling pill cart made her way down the hallway.

"Maybe you're right," Tyson said to Reed. "Maybe talking at the station would be better. Dad and I can come down there tomorrow, or the next day, and give a statement and a list of anyone we can remember who's been on the property. We'll call and set it up." And then to his father, "Come on, Dad. Let's go." He was already striding toward the exit doors on the other side of the Information Desk.

CHAPTER 6

Nikki felt another serious pang of guilt over Sylvie's condition. If only Reed's partner hadn't spied her in the river. Or for that matter, if only Nikki hadn't slipped and ended up in the water.

Things would be far different.

That's right. And Sylvie Morrisette wouldn't be fighting for her life, would she?

Angry with that horrid little nagging voice in her head, Nikki pushed that painful thought aside, adjusted her sling, then craned her neck, but Reed was nowhere in sight. In fact, the area around the nurses' station appeared to be empty.

One of the female nurses, the one with thick black hair pulled away from her face and sharp dark eyes over her mask, glanced down quickly, said something unintel-

ligible to her coworkers, then slipped off of her chair to
hurry out of sight.

Nikki couldn't help but wonder if the nurse had gone
to check on Morrisette, if something had happened,
though she knew that was unlikely. If Reed's partner were
in surgery, she would be on another floor or in another
wing, in an operating room, no longer a patient in the ER.

So where had Reed gone?

To check on his partner? Had Morrisette taken a turn
for the worse? God, she hoped not.

Or had Reed been called away because of a develop-
ment in the case? Maybe the bodies had been ID'd or
more corpses located? Had the crime team found some
evidence? A new lead? And what about Bronco Cravens?
Her mind spun with dozens of unanswered questions.

She kept her gaze glued to the door and wished he'd
return.

If only the damned doctor would release her.

Soon. It had to be soon. To pass the time, she concentrated on the case. What did she know? Two bodies had
been discovered by Bronco Cravens, a lowlife if there
ever was a lowlife, but she didn't know the identity of the
corpses or how long they'd been buried there, or even
where on the property they'd been located. In fact, she
hardly knew anything. She thought she'd spied someone
hiding beneath the curtain of willow tree branches, but
she wasn't even certain of that. Yes, she was certain she'd
seen the boat, but had she witnessed someone helming it?
It had definitely been moving. In her mind's eye she remembered that flash of red visible behind the curtain of
silver-green leaves turning in the wind.

Was it important?

Someone with something to hide?

Just a lookie-loo motoring on . . . on what? The rushing river filled with debris from the storm? Unlikely.

Another reporter?

She chewed on that and wished she could get out of here so that she could dig into the story. More details may have been released, but she had no way of checking right now. She wasn't expected to stay overnight but was waiting for a doctor's orders to release her. The holdup, as she understood it, wasn't her shoulder, just a matter of paperwork.

Good.

She shifted on the bed and felt her shoulder twinge again just as Reed reappeared. His anger had ebbed a bit, though he still wasn't smiling. "The doctor is supposed to be signing you out soon," he reported. "So, I'm going to check on Morrisette, then I'll swing over to the house and grab you a change of clothes."

"Wait," she said. "Have you heard anything about Sylvie?"

"Not yet."

"Still in surgery?"

"As far as I know."

"I need my phone."

That brought a wry smile. "It's dead."

"Wha—oh." She remembered sliding it into her back pocket before she'd fallen into the river. "I need one."

"Not tonight."

That thought made her heart sink. Yeah, there was a hospital phone on the nearby table, but it wasn't preprogrammed with the numbers in her contact list and every call would have to go through the hospital's switchboard.

He checked his watch and frowned. "Look, I'll be back in half an hour or so. Just sit tight."

"As if I could do anything else."

He actually barked out a short laugh.

"Where are you going?"

"Home. To let the dog out. And to change, maybe grab a shower. I'll bring you clean clothes."

"And a new phone."

"Dream on." He gave her a wink. "Hang in," and then he left.

And he was gone. As the door closed she caught a glimpse of a gurney being wheeled in the curtained hallway beyond, an orderly in scrubs pushing an elderly woman with pale skin and a bony hand clutching the rail, an IV pole attached.

Impatiently Nikki adjusted the ice pack on her shoulder, leaned back on her pillow and closed her eyes as she waited. She needed to get home, to check on Bronco Cravens, maybe schedule an interview with him. That would be a start. And then there was research on the old Beaumont estate. What had happened to it in recent years? Yeah, it had fallen into horrible disrepair, but there had been a time when it had been rented, right? After Beulah had moved into a retirement community? Or had it been after her death? She tried to think. Beulah and her husband had one son, Baxter . . . or had there been a girl as well? Maybe one who had drowned in the river.

She shuddered, knowing how cold that water could feel and now Morrisette . . . no, she wouldn't think about that now and pushed any worrisome thoughts aside. She wished she had her damned cell phone. She was clearheaded enough that she could connect to the Internet and do a little search on the Beaumont estate.

The phone on the bedside table rang sharply.

Thinking the caller had to be Reed, she stretched, winced and managed to get the awkward receiver to her ear.

"Hello?"

"Nikki? Oh my God, I just heard!" Charlene sounded breathless.

Of course.

Didn't she always?

"I saw it on the news and I tried to call you, but I couldn't get through, so I got hold of Reed and he filled me in . . . well, a bit. What happened?"

"It's a long story, Mom." Nikki's relationship with the woman who had borne her had always been complicated, never easy. An impossibly thin woman with fine graying hair, sharp features and eyes that missed very little, Charlene prided herself on being the boss while playing the victim. Forever trying to manipulate those around her while pretending to "go with the flow." That hadn't worked with her headstrong daughter and so they'd never gotten along all that well, and then there had been the big wedding that hadn't come off. Charlene had yet to forgive Nikki for eloping with Reed rather than go through with the over-the-top nuptials her mother had planned. Though Charlene always appeared on the edge of frail, Charlene Gillette had true inner grit and had survived a loveless marriage, as well as the death of her oldest son. A born survivor. And Charlene Gillette wasn't known to be all that great in times of crisis. No matter how many she'd lived through. Unfortunately, there was no avoiding Charlene. Not now.

You can do this.

"Are you all right?" Charlene asked.

"Fine, Mom. Dislocated shoulder. It's no big deal."

"You're sure?" Charlene was obviously unconvinced.

"Yes, of course."

"And the baby?"

"All good. And I have an appointment with Dr. Kasey tomorrow morning. She squeezed me in, just to make sure."

"She didn't come see you?"

"Not yet. Another doctor examined me here at the hospital. Really, Mom, it's okay. I'm going to be released soon, hopefully within the hour." She checked the clock and saw that it was after ten.

Charlene said, "Okay, good. That's good. But I've been watching the news. They've pulled two bodies from the old Beaumont home. I assume that's why you were there?"

Nikki closed her eyes as her mother rambled on and on about what she'd seen on television, where the crack news team from WKAM had filed the first report of two bodies being located in the basement of the Beaumont manor. "The reporter said that not only you but a police officer was pulled from the river, Detective Morrisette."

"That's right."

"Reed saved you? But she was trying to save you?"

Nikki wanted to argue that she hadn't needed saving but knew there was no reason to pick nits over what had happened. "Yes, essentially."

"Well, what were you doing? Nosing around again? Nicole, when will you ever learn? You seem to have some kind of death wish." She started rambling about Nikki's past near-death experiences, and she really did have a point. For someone in her midthirties Nikki Gillette had defied the grim reaper more than once. This—falling into the river—didn't compare with the other hair-raising times when she'd faced what she'd thought was certain death.

Charlene, though, wasn't convinced. "You have to be more careful! It's not just you this time, you know."

"Yeah, I do," Nikki agreed, though she didn't want to admit it.

"You're carrying my grandchild."

And our child, Reed's and mine. But she bit her tongue rather than start any kind of argument and said instead, "Look, Mom. Sorry, but I've got to go, the nurse is back." It was a bald-faced lie, but she had to end this conversation before Charlene really got going.

"Oh. Well. Fine." Her mother sounded disbelieving but didn't push it. "You'll call after you see Dr. Kasey tomorrow?"

"Yeah, of course." She was nodding as if her mother could see her.

A pause. Then, "Well. Okay, then, you . . . you take care and knock off all this investigating stuff, okay? You're a wife now, soon to be a mother."

Charlene was SO old school. It ticked Nikki off. Bigtime. And she didn't need any reminders of her mother's disapproval or a lecture—make that *another* lecture—on how to live her life. "Got it," she said, though that was another lie just to cut her mother off. They both knew Charlene was wasting her breath, and man, oh, man, did Nikki want to keep arguing, to push her mother out of the Dark Ages. But they'd been 'round and 'round on the subject before with neither woman ever backing down nor giving an inch. A waste of breath. It was time to end this. Past time. "I really have to go." And she didn't wait for her mother to respond, just hung up the bulky receiver and told herself to cool off.

She thought about the news reports. Charlene and the

rest of Georgia knew as much about the bodies located at the Beaumont estate as Nikki did. Despite being on the grounds at the crime scene and her husband being the lead investigator Nikki hadn't gotten any more information than the general public through the Public Information Officer. It was irritating and frustrating and . . . and just plain wrong.

However, Bronco Cravens's name hadn't been released.

Yet.

So Nikki still had a bit more insight into the case and if she could get Reed to open up a little—not enough to compromise the investigation, but give her something— she would have a little more to go on. She was trying and failing to remember Millie's cell phone number when the nurse who had helped admit her returned with the news that the doctor, having spoken to her obstetrician, had signed the discharge orders. Nikki, complete with sling, ice pack and instructions on care for her shoulder, was essentially released. Reed showed up ten minutes later with fresh clothes. While he again checked on Morrisette, Nikki, with an aide's help, managed to dress in the sweats her husband had plucked out of her closet. She was still trying to figure out how to broach the subject of the investigation when he returned, his face once again grim.

"Bad news?" she asked, immediately concerned as she adjusted her sling.

"Not good. She's still in surgery." He met the worry in her eyes. "Complications."

Her heart dropped. "What kind of complications?"

"I don't know. It's a brain injury, Nikki. I'm sure there can be lots of things." As he gathered her bag of wet clothes, he added, "Her kids are here. In the waiting room. With their father."

That surprised her. Morrisette had never had a kind word to say about Bart Yelkis and had often put him in the category of "deadbeat dad." "I didn't think they got along."

"They don't, but he's probably here to support his kids." He glanced around the small room. "Can we get out of here now?"

As if on cue, an orderly appeared with a wheelchair and soon enough she was home, where Mikado and Jennings greeted her at the front door. Mikado, a small mutt of undetermined heritage, wanted to lick her face and had to be ordered to sit, so he wriggled, tail swishing the floor, while Jennings twined between her legs before she gave them each a pet, then climbed the stairs to their bedroom.

"I might have to go out again," Reed told her as she sat on a bedside chair and kicked off the flip-flops Reed had brought to the hospital. "I just got a call from the station. We've located Bronco Cravens. You okay with that?"

She looked at him as if he'd just flown in from the moon. "It's only my shoulder, Reed. I think I'll be fine."

It didn't seem fine with him. "If you say so."

"I do." She knew what he was getting at: the pregnancy. But she let that elephant in the room remain invisible, for now. Wouldn't bring it up, not directly. Instead she said, "Seriously, I'm okay."

"I wouldn't even consider it, but since Morrisette's laid up, we're a body down."

"You're going alone?"

"Delacroix is going with me."

Making her way to the bed, she asked, "Delacroix?"

"A newbie. Assigned to the case. Computer wiz, as I understand it. Figured out it was Cravens who called."

"Good. Then go, go." She made shooing signs with one hand as she sat on the edge of the bed and tried to stifle a yawn. "You need to find out what he knows," she added, and winked at him. "You can fill me in when you get home."

"In your dreams, Gillette." But he rapped on the doorjamb with his knuckles. "I'll be back as soon as I can." As Mikado jumped onto the bed, Reed pointed a finger at the scrappy little mutt. "And you. You're in charge."

Nikki laughed, then winced at a sharp pain in her shoulder. "Damn."

Reed caught her grimace. "You okay?"

"Fine. Just got to remember the stupid shoulder. So go already. Go 'serve and protect' and most important: Find out what Bronco knows."

"Okay. If you're sure."

"I am. Just keep me in the loop."

"You never give up."

"And you love me for it."

"Oh!" He actually managed a grin. "Is that why I love you?"

"Pretty sure." Exhausted, she nestled under the blankets, her shoulder throbbing slightly. A very determined part of her still wanted to question her husband about the bodies that had been located and if the police expected to find any more, and she really needed to find out if Bronco

Cravens was somehow involved. But now wasn't the time. She'd learned long ago when to push it with her husband and when to bide her time, which, of course, wasn't in her DNA.

But she'd go with it.

For tonight.

Just for tonight.

CHAPTER 7

Delacroix was waiting for him at the station. Since Morrisette wasn't on active duty, Delacroix had been assigned, at least temporarily, as his partner. Reed wasn't pleased about it, but the department was short-handed and he didn't really have a choice, at least not for the time being, so he rolled with it. He didn't know much about her, only that she'd recently been hired and had some, if limited, experience at another department. New Orleans, maybe? Or Baton Rouge? He didn't recall and it didn't matter at the moment.

Jade Delacroix was young, in her early twenties, with shoulder-length auburn hair, hazel eyes and sharp features. She was lithe and trim, all of five-four, and wore a pair of thin-rimmed glasses, jeans and a black jacket over a gray T-shirt. After quick introductions, they settled into his Jeep, he behind the wheel, she in the passenger's seat, and just for a second Reed thought about Morrisette, who had occupied that spot for as long as he'd owned the Jeep.

As he pulled out of the parking space, she gave him the rundown on Bronco Cravens's whereabouts. "He was spotted at his favorite hangout, a dive bar called the Red Knuckle. It's not far from the university."

"I know it. It lucked out. Didn't get hit by the hurricane."

"Right. One of the lucky ones. Anyway, a deputy spotted his truck leaving the bar and followed him to his cabin. Called me and I said we'd want to interview him at his home, right?"

"At least give him the option." Reed was already heading out of the city to Settler's Road, backtracking a bit as the Cravens family's home was closer to the Beaumont estate than it was the city. In fact, it was situated on a parcel of land directly across the river from the old house and had once belonged to the Beaumont family. "Any idea how long Bronco was at the bar?"

He cracked his window, letting in the cool night air.

"Hours, mainly nursing beers, watching baseball according to the barkeep."

"You already talked to him?"

"Yeah, by phone. While waiting for you. He wasn't too happy about it as he was busy." She explained that Guy Thomas, the bartender, had said Bronco Cravens was a regular and had been hanging out there for hours, was there when Thomas had signed in for his shift at 4:00 p.m. and insisted that one of the TVs over the bar be tuned to the local news. "According to Thomas, Cravens seemed irritated that there was so much coverage of the hurricane and kept asking the bartender to flip the channel from one local station to the next. Really ticked the bartender off. Finally, about forty minutes ago, he left. That's when the deputies caught sight of his truck. I'd already put out a BOLO for it, so they called it in and I asked them to follow him. He led them home, I called you, told them just to make sure he didn't go anywhere but wait for us. And here we are."

Reed checked the clock on his dash. 1:23. Again he thought fleetingly of his partner. Surely Morrisette was out of surgery by now, but he hadn't received any calls.

A good sign?

Or bad?

No telling. He'd phone once he'd talked to Cravens.

He hit the gas, leaving the lights of the city behind. The road wound along the river and into the woods, where the brush was thick, moonlight barely filtering through the leaves. As they reached the lane leading to the property where Bronco Cravens had lived most of his life as far as Reed knew, they came across a cruiser for the department, parked fifty yards from a clearing where a small cabin sat, moonlight illuminating the dark structure. An older Ford Ranger was parked in the two ruts that stopped before a small garage, its door slightly askew.

The deputies hadn't gotten any closer as they'd seen a dog through the window, so they'd kept their distance while watching the cabin. The lane was, according to all maps, the only way in and out of the property, and the deputies had a view of the front and back doors as the cabin sat at an angle.

"Came home, let the dog out, went back in, cut the lights," the taller deputy, Marcel Van Houten, told him. "We got lucky, the dog didn't notice us."

"Okay, let's go," Reed said to Delacroix, and together they walked to the front door. As anticipated, the dog inside began going nuts, barking its fool head off, and a man responded, "Fender! Stop! No barking! Enough." But the dog ignored him, making a ruckus. "I said, enough already. Holy shit, stop!"

Reed rapped loudly on the front door as Delacroix stood a step to the side, her weapon drawn. Just in case.

Inside the rough-hewn home, the dog was growling, snarling and yapping out of control. But the man had turned quiet.

"Police!" Reed said to the door, pounding again. "Bruno Cravens, this is Detective Pierce Reed. Savannah-Chatham Police Department. Open up!"

Then he waited.

No response.

"Bronco!" Reed shouted, and this time he heard something other than the dog.

"Yeah, I'm comin'. You! Fender! Sit and shut up."

Finally, the dog went quiet and footsteps could be heard before the single bulb of the porch light turned on, a lock was turned, the door opened a crack, and Bronco, his brown hair mussed, one bleary eye peering past a small chain that connected the door to the jamb, asked, "Whadda ya want?"

"I think you know," Reed said. "We want to talk to you about what you know about the bodies discovered in the basement of the Beaumont home, downriver. We know you called in the report."

"I didn't—"

"You did, Bruno. We know it. Can prove it." Reed was too tired for the other man's denials. "So, don't argue. You won't win. Why don't you just open the door, let me and my partner, Detective Delacroix, in and you can tell us all about it?"

The eye just stayed focused on Reed.

"Otherwise, Bronco, we'll have this conversation down at the station. Your choice."

"Oh, man," Bronco whined as a moth, drawn to the light overhead, began flitting around. Bronco was distracted by the movement for a moment.

Reed brought him back to the conversation. "Work with us and you won't find yourself behind bars for trespassing."

"Behind—? Hey, look! Without me, you wouldn't have . . . oh, shit," he said, realizing he'd just admitted to the call. His eye refocused on Reed.

Reed nodded. "Right."

"Crap." Bronco let out a defeated sigh, waited a beat and finally said, "Fine. Okay. Just give me a sec to put on some pants."

"Two minutes," Reed said, and as Bronco turned from the door, added, "Just so you know, we're watching the front, back and sides of the house."

"Yeah, yeah, I know the drill." Bronco pulled the door behind him, leaving the porch light glowing and a second moth to join the first. Reed waited, Delacroix at his side, he watching the digital readout on his watch, she still focused on the door, her service weapon drawn.

Bronco snapped on interior lights and opened the door twelve seconds short of the two-minute limit. In a pair of battered jeans and a T-shirt, his hair still uncombed, he unlatched the chain and stepped aside, allowing them to pass into the squalor of his living area.

Reed stepped inside cautiously, his eyes scanning the small pine-paneled living room for the dog, who turned out to be a docile hound of some kind. Curled up on a small rag rug near the end of a stained couch, he watched the newcomers but couldn't keep his tail from wagging.

Delacroix was edgy, though she tried her best to keep her case of nerves under control as Bronco waved them into two beat-up recliners and settled onto a corner of the couch near his dog. The place smelled of old tobacco, stale beer and dog, ashtrays overflowing, beer cans left on a center coffee table that had seen better days.

"I figured you'd show up here," Bronco admitted. "Shit, man, it didn't take you long." He lit a cigarette and rubbed the stubble on his jaw. Exhaling in defeat, he let the smoke drift up to the yellowed ceiling and leaned forward, elbows on knees.

"You called in the bodies?" Delacroix asked. She was sitting tentatively on the edge of her seat, a battle-scarred brown recliner, her eyes laser-focused on Bronco, the fingers of her left hand rubbing together nervously, as if she were contemplating reaching for her service weapon.

"Yeah, yeah." He waved off the question as if it were a given. "I was up to the old house and I went into the basement and found the graves."

"Why?" Delacroix asked. "What were you doing there?"

That's when the lies began weaving in with the truth. Reed read it on the other man's face.

Bronco looked to one side, trying to come up with a plausible answer as he scratched his chin and took another drag. "Well, y'see I had the key. From my granddaddy."

"Wynn," Delacroix supplied.

"Yeah, he'd been the caretaker up there for years, y'know. Anyway, he, um, he passed away a few weeks back and I ended up with the keys to the place. I thought I should go up and see if everything was okay." He glanced to the window and the dark night beyond. "Because of the hurricane, y'know."

"And?" Reed pushed.

"And nothin'. I was checkin' out the basement and I found those bodies." He took a long pull on his cigarette again, and Reed noticed his hands shook a bit. "Scared the bejeezus out of me, if ya want to know the truth. Spooky as hell. I saw 'em, took off, and made the call. Figured I had to. Them two little bodies . . . shit." After a final drag, he shot a stream of smoke from the corner of his mouth and jabbed his cigarette out in the already-full ashtray. "Hope I never see a thing like that again." He looked up at Reed and motioned to the two cops. "You all. You see that kind of shit all the time, but me? I don't. And I sure as hell don't want to again. Not if I live to be a hundred!"

That part Reed believed.

But Delacroix wasn't moved. "So you waded through the muck in the basement to the far wall and found the latch to the crypt."

"Yeah, that's about it." He was nodding.

"Kind of intricate, isn't it?" she pointed out. "Not all that easy to get into."

Bronco frowned and Reed noticed a bead of sweat running from his temple. "Well, the damned door was open and I . . . I peeked in and damn, but one of those skulls seemed to be starin' straight at me!" He gave a shudder.

She asked, "What time was this?"

"'Bout ten minutes before I made the call. I got in my truck and me and the dog came here, I called, took a shower and . . . and drove into town."

"To the Red Knuckle?" Reed asked.

"Yeah." Bronco's head snapped up. "You had me followed?"

"Well, yeah. After we figured out who made the call, we started looking for you," Reed explained. "Do you have any idea how long those bodies have been up there?"

"Hell, no! I didn't know they were there."

Delacroix interjected, "What about identifying them? Do you know who they were?"

"Shit, no! They looked like girls, I guess. I mean, they were wearin' girl things, but . . . wait!" He focused on Reed. "What is this? How would I know who they were? Wait a minute? Are you . . . ? Are you suggestin' I knew something about how they got up there? What happened to them? Shit, I got no fuckin' . . . no clue!" He scraped his pack of Winstons from the table and shook out another cigarette. His hands visibly trembled as he snapped his lighter over the end of his filter tip. "What the hell are you trying to pull here?" He squinted through the smoke. "I did you all a favor. I found the bodies, got the hell out, called fu—effin' 911 and that's all I know."

Delacroix said, "But your grandfather, he might have—"

"He's fuckin' dead!"

"—might have told you about them?"

"No way! Wynn didn't know nothin' . . . or at least he didn't tell me 'bout any damned dead girls. The only dead one I know who died up there was that girl whose ghost that's hangin' out there. Nell or Nellie or whatever. But no."

"You know the bodies are girls?" Delacroix asked, dead serious.

"Well, hell, I think so. Like I just told you! One of 'em was wearin' a locket and a bra . . . oh, shit, I want a lawyer!"

"No need for that," Reed said, "though, of course, you could call one and we can go downtown, make this real official. But we're just asking about what you found."

"You're not arresting me?" he asked.

Delacroix asked, "Should we?"

"Hell, no! If I was guilty, would I have called the goddamned police? Huh? I was doin' my civic duty."

"Anonymously," she pointed out, and didn't bother to hide the irritation in her voice.

"No shit. Because of this. I didn't want to go through all this." Bronco rolled his eyes to the ceiling and let out a lungful of smoke on a sigh. "I shouldn't of done it. I knew it. Calling the cops is always a bad, bad idea."

"No one's arresting anyone," Reed said, sending a pointed look to his newbie of a partner. "We're just talking. That's all. Just trying to figure out what's going on."

"The way I look at it, you all should be grateful I even made the call," Bronco said.

"We are."

Delacroix shot him a glare that accused him of being a liar, but Reed ignored it and Bronco relaxed a little. "Fine then." Leaning back on the couch, he glowered at Delacroix, then focused on Reed and, with urging, told them what he knew, though Reed thought he was still holding back. On the way back to the station, Delacroix said, "He's lying. Not about everything, but he's holding something back." She rolled down the passenger window. "And I smell like an old cigarette butt. He was nervous, couldn't keep from playing with his pack and lighting one after another. He knows more than he's saying."

"Maybe he'll have a come-to-Jesus moment and tell us everything."

"That guy?" Delacroix snorted and pulled a face. "I'm not putting any money on that. He lies like that rug his dog was sleeping on."

Reed couldn't argue. He dropped her off at the station to pick up her car, then swung by the hospital to check on Morrisette.

But he was too late.

As he started for the main doors, Reed noticed Bart Yelkis huddled with Morrisette's two kids, both of whom were crying and crossing the parking area. Toby, a string bean with a Mohawk, was almost as tall as his spark plug of a father. He was sniffing and dashing away tears while trying to suck it up. Priscilla, as petite as her mother, was sobbing, hiding her head beneath a curtain of blond hair and refusing to be comforted by her father. Bart's expression was dark, a mixture of anger and angst.

Reed's stomach dropped. He felt the bad news. Knew, with sickening insight, what was to come.

Bart zeroed in on Reed and shepherded his kids into a jacked-up Dodge Ram, a black king cab with amber lights mounted on the roof of the cab. He slammed the door behind them, then whirled and, fists clenched, crossed the parking lot to square off with Reed.

"I'm suing your ass, Reed. You and that fucking department you work for. It's your fault she's dead."

Dead? Morrisette is dead? Oh. Jesus. "No . . ." He didn't want to believe it, though the truth was evident in the shorter man's eyes. "But I thought she was . . ." His voice trailed off. Hoping against hope he was reading Morrisette's ex all wrong, he wanted to deny what was becoming horribly evident, with a sinking sense of dread that Yelkis, for once, was telling the truth.

Sylvie Morrisette, his partner for over a decade, was gone.

"What? Wait. You didn't know?" Yelkis stepped over a raised flower bed separating one area of the lot from the next. To drive the point home, he said, "She died, Reed. Right there on the operating table." Advancing on Reed, he fought to keep control and failed. "Her life was snuffed out, just like that." He snapped his fat fingers as beneath the brim of his cap a vein throbbed visibly at one temple. "The way I hear it, your wife killed her." His jaw worked and his fists opened and closed, and Reed detected the lingering odor of his last beer on Yelkis's breath. "Did you hear me?" he demanded, pointing a finger at Reed's chest, his lips twisted in fury. "Your damned wife." For a second Reed thought Yelkis was going to take a swing at him, sucker-punch him right then and there.

But as his fists balled, the passenger window of his truck rolled down and Toby yelled, "Dad? You comin'?"

Yelkis held up an index finger and yelled over his shoulder, "In a sec!"

"No one killed anyone," Reed argued as a heavyset woman walked across the lot, aimed her remote at a silver Toyota, pressed a button and the little car beeped a response, its lights blinking.

"Hell, yeah, she did," Yelkis insisted. "Your reporter wife? She killed Sylvie just as sure as if she steered that damn boat right into her head." He pointed an accusing finger at Reed. "Sylvie dived in to save your bitch of a wife. And let me tell you, Nikki Gillette ain't gonna get away with it." He sneered Nikki's name and the muscles in Reed's back tightened reflexively even though he told himself not to take the bait.

"Yeah," Yelkis went on. "That wife of yours? Rich from the get-go. She's skated all her life, the daughter of a big-time judge and then married to a cop, but it ain't gonna work. Not this time!" His jaw jutted forward, silently daring Reed to lunge at him.

Reed's jaw was so tight it ached. "I don't think—"

"Good! Don't think and don't goddamned argue with me." Yelkis jabbed his finger straight at Reed's chest. "Nikki Gillette is the reason my Sylvie's gone! She's the reason my kids don't have a mother no more."

"I'm sorry for your loss," he said automatically, still seething inside.

"Yeah, sure."

From the corner of his eye, Reed saw Priscilla's pale face pressed against the truck's rear window and he hurt for the girl, understood Yelkis's frustration, but deep down wanted to argue with the man, defend Nikki, tell Yelkis to fuck the hell off. He didn't. Not when he noticed the streaks of mascara running down Priscilla's wan face.

Bart Yelkis was still raving. "You and your wife and the whole goddamned police department are going to pay. That was my kids' mama who died in there tonight." He hooked a thumb toward the hospital. "Don't think I'm gonna forget who's responsible!" With that he stalked back to his truck, snarled at his kids as he climbed in, then started the truck and backed up. He threw the pickup into gear. Tires chirped as he tore out of the lot, barely slowing to wheel onto the quiet street.

Reed wanted to disbelieve Yelkis.

But he knew it was the truth.

He wanted to rail at the heavens but didn't figure God was listening.

And he wanted to throttle his wayward, bullheaded wife. Instead he climbed behind the wheel of his Jeep and stared at the hospital through the bug-spattered windshield. Four stories of windows—patches glowing dimly in the night. Wide glass doors beneath a portico where a glowing red sign read: EMERGENCY ENTRANCE. Sprawled before it all, a wide, nearly empty parking lot illuminated by lampposts and the blue of moonlight.

His cell phone buzzed and he saw it was Delacroix. The word, it seemed, was out. He hesitated, then answered.

"You heard?" she asked. "About Detective Morrisette?"

"Yeah." A knot swelled in his throat.

"I'm sorry."

"Yeah," he forced out. "Me too." Tears stung at the back of his eyes. Hot, unwanted drops of anger, frustration and grief.

"You okay?"

No! I'm not okay. I don't even know what "okay" is right now! "Yeah," he lied. "Fine."

"You sure?"

Shit no. I'm not sure about any damned thing right now.

"Reed?" she asked.

"I said I'm fine," he said sharply. His chin wobbled, and tears began to drizzle down his face. But he kept his voice steady. Somehow. "I'm good. I'll talk to you tomorrow." He swiped the hot tears away.

"Okay. Hang in there."

He clicked off and slid a glance at the passenger seat, where Morrisette had spent so many hours navigating, swearing, checking her phone, confiding in him and just bullshitting about the world. He could almost see her spiked platinum hair, the eyebrow stud she once wore and the ever-present snakeskin boots.

Shit. He pounded a fist into the dash.

Shit, shit, shit!

She was gone.

The idea was nearly inconceivable that someone so vibrant, so passionate, so full of life could be dead.

Pull yourself together. You see life and death all the time. In your job, it's what you deal with. Everyone dies. You can deal with this. You've got a wife and a kid on the way. And a damned case to solve. Get on with it, Reed.

He started the engine, dropped the Jeep into gear, then stopped. Even though he knew the truth, believed what he'd heard from Yelkis and had the information confirmed by Delacroix, he had to hear it for himself. He shoved the Jeep into park, cut the engine and got out of the Jeep. Pocketing his keys, he half jogged to the wide glass doors of the ER.

Maybe, just maybe this was all a mistake.

Or a bad dream.

He had to hear it for himself.

But even as he showed his badge to bully his way to see the doctor who had been tending to his partner, he knew deep in his gut it was an exercise in futility.

Detective Sylvie Morrisette, four times married, four times divorced, mother of two, with her west Texas drawl and caustic sense of humor was dead.

All because his damned wife didn't know when to back the hell off.

CHAPTER 8

"Dead?" Nikki whispered, staring up at her husband from the bed. He'd walked into their bedroom and snapped on the bedside lamp to wake her and tell her the horrifying news. "Oh, God. Morrisette . . . she . . . died?" Suddenly numb inside, Nikki took a minute to process what he was saying, but she still couldn't believe it. No . . . not sharp-tongued, balls-to-the-wall, take-no-prisoners Sylvie Morrisette. That was impossible. It had to be.

But Reed's face said it all.

His tortured expression convinced her.

"Oh, dear God." Her insides turned to lead. She scooted up against the pillows at the head of the bed and ignored the jab of pain in her shoulder and patted the edge of the mattress. "What happened?"

"Neurosurgeon couldn't save her." He closed his eyes, sat on the edge of the bed, the mattress sagging, then let his head fall into his hands.

"But . . . I mean . . ." She had no words, was cold to her core.

"They did their best, but she died while she was still in surgery. Blood pressure went down, heart failed, oh, hell, I don't know exactly what the hell happened." His voice cracked and he cleared his throat, trying to grab on to the rags of his composure. "I'm not sure anyone knows yet. The thing is: She's gone, Nikki. It's over."

Nikki's heart broke. Not just for her grieving husband, but for Morrisette's family, those close to her. "What about her kids?" she asked softly as beside her, nestled in the pillows, Mikado, who had been sleeping, blinked his eyes open and wagged his scruffy tail.

"With their dad." Reed's jaw tightened and he sniffed loudly. "Morrisette would've hated the thought of that."

Nikki grew cold inside. "I'm . . . I'm so sorry."

He lifted his head, his gaze hard, his eyes red as he looked at her. "You should be."

A beat. Just long enough for her to process.

Her throat closed and she blinked back tears. Shaking her head, she whispered in disbelief, "You're . . . ? You're blaming *me*?"

He seemed about to snap back at her but somehow held his tongue, his jaw working. For a second she thought he would point out her flaws—stupid curiosity, her insatiable need to follow a story and her carelessness of falling into the river. As if she were the direct cause of his partner's death. Instead he didn't say a word. Just stared at her with grief-riddled eyes that, if she looked close, simmered with a quiet, condemning rage.

"I didn't . . . I mean . . . yeah, I shouldn't have been there and yeah, I slipped into the river, but I was perfectly fine. I'm a good swimmer. I could've—"

"Morrisette had no idea what kind of swimmer you were. She saw a person in danger, a person being swept away, a person who could drown, and she reacted like the good cop she is . . . er, was! No, Nikki, you didn't personally drag her into the river; you were just the eager, unwitting bait."

"No . . . I—"

He cut her off. "Detective Sylvie Morrisette took an oath to protect and serve, and that was what she was doing when she died! Protecting you."

She gasped. "Jesus, Pierce."

He stood then, towering over the bed, staring down at her. "I'm not blaming you. Not directly. But if you hadn't sneaked into the crime scene against department warnings and orders, this all wouldn't have happened and Sylvie Morrisette would be alive right now, working the case, bitching about her exes, all four of them, and being able to be the good mother and officer she always strived to be." He squeezed his eyes shut and threw back his head, willing himself to gain control. "No," he said, blinking up at the ceiling. "It's not your fault that she's dead, but because of your actions she took a risk and ended up losing her life."

"Oh, Reed, you seriously can't blame—"

But he was already walking out of the bedroom, heading down the hallway to the stairs, his footsteps echoing behind him. Mikado hopped off the bed and followed Reed down the stairs.

This was all wrong. So wrong.

Nikki felt miserable. Her heart was heavy, her head ached, her shoulder began to throb and she was pummeled with guilt. Throwing herself back against the pillows, she closed her eyes and fought tears. She'd never been one to cry, but now her throat grew thick and her eyes burned. She blinked and dashed the tears away. If she hadn't gone against Reed's orders, if she hadn't gone to the Beaumont estate, if she hadn't slipped and fallen, if . . .

"Stop it!" she said aloud, and sniffed back any remaining tears. Weeping wouldn't change things. Bawling her eyes out wouldn't help. She was and always had been a woman of action. Could never lie around idly. Not even now. She threw back the covers and got out of bed to walk into the adjoining bathroom. Using her good hand, she splashed water on her face over the sink, then caught sight of her reflection. Mussed red-blond hair, green eyes puffy from lack of sleep and the sudden spate of tears, her freckles still visible in her flushed face. Not a good look. But did it even matter? Probably not. Still, she glared at her image and said, "Get a grip, Gillette."

Back in the bedroom, she found her robe slung over the back of a chair and slipped her good arm through one sleeve, letting the other sleeve hang over her shoulder with the sling. She couldn't cinch the damned thing around her waist, so the robe gapped slightly, billowing behind her as she headed downstairs.

She found Reed in the kitchen.

He hadn't turned on any lights, but a bit of moonlight filtering through the windows offered a weak, bluish illumination.

Reed was drinking.

Seated on a barstool at the kitchen island, a half-empty bottle of scotch and a short glass filled with ice cubes and dark liquid on the counter in front of him, he glanced up as Nikki approached. "Figured I'd have a drink in her honor." He held up his glass. "Or two."

"Sure." The digital readout on the stove glowed a soft blue. 4:17. The dog had settled into a bed near the back door. "Sounds like a good idea to me." Leaning a hip against the island, she added, "I think Morrisette would've appreciated it."

"Damned straight, she would." He took a long swallow, then slammed his glass down with a hard smack against the counter. Ice cubes rattled and danced. A bit of scotch sloshed over the rim.

"I would join you, but . . . well, the baby."

"Yeah." He nodded as if lost in thought. "Right," he finally said. "The baby."

"*Our* baby."

"I know."

But that was the end of the conversation; he was somewhere else.

A silence ensued, stretching long between them. Awkward. Almost intimidating. The clock counting off the minutes.

For once, Nikki was at a loss for words. To fill the void, she opened the refrigerator, the light from its interior illuminating a swath of the room. "Maybe you'd like a couple of eggs and a slice or two of toast? Or something?" She glanced over her shoulder. "It is morning, y'know."

"Yeah, I know." Another swallow, another noisy drop of his glass onto the counter top. "And it's too late to be drinking. But . . . what the fucking hell? Right?" He drained the glass as she retrieved a carton of eggs from the fridge, let the door close, then switched on the light over the stove.

"You're serious about making breakfast?" He let out a snort. "Unreal."

"I just thought it might help."

"Well, you were wrong." His eyes were like lasers as he looked at her. "Nothing's gonna help. It'll all just take time."

"Then come to bed."

"Won't be able to sleep."

"There are other things we could do," she said with a flirty lift of her eyebrow, giving him the look he usually found irresistible.

"You're injured," he reminded her, nose in his glass, and polished off his drink.

"Oh, I think I can manage." She managed a bit of a smile, a little come-on.

He eyed her in disbelief. Uncapped the bottle. "Not now."

Never could she remember him turning down a sexy invitation. "So you're going to drink away the rest of the night?" she asked, deflated, an edge in her voice.

"Don't know." He poured another stiff shot. Studied the glass. Gave a quick nod. "This is only drink number two. But . . . Yeah." He nodded. "Maybe."

"Reed—"

"Let it go, Nikki." Again he pinned her with his gaze. "I'm dealing, okay? I don't need judgments. I don't need lectures. And most of all I don't need you trying to coddle me or make me feel better."

"I'm just trying to help."

"Well, thank you," he said sarcastically. "But right now, I don't want your help. I think you've done enough."

Her temper ignited. "Wow. As if I don't feel bad enough."

"Do you?" He eyed her in disbelief. "'Feel bad?'"

"Of course I do. You're not the only one hurting tonight."

"You? You're hurting?" he threw back at her. "Seriously? Geez . . . But then you didn't see her kids, though, did you? Priscilla and Toby. They're the ones hurting. They're the ones who have to live with what you . . . with what happened."

Stung, she stared at her husband with new eyes. "You were going to say, 'They have to live with what I've done.'" She couldn't believe it. "Admit it. That's what you were going to say!"

"If the stiletto fits—"

"Oh, my God! Enough! Pierce, just stop! If . . . If you wanted to make me feel guilty, then you've done it. Okay? Mission accomplished!" Furious and hurting, she snapped off the range light, leaving him in darkness. "You made your point. Loud and clear." With that she stormed out of the room. He could drown himself in his sorrows for all she cared, she thought, her housecoat sliding off her shoulder. Angrily she yanked it into place as she started up the stairs, the dog at her heels.

"Well, since you're listening," he yelled after her. "Stay the hell away from my case. Leave it alone. You've done enough damage for one day."

That stung. *Damage—as in causing his partner's death.*

As if she didn't feel bad enough! She stopped on the

fifth step, deciding whether or not to stalk down and give him a piece of her mind. Yeah, she'd made a mistake. A horrible, *fatal* mistake. And she felt guilty about it. Seriously guilty. It was eating her up inside. But he—her damned husband—didn't have to pour salt in her already burning, open wound.

And if he thought he could order her to . . . what? *Leave it alone?*

Fat chance!

Now, more than ever, she was committed to finding out what had happened out there at the Beaumont property. Who were in the graves? Why was there one left empty? How long had the bodies been up there? Again, her mind reeled with dozens of questions.

Reed really thought she would just let it go?

Maybe he didn't know his wife that well after all.

If he thought he could get away with brooding all night, sulking in the kitchen, drinking himself into oblivion, then he had another think—and probably drink—coming! She was a reporter and had been since they'd met. So he knew how she felt about her job, how writing about crime, even solving cases was a part of her, as it was a part of him.

She spun quickly, determined to have it out with him. As she did, her foot caught in the sagging hem of her robe, the loose material tangling around her ankle.

She slipped on the step.

She scrabbled for the rail, gravity pulling her down swiftly.

Her fingers slid down a baluster.

Her feet slipped to the next step.

Thud!

She landed on her back. Pain ricocheted down her

spine. Agony ripped through her shoulder as she tumbled. She let out a yell. "Noooo!" The dog barked and scrambled out of her way. "Reed!" She fell to the base of the step.

"Nikki!" Reed's voice was sharp. Anxious. Echoing over the sound of a stool scraping backward and running footsteps. "Nikki!"

She felt something break within her. Something tender and fragile.

Oh. Dear. God.

Sprawled on the last two steps, rattled to her core, she spied her husband careening around the corner to the kitchen. He was at her side in an instant, on his knees and hovering over her. "Oh, God, Nikki, are you okay?" His face was a mask of worry, his anxious eyes scanning her features.

Was she? She blinked. Moved slightly. Testing her arms and legs. "Yeah, I think so," she said, though she wasn't certain.

"Your shoulder?"

"It's . . . it hurts," she admitted as her head cleared, and she knew in that instant her shoulder wasn't the problem. Nor was her back, nor her arms or legs. No . . . oh, please . . . no.

"Thank God."

She heard his voice as if from a distance.

A deep, clawing sadness took hold of her soul as she recognized the feeling of wetness between her legs. She had trouble finding her voice. "I think you'd better call Dr. Kasey," she said, forcing the horrid words past her lips.

"Dr. Ka . . . Oh, no," he whispered, letting his gaze slide down her body. "You mean . . ."

She followed his gaze but knew what she'd find. A crimson stain was blooming on her nightgown, visible where her dressing gown had parted. "Oh, Jesus, Nikki."

"Call her," she said again, more forcefully, even though she was certain it was too late.

There was no baby.

Not anymore.

CHAPTER 9

Two days later, Reed was at the station. He tossed back the cold dregs of his coffee and threw the disposable cup into the trash near his desk. The door to his office was slightly ajar, and he heard the buzz and hum of activity from the outer hallway. Someone was laughing. He thought it sounded like Van Houten's deep rumble as it faded away.

It was nearly five, the shift would be changing soon, and voices and ringing phones carried over the wheeze of the air-conditioning unit that was struggling against the thick Georgia heat.

Though the flood waters from the storm had receded and most of the power had been restored, the city of Savannah was still in the midst of a major cleanup. Emergency crews for the city and electric or cable companies continued to work around the clock. The streets had been cleared of debris for the most part, but now the roadways were filled with vans from the media, trucks for the road crews or construction companies, and insurance adjustors assessing the damage.

Getting through town was still a challenge.

But then, what wasn't?

Reed considered another cup of coffee, then discarded the idea as it was late afternoon, bright sunlight visible through the grimy window.

He rotated the kinks from his neck.

Because of the hurricane, the police department was stretched thin.

Losing an officer, especially a detective of Morrisette's caliber, didn't help. She'd been a good cop. A dedicated cop. A do-anything-for-justice cop. The department missed her. Hell, Reed missed her.

He glanced over at Morrisette's empty desk and frowned, a hollow feeling in his gut.

It would ebb in time.

He knew that.

But for now there was a distinct void in his life.

More than one, he thought sadly as he remembered the panicked early-morning drive to the hospital with Nikki, her face white as chalk, the deep regret and aching sadness in her eyes despite him saying over and over again, "It'll be all right, Nikki. Hang in there. It's all gonna be all right." He'd known differently, of course, as he'd punched the accelerator and sped through the near-empty streets, the Jeep's emergency lights flashing on the short, frantic trip to the hospital. He'd slid a glance in her direction. "We're gonna be okay."

Nikki had seen through his lie and nervously cracked

the window. "I don't know if we'll ever be 'okay,'" she'd admitted as he'd careened into the parking lot. The Jeep slid to a stop at the glass doors of the emergency room, the same doors he'd walked through only an hour earlier, and he'd hustled her inside.

From then on it had been a blur, a tangle of emotion.

Nikki's OB/GYN had met them in the ER.

Devoid of makeup, her hair in a loose, messy bun, Dr. Kasey had taken the call from the answering service and rushed to the hospital. After a quick exam in the ER, she'd somberly delivered the news they'd already expected: Nikki was miscarrying. There would be no baby. Not now. They would have to wait, but in a few months and blah, blah, blah. The same litany they'd heard before.

He wondered if it would ever happen, if they would ever have a pregnancy go to term, and told himself if it didn't happen, he would be okay. Maybe. But Nikki? He felt a bitter sadness deep inside. As hard as it was on him, it was worse for Nikki. He knew that. He'd seen it in the pain in her eyes. The misery. And the regret.

"Hell," he muttered under his breath, and rolled his chair back to the desk again. He wouldn't think about all that now. Nor would he consider the tension that existed in his marriage. So many harsh words had been uttered, so many apologies left unspoken.

He glanced over to Morrisette's empty desk again. He'd been out when someone had cleaned out her desk and he hadn't seen who had taken all of Morrisette's things—her pictures of her kids, a silver boot paperweight, a sharpshooter award all hidden in a messy stack of paperwork, coffee cups and half-empty packs of gum. There had been a pot with a half-dead cactus that she'd never watered in one corner, neglected but too stubborn to die. Now the workspace was empty, the computer monitor dark, her chair tucked neatly into place.

So unfamiliar.

So sterile.

He'd managed to snag one memento from Morrisette's desk drawer before someone had cleaned everything from her workspace. A ring of keys with a Lone Star. He'd slipped the keys from the ring, left them in her desk drawer, and fingering the sharp points of the star, pocketed the token. He figured she would've wanted him to have it. And even if not, too bad.

A reminder.

At least for now.

But the loss of his unborn child was different. No memento for a kid who hadn't come into the world. Just heartbreak.

The desk wouldn't be empty long. He'd been advised that Delacroix would soon occupy the space, that she, a junior detective, efficient but still a newbie to the department, would be his new partner.

"A temporary move," Sergeant Sanya Jones, her words emphasized by the slightest of Jamaican accents, had told him. She'd transferred from Miami several years ago and ran the department with an easy smile and an iron fist. "Let's just see if it works out."

He'd wanted to argue, not so much that he had anything against Delacroix other than she was a little wet behind the ears, but because neither Delacroix nor anyone else would be able to fill Sylvie Morrisette's beat-up boots.

God, he'd miss her.

There was a sharp rap on the half-open door to his office. Reed looked up to spy Jade Delacroix poking her head inside. "Got a sec?"

"Sure."

In a pair of jeans, black T-shirt and jacket, Delacroix slipped into the room. Her badge was visible, clipped to her waistband, and she carried a slim iPad with her. She let the door close a bit behind her, but the noise from the outer hallway still drifted into the room.

"Take a load off." He motioned to the vacant chair and desk. "I hear this is yours now."

"Yeah, I guess." She glanced at Morrisette's chair but didn't move to it. Instead she remained standing, fidgeting and looking uncomfortable. "I, um . . . I just wanted to say I'm sorry. You know. About Morrisette."

"Me too." He'd been getting the same sad faces and quick condolences from everyone he'd met at the station.

She plowed on. "Yeah . . . and well . . . I heard, you know, about the baby. The miscarriage. That's . . ." Biting her lip, she glanced out the window and squinted behind her glasses. Her jaw was tight, her auburn hair catching in the light. "That's rough." She was nodding, as if agreeing with herself, as if she'd suffered a similar experience or at least known someone close who had.

"Yeah, thanks." That unhappy news, too, had swept through the department. Most people had heard that he and Nikki had been expecting, so again, he'd dealt with more than a handful of condolences. Hopefully, this was the last and they all could move on.

"So, what's up?" he asked, effectively changing the subject as he leaned back in his desk chair. "You got something on the Beaumont victims?"

"A good possibility. Narrowed things down," she said, adjusting her glasses.

He waited. This was good news. The morgue and ME were overworked, as was everyone after the hurricane, but they'd rushed the autopsies of the decayed skeletons through.

"Dental records confirmed that the girls in the graves are the Duval sisters."

"Really?" He'd wondered, as had others. He'd known about the missing girls. Almost anyone who had lived in Savannah in the last twenty years had heard their tragic story: three sisters who had disappeared after going to the movies.

"IDs verified on the older two girls," Delacroix explained, flipping open her iPad cover and checking her notes. "Holly, the oldest, was twelve at the time and the middle sister, Poppy, was ten."

He said, "But there were three."

"Yes, Rose, the youngest." She glanced up at him. "Still missing."

He felt the muscles of his back tense. "How old was she?"

"Almost five." Again she looked at her screen.

"So we can assume the youngest was supposed to go in that last spot, the empty grave. That had been the killer's plan."

Her lips tightened. "Possibly."

Of course there were other options, but that seemed the most likely. "Do we have cause of death for the two?"

"Not completely confirmed, but the guess is strangulation." Her jaw grew hard. "Fractured hyoid bones in both bodies."

"So they were dead when they were placed in the tomb."

"And staged," she said, reminding him of the victims' interlocking fingers.

"Right." He rubbed the back of his suddenly tense neck. He'd dealt with his share of sickos. It came with the territory, but the crimes against children really got to him. "Has anyone notified next of kin?" The worst part of the job.

"Happening now," she said. "The mother still lives in the area. Her name is . . ." Again she referred to the screen.

"Margaret," he remembered.

"Yeah." Nodding, she kept her eyes on her device. "Margaret, but no longer Duval. She's remarried. Her name is . . . Where is it? . . . Oh, here we go: Margaret Le Roy. Her husband is Ezra. He's a minister at the Second United Christian Church. It's off of Derenne, not far from the hospital and medical center."

"I know it." Reed pictured the building with its prominent white spire and tracery windows cut into sand-colored bricks. "What about the father of the girls?"

"Harvey Duval," she said. "He moved. Out of state. Now in . . . let me see." Deftly Delacroix moved her cursor and said, "Okay. He's in California."

"Who isn't?" he asked.

"Right." She smiled, some of the tension breaking. Leaning a hip against Morrisette's desk, she said, "Harvey landed in Fremont, which is a big tech center, I think. Southeast from San Francisco, closer to San Jose. Anyway, Harvey was in insurance. For a time after the girls disappeared, he and Margaret hung together and lived here in Savannah. But then the marriage fell apart and they split." She was reading her notes, skimming details.

"So the talk was that he wanted to get over the disappearances and try to move on. She, Margaret, couldn't. Or wouldn't. She became obsessed." Delacroix looked over the tops of her glasses, pinning Reed in her gaze. "I can't say that I blame her. Anyway, the upshot is that they divorced and she lost her job as an RN at Oswald General Hospital, because finding her daughters was all she could think about. She was coming in late and having trouble concentrating and, well, that's not hard to imagine given what she was going through." She scanned the notes. "Anyway, the upshot is that he moved away, to the West Coast, and she stayed. She began working as a private nurse and part time at a clinic here in town."

"And all the while kept hounding the department," he said.

"Yep, never stopped reminding us that the case hadn't been solved, didn't want it to go cold, which, of course, it did."

That was right. He'd heard some of the staff in the Missing Persons department complain. Also, every year on the anniversary of her daughters' disappearance Margaret had taken out a full-page ad in the *Sentinel* in an effort to renew interest in the case and keep the public informed, all in the hopes that someone—anyone—would have some information leading her to her children.

Reed got it. The woman had lost her three daughters in one fell swoop. But there was more to the story. Something about a brother, he thought. Something that was suspicious.

"Who was the lead?"

"Detective in charge of the investigation?" she said, then answered before he could confirm. "Charles Easterling, retired the next year, after the Duval girls went missing, and died three years ago at eighty-three. Congenital heart disease."

"Who was assigned?"

"Someone named Woodrow Stevens, who moved to Chicago last year."

"Woody," Reed said.

"And now, it looks like you're up."

Waving Delacroix into the visitor's seat, he leaned back in his chair and tented his fingers. "So give me the rundown. Fill me in on what actually happened the day the girls were last seen." He hadn't been a police officer yet when the girls had been abducted twenty years earlier, but he'd heard bits and pieces over the years. The case had never been kicked to Homicide because no bodies had ever been located and the mother had stalwartly insisted the girls were alive. That they'd been abducted. That they just needed to be found.

To add credence to her beliefs, there had been sightings over the years, calls from people who had sworn they'd seen one or more of the Duval sisters in different parts of the country, one as far away as Alaska if he remembered correctly.

With the aid of computers, police artists had come up with images of what the girls would look like today as young women, and so, over the years, every once in a while, there had been reported sightings of Holly or Poppy or Rose.

When Reed had first met Nikki, she had recently interviewed a woman who had sworn she'd seen all three girls with an older couple when she'd been visiting Disney World in Orlando, though, as with the other rumored glimpses of the girls, the story hadn't panned out.

None had.

Until now.

"Okay. The rundown. And by the way, I sent you copies of everything I've got." She glanced up. "Check your e-mail."

"Will do."

"Okay." Rather than sitting at Morrisette's old desk, Delacroix settled into the visitor's chair, her fingers skating over the keys of her device as she brought him up to speed.

In essence, the three Duval sisters, curly-headed blondes with bright blue eyes, disappeared nearly twenty years earlier. They'd gone to the movies at a theater five blocks from their house with their older half brother, Owen, who had dropped them off, then claimed when he came to pick them up after the movie had let out, they were gone. He insisted he searched for them to no avail. Witnesses had seen the girls at the movie, but no one remembered their half brother. He was supposed to stay with them throughout the flick, but he swore he bribed them with candy for their silence so he could duck out early. When he returned and went home, the parents were frantic and called 911 to report them missing.

"Owen became the primary suspect or 'person of interest,'" Delacroix said, lifting one hand and making air quotes with her fingers, "and actually he still is, but he had an airtight alibi with a girlfriend and since there were no bodies and no one saw him with the girls, no witnesses, he walked. The press crucified him, of course, but he's always maintained his innocence."

"And where is he now?"

"He moved to Atlanta not long after the girls disappeared and since then relocated to Jacksonville. People assumed he left Savannah to get away from the scandal and persecution, but who knows? Same for the move to Florida, no one knows why he landed there.

"However, the interview notes seem to indicate that his reaction, to the girls going missing, wasn't expected. Instead of being upset and worried, or even feeling guilt or regret for losing the girls, he seemed angry and distant."

"Anyone talk to him since the bodies were located?"

"Not from the department. I can't say about his mother. She got the word about the IDs this morning, so she could've called him or texted him or whatever. And then there's this," she added, her lips tightening a bit, "he hasn't exactly kept his nose clean. A girlfriend, Maria Coronado, filed charges against him for assault about seven years ago, that was when he was still in Atlanta, but then changed her mind, dropped the charges and the case never went to court. From the looks of it, the cops were called to their shared apartment twice and then the arrest, but, like I said, Coronado changed her mind."

"Let me guess, they got back together?"

"For a while, then he split for Jacksonville."

"Without her."

"Uh . . . doesn't say, but I'll check. And he may have moved since. I checked with the Jacksonville PD, and they cruised by his apartment. Looks vacant and has a FOR RENT sign in the window."

Reed thought that over. "His mother might know."

"You'd think."

"Anything on the biological father?" He rubbed his chin, feeling the stubble from his five-o'clock shadow. "I know Harvey adopted him early on, but was the real father ever around?"

"No info on that. Yet."

"Huh." Reed made a mental note. "What about Owen Duval? Anything new?"

She shook her head. "Nothing serious. A few traffic tickets, one for expired plates and one for running a red light. And a neighbor complained that he played his music too loud and too late, that was when he was in Atlanta with the girlfriend, but since then, nothing." She looked over the tops of her glasses at Reed. "At least that we know of."

"Right. Let's find him," Reed said. "See what he has to say for himself."

"You got it."

"And I want to run down the girlfriend who gave him the alibi as well. Do we know where she is?"

"Still working on that. Her name is Ashley McDonnell, or was, she could be married by now."

"What about anyone else close to the Duval girls? Friends? Cousins?"

"Lots of people interviewed way back when. I've got a list and I've sent it along with all the case files to you—e-mail."

"Okay."

She said, "Here's something else: There were only two security cameras at the theater at the time, one at the ticket booth outside and then one in the lobby. Neither one showed anything out of the ordinary, no abduction during the intermission between films—it was a double-header that evening."

"But there is some footage?"

"Yeah, we've got a copy."

"Let's look it over."

"What about other security cameras in the area?"

"Nothing. Back then there were few street cams or security cams outside, so there was nothing to go on. An Amber Alert was issued, but you know, technology wasn't anything like it is now and the alert system hadn't been in existence all that long, so the Duval girls fell through the cracks.

"A tip line was set up and at first all kinds of calls came in. Just like you'd expect. Everything from those that seemed legit to some of the most bizarre, but, as you know, none paid off. Eventually, sadly the case went ice-cold and if it weren't for Margaret stoking the fires of interest every year, people would've forgotten all about it."

"Until now," he said, and she nodded.

"Until now."

He stood and grabbed his jacket off the back of his chair. "Let's go and see what Margaret Duval has to say." His guts twisted at the thought of speaking with the grieving mother, but it had to be done.

"All right." Delacroix snapped her iPad shut, retrieved her phone from the back pocket of her jeans and was heading out the door. A step or two behind, Reed circumvented a couple of detectives walking the opposite direction down the hall and caught up with Delacroix at the top of the stairs. As he reached her, her cell went off in her hand. She slanted a gaze at the screen, then sighed. "Crap."

"What?"

"Wouldn't ya know?" She started down the steps. "It's the morgue. I asked them to keep the clothing and jewelry from the bodies and let me know when I could take a look. Examine the locket before they processed and bagged it."

"That hasn't been done?"

She sent him a glance over her shoulder and was jostled by a beefy uniformed cop hurrying up the stairs. "Backlog, remember? They were already behind when the hurricane hit. They rushed the autopsies and ID of the girls through and now want to clear them out. So I gotta go." She slid him a glance as they reached the first floor. "Why don't you go on ahead and I'll meet up with you," she suggested. "For all we know Margaret might not even be home."

"She might be at the morgue already. You might run into her there."

"Oh, God, I hope not . . . she shouldn't see the bodies." Delacroix's eyebrows slammed downward over her glasses. Shaking her head, she added, "They're just skeletons. Nothing a mother should ever view."

He couldn't disagree. "If I see her first, I'll try to dissuade her."

"Do that. Definitely. After I check out the locket, I'll try to catch up with the father, Harvey, in California, talk to him on the phone. Then I'll meet you back here. Okay?"

"Works for me," he said as they reached the main door.

"Good. Later."

Once outside they split up.

Reed climbed into the sweltering interior of his Jeep, slid on a pair of Ray-Bans, then started the engine. With the windows rolled down, he maneuvered through one detour, hit the Truman Parkway, melding into traffic and rolling up the windows as he remembered how Morrisette had an irritating habit of playing with the automatic windows. It had driven him crazy. Now, he'd have to get used to a new partner and all her idiosyncrasies. Delacroix? Would he be partnered with her permanently? Or would he have to get used to flying solo?

Maybe, for the time being, having some time alone was a good thing.

CHAPTER 10

With the cat curled up beside her, Nikki lay on her back in the bed and stared at the slowly turning blades of the ceiling fan. She felt awful.

Never had she liked lying around, she'd never even been one to sun herself on a beach and soak up rays or spend hours on the couch watching television or reading. She'd always been athletic and ready for action, so this . . . this ennui was getting to her.

Add to that a mountain of regret and guilt eating away at her brain.

Which hadn't been helped by her husband.

She was still steamed at Reed. Oh, she got where he was coming from, she didn't blame him for that, but it was time to move on. They were both incredibly sad at the loss of the child, but she couldn't stand recuperating and doing nothing despite her doctor's suggestion to take it easy. She grabbed her new phone, the one she'd picked up after her visit with Dr. Kasey. Somehow she'd managed to transfer all the data to her new iPhone, but she'd done it by rote as her thoughts had been with the baby she'd lost. Even now, she blinked back tears.

"You need to give yourself permission to heal, to take the time," Dr. Kasey had said, her dark eyes kind, her smile understanding. But what the doctor and her husband didn't understand was that Nikki was better off doing something, anything, and the fact that there was potentially the story of the century at her fingertips only added to her need to get up and get going.

Worse yet, Norm Metzger had the nerve to call her for information on the investigation.

"What is it about 'I'm recovering and shouldn't be bothered' you don't understand?" she'd asked him when he'd identified himself and explained that he was looking for information on the bodies found at the Beaumont estate. Nikki would never have taken the call, but she'd recognized the number for the *Sentinel* and assumed erroneously that Millie was phoning her with information.

"But you were there," Metzger had argued, "and you're married to the lead investigator on the case."

"So?"

"And it's *my* story, Gillette. Not yours. Not anyone else's at the paper." He couldn't hide the irritation in his voice.

Nikki got it. Metzger was still burned about the other crime cases she'd been a part of while he, ostensibly, was the police beat/crime reporter for the paper. He'd also seethed about her brush with fame as a published true crime author of three—count 'em!—three books. As close as he was to the editor, Norm probably figured his job was on the line. And it should be. If he wasn't such a close golfing/poker buddy of Tom Fink, he would have been fired years before.

"Look, we're on the same team here. We both work for the *Sentinel*, and God knows the paper needs a shot in the arm. So help me out here. What did you see at the Beaumont estate, and where are the police on this? The bodies have been ID'd as a couple of the Duval sisters, the girls that have been missing for about twenty years, the ones where their mother takes out ads in the newspaper to keep the public aware."

"Right."

"So you must have the inside track on the investigation."

She bristled. "You know Detective Reed and I don't discuss his cases."

"Oh, come on, Gillette. You expect me to believe that?"

She bit her tongue, but her temper was rising and she clenched the phone so hard her hand hurt.

"I can't believe it!" he said, his voice rising. "Listen, I know you've got the inside track on this one. Just like you did before with Blondell O'Henry and *The Grave Robber*. Nearly cost me my job, last time."

She snapped. Could control herself not a second longer. "You don't know anything, Metzger," she charged. "And that's the problem: You never have. If you really cared about your beat, you'd put more into it. Instead of phoning it in. You're right, the paper's in trouble and you aren't helping."

"You little bitch," he said, almost snarling, all of his pent-up rage and jealousy boiling to the surface. "Born with a silver spoon, always getting into trouble, thinking you're some hotshot author when you've got it made being married to the damned department! Like I said, 'inside track.'"

"Don't call again!" she advised, and as she clicked off heard him mutter, "Hormonal bitch."

She wished she could have slammed down a receiver rather than just press a button. Geez, he pissed her off! And the remark about hormones. Obviously Metzger hadn't heard of the Me Too movement. And considering her condition after the miscarriage, the barb cut deep.

Don't let him get to you. He's scared. Backed into a corner. Needs his job. Just do yours.

But his jab cut deep. She felt hot tears burn the back of her eyes.

"Screw it!"

She threw off the covers. Refused to cry.

Would not.

No more tears, she told herself, though her throat was clogged.

It was past time to get up and get going and yeah, her shoulder still ached and her arm was in a sling, and yeah, she felt horrible, just horrible about losing the baby. Then, oh, God, Morrisette. So awful. But lying in bed and stewing wouldn't help anything.

She'd promised Reed she would take the doctor's orders seriously and she would, but it wouldn't help her to do nothing and go quietly out of her mind.

Besides, there was a story to write.

And it was still hers, damn it. No matter what Metzger thought.

She'd already seen news reports on TV. With the bodies identified, reporters were already on the scene, not only at the Beaumont estate, but had collected at the home and business of Tyson Beaumont, who along with his father, Baxter, owned the property where the bodies of the Duval sisters had been found.

Nikki should have been there. In the crowd. With questions and a microphone. It was all so frustrating. When she should have had a damned exclusive. She'd even read Metzger's account of the discovery of the bodies. It had been accurate, but, in her estimation, thin.

She could do better.

She *would* do better.

Besides, she did have an ace or two up her sleeve. And not because of Reed. First, there was the boat she was certain she'd seen beneath the willow tree. It had been red and hard to distinguish, but she kept mixing it up in her mind with the prow of the boat that had struck Morrisette. Different boats, right? Had to be, but she wasn't certain; that part of the tragedy was still murky in her mind. And then there was Bronco Cravens. So far she'd seen no interviews with him. His anonymous tip to the police department hadn't yet been leaked to the press, but she knew about it.

That, though not much, was something.

A different angle.

The Cravens and Beaumont families, though from vastly different social strata, had been connected for years, and no one, so far, had delved into that side story.

And she knew Tyson Beaumont, who was a year or possibly two younger than Andrew but, she thought, had played ball with him in high school. Way back when.

She hadn't really known the Duval girls, though Holly hadn't been that much younger than her, maybe a couple of years? She'd have to check. There was a chance that she might have been friends with someone Nikki had hung out with in junior high, though that was a stretch. She certainly didn't remember it.

Also, so far the victims' mother, Margaret Duval Le Roy, had not spoken to the press despite the small group who had collected on the lawn in front of her house. But that would probably happen. And soon. Nikki only wished she could be the first reporter to interview the victims' mother, but considering the fact she was still laid up, it seemed unlikely. She tested her arm, felt a painful twinge in her shoulder and silently swore at her bad luck.

But a sore shoulder didn't mean she was bed-bound.

Nor did a miscarriage, sad as it may be.

"So do something," she said aloud. As if she needed any motivation.

On the bed, Jennings stretched and yawned. His pink tongue curling, his needle-sharp teeth visible.

"I wasn't talking to you," she said, but couldn't resist patting him on the head before she made her way to the steps leading to the third-floor loft and her office. Ignoring the pain in her shoulder, she flopped onto the daybed with her laptop, then started scouring the Internet for more information on the bodies located at the Beaumont estate. All she knew was that they'd been ID'd as the older two of the long-missing Duval sisters, Holly and Poppy. But Rose, the youngest, was still missing. So what happened to her? Was she buried elsewhere? Or were her remains scattered, found by animals? No, that didn't make sense, not if the reports were accurate because the other two bodies hadn't been disturbed. So—had she escaped? Was it possible the youngest sibling alone had survived? What were the chances of that?

In her mind she was already writing her story, using her unique perspective as a person who had been at the historic home as a child. She knew a portion of the history of the old home, most of the rumors and scandals, secrets and lies. Those that she didn't, she could find out. If Google couldn't help her, Charlene probably could. All she had to do was ask her mother. . . .

Her heart sank at that thought. She'd barely spoken to Charlene since losing the baby. One quick call delivering the heartbreaking news and a promise to phone again when she was feeling better.

"No time like the present," she said aloud as she heard Mikado's nails clicking on the stairs as the old dog came up to join her. As the phone rang in her ear, he looked up expectantly and Nikki patted the mattress beside her. He sprang onto the bed and settled in beside her. "We need to go outside, you and I, to get some exercise," she said as the phone call went to voice mail.

Relieved, Nikki left a quick message saying she was feeling better and would call Charlene back. Then she dived into the information her laptop provided. A lot had happened since she'd been laid up, the essence of the information as she sifted through it that the two bodies had been identified, as many had speculated, to be the two older Duval sisters. Holly and Poppy. The youngest girl wasn't in the basement, her whereabouts unknown.

Dead? Or alive? If dead, where was she buried, and would she be found? And if alive, where was she? Did she remember? Was she living another life and didn't realize who she was? And what about the older half brother, Owen, Margaret's only son. He'd been the prime suspect in his sisters' disappearance. What had happened to him?

Was he around? Did he know that Holly's and Poppy's bodies had been discovered? What, if any, connection did the Duval family have with the Beaumonts?

Dozens of questions swirling through her brain, she accessed the newspaper's archives remotely and pulled up story after story about the Duval sisters and started making a list of people to interview. At the top of the list was Owen Duval. She didn't know much about him, only that he'd been adopted by Harvey Duval soon after Harvey married Margaret. So where was Owen's biological father? She made a note to track him down.

She spent over an hour searching through the files she could access, as well as online yearbooks, cross-checking the pictures and names with a list of the acquaintances she'd found in old newspaper articles. There were several names of classmates that rang distant bells with her. When she'd looked up those names in old yearbooks, she vaguely remembered some of the kids, all of whom would be in their midthirties now. She noted a few of the names and was about to call Millie when Mikado placed his nose on her leg and whined.

"That's right. I promised," she said, and reluctantly climbed down the stairs to the kitchen and opened the slider. The dog shot outside. He sniffed around the backyard, chased a ball she threw with her good hand, then flopped on the flagstones in a patch of sunlight to sun himself. "Feel good?" she asked, scratching his scruffy head behind his ears, though she was thinking of the case and how she would unravel the mystery. She'd need the help of the police department but didn't dare talk to Reed. Not yet. She knew other people at the department but figured she was persona non grata with the PD. At least for now.

She left the dog snoozing in the warm sunlight and returned to the third floor again.

She dialed Millie's cell number and put her phone on speaker while her fingers flew over the keyboard. Yeah, her left hand twinged, hurting as she typed, but at least it still worked.

Millie clicked on before the phone rang twice, but Nikki didn't wait for her to answer. "I see the bodies have been ID'd."

"Yeah, next of kin—the mother—was just notified a couple of hours ago."

"Metzger called trying to get info from me."

"Yeah." A pause. "He's here at the office, doing some research. Or whatever. Maybe playing games on his computer. Or placing a bet or two. He's big on the online gambling."

"What about the third sister? The little one?"

"No sign of her or her remains," Millie said, then, "unless you know more than I do."

Nikki got the implication. "From Reed? Are you kidding? His lips are sealed. Like permanently." And it was frustrating as hell.

There was a brief pause, then Millie asked, "So, Nikki, how're you doing?"

The question was inevitable. "I'm okay." That was a bit of a lie, but she went with it.

"How's your shoulder?"

"It'll be fine."

"And—?"

Nikki let out a sigh. Millie wanted to know about the baby. Okay. That was fair. They were friends. "I'm . . . it's . . . it's okay," she hedged, spying the cat stroll into the loft and hop onto her desk. "It, um, it might take a little while to get over, but I've been through it before. I'll be fine. *We'll* be fine." Another lie, this one a little larger because right now she and Reed were not okay. Not okay at all.

"It's rough."

A lump formed in Nikki's throat. She could handle a lot, but when someone was kind to her . . . "Yeah, it is. But . . ." She blinked. Stupid tears. "But there it is. So, I've decided to concentrate on work. For now."

"Good idea."

"So, to that end, I can access a lot of the newspaper's files remotely, here, but that might not be enough. I might need your help."

"You got it. What do you want?"

She watched as Jennings gathered himself, then leaped to the window ledge to stare out at the upper limb of a magnolia tree, where a magpie was perched, screeching and flapping its wings. "I'm hoping you can run down some contact info for me," Nikki said. "Lots of people were quoted in the original reports, like friends of the victims, neighbors of the family, people who were at the movie theater on the day the girls disappeared, so I'd like to talk to some of them. You know, like the ticket taker or the person who worked the refreshment counter, that kind of thing, anyone who can remember them that day. Do you think you can find them? Especially any that are still local, that haven't moved away?"

"Mmm, yeah. I'll see what I can do. You got a list?"

"I'll e-mail it to you."

"Good."

"Also," Nikki said, flipping through her notes, "if there's any info on Owen Duval, the brother, let me know because the police had zeroed in on him and if you can locate Owen's alibi, her name was Ashley McDonnell."

"McDonnell, got it. Is that all?" Millie asked sarcastically.

"Actually, no." Nikki was thinking fast now. "I think I might have known some of the people close to the Duvals, so if you can find a list of people the police interviewed, the girls' friends and relatives, that would help. If there's any way to get a peek at their statements, I'd love it."

"If it's not public, you've got a better lead on that."

"Through Reed," she said, flopping back on the daybed.

"Yeah."

That would never work, but she had to move on, couldn't be waylaid. "So, if you could just, you know, keep an eye on the story, whatever comes in to the paper, over the wires or tips or whatever, and give me a heads-up and send me links, that kind of thing, so I can be on top of it until I can come back into the office myself, that would be great."

"Okay. I think I can do it. No problem."

"Oh, and let me know what Metzger's got going on this."

"Sure," Millie said, and Nikki could hear the smile in the other woman's voice. "You got it."

CHAPTER 11

Reed cut the engine.

He'd parked his Jeep in the shade of one of the large live oaks that separated the church lot from the parsonage, a white brick bungalow, and now was walking along a stone path leading to the porch.

The door opened before he could press the doorbell and a small, bird-like woman peered at him through the screen. Her eyes, behind rimless glasses, were red from crying, her skin blotchy. Blond hair shot with silver was cut short and swept away from her face.

"Mrs. Le Roy? Margaret Le Roy?" he said, showing his ID, then introducing himself.

"We've been expecting you," she said, her voice husky. "The first officer who was here . . . The deputy who told us about"—she cleared her throat and forced herself to continue—"who explained that . . . that the girls had been found said . . . said that someone would be coming." She opened the screen door. "Come in, please." In jeans, a light T-shirt and pink cardigan despite the heat, she led him to a living room just off the entry. Waving him into one of the floral wingback chairs positioned in front of the picture window, she dropped onto a faded couch pushed against the opposite wall where a large print of *The Last Supper* was mounted.

"I'm sorry for your loss," he said, and she closed her eyes, nodding.

"Thank you. Yes . . . it's . . . it's hard."

"I can't even begin to imagine."

"You wouldn't want to."

"No." He faced her across the coffee table, where a large Bible lay open. A canary twittered from a cage on the side table. Upon the mantel of the fireplace were several family photos; a group shot of three blond girls, arms linked as they squinted into the sun, was front and center. Reed's heart twisted as he recognized Holly, Poppy and Rosie Duval. The two older girls were nearly twins, they looked so much alike, the main difference being one was taller, but only by a couple of inches. Both dark blond, both with short, little, freckled noses. The littlest was too young to have had such a clear resemblance.

"My husband will be joining us. He's on the phone, I think." Margaret glanced to the empty hallway, then back at Reed. "Are you certain?" she asked, a hushed, desperate note in her voice. As if she were afraid to say the words. "I mean, are you sure the girls are really Holly and Poppy?"

"Yes, the dental records were a match." No reason to sugarcoat the truth. "We're waiting for DNA, but there's really no doubt. I'm so sorry for your loss."

"I want to see them."

He'd been expecting that. "I don't think it's a good idea."

"They're my daughters!"

"And . . . unrecognizable."

"But—"

"Mrs. Le Roy, I would strongly advise against viewing the remains."

"I am a nurse. Retired now, but still," she said. "And I've seen bodies before. Many bodies."

"Again, I don't think it's a good idea."

She shook her head, wiped the edge of her eyes with a handkerchief. "But my daughters—"

"I know."

"And . . . and by the way, there are three of them. You say you found Holly and Poppy, but what about little Rosie . . ." Her voice trailed off before she spoke quietly. "You haven't come to tell me you've found her, have you?" Behind her glasses, her eyes focused hard, drilling into him.

"No. No, I haven't."

"Good." She swallowed hard. "Maybe she . . . maybe she somehow . . . Oh, no, I won't let myself think it." She sketched a sign of the cross over her thin chest and then caught herself. "Old habit," she admitted. "And it's true what they say, old habits really do die hard. I was born and raised Catholic. But then, well, I met Ezra and . . . well, he convinced me to start attending his service and I did." She looked over her shoulder again. "He said he wouldn't be long—oh, I think I hear him."

She did. Heavy footsteps heralded her husband's approach and he appeared, a big bear of a man with snow-white hair and a thin white beard that just traced the edge of his jaw. "Reverend Ezra Le Roy," he said, extending his hand as Reed stood.

"Detective Reed," Margaret explained. "He won't let me see the girls."

"Oh."

Reed ended the handshake. "No, I just suggested that it might not be a good idea because of the years that have passed, the condition of the bodies."

Margaret let out a little squeak of protest.

"I see." Her husband sighed heavily. "It's probably for the best."

"If you think so." She wasn't convinced.

Her husband was nodding his near-bald head. "I do."

"Well . . . well, I was . . ." She pulled herself together and said, "I was just asking about little Rosie."

"You found her?" Le Roy's eyebrows quirked up expectantly.

"No, not yet."

"But you're still looking."

"Of course. I just came by to ask some questions."

"Oh." Margaret's face fell, but she bravely sniffed back her tears. "I guess I should be glad about that. I've been after the police for years and no one seemed to care . . . but then maybe it doesn't matter. The girls were already gone." Her gaze slid to the canary. From its perch, it pecked incessantly at a tiny mirror dangling from the top of its cage.

"If you could tell me about the day they went missing," he suggested.

Margaret sighed. "What good will that do?"

"We need to find out who did this to your girls, Mrs. Le Roy. And we need to find Rose."

Her eyes filled. "Yes, yes, of course. It's just that it's been so long and I thought, I *prayed* that the girls would be found. Alive." Her voice cracked and she swiped at her eyes. "And why now? After all these years? Why couldn't you have found them earlier? Before . . . before . . ." She took in a shaky breath. "This should never have happened to the girls, never! I don't know how many times I was down at the police department! If you people had located them when they went missing, if you'd done your job then, they might be alive today! Oh . . . oh . . . dear God." She was weeping, her shoulders shaking.

"Oh, baby." Ezra took a spot next to her on the couch and wrapped his arms around her. "Come on, Margie, honey. The detective is just doing his job. Maybe you and I, we should pray, huh? How about that?" He placed his forehead onto hers and began to whisper a prayer.

Reed looked down at his hands, giving them time, the canary pecking softly against its own reflection.

". . . and please, Lord, help us locate Rose and may she be found healthy, a now-grown woman . . ."

Reed's heart sank. What were the chances? This was probably just false hope, but he didn't interrupt.

". . . accept them into heaven . . ."

Reed waited.

". . . in the name of our savior, Jesus Christ, we pray. Amen."

"Amen," Margaret repeated, calmer, her eyes dry. Her husband released her, and she focused on Reed again. "Forgive me, Detective," she said calmly, though her face was still blotchy from her spate of tears. "I know you're here to help us. What . . . what can I tell you?"

"How about we start with the day that the girls went missing?"

She let out her breath slowly and told them the story, just as he'd heard it from Delacroix and read for himself before driving here. Margaret explained that she and her husband at the time, Harvey Duval, had been together, going through open houses as they had been planning to move, and they'd had dinner later at a crowded restaurant. They'd allowed the girls, even the youngest, to go to the local cinema with their older brother, Owen.

At the mention of her son, Margaret looked away, to the window, her hands working the handkerchief in her lap. "Oh, dear," she said, and Reed followed her gaze. At the edge of the yard a large news van was rolling to a stop, its satellite scraping the lowest branches of one of the live oaks.

"I'll handle them," the reverend said, on his feet quickly. He snapped the blinds shut and headed out the front door.

Margaret licked her lips. "You know," she admitted, "for years I called the newspaper and TV stations and tried to drum up interest, attempted to keep the story alive, if you will." She swallowed hard. "I think I talked to your wife, she's a reporter for the *Sentinel*, right?"

"Yes."

"But time goes by, other stories become more interesting, more 'relevant.' And so my girls faded away and now . . ." She shook her head, her graying hair sweeping the back of her neck. Her lips pursed. "Now we have to find Rose." Her eyes met his. "That's your job, Detective."

"Yes. So, about the day the girls disappeared."

"Worst day of my life . . . well, if you don't count this

one, I suppose." She went on with her story. She and her husband had come home and learned that Owen had lost his sisters. He hadn't gone to the movies with them but instead had spent the late afternoon and evening with his girlfriend, Ashley McDonnell. Her lips had tightened at the mention of the girl. "She's a piece of work, let me tell you. She's married now, has children of her own. But back then she and Owen were hot and heavy, if you know what I mean." One eyebrow arched over the rim of her glasses in obvious disapproval. "Owen was hot to trot. Couldn't get enough of that little tease." Her lips pinched down in disapproval. "But then, after . . . after the girls vanished, well, of course they broke up. She dropped him like a hot potato."

"Does she still live around here?"

"Yes." Again the expression of disapproval. "After dating a plethora of local boys, especially the rich ones like Tyson Beaumont and Jacob Channing, she married a local boy who made good, some kind of software developer or something. Lives out on Tybee . . . fancy place."

"You've been there?" he asked, as Tybee Island wasn't far, about half an hour by car.

"Oh, my, no. I mean, I've been out on the island and drove by, but I haven't been in. Don't want to."

"What about your son?"

"Innocent!" she snapped, indignance flaring in her eyes. "Don't go there, Detective. The police have dragged Owen's name through the mud. Over and over again. I know you all think he's a prime suspect, but he would never, *never* have harmed his sisters. He adored those girls!"

"He was adopted by Harvey Duval?"

"Yes."

"And his biological father?"

Her cheeks flushed crimson. "Out of the picture. Was from the time before Owen was born." She inched her chin upward. "Owen's never known him, and that's for the best."

"But he has a name."

"He's not involved! For all I know that son of a . . . he might be dead. He's absolutely irrelevant, so just leave his name out of it!"

Making a mental note to find out about the man who elicited such a harsh response from Margaret, Reed heard the front door open, then close with a soft thud. A few seconds later, Ezra returned. He handed Margaret a business card. "Kimberly Mason. With WKAM. Says she's talked to you before."

"Barely gave me the time of day." Margaret sniffed, but clutched the card.

"She wants an interview. I asked her to call and we would work it out. Possibly later this afternoon."

"Fine." She turned her eyes back to Reed. "We're about done here, I think."

"Just about," Reed said. "I'd like to talk to your son, so if you have a phone number, e-mail or an address, I'd appreciate it."

Margaret's shoulders stiffened, but the reverend was nodding. "No problem. Margaret has that information and probably a lot more that would help the police." He smiled benignly at his wife as she silently bristled. "She's kept up with the case, of course, and made certain she updated the names and numbers of anyone who knew the girls. Isn't that right, honey?"

Obviously irritated with her husband for being so forthcoming, she nodded curtly.

"If I could see it?"

"I'll make copies," she said. "And e-mail the information to you."

The reverend said, "I know, I mean the detective and I know this is hard, honey, but the police are just trying to help."

"Too late for that."

"Maybe not for Rose. You have to have faith." Her husband gave her a squeeze. "Remember: 'Don't be afraid; just believe.'"

"Mark 5:36," she whispered, and cast her eyes downward.

"Right."

"Think of Rose," her husband said softly.

"Of . . . of course." She stared at the floor for a second, then added, "Owen's not in Jacksonville any longer. He moved back here about two"—she glanced at her husband as she thought—"no, almost three months ago. He rents a place in Bloomingdale, well, just outside of it. Give me a sec." She stood and headed toward the back of the house.

When she was out of earshot her husband said, "You have to understand, Detective Reed, that this is hard on her. Very hard." His brow furrowed. "I worry about her. She's a strong woman, but there's only so much a mother can take. Do you have any children?"

Reed hesitated, felt a pang of regret, then shook his head.

"Well, this is tough. Let me tell you. I don't have any of my own, but I've seen what it's done to Margaret and then, of course, I deal with all kinds of family crises with my congregation—"

Footsteps heralded his wife's return and she handed Reed a sheet of paper, lined and frayed from where it had been torn from a spiral tablet. Owen Duval's name, address, e-mail and phone number were written in a smooth, flowing hand. "He's innocent," she said.

Reed knew she'd given as much as she would. He handed her his card. "If you think of anything else that might help us, please call."

She bit her lip and crushed his card in the fist that still clutched a similar card from the newswoman. "I'm sorry. I didn't mean to be mean, to be rude. It's just that after all the years I tried to give the police the information I'd gathered and then was treated like I was a nutcase, you know, like there was something wrong with me for trying to find out what happened to my daughters, it's a little unsettling that now . . . now you want my help."

Reed stood. "Yes, yes, I do. Thanks. I can't change what happened in the past, but I'm sure the department has always sought to find your daughters. Now we want to locate whoever did this and bring him to justice, as well as find Rose."

"You think the kidnapper, the murderer is a man?"

"Don't know," Reed said, tucking the note with information on Owen Duval into his pocket, "but we will find out."

"Just find my daughter." Again Margaret's eyes shone with unshed tears. "And please, oh, God, please, when you do locate her, bring her back to me alive."

*　*　*

I wondered when they would be discovered, when the bodies would show themselves. I've waited. And I've worried. And I've anticipated. Expecting this day. Finally, now, the truth will be exposed, and I will have to be oh, so careful. Too easily I could give myself away, too easily I could be found out. And I just can't let that happen.

CHAPTER 12

*R*eed *will kill you! You'd better think twice about this,*
Nicole . . .

Nikki's conscience harangued her as she parked at the
park two blocks away from the house where once the
Duval family had lived. As far as she could tell, she was
alone. No other reporters staking out a home that had
been bought and sold three times in the twenty years
since the girls had gone missing.

Well, he won't really kill you, of course, but he could
divorce you. Is that what you want?

"Of course not," she argued with herself as she locked
the car and felt her shoulder begin to ache. Too bad. It had
been four days since she'd been released from the hospital and she was feeling better. She'd always healed
quickly, and this time proved no different. Her shoulder

gave her just a twinge of pain now and again, and the other . . . well, she was healing inside as well. Even emotionally, she decided.

Besides, she'd been through worse, she thought, as she walked along the sidewalk that rimmed the park, and now she had the list of names, numbers and addresses Millie had e-mailed her. Yeah, she had to get some things straight with her husband, but come on, he'd proposed and married her knowing full well she would never let a story go, especially a mystery that had swirled around Savannah as the Duval girls' story had, especially one involving people she'd known, girls she should have grown up with.

A thicket of trees had been uprooted by the hurricane, the sidewalk buckled and cordoned off with neon cones and yellow tape for several yards, so she jaywalked across the street and eyed the small home where the family had resided. The stucco exterior was painted a soft gray with white paned windows with black shutters and flower boxes filled with trailing petunias in pink and white. The yard was tended, any debris from the storm already raked away. The house appeared to be one story, but the pitch of the roof and windows cut into the eaves on either end suggested a bedroom or two upstairs.

This was where the girls had lived.

Where Harvey and Margaret had raised their family.

Where Owen Duval, too, had made his home. She'd tried to contact him already, using the phone number that Millie had found, but he hadn't picked up and she'd left her name and number asking him to call. So far, he hadn't.

As she stared at the house, she tried to remember Owen, to conjure up something she'd known about him when they were in school, but couldn't recall ever speaking with him. Even though he'd lived in the area, she'd never run into the boy who had lost his sisters that fateful day.

She'd looked up pictures of him, from the high school yearbook and from any photos she'd located on the Internet. But she'd found no recent shots of Duval, so she was stuck with the image of a dark-haired sullen youth with a perpetual frown and thick black eyebrows.

She wondered where he'd slept in this house. The people who owned the place now were an elderly couple with the neat front yard, tidy detached single garage and a lush, if hurricane-ravaged vegetable garden of squash, pumpkins, pole beans and rows of corn visible through the opening between garage and house.

Nikki had come here on a whim, thinking that seeing the home where the Duval family had once resided might give her some insight, a different slant on the story, but the house was like so many others on this street.

Had pure evil resided here?

Hidden by the charming facade?

She felt a chill run down her spine as she stared at the upper windows, but told herself she was letting her imagination run away with her. Whatever malevolence may have resided here, it had left when the Duval family moved on.

Still bothered, she walked the few blocks east, toward the street where the cinema had been built, a wide boulevard skirted with storefronts, cafés, a couple of bars and an apartment building. The theater, a staple in this part of town for over a hundred years, had closed not long after the Duval girls' disappearance. It had been on the market, empty for years before the owner had sold to a developer, who had converted it to this mini-mall, but the original ticket-taking booth was still positioned in front of a double set of glass doors.

Inside, of course, everything had changed. Where once the floor had descended with row upon row of seats, it was now level, skylights cut high into the domed ceiling. The lobby with its old-fashioned refreshment counter, alcove leading to separate restrooms and doorways to the stairs leading to a projection room and offices one floor above were gone, replaced by two stories of small shops and kiosks tucked against the walls, all of which opened to the center courtyard where café tables had been strewn around an old caboose from a train that had been converted into a bakery and coffee shop. A balcony rimmed the entire building, with staircases at each corner. In one glance Nikki noticed a florist, a T-shirt shop, a sunglasses "emporium," a wine shop and a kiosk that promised "the freshest homemade candy in all of Savannah."

Her phone buzzed as she was passing a small deli, and she saw the call was from her mother. She walked out a side entrance and took the call. "Hi, Mom."

"Nikki? Where the devil are you?"

"Out. Why?"

"I stopped by. Well, we did. I was with Lily. Your sister and I wanted to see how you were doing."

"I'm fine, Mom." Nikki didn't say it, but she wasn't all that sure Lily had wanted to visit, or spend any time with Charlene. A free spirit, Lily was a musician and a pseudointellectual and a single mother by choice. She and her straitlaced, by-the-book, churchgoing mother were always at odds. It said something that Lily was concerned enough to put aside her feelings for her mother to visit Nikki.

"But shouldn't you be resting? In bed?" Charlene asked.

"Seriously, Mom. I'm okay."

"Well—"

"I'm following doctor's orders, okay?" That was a bit of a lie, but there was no way Nikki could spend another day or hour or even damn minute holed up in her supposed misery.

"If you say so."

"I do. Sorry I missed you."

A beat. Then, "Me too. Be careful, Nikki," she added. Then her voice was softer as if she'd turned away from the phone. "Lily, is there anything you wanted to say to your sister? Here, talk to her. I need to freshen up. And don't go out onto the veranda to sneak a cigarette. You know how I feel about that. You're a mother, for God's sake. What kind of example are you setting?"

"You know what they say about reformed sinners," was the husky response.

"I quit years ago. Years! Now, here. Talk to Nicole."

A second later, Lily's husky voice was clearer. "Hey, Nikki. We were just checking on you, no big deal, and if you say you're cool, then we'll touch base later."

"I'm fine. Mom just won't believe it."

"Some things never change."

"I guess not."

"I'll call later, or, more likely, Mom will." Her voice lowered to a whisper. "Okay, she's gone now, into the powder room. Oh, God, she is in *such* a mood. The thing is, she's all about baking you something, if you can believe it, like peanut butter cookies or an apple pie or something. She keeps obsessing about it."

"I don't even like peanut butter cookies."

"I know, I know, but I do, and sometimes she gets us—or what we like—mixed up. Remember the time she bought me that series of crime novels for Christmas and gave you the poetry books? I mean, really? She didn't even realize what she'd done."

"That was right after Dad died," Nikki said, remembering. Charlene had been in a fog for nearly a year, even though her marriage to Nikki's father had been far from perfect. "She was a little out of it."

"Still is, if you ask me," Lily said. "Anyway, right now she feels like she has to do something motherly." Her voice lowered. "Actually, I think she planned to pick something up at a bakery, she *detests* getting the kitchen dirty."

"I know." Nikki almost smiled. She and Lily were direct opposites, but they had one thing in common: They understood their mother's need to control them and fought it at every turn. "I need to talk to her. About what she remembers about the Duvals."

"Oh, God. Once she starts, she'll never stop."

"Has to be done."

"Well, fine, then it's your funeral."

"Very funny."

"If you say so. She's coming back—"

"Not now." Nikki wasn't ready to deal with Charlene. Not yet. "I'll talk to her and you later."

"Okay. Take care of yourself. Ciao," Lily said with a perfect Italian accent that ended the call.

Nikki stuffed her phone in her pocket and tried once again to remember the theater as it had been. Standing in what had been the middle of the seating area but was now occupied by a coffee kiosk, Nikki imagined the three sisters, huddled together in the middle rows, maybe popcorn and sodas or red licorice in hand. They'd been watching *Shrek*, a recently released kids' movie. And what had happened? Had they left during the film? Why? On their own? Or lured? Or coerced? Some other moviegoers had reported seeing them before and during the show, but not after. So what had happened? Why had they left?

She glanced up to the area where the projection room had been situated, the small windows still visible, and as she did she felt as if someone were staring at her, someone located in a dark corner, or on the balcony, or . . .

Oh, get over your bad self! There is nothing wicked, nothing degenerate here.

But in her mind's eye she saw those three blond, blue-eyed girls in the darkened theater being lured even farther into the shadows . . .

"Nikki? Nikki Gillette!" A woman's voice cracked into her reverie and she actually jumped.

She whipped around to spy a tall brunette in a summer dress and green apron heading her way. Her long hair was wound tight onto the back of her head, and huge gold hoops glinted as they swung from her ears.

"I thought that was you!" She smiled, a wide, toothy grin rimmed by shiny pink lips. "I work at the flower shop now. Who woulda thunk, right?" Rolling her eyes, she hooked her thumb toward the door of the storefront flanked by risers of colorful cut flowers. As she passed by the coffee shop situated in the middle of the mall, Nikki got a better view of her. "You don't recognize me, do you?" She seemed amused and rolled her palms upward. "It's me, Maxie."

"Maxie Johnson?" Nikki asked. This outgoing woman was the girl with whom Nikki had taken horseback riding lessons when she'd been in junior high. Maxine "Maxie"

Johnson had been the youngest in the class, a doe-eyed girl who had shied away from even the gentlest horse in the paddock even though her mother had been the riding instructor.

"Yeah, yeah! Well, it's Maxie Kendall now, I'm married—well, I was." She shrugged. "Just got divorced and here I am working at the florist shop. I guess that's what I get for marrying a lawyer."

"I'm sorry."

"Don't be. He was a jerk. Cheated on me from the get-go. I'm even thinking of taking my maiden name back." She frowned a bit, then waved a hand as if dismissing her ex as if he were a bothersome mosquito. "I just read that you were in some kind of accident in the river . . . after the hurricane."

"Yeah, well . . ." She nodded toward the sling on her shoulder. "I'm okay."

"Oh, yikes." Maxie pulled a face. "Hurt?"

"Not too bad."

"You got that in the river, right? At the Beaumont estate. I heard about it."

"Bad news travels fast."

"Right. I guess. Anyway, you know, I knew those girls. The Duvals? Well, not so much Rose, she was too little, but Holly and Poppy, yeah. They were in the neighborhood. They lived down the street from me, just down the block. We—my parents and me—our house was just across from the park until they finally bought the arena and that dump of a house that came with it. We all moved out there, you know, to Heritage Equestrian Acres. Geez, that name's a mouthful, isn't it? Look, I'm on a break, only fifteen minutes, thought I'd grab an iced coffee. You?"

"No, no, I'm good."

"Okay." She stepped to the window and placed her order. "Yeah, iced mocha, light whip . . . what? Sure. Sprinkles. Why not?" She sent the barista another brilliant smile and while she waited for the concoction to be created, said to Nikki, "It's weird, you know. Working here, where it happened. I mean, those girls were literally right about here the last time they were seen." She pointed to the floor. "Freaky."

"What do you think happened?"

"Dunno." She shook her head. "But Mom has her theories . . . oh, thank you." She paid for her drink, took it and took a sip. "My one indulgence."

"What does your mom think?"

"What everyone does, that Owen, the brother, did it, but with Mom it's different. She's kind of a psychic, you know. Gets all these 'vibes.' Or at least she used to. She doesn't do much predicting anymore. But back then, when I was taking lessons with you? Mom told me she could tell I'd never be a horsewoman from the moment I stepped into the stable. She was sure right on that one."

It hadn't taken a psychic to see that Maxie had been deathly afraid of horses during the lessons. Nikki could have called that one.

"So you knew the Duval sisters?"

"Yeah, some. Holly, mainly. She was one year younger in school, but we hung out a bit. Usually with Andrea. You know her, right? Andrea Bennett, no, she got married. What was the guy's name? He wasn't from around here, someone she met while going to school . . . oh, God. Wait! Clancy. His name's John or Josh or something like that, but Clancy, that's her last name. Andrea and Holly and Brit—that's Brittany Sully, I don't know if she's married or not, but they were all real tight." Maxie smiled, proud of herself for coming up with it. "I haven't thought of Andrea in years." She took another sip, then checked her watch. "Oops! My break's about over and I have to run. My boss—a real stickler about clocking in and out, he's got an OCD thing about it. That's right, isn't it? OCD? Obsessive-compulsive whatever."

"Disorder."

"Right. That's it. Anyway, he's beyond anal and I don't want to lose my job." She started walking toward the florist shop.

"But your mom—is she around?" Nikki asked.

"Oh, she's always at the arena. If you want, you can probably catch her there." And then she was off, hurrying back to the shop, where a short man in his own green apron stood in the door scowling at Maxie as she scurried past the rows of cut carnations and roses to disappear into the store behind him.

Nikki thought about it.

She needed to begin digging deeper into the people who knew the Duval sisters. She'd look up Andrea Clancy and Brit Sully, as well as any other friend of the victims, but for now, Nikki decided to start with Maxie's mother, Chandra "the psychic horsewoman" Johnson.

"So it's true, then," Harvey Duval said over the wireless connection, when Reed, sitting in his office at the station, finally reached the victims' father. "My daughters are really gone. An officer came by the other day, but I still held out a little bit of hope. Silly, I know, but . . . it's funny what you can tell yourself. The lies. The platitudes." There was a soft, resigned sadness to his voice, and he let out an audible sigh. "I'd expected it, of course, after all this time. At least I'd convinced myself that I would be ready for any kind of news, but it's still a punch to the gut. They . . . they were so beautiful. So innocent. Dear God."

"I'm sorry for your loss," Reed offered. He was recording the conversation but still wrote notes to himself.

"Me too." Harvey cleared his throat. "Do you have any idea who did this?"

"Not yet."

"Margaret's devastated, of course. I called her after the deputy who gave me the news left. I thought it was the right thing to do even though it's no secret that ours wasn't the happiest of marriages." There was still a bite to his words, even years later.

"You didn't get along?"

He snorted. "She expected me to claim a child as my own, and then when we lost the girls . . . Well, it was too much. We were already about to split up. When we were house hunting, we were really looking for an apartment. She needed me to sign on the lease, and I thought it was the decent thing to do." He cleared his throat. "But then decency's pretty hard to come by. Anyway, then we lost the girls and so we tried to put it back together, the marriage. Of course it didn't work. Too much water under the bridge. The girls disappearing was the final straw." Another sigh, then, "There's some finality to this, I suppose."

"Except that Rose is still missing."

A beat. "Right. But it's only a matter of time, isn't it?" he said defeatedly. "And then, no doubt, you'll locate her, too. Look, I've got to go. I told the police everything I know over and over again. Nothing's changed."

Except that two bodies were located.

Harvey ended the call.

In Reed's estimation, quite a bit had changed. He pulled up Harvey Duval's statement and reread it, but it was almost word for word what Margaret's had been; basically, the kids were at the movies, Owen was in charge of the girls, while Margaret and Harvey had looked at some open houses, then went out to dinner, and when they got back all three of the girls had disappeared. He hadn't even been that concerned to begin with as the oldest daughter, Holly, was on the threshold of becoming a teenager, had been feeling her "wild oats" and been rebelling. They'd caught her smoking and sneaking out, but until the day they'd gone missing had never involved her sisters, other than insisting Poppy "cover" for her, which meant lying, and according to Harvey, Poppy had done it on several occasions. Rose, too young, hadn't really been aware of her older sister's open defiance.

Reed shuffled backward, through all of Margaret's statements over the years. She'd never mentioned that her eldest daughter had been any kind of trouble. When asked about it, she'd dismissed Holly's disobedience as nothing but a teenager pushing her limits, testing her parents, and had indicated that Harvey, ever the dictator, had overreacted to his daughter's "antics."

He read her direct quote: "It's all just a part of growing up, you know, but Harvey didn't have a normal childhood, didn't understand that kids push boundaries. His own parents were of the 'spare the rod and spoil the child' mentality. But then I knew he didn't care that much, not really. The fact that he left me, in all of my grief and despair, when our daughters were missing, for the love of

God. Who does that and remarries and starts another family? It's like he just didn't care."

Or couldn't face the horror of the truth.

Delacroix appeared as he was still going over the statements. "What did you find out from the father?" she asked.

"Not a lot. He seems to be devastated, but then who wouldn't be?"

"Right."

"Catch me up," he suggested, as in the interest of speeding the investigation along, they'd split up and interviewed different people during the past day and a half.

"Okay." She sat on the corner of Morrisette's desk and scrolled through her phone. "First up, Tyson and Baxter Beaumont, the father and son, came in and gave statements about the property where the victims were found. I typed them up, they signed, and I sent you a copy just this morning." She glanced up from her screen. "Nothing of importance that I could find. Nothing we didn't really know. I asked them why they thought Bronco was on the property, and they agreed he was probably there to steal whatever he could find since his grandfather had a key and was now dead so he couldn't keep an eye on the estate or Bronco."

"Did they say anyone else was ever on the property?"

"No." She shook her head. "Not even squatters, but they mentioned they were going to put up some kind of security system and new signs. They seemed pissed about the whole thing, more worried about the notoriety of bodies being found there and what it would do to their property values. They seemed to care more about money than they were concerned that those kids were buried there."

She frowned. "My take: coldhearted pricks. But I didn't put that in the file."

"Good." He nodded.

"Then I called Ashley McDonnell, now Ashley Jefferson, Owen Duval's alibi. She's married now, got a couple of kids and lives out on Tybee." Delacroix scrolled down on her phone, then looked at him and shook her head. "Piece of work. She was more concerned with getting her power on after the storm and having her yard cleaned up than she was about the bodies."

"Old news?"

"I guess. She was actually irritated that I was bothering her. Worried aloud about not being connected to the Internet even though her husband is some kind of computer wiz. She was late posting to her blog." Her eyebrows elevated. "As I said, 'piece of work.'"

He leaned back in his chair. "Does she still keep in contact with Owen?"

"Nope, acted as if he was 'just a friend' in high school. I got the impression that she thought she was doing him a favor hanging out with him."

"You buy that?"

"Nuh-uh, that woman is too self-centered to have taken on a charity case. People don't get meaner after high school, you know? They usually grow up, become kinder, not the other way around."

"She was Owen's alibi."

"Still is. Said they just hung out at her folks' place as the parents were away for the weekend."

"Doing what?"

"Watching TV." Her eyes held his. "I call 'bullshit' on it, but she wouldn't budge. I think we might need to talk to her in person, get a bead on her."

"Everything she said matches what Owen Duval said in his statement."

"Hmmm." Her eyebrows knitted. "No one else seemed to think they were a couple. Check out the old statements."

"I know. Maybe someone will change their tune."

She hopped off the corner of the desk and walked to the window, staring through the glass. "I just get the feeling that someone's lying. No . . . that's not right. I get the feeling that a lot of people are lying and I'm not sure why. What did Margaret Duval say?"

"A lot. She's pretty broken up of course. Had held on to the belief that her daughters were alive."

"I guess there's always hope," she said, biting her lip thoughtfully.

"Apparently." Reed explained about his meeting at the parsonage and ended with, "She told me to bring her youngest daughter back alive."

Delacroix took the visitor's chair. "Did she? And how did you respond?"

"I didn't."

"Because you think it's impossible?"

"No, because I don't like to make promises I can't keep. What did you find out about the locket?" he asked, and noted that she was taller than his previous partner. Delacroix sat up taller and straighter in the chair than Morrisette had.

"Nothing. Empty." She raised a shoulder. "It was worth a shot, but no, it wasn't like some kind of Nancy Drew moment when the final and dangerous clue to the mystery is revealed within the clasp of a small piece of jewelry. So I just put it back with everything else."

"Damn. That would've made things so much easier."

She actually smiled, showing off a bit of white teeth.

"I know, right? Well, here's something. I did get hold of Owen Duval. He wasn't all that talkative, insisted upon lawyering up as if he expected to be arrested or something."

"Really?"

"He claimed that he was railroaded when the girls disappeared, that the cops didn't look any further than him."

"Could be true," Reed said, motioning toward the files. "The detective in charge at the time zeroed in on Owen Duval from the get-go."

"He shouldn't have?" Delacroix was surprised.

"Don't know. He was the likely suspect, but even with his solid alibi, the detective, Charles Easterling, was set on Owen."

"You talk to him? Easterling."

"Can't. He was near retirement at the time and died a couple of years ago. The cop who inherited the case retired, too. Moved to Chicago. I did talk to him, but he couldn't tell me any more than what was in the files. So, here we are."

"With Owen Duval as our number one suspect. Some things don't change over the years," she said. "Be interesting to see what he has to say. It's all set up to meet him at his lawyer's office."

"He's already hired an attorney?"

"I guess, but the place is out of town. Attorney's name is Austin Wells." Her eyes narrowed behind her glasses. "You know him?"

"Of him. Thought he was retired."

"Apparently not. We're scheduled to meet him at five thirty. Gives Owen time to get off work. He works at the Chevy dealership. Mechanic. Gets off at five. Oh, and we're not meeting at the law office; it's located in the

Winslow Building, damaged in the hurricane. We have to go to Wells's home."

"They could have come down here."

"Apparently Owen Duval refused to step inside the building. Something about hating police stations and interrogation rooms. He spent a lot of time here twenty years ago."

"He might not have a choice."

"I know, but for now, I figured we could be somewhat accommodating." She slid him a sly smile. "If we don't like what he has to say or think he's holding out, we can always change our minds and haul his ass down here." Arching a brow, she said, "My grandma always said, 'you catch more flies with honey than with vinegar.'"

"Did she?"

"Yeah, but then she'd always add, 'but if the honey don't work, haul out the fly swatter and smack that son of a bitch dead.'"

Reed had to laugh as he reached for his jacket. "A woman I'd like to meet."

"Too late. She's long gone. I barely remember her. Come on, let's roll."

CHAPTER 13

"If you ask me, the whole family was a little off, if you know what I mean," Chandra Johnson said to Nikki. They were standing on one side of a rail fence at the equestrian center while a girl of about eight in riding clothes and a helmet was astride a prancing bay horse with a wide white blaze, trying and failing to gain some control of the gelding.

The place was much as Nikki remembered it, with a huge covered arena, wide barn doors opening to this out-door paddock, the acres around it grassy aside from an occasional pine tree and an orchard nearer to the house. Across a gravel lot, a two-story brick house that had seen better days stood in a grove of pecan trees, a weedy garden to one side.

Nikki had parked on the wide gravel strip between the

house and arena. Inside the enclosure, the horse shook his head, dark mane shivering in the late-afternoon sunlight. To the rider, Chandra instructed, "Ease off on the reins, Willa, quit fighting him." Under her breath, she muttered, "That girl has the touch of a blacksmith. Oh, for the love of God!" To Nikki, she said, "Give me a second, will ya?" And then she was through the gate of the fenced enclosure and striding toward the horse. "Whoa," she said softly as she approached horse and rider. She took hold of the reins and laid a hand gently on the gelding's shoulder, then spoke softly. Nikki couldn't hear any of the one-sided conversation, but it seemed to calm both horse and rider.

She remembered being the girl on the horse and Chandra's annoyance and advice and way with horses. Chandra, a woman who might be more comfortable with animals than people, was older now, thicker around the middle, her brown hair still plaited in a single braid that snaked down her back, though now the plait was dull and dyed, gray roots visible surrounding a rounded, tanned face. She was wearing a dingy orange T-shirt with a Grateful Dead logo and faded, dusty jeans that seemed identical to the battered pair she'd worn twenty years earlier.

"Now give it another try, and remember, hold the reins lightly," she said more loudly as she backed up. "Remember, Oliver can feel what you want. Communicate with the horse. Trust him." With those parting words she slipped through the gate again, her eyes rolling toward the sky. "Lost cause," she said to Nikki, then watched as the rider urged the horse forward and he started at a quick trot around the perimeter of the oval arena.

A chain saw started to roar in an orchard nearby as a

wiry jean-clad man bent over a downed peach tree, but the horse didn't flinch, just kept his pace, the little rider teetering slightly. "Oh, for . . . would you look at that? I told Chuck *not* to clear the damned trees until *after* Willa's lesson." She sighed, then waved frantically, finally getting the grizzled man's attention. She made a slashing motion across her throat and the chain saw died as Chuck frowned, lifted a baseball cap from his balding head, but nodded, getting the message.

"One more idiot to deal with," Chandra confided. "Now, what was I saying? Oh, right, you were asking about that Duval family who lived up the street from us. I got a weird vibe from them, but it was probably because of the older boy, what was his name? Owen. Yeah, that's right. Sullen little bastard. Always staring at you from behind a mop of dark hair, like he was hiding; y'know, a predator in a cave." She gave a little involuntary shudder.

"You think he was behind the girls disappearing?"

Chandra let out a snort. "Course he was. Who else? And he was supposed to be in charge, now, wasn't he?" She glanced at the rider as the horse trotted past. "That's better, Willa, now, slow him down. We're about done here."

Bouncing atop Oliver, the waif of a girl nodded, her face ashen, her eyes round, the helmet slipping a bit. If she was enjoying her lesson, she was hiding it well. She yanked back on the reins and the horse stopped suddenly.

Chandra bolted through the gate. "That's good, that's good," she said, snagging the reins just as a gray minivan rolled down the lane to park behind Nikki's Honda. A frazzled-looking red-haired woman climbed quickly out from behind the wheel. With a runner's body, she was lean and taut, her age landing somewhere in her forties.

"Come on, Willa," she called, waving at her daughter as Willa, with Chandra's help, dismounted. Yanking off what appeared to be a hated riding helmet, the girl bounded through the open gate. Chandra tied the reins loosely over one of the rails beneath a shade tree, then followed.

"How'd she do?" Mom asked, checking her watch and ruffling her daughter's hair.

Chandra equivocated. "Improving."

"Good, good," Mom said, not really interested. To her daughter, she added, "Look, honey, you get in the car. Quick. Chop. Chop."

The girl didn't need any more encouragement and dived into the minivan.

Mother apologized, "Sorry. We're already late for the boys' lessons."

"Do I have to go?" Willa whined from the interior of the minivan, but Mom ignored it. To Nikki, she offered an apologetic smile. "Martial arts. Tae kwon do and we're late. Well, I'm always late. Twins. Six-year-old boys. Willa hates waiting, and I can't say that I blame her, but, well, you know, it is what it is." She shook her head as if she couldn't believe her life. "After martial arts, it's swim lessons for all of them." She was flustered and breathless. "Crazy, I know."

"Mo-om," Willa called from the interior of the van. "Can we just go now?"

"Yeah, yeah, I'm coming," she threw over her shoulder, then, turning back to Chandra, "Oh, damn. I forgot the check. I'll . . . I'll Venmo the next month's lessons when I get home. Okay?" She was already heading back to her vehicle.

Chandra's smile faded. "And this month's."

"Right, oh, yeah, right, right! That's totally what I meant." Blushing, she threw Chandra an oh-silly-forgetful-me look, then was off, diving into the minivan, getting behind the wheel and slamming the door shut in one quick motion. She maneuvered a quick three-point turn before driving quickly down the lane, dust kicking up in the gravel in her wake.

"I'm not going to count on that, the Venmo thing," Chandra said, almost to herself, then turned back to Nikki. "Sorry. Business. You were asking about that Duval family." She shook her head. "They were a strange lot."

"They were? How so?"

"First of all, the parents weren't happy. I felt it in their faces, saw it in the way they interacted with each other. That's no crime, of course, happens all the time, but they were different. It was"—she squinted up at the sky, where thin white clouds slid over the sun—"it was this weird vibe. It went beyond unhappiness or not trusting each other to, like, wariness."

"Before the girls went missing," Nikki clarified.

"Before, during, and after. It was just always there. And the kids felt it, too, at least the oldest one, uh, Holly did. I sensed it. She was always edgy around her folks. Clammed up, like she was afraid to say anything. But—a lot of people are odd or have different kinds of relationships. As for the Duvals, the entire family seemed, I don't know, 'off,' I'd say. Frankly, I was surprised that Harvey and Margaret stayed together for as long as they did because before the girls went missing, there was talk of them not getting along or having affairs or whatever." She scratched the back of her neck, beneath her braid. "I never saw any sign of it myself, and gossip runs through

Savannah like wildfire through tinder, but who knows? Where there's smoke, there's fire, y'know? Smoldering somewhere, but it's a damned shame about the kids." She clucked her tongue. "Cute little things, all of 'em. And that little Rose, she had a special spark. Holly, she was suspicious, and the middle one . . . uh, Poppy, she was kind of sneaky and a really good student, I think, and like I said, little Rose, she took after her mother, looked more like Margaret than the other two. They favored Harvey, but that wasn't bad. They were a good-looking group, just . . . off somehow."

"Maxie seemed to think that you had a special insight into them."

"Oh. Well." She rubbed her chin. "I can see things sometimes, especially if I concentrate, but all I saw about that family was trouble, lots of strife, and the cause of it? The older brother. He's just a bad seed."

"And you know this how?" Nikki asked. Just because a teenager didn't meet your gaze didn't indicate that he was troubled.

Chandra bit her lip. "Well . . . okay . . . I guess I can tell you, but don't you print it. Got it? Anything I tell you is from an 'anonymous source,' right? Otherwise it's got to be completely off the record."

"Understood."

"Good." Leaning against the top rail, she glanced at the horse, still saddled, switching his tail at a bothersome fly. "Maxie probably told you, or you've heard that I sometimes see things, you know. It's not like it happens all the time, but sometimes. Definitely." She rubbed her chin, her eyes narrowing as she remembered. "And it happened with that family once, at the Marianne Inn, just up the river, here." She hooked her thumb toward the north. "I took a trail ride up that way with a couple of friends, oh, God, it's been over twenty years, of course. I was riding in the lead, I remember, on Zeus—he was my favorite gelding at the time. Sorrel with a stubborn streak but could race like the wind. Man, I loved that horse . . ." She was squinting, thinking, her mind turned inward. "Anyway, that's when I came across them and there was this, this . . . oh, just something that gave me pause."

"An aura around Harvey and Margaret?"

"No . . . it was the girls—no, that's wrong." She paused, her eyebrows drawing together. "Just the oldest one, Holly. I sensed some sadness in her, more like a wave of despair. And then, upon hearing the horses, she looked up, saw us coming, and the tears that I'd seen falling dried quickly." Chandra's voice was quieter. "The feeling I got, the energy from her, changed immediately. She just forced a smile, then ran off."

"To the lodge?"

"Yes." She nodded thoughtfully as the horse nickered softly. "It was open back then." Clearing her throat, she added, "I'd better see to Oliver." She stepped to the still-open gate.

"You said, 'them.' You saw 'them.' So who besides Holly?"

"That's just it. I sensed there was someone else there, saw a flicker of something, or someone, but not sure who . . . or even what. A shadow. I remember there were bees that day—wasps, no hornets, I think. I remember swatting at them and urging the horse forward. To get away from them." Her brows drew together and she rubbed her forehead, leaving a smudge. "Funny the things you recall."

"But you saw someone else. With Holly."

"Yeah, I *felt* a presence. Maybe the brother—Owen. Coulda been him."

"And you think he's capable of murder?"

"Now, don't you go twisting my words. I don't know what he's capable of, I just said he's a bad seed. That's all." She was getting angry now, as if feeling Nikki was reading more into what she was saying than she meant.

"What was Holly Duval doing at the Marianne Inn?"

"Beats me." She shrugged as she untied the bay. "That, I can't tell you." She waved to the man in the orchard, making a swirling motion over her head, and he got the message. The chain saw screamed, biting into wood again.

Nikki watched Chandra lead the horse to the trough and as he dipped his head and drank, she wondered about Chandra's claim. If the woman fancied herself some kind of prognosticator or seer, she was a damned poor one. And there was something more to the woman, Nikki thought. Beneath the civil, rancher-like exterior was something darker, something Chandra worked to keep hidden. As Nikki drove away, checking her rearview and spying Chandra Johnson staring at her through a cloud of dust, Nikki couldn't shake the uneasy feeling that she'd just been speaking with a charlatan rather than a psychic.

Reed slid a pair of sunglasses over the bridge of his nose while Delacroix sat in the passenger seat of his Jeep, riding shotgun, her eyes focused, as usual, on the screen of her cell phone as they drove along the river.

"We're about to Wells's place."

"Mmm." She nodded, looking up, her own pair of Ray-Bans hanging from the neckline of her shirt. "I don't think his story is going to change. He was interviewed three times and I watched them all twice."

"Me too."

"Nervous, wasn't he?"

"Very." In the interviews, each a little more intense than the one before, Owen Duval, only sixteen, had come in voluntarily. But he'd stared at the interviewing officer belligerently, his arms crossed over his chest, his right leg visibly jumping beneath the table in the interview room. Each time, he'd held fast to his story, barely changing the wording, and each time he was backed up by an airtight alibi from his girlfriend, Ashley McDonnell, at the time.

As if she'd read Reed's mind, Delacroix said, "Ashley McDonnell, who is now Ashley Jefferson, still lives in the area. Married, a couple of kids, rocking the island lifestyle out on Tybee."

"You get hold of her?"

"Yeah, but she tried to brush me off. Too 'busy' with the kids, hubby and some sort of mommy blog, you know, but I used my considerable powers of persuasion to convince her otherwise. She agreed to meet me, albeit reluctantly, later, probably today or tomorrow. Worked for me. I wanted to see what Owen has to say first."

"What 'powers of persuasion' are those?" he asked, spying the turnoff and driving down a smooth lane.

"The power behind the badge," she said, staring through the windshield as they drove through a grove of pecan trees and up a small rise to a large, plantation-style home of two stories. With gleaming white siding, a wide front porch, huge pillars and tall windows that winked in the dying afternoon sun, the house was surrounded by a trimmed lawn and the front doors flanked by huge ceramic pots overflowing with trailing flowers.

"Man, oh, man," Delacroix said, clucking her tongue while Reed parked behind a triple garage and next to a dusty, ten-year-old Chevrolet Silverado, the windows tinted, and from the plates, Reed knew the vehicle belonged to Duval. "Wells isn't exactly a public defender, now, is he? How in the world does a guy like Owen Duval afford this kind of lawyer?"

"Pro bono, I'd guess. Wells is probably doing it for the publicity. So people get to know his name. He's got ambitions."

"Such as?"

"Governor." Reed shrugged. "Or senator, maybe."

"You know this how?" she asked dubiously, as he pocketed his keys and they both climbed out of his Jeep.

"Common knowledge. And who knows? Maybe he's looking to get a book deal out of it."

"Like your wife?" she said, shooting him a knowing look.

"Maybe."

"Pretty hard with attorney-client privilege."

"Been known to happen."

"Hmm." As they reached the edge of the lawn, she said, "I'm going to push Duval a little."

"Okay."

"So don't get in my way."

"Why would I?"

"You know, the lead detective thing. And the man thing. Just go along."

"If I can," he said, slightly annoyed, but maybe it would be good to see her in action, see if they really could make a team out of their new partnership. He doubted it but was game.

For now.

They walked along a brick pathway to the front door, which was opened as Reed pressed the doorbell and chimes pealed softly from within.

"Detectives," a tall, slim man with a shock of white hair and rimless glasses over deep-set blue eyes answered. Austin Wells was in slacks and a white shirt, sleeves rolled up, an easy smile sliding across his tanned jaw, his voice deep, with just a hint of Georgia drawl. "We've been expecting you."

Reed and Delacroix introduced themselves while Wells led them inside, through a two-storied foyer to a den at the base of a sweeping staircase. The room was an octagon with several sets of French doors cut between floor-to-ceiling bookcases, each entryway offering a different view of the surrounding grounds.

Owen Duval, dressed in clean jeans and a polo shirt, sat in a side chair near a massive wooden desk. His hair was still dark, but cropped close, a goatee surrounding his lips, his eyes dark and gray and haunted. His hands were clasped in front of him, and he didn't get up when they entered.

To Reed, Duval looked guilty as hell.

But of what?

Wells motioned them into chairs that faced the desk, angled across from Duval, so they sat as quick introductions were made, Duval eyeing them suspiciously.

A glass pitcher of sweet tea was sweating on a silver tray next to several glasses, and Wells offered them each something to drink, but no one was interested. "Okay, then, let's get down to it," Wells said, and sat behind the desk. "This is all for the record, and please note that Mr. Duval has agreed to be questioned *again* of his own volition." He set his phone on the desk and hit the record button, and Delacroix did the same.

Before a question could be posed, Owen looked up and met Reed's eyes. "I don't know why you all want to talk to me. Nothin's changed. Yeah, I guess you all found some bodies, right, up at the Beaumont place, but I know nothin' and I mean nothin' about that."

"Hey," Wells intervened, holding up a hand. "Just let the detectives ask the questions, okay?" He sent him a we-talked-about-this look.

Duval nodded several times. "Yeah. Okay." He rubbed his jean-clad knees.

"So, tell us what happened on the day that your sisters went missing," Delacroix asked, and his hands stopped their incessant movement as he stared at her, his eyebrows pulling together. For a second Reed thought he was about to alter his story, that in the seconds he was staring at Delacroix, sizing her up, he was coming up with an alternative tale.

Instead, he blinked and gave a tiny shake of his head, as if dismissing the idea.

"I've already told you," Duval said. "Jesus . . . will this never end?" And then after another stern look from his attorney, he repeated his story. "I was supposed to watch the movies with the girls. Instead, I dropped them off. It wasn't that big of a deal, or it shouldn't have been," he added, rubbing a hand through his short hair. "It wasn't as if Mom hadn't left the girls with Holly—she was twelve and babysat all the time!"

"But you left."

"Yeah, yeah." He shook his head as if he still couldn't believe how everything had turned out, how dark it had become. How deadly. "I, um, I ditched the kids, told Holly about it and she was kinda pissed, but I thought, oh, big deal. She was mad at me all the time anyway. I thought she could handle it. I would be back before the movie got out and so, no harm, no foul." His eyebrows drew together and the cords in the back of his neck tightened as he thought about it. "Then I took off to be with Ashley . . . Ashley McDonnell, she was my girlfriend at the time, and you know when you're a teenager you just can't get enough alone time, or any. My folks were strict and they acted like I was supposed to take care of the girls whenever they wanted. Mom, she kinda understood, but Harvey, he was"—Owen's fists curled and relaxed, curled and relaxed as he searched for the right word—"a real ballbuster. He was a 'my way or the highway' kind of guy."

"He adopted you."

"Yeah . . . right after Holly was born. Mom made a big deal about it. We were all a 'real family.'" He made air quotes and rolled his eyes. "That's what she said." He snorted. "As if."

"And your biological father? I just got the records. He's Reggie Scott? Right?"

Owen's lips curled. "I met him. A couple of times . . . well, I might've met him as a baby, but I don't remember him. It was just me and Mom and then Harvey. I can't even recall a time when Harvey wasn't around."

All this wasn't new information.

"Where did you meet him?"

"The last time was at a bar downtown. When I was . . . maybe twenty-two. Out of the blue he wants to talk to me, see how I'm doing. Just out of prison. Again." Duval's lips twisted at the memory. "He was all 'hey, it's great to see you,' and 'Wow, you're a man, now,' and 'gee, I'm sorry I wasn't around when you were growing up.' You know, all that bullshit." He glanced out the doors with a view of a pergola and pool. "And it was all a big con. All he wanted really was to hit me up for some money. Didn't even buy my damned beer." Frowning, he glared at Reed. "Why are we talking about my dirtbag of an old man? I never knew him and I never will."

"Just checking details," Delacroix said.

"Scott's not a detail. He's nothing. And by the way, I wouldn't mention any of this to my mother. The last thing Margaret ever wanted me to do was get in contact with my old man. Now I know why."

Delacroix didn't let up. "You're single, right?"

His jaw tightened. "Yeah."

"But you've been through several girlfriends?"

"So what?" He lifted a shoulder.

"Starting with Ashley McDonnell."

Owen waited, but he was silently seething, his eyes narrowing on Delacroix.

"What happened there? Why'd you break up?" she asked.

"What? What's this got to do with . . . ?" Irritated, Duval threw up a hand. "We were kids. We dated, we broke up. It happens all the time and it was, like, a million years ago."

Wells said, "I don't see what this has to do with anything."

"And you dated a girl named Maria Coronado, isn't that right?" Delacroix asked.

"A few years back when I lived in Atlanta, yeah—hey, wait!" A vein started to throb near his temple. "What the hell is this?"

"She had you arrested for domestic violence."

"What the—no! That . . . it was all a mistake. Blown way out of proportion." He looked to his attorney for help but kept talking. "We got into a fight, that's all. She thought I was cheating on her."

"Were you?"

"No, but she was batshit crazy jealous. As I said, we got into it. Harsh words and then *she* hit me with a god-damned metal spatula. Split my lip. She was screaming and yelling and the neighbors called 911. The cops hauled me in, but it was all a big mistake. Nothin' happened. She didn't have a scratch on her and she dropped the charges!"

"Okay . . . let's get back to the day you were supposed to be looking after your sisters," Delacroix suggested, and Duval, already agitated, started to bristle. "So you left in your car and went to pick up Ashley," Delacroix prodded.

"No, no, no. Are you kiddin'? What is this? Do you think Harvey would trust me with the Taurus? No way! I walked the girls to the theater and jogged over to Ashley's. Harvey and Mom took the car to look at the open house. Ashley's folks were out, so we hung out at her place. I already told you all this!"

Again—his story was just as he'd previously said. Unshaken. Despite Delacroix's best efforts. She'd watched his interviews and read the transcripts. She knew that he'd walked his sisters to the theater. She was just trying to rattle Owen, Reed guessed, to try to shake him from his story. The play hadn't worked.

In twenty years, his story hadn't changed. Not one iota. But he was irritated, his face red.

"Look." His gaze was laser sharp on Delacroix. "I don't know why you all think I did it. Why? Why would I kidnap my sisters? And how? God, I just told you I didn't even have a car!"

"Did Ashley have access to one?" Delacroix asked.

"I don't know! Holy shit!" Owen glanced over to Wells. "I told you this would be a waste of time. I don't know why I even agreed to do it in the first place. They"— he hooked a thumb toward Reed and Delacroix—"don't listen. After all this time. It's pointless. I can't tell them anything I don't know."

"He's right," the attorney cut in suddenly. Looking directly at the detectives, Wells, no longer affable, said, "My client's cooperated over and over again to the point that he's nearly being harassed." Before they could argue, he held up a hand, palm toward Reed. "I think we're done here."

Reed glanced at Delacroix. "We got what we came for."

"Good! I need a break." Owen shot to his feet and without a look over his shoulder walked out the French doors, reached into his jeans pocket and withdrew a crumpled pack of cigarettes and a lighter. His hands shook as he lit up. Through the glass Reed watched him inhale deeply, pacing back and forth in front of the panes, water in the swimming pool shimmering behind him. He was shaking his head, his lips moving as if he were having a conversation with himself.

Wells stood and rounded the desk. "He didn't want to talk to you, thought it was a bad idea, but I convinced him to cooperate once more. I don't think I can do it again, and really, I wouldn't want to. He's told you everything he knows."

Reed silently agreed, though Delacroix seemed about to argue.

"If he thinks of anything else," she said, handing Wells her card.

"I'll let you know." This time his smile was a little colder as he escorted them to the front door. "But I wouldn't hold my breath if I were you."

Only when they'd driven away from the house and through the rows of pecan trees did Delacroix turn to him. "You notice anything strange about Duval?"

"Such as?"

"Such as he didn't so much as ask one question about what happened to his sisters. All he knows is what he's read in the papers or seen on TV. Don't you think it's odd that he didn't ask how they died? How long they'd been there? Why was there only two of them? What happened to the youngest?" She angled her chin up at him.

"Maybe."

"And maybe he didn't ask because he already knew," she ventured, rolling down the window a crack, then closing it again.

Just like Morrisette.

He felt a little pang of regret, a sense of déjà vu that gave him pause, but dismissed it.

For now.

"He's lying."

"Lying?" Reed accelerated onto the main road.

"Yeah, I can feel it, y'know. He's got secrets." She chewed on her lower lip, the fingers of her right hand drumming against the window's ledge. "It's just not right, he's holding back. I just needed to push him harder."

"Any harder and he'd just clam up."

She sent him a look. "Or come clean. There's got to be a way. Probably through the girlfriend. Ashley Jefferson. She's Duval's alibi, so she's the key." She whipped out her phone. "Time to reset her priorities, I think. I'll call. If I don't get through, we'll just run out there, right?" She slid him a smile as she punched in a number. "I'm thinking the mommy blog can wait."

CHAPTER 14

Nikki couldn't help herself. She drove out of town with the windows down, letting the heat of the day rush through the windows and blow through her hair. She'd felt cooped up, antsy, as if she were spinning her wheels.

As she stepped on the gas and passed a slow-moving sedan that was plastered with a STUDENT DRIVER sign, she thought about the story she couldn't push aside, no matter how much her husband wanted her to abandon the project.

She knew that a lot of the answers to the Duval girls' disappearance could be answered at the Beaumont estate, where the bodies had been found. She hadn't been back since all hell had broken loose the last time she'd gone out there, and she felt that if she actually walked on the property she might gain some insight.

Really? Even though the police have already combed the place—detectives, deputies, crime scene techs, all with more equipment than you? You think they might have missed something you'll just happen to stumble over?

Her fingers were sweaty on the steering wheel. It was unnerving to drive out to the place again, but she felt in her gut that she needed to actually feel the aura of the old, decrepit mansion that had once been so grand and where so much tragedy had occurred. Nell Beaumont had drowned in the river, Holly and Poppy Duval had been sealed in their tomb and Sylvie Morrisette had lost her life trying to save Nikki. Even the loss of Nikki's own unborn child could be tied to the place, she thought sadly.

What other secrets did that old graying mansion hold?

She slowed as she passed Channing Vineyards and the rows upon rows of vines gracing the rolling hills, and made a final turn where the two huge pieces of property were separated by a moldering fence. A quarter of a mile later, she turned into the lane leading to the heart of the Beaumont estate. Today, she thought, she wouldn't have to sneak in the back way through the woods and along the edge of the river.

But she was wrong. As she pulled into the lane, she spied another SUV, a white Lexus, parked near the open gate, the driver's side door hanging open. Tyson Beaumont, in jeans and a faded T-shirt, was behind the wheel, a cell phone pressed to his ear. She wouldn't be able to get into the grounds without him knowing, so she'd have to wait, but she'd hoped to talk to him anyway and now seemed as good a time as any.

Nikki pulled into a spot next to his Lexus, cut the engine and slipped out of her sling before she got out of her car. Approaching his vehicle, she overheard his end of the conversation. "I'm handling it now . . . what? Yeah, I'm putting up the last sign, and the security company should be finished by the end of next week . . . I know, I know, but they're all jammed up because of the hurricane . . . it'll happen. They promised we're at the top of the list. I've got something going for now, not all that great, but it'll have to do . . . What? . . . Okay. Do that." Glancing up, he spied Nikki. He held up a finger and nodded, as if whoever he was talking to could see him. "Yeah. Right . . . I know. Tell Mom I'll be by soon . . . what?"

A pause in his side of the conversation, then he rolled his eyes.

"I don't know, Dad. Probably a couple of days . . . sure . . . okay, I've got to go." And he hit a button on his phone before sliding it into the pocket of his jeans. "Nikki?" he asked. "What're you doing here? I heard you nearly drowned, that you were prowling around or something when the cops were here."

What could she say? "You know me, I can't ever resist a story."

"Your brother used to say that you were just nosy."

"That's right." She smiled, remembering her oldest sibling as a gust of wind scattered dry leaves across the sparse gravel and past a toolbox lying open near the gate. "You knew Andrew."

"Played ball with him." He swatted at a yellow jacket that hovered near his head. "Damned bees." Then, he added, "We're closing up the place." For the first time she noticed the NO TRESPASSING signs that warned that violators would be prosecuted to the full extent of the law.

"Too many lookie-loos and people trying to break in while we're trying to sell the place. Now, since the bodies were found here, it's gotten crazy." He rubbed his upper lip where it seemed he was starting to grow a blond moustache. "You're not the first reporter to come poking around, you know."

Oh, she knew. She thought of Metzger from her own paper and the news stations and their teams of reporters.

"I was just talking to Dad about it," Tyson went on. "We've been trying to sell the place for years, as is, but now with all this bad publicity and the fact that the old house is literally crumbling down, maybe we should tear the old house down."

"Oh."

"I know. The historical society is already making noise about it. Dad calls them the 'hysterical society.'"

"The society has a point."

"Yeah, I know. But so do we. We need to sell this place, at least most of it. Crap!" The yellow jacket was back and he swiped the air vainly again. "Must be a nest somewhere." The wasp wouldn't give up, buzzing around his shiny head. He grabbed a baseball cap from the front seat, jammed it on and walked closer to Nikki's car. "They're scavengers, you know. Eat meat, even their own kind. Little cannibal bastards." He walked over and pulled the gate shut, then tested what appeared to be a new electronic locking system on the gate. He pointed a remote device at it and the lock clicked loudly before he tried to open it manually, pulling on the rails. It didn't budge.

"This won't keep anyone who really wants to get in out," he admitted, "but if someone shows up, we'll know immediately. Well, eventually." He pointed to a camera poised in a tree just on the other side of the gate. "And we'll see who it is. Digital camera, sends the images constantly. I put that one up, but it's just a stopgap until the security company puts in a whole system. Should be all hooked up by the end of next week. It would be sooner, but the security company's on overload, trying to restore everything that got knocked down during the hurricane."

She eyed the camera and nodded.

"Soon, we'll have more of the same around the house, too." He spied a piece of remaining yellow crime scene tape, swore under his breath and yanked it off the fence, then wadded it up and stuffed it into his pocket. "This is the kind of publicity we *don't* need." He glanced up at the camera again. "Once we're operational, if anyone had the stones to try and bury any more dead bodies, we'll catch them."

"Let's hope no one does."

"Amen to that."

She changed the subject. "You lived here for years, right?"

He nodded. "Me, Dad and Mom and Grandma."

"And the staff."

"Yeah, oh, yeah. Only the maids stayed at the house, though. The others, like Wynn Cravens or Margaret Duval, they didn't live in."

"Margaret Duval?" she repeated.

"Yeah, she was Nana Beulah's nurse, so she was there a lot, even spent some nights at the house, I think."

"Before you moved into Savannah?"

"Yeah." He nodded, his blue eyes watching a squirrel scamper up the trunk of one of the live oaks just beyond the fence. "Nana Beulah stayed on for a few more years—

God, was it, like, maybe ten? I don't really remember. Anyway, eventually she needed round-the-clock care in a modern facility, one without all the steps that are in the house here, and eventually we closed everything down. The only one who stayed on the payroll was Wynn for a while. We needed someone to look after the place, but eventually we had to let him go, too."

"Twenty years ago," she said, thinking aloud. "You all still lived here then? When the Duval girls went missing?"

"I guess." He turned to look at her and she had a flash of memory from her own youth. He was much younger, a tall, cocky youth who knew he was handsome, athletic and rich. She remembered him playing football on the backyard behind the house with her brother Andrew and a couple of other boys, Jacob Channing and Bronco Cravens. All shirtless and sweating, muscles gleaming as they ran over the grass of the terraced lawn. They were all connected by this piece of property with its shadowy history.

Now, Tyson, heavier and harder-edged than the boy she remembered, was nodding, his eyebrows knitting. "Yeah. Mom, she'd wanted to move for years, ever since we lost Nell, but Dad and Nana, they didn't want to leave. Eventually, Mom convinced Dad and so we did." He lifted a shoulder. "Like I said, Nana stayed on. Wouldn't budge. Until she absolutely had to." He eyed her quizzically, his arms folding over his chest.

"I never met Nell," she said.

"She died a long time ago." His countenance changed, growing more solemn.

"You were there?" Nikki asked. "The day she drowned."

He closed his eyes for a second and sighed through his nose. "Yeah, not a good day. Jacob and I were swimming in the river. She saw us and followed. But she didn't know how to swim, and we were into what we were doing, jumping off this log into the river, we didn't see. Didn't even know it until it was too late. We tried to save her, but—" He lifted the hat from his head and rubbed his scalp. "Not something I like to think about."

"You were swimming with Jacob? Jacob Channing?"

"Yeah, we were neighbors. Hung out a lot in the summer. Just had to be careful, sometimes a gator is up here, but that day—?" He squinted and looked up at the sky. "That day the gators weren't the problem. Look, I don't even know why we're talking about this. It was a really tough time. Especially for my mom. It's one of the main reasons we moved."

He looked as if he was about to end the impromptu interview. Nikki said quickly, "You dated Ashley McDonnell in high school, didn't you?"

"What?" He appeared surprised. "Where did that come from?"

"She said so and I'm just confirming. She's Owen Duval's alibi."

"I heard." He shrugged. "I dated a lot of girls back then. Ashley was one of them. And for the record, she dated around a lot, too. If you could call it that."

"What would you call it?"

He raised an eyebrow. "These days I think they refer to it as 'hooking up.' And she was always with Owen. Not necessarily a sexual thing, I think. Even back then when everything was, but she and Owen—it was weird if you ask me. But what does this have to do with anything?

Who I dated? Who she dated? Geez, that was a lifetime ago." He picked up his toolbox, snapped it closed and loaded it into the back of his vehicle. "So what's with all of the questions?"

"Just for the story."

"About the Duval sisters?" he asked, but before she could answer his cell phone rang and he yanked it from his pocket. "I gotta take this," and he answered the phone, effectively ending the interview. "Tyson Beaumont," he said, slamming the back door of his SUV shut, then getting into the driver's seat and turning on the ignition.

She got the message.

And she knew that if she wanted to go back to the grounds and see the house for herself, she'd have to do it quickly before the new security system was activated. She couldn't tip off the Beaumonts, or her husband.

That part bothered her.

As she drove toward Savannah, past the open fields and into the city, slowing with traffic, she thought about what Tyson had told her, about the timeline of his family living at the estate; something about it nagged at her, but she couldn't put her finger on it.

Before heading home, she stopped at Wilda's Ribs for takeout, her stomach growling at the spicy scent of barbecue sauce filling the interior of the SUV. She pulled into the garage and cut the engine. As she reached for the door handle and was about to pick up the white sack on the passenger seat, her phone rang. She recognized the number, so she picked up. Andrea Clancy, one of Holly Duval's friends from junior high, was returning her call. "Hello."

"Nikki? Nikki Gillette? You called me?" a woman inquired. She was speaking loudly over a cacophony of background noise and breathing hard, as if she were moving fast. "It's Andrea Clancy and I'm at the airport, here in Cincy."

"That's right, Andrea. I did call you. Thanks for calling back." Nikki remained behind the wheel of her Honda, unwilling to take a chance that the wireless connection might fail if she moved from her spot in the garage. "I'm a reporter with the *Sentinel*."

"Yeah, yeah, I know that. Look, what is it you want to know? I'm on my way to Seattle for a conference and I've got a tight connection."

"I'm calling about Holly Duval."

"I figured. I saw online that they found her body. And her sister's. I . . . I just can't believe it. I mean, I knew everyone kind of assumed that they might not be alive but . . ." Her voice faded for a second.

Nikki heard the roar of a jet engine and a woman's muffled voice instructing passengers about boarding. "Anyone with small children or needing assistance please . . ."

"I'm just having trouble processing it. That she's actually dead. *Murdered!* Dear God. I just hoped there would be a different ending," Andrea said a little breathlessly. "Look, the connection's kind of crappy here. I just got through security and am heading to my gate—oh, excuse me—sorry. Nearly ran down a woman with a stroller. God, I'm late."

"But you two were close?" Nikki pressed on for fear the connection would be lost. "You and Holly?"

"BFFs as they would say today. But that was in junior high school, of course, because . . . well, you know she didn't get to go on. Didn't get the chance. It was sad, so sad, all of it." She was still walking it seemed, bits of conversation playing in the background, a crying baby audible. "But then Holly hadn't been happy in a long time. No one in the family was. Still, this is bad. I mean, *murder?* Really? Scary stuff."

"No one was happy?" Nikki asked.

"I don't think so. Not according to Holly. She always thought her parents were on the verge of divorce, you know."

"Why?"

"I don't know. I guess it was always tense there. She said her mom and dad were never all that happy and things just got worse."

But the parents had stuck together for a while, after their daughters had disappeared.

"I thought that Harvey and Margaret split because of the pain of the girls going missing."

"Well, that didn't help, I'm sure, but according to Holly there had been trouble all along, well, at least in the last few years. Her mom and dad were always fighting."

"About what?"

"I don't know . . . Maybe it was money . . . or her job."

"Hers? Margaret's?"

"Yeah, I think. She was a private nurse or something after she got fired from the hospital or . . . Oh, wait . . . Crap . . . this isn't the right gate! Oh . . . never mind. Next one over. But . . . damn . . . I think they're calling my flight." She hesitated and for a few seconds Nikki heard the noise of the airport crackling over the line. Then Andrea was back. "Look, I've got to run."

Nikki didn't want to lose her. "So you think Holly's parents weren't getting along?"

"I don't know. Not really, but I've thought about it, of

course. Holly had just complained about it, mentioned that things had gotten tense at the house around the time her mom switched jobs and there were all sorts of other things. Owen, he was getting into trouble—teenage boy stuff like a minor in possession, y'know, getting caught drinking by the cops. Maybe even getting high. I don't really know. And then there were financial issues, always. I know because Holly couldn't afford new clothes or CDs or jewelry, whatever we were into at the time. I think—and I don't know this—but I think she was shoplifting. Wouldn't buy like a pair of earrings when we went shopping, then ended up with the same pair a week later and swore it was a 'gift' from some aunt I'd never heard of. But don't quote me on that, cuz I'm not sure. I wouldn't want to disparage the dead, or whatever it's called."

She was talking fast and on the move again, it seemed. "I really can't remember all the details, even if I knew them. But, come on, they had four kids. That's gotta be rough. And expensive—oops! Look, I gotta go. Really. We're boarding and I have to use my phone to get on the plane and I don't really know anything else anyway." She clicked off, leaving Nikki to stare out the windshield to the workbench beyond the hood of her car and think about the Duval family. So there was some trouble at home. So finances were tight. Those were normal problems, not unique to the Duvals. But what about Margaret's job? And why had she been fired from the hospital?

What could tension between mother and father have to do with their children being somehow kidnapped, and ultimately murdered, their bodies hidden in the crumbling basement of the Beaumont mansion?

She thought about it all.

Three girls missing; two bodies found. What had happened to Rose, the youngest? She listened as the car engine ticked, cooling.

Her phone buzzed in her hand.

A text from Reed: **Working late. Don't wait dinner on me.**

"Great." She tossed her phone into her purse and felt a well of disappointment. She wanted to call him. Talk things out. Bring out into the open the rift that seemed to be widening between them. Things had been tense for the last couple of days, really tense, and it was getting to her. She was a big believer in working through problems, acknowledging them and getting everything out in the open—well, for the most part. If she were being honest, she sometimes held back a little and was working on |becoming more forthcoming. Reed, though, was more introspective, held things in, waited for just the right moment, or so he thought, but then she was rash, she knew it and owned it, and he was more methodical and careful. So their arguments tended to be one-sided and more than once she'd accused him of "holding back" or "not coming clean" or "being silently judgmental."

But she did feel more than a little bit of guilt. Hadn't she just been at the Beaumont estate, essentially going behind his back? "Crap," she muttered. What a mess.

She didn't doubt he was working, not for a second, because this was his MO when he was on a big case, but she also knew he was avoiding coming home, giving them both some space, some time to cool off.

If that were possible.

The phone rang and she expected to see Reed's number, but it was another anonymous set of digits. She wouldn't have answered, but she had several calls out to numbers she didn't have memorized, people who had known the Duval family. "Hello?"

"Nikki Gillette?" a female voice asked and before she could confirm, went on, "Hi, this is Sherry Culver, we've met before. I'm with the *Charleston Star*, working on an article about the Duval homicides, and I'd like to ask you a few questions. You were there when the bodies were found on the Beaumont estate outside of Savannah, right?"

Nikki was stunned. "I can't talk about—"

"Yes, yes, I know you're married to the lead investigator, but since you're part of the press, I thought you'd be able to give me a little more information. You were injured, I know, and a police officer unfortunately died that day while trying to save you, right?"

"I said I have no comment." Nikki was starting to get steamed and realized how it felt to be on the receiving end of an interview by a pushy reporter.

"Listen, Nikki, this can be on the down low. You know how it works, I quote 'a source close to the investigation' and no one's the wiser that you gave me the information."

"No, really, I can't."

"Hey, from one woman reporter to another? We all need a break here. We're all in this together, you know—"

"From one reporter to another?" Nikki repeated. "Right. Well, my answer is still 'No comment!'"

Flustered, she clicked off. Juggling her laptop bag and the takeout sack, she was irritated and a little humiliated. How many times had she been on the other end of that particular conversation, trying to persuade information from an unwilling source? She was still silently going over the conversation in her mind, trying to figure out how she could have handled the call as she unlocked the door and let herself into the house.

I always knew the press would be involved, that I would have to tread carefully, as if I were stepping through a nest of vipers, but I didn't expect anyone like that damned muleheaded Nikki Gillette. I hadn't anticipated I'd have to deal with the likes of her, as well as all the others, when it happened. Somehow, I'll have to remove her from the situation, but that will be tricky since she's married to Detective Pierce Reed. He's enough of a problem, but I can handle him. It's his brash, ultra-curious wife who is the real stumbling block, the serious threat. That said, I'm more than up to the challenge. Bring it on!

CHAPTER 15

Nikki's dog and cat greeted her enthusiastically, Mikado spinning in sharp circles, his tail wagging crazily, while Jennings, a little less wild, wound figure eights between her legs. She took the time to put her things down and pick up the tabby, nuzzling his face while he purred, then paying attention to Mikado, bending down and getting her face washed. "I missed you, too," she told them, and tried to ignore Mikado's eager eyes as he stared at the white bag, his nose in the air sniffing. "Not this time, bud," she said.

Instead, she fed both dog and cat their usual meals, Mikado scarfing up his kibble from his bowl set next to his crate in the laundry room, Jennings picking at his similar meal placed on the counter and out of the dog's reach. Jennings flicked his striped tail in disgust.

"Sorry. It's what the vet ordered," Nikki explained. Jennings, though he could still hop onto the washer and dryer and displayed more than a spark of interest in the birds who bathed in the fountain in the backyard, was aging, showing a few bones, his appetite fading. She stroked his head gently and he purred a bit before finally settling down to his meal. "There you go." The cat had been with her since college, a friend and confidant all of her adult life, longer than she'd known Reed.

Back in the kitchen she snapped on the small television on the counter, found a news station and while she was portioning out some of the ribs, cornbread and slaw onto a plate, she kept one eye on the screen, listening through the weather report—more sunshine on the way!, an update on the city's cleanup efforts, and good news! Saint Andrews School would open on schedule, though PE classes would have to be relegated to outdoor activities due to damage to the gym—until the solemn-faced reporter turned to the Duval case. Thirtyish and blonde, with big brown eyes, white teeth and flawless skin, she stared into the camera and reported that two of the missing Duval girls had been located, their bodies discovered in the basement of the Beaumont mansion.

A montage of pictures of the Beaumont estate ensued as the anchor described how the bodies were located by an anonymous tip to the police department. No mention of Bronco Cravens. Yet. Surely his name would come up. Nikki ate as she watched. Most of the information in the report Nikki already knew firsthand and steeled herself for the inevitable that came within minutes. She watched as old film of the Beaumont estate rolled onto the screen, the huge house, rose garden and terraced lawns, Beulah Beaumont with her son, Baxter, as a young man, and his

daughter, Nell. There was mention of tragedy being associated with the place and then pictures from a few days
ago of the gates guarding the grounds with police cruis-
ers' lights flashing. Also included were the same pictures
of the Duval girls that had been circulating for years, individual school pictures that showed blond, blue-eyed
Holly staring into the camera with a shy smile and a similar shot of Poppy, her light hair pulled back in a ponytail,
her teeth not quite straight and a little large for her face.
Then there were a few seconds of the three girls caught
on film, in front of a brightly lit Christmas tree, little
Rose, at five still a towhead, her white-blond hair in wild
ringlets, her face still baby chubby, her smile infectious.

Nikki's heart broke for the family all over again as the
screen changed to show a picture of Detective Sylvie
Morrisette and the reporter, off camera, explaining that
she'd died in the line of duty while trying to rescue Nikki
Gillette, a reporter for the *Savannah Sentinel* and local
true-crime author. "Oh, no," she mouthed.

The story only got worse as the anchor mentioned that
Nikki was married to Detective Pierce Reed, lead investigator on the case who had been partnered with Morrisette. Mention was made that the funeral for the fallen
policewoman was slated for early next week.

"Crap." Nikki dropped her half-eaten rib onto her
plate as the screen switched and Abbey Marlow, in full
uniform, her red hair pulled back from her face, gave a
quick update to the press about the case, mentioning that
the police were looking for the third Duval girl in this so-
far double homicide. Abbey was succinct and short, not
offering up any more information and asking for the public's help in finding the missing daughter, now twenty-
five. A computer-generated image of what Rose Duval

might look like came onto the screen, along with the number of the police department.

Nikki found herself staring at the flat image of a pretty woman with high cheekbones, light hair and blue eyes, a small scar near her hairline at her left temple.

For half a beat, she thought she recognized the woman on the screen but couldn't place her. A second image of the woman in profile appeared, and Nikki decided she was wrong, grasping at straws, hoping beyond hope that little Rose Duval had somehow survived.

She finished what was left of her meal, then stuffed Reed's portion, still in the takeout bag from Wilda's Ribs, into the refrigerator. Her shoulder was starting to bother her as she climbed up to the third floor and settled into her chair at her computer where she wrote notes about the case. She had more people to interview and would like to look into the history of the Beaumont estate. Why had the killer chosen that location? What had happened to Rose? And what about the Duval family finances, the rumors of the parents splitting up? What about all the bad karma Chandra claimed to have felt about the family?

At nine thirty she went down to the bedroom, took off her sling and clothes, and did the best she could at showering. Her arm was feeling better and the warm water cascading over her helped in washing off any dirt and sweat from the day. She managed to shampoo, though she did drop the plastic bottle once and swore under her breath, but still, the spray felt good, as if she were exorcising the demons that had plagued her, washing away her guilt and pain. Only a few days ago, she was exuberant about the prospect of being a mother and Sylvie Morrisette was still alive, the Duval girls' fate a mystery.

As the room filled with steam, she scrubbed hard

against her skin, rinsed the conditioner from her hair and closed her eyes. She needed to find a way to fix things with Reed. Of course she would still work on the Duval story, but she had to work things out with her husband.

And he needs to work things out with you.

"Right," she said aloud as she twisted off the spray.

Reaching for her towel on the hook near the shower, she heard the dog bark.

Maybe Reed was home!

Then the bark changed to a deep, guttural growl.

A low warning.

She stopped short.

What the hell?

The hairs on the back of her neck rose in trepidation.

Dropping the towel, she snagged her robe, her shoulder protesting. But she threw the housecoat on.

More growling, then a hard, sharp bark.

Oh, God.

Footsteps.

Human footsteps.

Running.

Fast. Frantically.

What?

Who?

Not Reed.

Dear God. An intruder was in the house!

Her heart went into overdrive.

Who was it?

Why were they inside?

For no good reason.

Did they have a weapon?

Her phone! She needed her phone . . . anxiously, silently praying, Nikki patted the pockets of her robe as if by some chance it could be there while through the mist of the bathroom her gaze scraped the counter, but of course, it wasn't there. Nope. She'd left it on the charger downstairs.

Crap!

A kaleidoscope of jagged images spun through her mind, of all the times she had been at a killer's mercy, the sheer terror of fighting for her life. Her fingers clenched in the terry cloth. For a second she remained frozen and dripping onto the bathroom tiles.

Then the adrenaline kicked in.

Pull it together, Gillette!

Cinching her robe tight, she crept to the door, reached for the doorknob and twisted, realizing she hadn't locked it. She stepped into her bedroom, crossed the hardwood on bare, damp feet.

The footsteps were fleeing, sounding farther away as whoever it was raced down the steps in frantic, rapid succession. The dog hadn't given up. Mikado was barking out of control, his toenails, too, clicking frantically against the steps.

"Who's there?" Nikki demanded, slipping through the bedroom to crack the door to check the near-dark hallway.

Nothing.

Her eyes adjusted to the darkness, her ears strained as she heard the scuffling downstairs.

She steeled herself. Tried to think.

Her phone was downstairs.

But Reed's gun was locked in a safe in the bedroom closet.

Only steps away!

It would just take a few seconds to retrieve it as whoever was in the house could be armed. Heart thudding, she turned toward the closet.

"Yeowww!" A pained scream echoed through the house, and then the intruder snarled in a harsh whisper. "You bit me? You fuckin' bit me?"

More growling and barking.

"Back the fuck off! Shit! Let go of me! I'll kill you, you goddamned mutt!" a gravelly whispered voice warned.

"No!" Nikki screamed, dashing into the hall.

Too late!

Thud!

Mikado let out an anguished howl.

"Mikado!" she cried, her heart wrenching. *No, no, no!* She heard the back door open.

Nikki flew down the stairs as the door slammed.

She slid around the corner, racing into the kitchen.

Mikado was scrambling to his feet.

"Oh, baby, are you okay?" She was on her knees, trying to cradle her pup, but Mikado was having none of it. Incensed, he lunged toward the door, snarling and snapping and whining, ready to go after the prowler and tear him to pieces.

"Stop!" she ordered as he scratched furiously at the door. "No! Mikado! Not happening." Her pulse was still in the stratosphere as she twisted the dead bolt to lock the door. The guy could come back. Get a weapon and return. Why the hell was he in here in the first place? What was he after? "You are *not* going out there!" she said, and while the dog whined to be let out and go after the intruder, she stood to peer through the blinds to the backyard. She was sweating, her throat tight, her mind spinning with all kinds of horrid scenarios.

But everything appeared calm. The house now quiet. The backyard fountain was still gurgling serenely. The pathway lanterns illuminated a rock wall near the fence line and up-lighting washed a soft glow up the trunk and spreading branches of the magnolia tree. No dark figure seemed to be lurking in the shadows, and the creak of the back gate as it moved in the wind suggested he'd run out of the yard. Her heart pounding, she hurried to the front of the house and squinted through the sidelights of the front door, searching the empty street for a car speeding away. She expected to see the red glow of taillights or hear the sound of a fading engine disappearing into the night, but she heard nothing other than the rush of distant traffic and the sigh of the wind moving through the branches of the trees flanking the house.

Turning, she spied Mikado, apparently without injury, trotting up to her. "You're a good boy," she said, bending down and patting his head. "Such a good, good boy." He wiggled happily and seemed uninjured, thankfully.

Next, she checked all the doors and windows and found them all locked. All secure. So how had the intruder gotten in? With a sinking feeling, she wondered if she'd forgotten to lock the back door when she'd come home. Mentally she retraced her steps, coming into the house from the garage, wearing her sling, hauling her laptop bag and the takeout sack. Hadn't she locked the door behind her? She'd been on the phone with that pushy reporter and walked inside and . . .

She didn't remember.

Once more she went through a perimeter check, making certain she was alone and that every way into the house, even the dog door, was battened down. She thought about calling Reed and picked up her phone and hesitated. It would only upset him and she was safe now. And he'd be home soon. Right?

She decided to text and typed quickly.

FYI—Letting you know we had an intruder. Mikado chased him out. Never caught sight of him. Nothing stolen. Everything is okay. I'm fine. House is locked. See you soon.

She hesitated, then hit the send button and with one last glance around spied Jennings standing atop the bookcase in the den. "Come on. You too." With the dog following, adrenaline still pumping through her veins, she headed upstairs.

The phone rang before she reached the second floor.

It was Reed. Of course.

"I'm on my way!" he shouted as she answered. He sounded out of breath. "You're sure you're okay?"

"I'm fine." Aside from being still terrified.

"What the hell happened?" She heard a car door open and close.

"Just what I said. There was someone in the house. He's gone now. Mikado scared him off."

"Hell."

"It's okay."

"It's not! Stay put."

"Reed, really, I'm fine. Mikado's fine."

"Why wouldn't he be?"

"He was kicked."

"Fuck! Seriously?"

"Yeah. But, really, he's okay. I checked."

"Good. I'll be right there." She heard an engine spark to life, a gearshift being rammed into gear. "Stay on the line with me."

"I don't need to—"

"For God's sake, Nikki, just stay on the damned line."

This time she didn't argue. "Okay."

"I'll be home in ten minutes."

He made it in eight.

CHAPTER 16

It was after midnight when the officer taking the report had left and Reed was satisfied that the house was secure, his wife was unharmed and the damned dog, who had apparently saved the day, wasn't injured.

"This has something to do with the investigation," he decided, forgoing a nightcap and stripping off his clothes. They were in the master bedroom and Nikki had already slipped between the covers. Her hair was still damp, surrounding her face in ringlets, her face without any make-up, her eyes following his every move.

God, he loved her.

Never had he met a woman who could stir so much passion in him.

And no one could piss him off so deeply.

"So from now on—"

"I know, I know, you've said it, like, twenty times or maybe thirty. 'Double-check all the locks, keep my phone with me at all times and keep the dog at my side.' Is that about it, Detective?"

"About," he admitted, tossing his slacks over the back of a side chair where his crumpled shirt and tie were already draped. He threw his T-shirt onto the growing pile. "Just be careful."

"Got it."

He sank onto the bed beside her and decided it was time to be totally honest. "I just don't want to lose you."

She smiled and cuddled up to him. "And I don't want to lose you."

"I think this has something to do with the investigation."

"So you've said." Her head was propped against his shoulder, her hair smelling fresh and clean, her skin warm. "You've been asking around."

"Mmm." No denial.

"You should stop."

"Says you."

"Right."

"It's my job, Reed. And look, I don't need a lecture, okay?" She propped herself up on her elbow to stare at him, then winced from the pain and slid back to lying next to him, head back in the cradle of his arm. "I feel awful. Just awful. Guilty and sad and worried and ashamed and . . . and everything." She blinked and let out a sigh. "But I never intended for any of this to happen. I had no idea Morrisette would jump into the river, that she'd be hit by debris that . . ." Her voice trailed off and he waited. "Okay, I should have, I know. I was trespassing, potentially messing up a crime scene and . . . and I was pregnant." Her voice caught and she had to clear her throat. Her expression turned regretful. "But even though I'd . . . I'd miscarried before, I didn't think, I mean, I didn't believe I'd have to be like this hothouse flower who couldn't do anything."

His arm tightened around her. Being this introspective was hard for Nikki, facing her flaws almost impossible, but then, wasn't it for everyone?

"You get it," she charged, "but yeah, if I could do it all over again, I would make different choices. Better ones."

"And you'd listen to me."

"I always do, but, hey, you can't just order me around, Reed. Even if you think it's for my own good. Or . . . our own good." He caught the movement of her hand touching her naked belly and he felt his own sliver of pain.

"You haven't been known to be willing to talk things out," he said gently.

"I'm trying, okay? And I'll try harder, but I am who I am. The woman you married."

"I know." And he did. He kissed her forehead. "Just try to be careful and I'll try not to be so . . ."

"Closed off? Distant? Self-righteous. So damned authoritative—"

"Whoa, whoa, whoa! Slow down. One flaw at a time, okay?" He stared into her eyes and noticed a spark of wicked amusement in their green depths. She was pulling his chain and trying to smother a smile. "You talked about your job. Don't forget mine. I'm in charge of the investigation."

"We could work together."

"Yeah, right."

"We have before."

"Not by my choice."

"I'm just saying—"

"Okay, well, here's the deal," he said with a sigh. "First and foremost, you be careful. I don't want to lose you. Ever." He gave her another squeeze and she snuggled closer, her skin so warm and inviting he had trouble concentrating, but he forced himself. "And secondly, you talk to me about what you're doing. You can't be doing anything that could compromise the police investigation."

"Yeah, yeah, I know this."

"I'm serious. Nikki, someone broke into our house."

"Well, I think I didn't lock the door."

"I know, so you said, but whoever it was, it wasn't a social call. So—"

"I get it. I'll be careful. I'll check with you—" She turned her face to his and kissed him, her lips warm and supple, her body so tight and close.

"Wait," he forced out against his own body's desires, the heat that was flowing in his blood. "You're still healing."

"I know, but the doctor said everything was okay, whenever I felt like it we could, you know . . ." Her breath played against his chest. "There are things we could do . . ."

"Nikki, please, I don't want to hurt you."

"Hurt me, Reed," she whispered, breathing against his abdomen. "Please . . . hurt me. Or—wait." She paused and looked up at him from beneath the covers, green eyes peering up through the tousle of red-blond curls. "I've got a better idea."

Again her breath was playing havoc with his mind. "Do you?" he managed to get out.

"Um-hmm. Let me hurt you." Still gazing up at him, she smiled mischievously. "Let me hurt you real good."

The woman was impossible to resist.

At least she and Reed were talking again, in the same book, so to speak, if not exactly on the same page. They'd woken up later than usual, and Reed had run through the shower and shaved, dressed hurriedly and said to Nikki, who was still in the bed, "Just promise me that you won't do anything crazy," as he'd stuffed his keys and wallet into his pockets.

"No craziness," she'd said with mock sincerity as she'd raised her arm as if taking an oath and Jennings had hopped onto Reed's recently vacated pillow to curl up.

"I'm serious. Be safe. Keep everything locked and let me know when you go out."

"Aye, aye, captain."

"I said, I'm serious!"

"And I'm Nikki Gillette, glad to meet you."

"Ugh. So corny, Nik. And so old school."

"I know. But just try to lighten up, okay?"

"Lighten up? Last night—"

"Is over. Okay? Besides, I've got this guy"—she motioned to the dog bed, where Mikado raised his head and yawned, showing his teeth—"to protect me."

"God save us," Reed said, glancing at the pup, who thumped his tail against the side of his bed. "And who knows why the intruder came in. Was it about the investigation? Or something else? Random because the door was left unlocked, a burglar in the neighborhood, or something else?"

She leaned forward. "You tell me. You're the detective."

"And you're impossible." He glanced at the bedside clock and swore under his breath. "Call and text me if you decide to go out."

"Um-hmm." She listened to him hurry down the hallway, his feet clicking down the stairs, and she let out a long sigh. At least some of the tension—well, most of it—had dissipated. "I'll be careful," she whispered to the cat, and Jennings opened one suspicious eye as if doubting anything she said this morning.

When Reed walked into the office, he noticed things had changed. Delacroix had taken over Morrisette's desk and was sitting in the desk chair, leaning forward, her eyes glued to her computer screen as she used the mouse to scroll through images. Any reticence she'd felt about moving her things into the office had dissipated and she was working at the computer, a Diet Coke can unopened but sweating on a corner of the desk, a cup of pens and pencils, her cell phone and a few papers collected in a mesh basket.

The only personal items were a Loyola University cap turned upside down on the desk, her keys and small wallet tucked inside. She'd slung a lightweight jacket over the back of her chair and was wearing tight jeans and a black T-shirt.

"Hey," she said, not looking up from the monitor as he settled into his own chair and it creaked from his weight.

He asked, "What's up?"

"What's up with you?" Still her gaze was fastened to

the screen as the noise from the hallway, the buzz of conversation punctuated with laughter and the jangle of cell phones filtered in, colliding with the rush of air being pumped through the ducts from the air conditioner. "I heard there was a break-in at your place last night."

"That's right."

"No one hurt? Nothing taken?" She finally glanced over her shoulder.

"No."

"Your wife okay?"

"Yes." He hoped so.

"She's been through a lot lately."

Amen to that. "Seems to be pretty commonplace with Nikki."

"Yeah, I heard she gets herself into trouble," she said, one eyebrow arching over the rim of her glasses.

"Occasionally."

"How do you do that?" she asked, finally settling back in her chair and giving him her full attention.

"Do what?"

"Work with a reporter who's always butting into your cases?"

He wanted to argue but saw no point. He was going to be working with this woman now, so they'd better clear the air and set some ground rules about privacy.

"It's a work in progress," he admitted, "but we handle it." Like hell.

"A balancing act?"

"I guess." But the scales always seemed tipped a bit. "What've we got?" He was hoping for a new lead because their interview with Ashley Jefferson hadn't gone well. She'd stuck to her original statement and when they'd pushed her, she'd asked if she needed a lawyer.

Delacroix had planned to crack her and have her admit her alibi for Owen Duval was bullshit, but Ashley Jefferson had held firm, all of which had pissed off Delacroix.

"We've got a couple of things." She pointed to a graying box on the other side of her desk. "Original case files. You requested?"

"Yeah."

"They're dusty and I think I might be allergic." She took off her glasses and set them on the desk, then found a tissue and rubbed her eyes. They did look a little red and she was blinking away tears.

"Sorry."

"I'll live." She dug into a desk drawer, found a bottle of eyedrops and deftly administered them. "You know, everything's digital now."

"I know."

"So why bother?"

"Helps me get into it."

"Seems like you already were 'into it.'"

How could he explain that he liked to see the evidence as it had come in, to touch it and smell it, to feel as if the details of the case were surrounding him in the twenty-year-old dust? Delacroix had grown up in the digital/virtual age where everyone had a cell phone and friends via social platforms. Reed needed more, something tactile and real. He needed to get his hands dirty.

But she was already back at the computer screen. "Also, a couple of things. According to the ME, the victims weren't sexually molested."

He felt a sense of relief. "Good."

"I know. Right?" Her eyes met his. "Not that it matters now, I suppose, but . . . glad they didn't have to suffer that on top of whatever else happened to them."

Reaching for her can of soda, she hit her glasses to send them skating across her desk and flying across the space between their desks. "Geez, I'm such a klutz," she said as he picked up the pair, glanced through the lenses to see that they weren't cracked, then handed them back to her.

"Not much of a prescription." The lenses seemed clear, without any correction.

"I know." She seemed embarrassed. "I've had them for years. Because I have what's commonly called a 'lazy eye.' I guess I should have surgery, but I keep putting it off, you know. I mean, what if something goes wrong? I'm better off with these." She held up the glasses by the bow, then slid them onto her nose, opened her can of soda, took a swig and was back to business. "Anyway, I talked to a few people who were at the theater that day, people who made statements."

"And?"

"They are all sticking to their stories, which isn't a surprise, but I was hoping for something that might change things up. But so far, no luck." Another long swallow from her can. "I talked to most of the people who'd been at the theater that night, except for three I couldn't locate as they'd moved and one who'd passed away. The others, let me see—nine of them, including the guy working the refreshment stand who also was the ticket taker and the cashier in the booth outside the front doors—but none of them had anything more to add."

He wasn't surprised, but it was still disappointing.

"No one saw Owen Duval go into the theater, that's the thing, and if you look at the security footage, such as it is, he's nowhere to be seen even though he bought a ticket. I sent you the link, by the way."

Reed faced his desk, switched on the computer and scrolled through his e-mails until he discovered the link and opened it. The first footage was of people entering the theater. There weren't many trickling in, so it was easy to spot the three blond girls. "There they are . . ." Delacroix said, rolling her chair over to his and pointing at the screen. Owen appeared in the camera's eye as he approached, then slipped cash through a hole cut into the glass. The ticket taker slid four tickets back to him, along with some change, and he appeared to mutter a "thanks" as he passed out the tickets and placed his ticket and two dollars into his wallet.

"So he never went inside," Reed said.

"Looks like." Her eyes were narrowed as she stared at the images. "Now, watch, the camera angle changes because the department put all the film together."

She was right. After the girls entered the building, the screen went dark for a few seconds, then the new black-and-white image of the lobby appeared; the girls waited for an older couple to order and take their drinks and popcorn before stepping up to the glass case and making their own selections, one big barrel of popcorn, three drinks and a box of some kind of candy.

"Red Vines," Delacroix said as if it made any difference. "I talked to Gary Garvin, the guy behind the counter, and he remembered because the girls argued about what to buy, only had so much money so they had to split. He said the oldest girl, Holly, made the final choice and the middle girl, Poppy, wasn't happy about it." True enough; as the girls edged away from the counter, the middle girl was scowling, holding her drink but obviously mad as two teenaged boys approached the counter. "Did you talk to any of these guys?" he asked, motioning to the boys pushing each other and laughing, screwing around as they ordered.

"No, they were never located."

"Seriously? Because they could have known Owen Duval, and because of it, might have paid more attention to what happened to him."

"I sent you a list of everyone who was questioned. These guys weren't located. No one recognized them."

As Delacroix's cell phone beeped and she checked an incoming text, Reed reversed the footage until it fell on the boys again. "One of them has braces." He pointed to the blond with the long hair, his eyes nearly obscured by the pale fringe, a burst of freckles over a Roman nose. He was wearing a tank top, jacket and shorts and looked all of fourteen. The other was taller and seemed slightly more mature, more filled out, his face a roadmap of pimples, his dark hair curly and wild, his shoulders broad and straining the shoulders of a long-sleeved T-shirt that barely covered the waistband of his shorts, which were so low slung they nearly fell off his narrow hips. "We need to find these guys."

"They tried," she said, pocketing her phone. "At least Charles Easterling tried originally."

"Well, we gotta try again. Let's get a picture from the film of each boy. Make it as clear as possible and give it to the press, get it out there, see if anyone remembers them or if they come forward. They'll be in their early to midthirties by now. If that doesn't work, we'll do computer enhancements, show what they look like today, like we did with Rose Duval, and see if we get a hit."

Delacroix had retrieved her cell from her pocket and was nodding as she made notes on the device, but she paused, looking up. "You think that will work—the computer-generated images?"

"Won't know until we give it a try."

"But nothing's come through on the youngest Duval girl, right, the one where we sent out the images?"

"Not yet, but it's still early. Been less than twenty-four hours that it's been with the media." He managed a smile he didn't feel because they both knew that the chances of the youngest sister being alive were slim, almost nonexistent. And even if she somehow had managed to survive, locating her was a long shot, an extremely long shot. "Let's do it and see what we come up with. Who knows?" His gaze locked with hers. "We might just get lucky."

CHAPTER 17

"Yeah, I can meet." Brit Sully's voice sounded a little faint over the wireless connection.

Nikki sat a little straighter in her desk chair. After over a week of trying to reach the woman, Brit, who was part of a clique that had included Andrea Clancy and Ashley McDonnell, had finally called her back.

"Awesome," Nikki said. She'd been searching for and going through all the social media accounts of the people associated with the Duval case. If anyone who knew Holly, Poppy, or Rose Duval had a Facebook, Instagram, Twitter, or other social platform account, Nikki had been trying to track them down or, if she could get into the account, take a look at their psyches, as well as their friends and contacts and interests and groups.

Now, finally, she could actually talk to someone about

the case. Someone who'd actually known Holly Duval. Besides the girls' parents, with whom she'd had short, emotional conversations.

Margaret, the girls' mother, had been eager to talk, though unable or unwilling to offer any real insight, preferring instead to rail against the police for not finding her daughters earlier, and held tight to the belief that her youngest was alive somewhere.

"And where is Rose?" Margaret had wailed. "Where's my baby? Why can't the police locate her?"

Harvey said little more than "It's a real shame." And when asked about his still-missing youngest daughter, Harvey had been more resigned. "I doubt we'll ever see her again. Look, I can't talk about this anymore. Please, don't call again."

So far, she hadn't.

Everyone else she'd tried to contact about the Duval case had denied her. Until now. Her pulse ticked up as Brit suggested, "How about in half an hour? Ten thirty, I know that's kind of short notice, but I didn't really know if I should talk to you, and the rest of the day is pretty full."

"Sure. Fine. Half an hour works!" She didn't want to lose this lead, didn't want to give Brit a chance to back out. "Where?"

"I was thinking the Buzz, that coffee shop that's not far from Forsyth Park? You know where it is?"

"Yes. Perfect!" She frequented the Buzz often enough as it was only across the park, a few blocks from where she lived. "I'll be there." She stood quickly and heard a series of pops as her spine lengthened.

Finally! After two days of spinning her wheels. She'd spent most of the past forty-eight hours at home, working on her laptop, checking the Internet, arranging her own timeline of when events in the Duval murders had taken place, and making calls for interviews where she'd left messages one after another. Texts, e-mails and voice mails had been left unanswered.

Until now.

Of course Reed had been as tight-lipped about the case as ever, and rather than risking another rift with him, she hadn't badgered him about the investigation and had barely mentioned it. He was absorbed in it, though he did ask about what she'd done each day and if there had been anything the least bit suspicious here at the house.

There hadn't been.

No bogeyman lurking in the shadows.

No dark figure leaping at her as she rounded a corner.

And though she still had the uncanny sensation that she was being watched or followed, she'd chalked it all up to some lingering paranoia that she dismissed because one thing she was not was a wimp!

There had been a couple of times when the cat had looked out the window, his tail twitching, and Nikki had followed his gaze to land on a bird at the fountain or a squirrel scampering brazenly along the top of the back fence, but that had been it.

Nothing the least bit evil or scary or threatening.

No one had been hurt.

Nothing had been stolen.

Everything was quiet again.

Now, she hurried downstairs and felt a twinge in her arm, reminding her she wasn't quite healed, though she'd been wearing her sling less and less and she wasn't going to bother with it now. She put her iPad, phone and keys into her bag and caught sight of Mikado at the door, looking up at her hopefully. "Next time," she promised. "You're in charge." His tail swept the floor. "That's right, because we can't trust him, now, can we?" She pointed to the cat, who was creeping along the windowsill, staring into the back garden.

And then she was off.

Nikki half jogged crossing the park where the live oaks spread their branches across the wide walkways. She passed a man in a fedora and overcoat despite the heat, a teenager walking four dogs of different shapes and sizes, and two women power walking for their morning exercise.

She was starting to sweat a bit when she caught up with Brit at the Buzz, where she had already ordered a tall coffee drink and was seated at a tall café table in the front courtyard while scrolling on her phone.

"Hi! So glad to finally connect," Nikki said, taking the stool across from her.

"Yeah." She looked up from the screen. In her late thirties, Brit was petite and trim, wearing running clothes that suggested she kept fit by logging in miles jogging. Her thick black hair was pulled into a ponytail, a few silver hairs catching in the morning light. "Don't you want to grab something to drink?"

"I'm fine," Nikki assured her as she pulled out her phone and iPad. She didn't want Brit to have a chance to second-guess herself. "As I said, I just wanted to ask you some questions about the Duval family."

"You and a million others," she said, taking a sip from her cup.

"Other reporters?" That worried her and she considered Norm Metzger—God, he was a pain in her side.

"Oh, yeah. Like tons. But not the cops. Well, at least

not yet. Anyway, I didn't know what to do, but I wanted to help since I was a friend of Holly's, you know. Maxie said you were cool, so"—she shrugged—"ask away." She licked off a remaining bit of foam from the rim of her drink.

Nikki decided to get right to the heart of it, what had been nagging at her. "Tell me about Ashley McDonnell and Owen Duval, how close they were."

"They weren't." Brit leaned forward, the tall table wobbling slightly on the cobblestones. "That—the two of them—was definitely *not* a thing. At least not *that* kind of thing."

"But she's his alibi. She swore she was with him that night."

"I know. I know," Brit said. "But I'm telling you, Ashley McDonnell was out of Owen Duval's league. Like waaay out!" Brit's eyebrows lifted as she took a long sip from her latte. "I really never understood why Ashley hung out with him, you know. He was so quiet and aloof, kind of kept to himself."

"Maybe that appealed to her."

Another long swallow of her latte. "I guess, but Ashley was always a girl who had her eyes on the prize."

"Meaning?"

Brit cocked her head and stared at Nikki as if she couldn't believe she had to explain the obvious. "Ashley was only interested in running with the 'it' crowd, the popular kids. Cheerleaders, jocks, especially the ones who had money. Even at fourteen or fifteen, she knew what she wanted."

"Which was?"

"A rich husband, obviously. And she got one, didn't she?"

"In Ryan Jefferson?"

"Right!" Brit rubbed her thumb over the tips of her fingers to indicate cold, hard cash. "Ryan developed some kind of medical software—for heart patients, I think, but I could be wrong and it doesn't matter. Anyway, he built up his own company, made a fortune, then sold it before he was forty for, like, millions of dollars, probably tens of millions, but I don't really know."

"And Owen didn't have any?"

"Nah, he was more of a bad boy." She drained her drink and squinted, thinking. "The thing that really doesn't make sense to me is that Ryan is a nerd. Always was, always will be."

"A 'nerd'?"

"Okay, I know that's not PC, but it's true. He's a computer geek, still. With all his money, he drives an old minivan, you know, so he can haul stuff. Ashley—who drives a Bentley, by the way—tried to talk him into a Range Rover or Lexus SUV or Tesla or whatever, but he runs around in beat-up jeans and not the expensive ones, but real old jeans and T-shirts." She rolled her eyes. "Drives Ashley crazy. It's not like he wears glasses duct-taped together, but he really doesn't give a crap about anything fancy. She's the one who talked him into moving into a gated community out on Tybee. On the water, of course. Nothing but the best for Ashley. That's what I mean. And they have a country club membership, maybe more than one, but that's for her and maybe his business contacts. Not him. She golfs and plays tennis and he . . . he has a 'garage' that's really a huge office filled with all kinds of computers and technical stuff. Like I said, 'a nerd.'"

"She met him in high school?"

"Well, she probably knew him then. He's older by a

couple of years, but they got together later, after he went to college and had his business going, I think."

"So she dated Owen in high school?"

"Not really 'dated.' Not seriously. They weren't, like, going together or anything like that. They weren't a couple."

"So why, then, would she protect Owen Duval?"

"You tell me? It didn't make any sense. Still doesn't. Back in the day he was sorta cute, I guess." She squinched up her face as if she didn't believe what she was saying. "But in kind of a mysterious way, I guess. And he could be funny—real sharp sense of humor. Sarcastic. But really, he was a dirtbag. Right. He shoulda been there for his sisters!" She tossed her empty cup into a nearby wastebasket. "I don't get it. As I said, Ashley always had her eyes on the prize, and she liked keeping her options open, so she dated a lot of guys."

"Owen called her his girlfriend," Nikki reminded her.

"That might have been the way he saw it, or wanted it to be. He might've even thought they were a couple or exclusive or whatever, but Ashley definitely didn't. She had a ton of boyfriends. A ton."

"Such as?" Nikki asked. She knew the crowd because her siblings had been in school with them.

"God, I can't remember. Not really. Uh . . . let's see. Jacob, she hung out with him a lot."

"Jacob Channing?" Wasn't that the name Margaret had mentioned?

"Yeah." She nodded. "Jacob was a real jock and he was the richest kid in our class, well, next to Tyson." She took another sip of her drink. "The Beaumonts. They had the most money. Everyone knew it. But Jacob was right up there, and he and Tyson were friends."

"And both dated Ashley?"

"Not at the same time." She wrinkled her nose. "But yeah."

"While she was seeing Owen."

"'Seeing him' isn't what I'd call it. Did they hook up?" Brit thought about it a second. "I don't know. She liked him, yeah. Owen held some weird fascination with her because he was different, I suppose, but . . . it was never serious. He wasn't the kind of guy she went for, not in the long term anyway." Brit shrugged as three women in their sixties climbed onto stools a couple of tables away. They were laughing and talking, hooking their purses over the back of their chairs and caught up in their conversation. Ashley leaned across the table and lowered her voice as if afraid the trio might overhear her. "If you want to know the truth, I was surprised that she was his alibi."

"Why?"

"Because"—she let out her breath—"well, because it would get her into trouble, you know, with her parents, and it also kind of messed with her rep."

"Her rep?"

"Reputation. It was one thing to be friends with Owen the outcast, you know, but to be his alibi, to be cast as the girl he'd been with that night, was weird. Ashley was always so worried about appearances: what she wore, who she hung with, her grades . . . everything."

"You're saying she's lying?"

"No—I mean, I don't *think* so."

Which seemed to indicate she did.

Nikki asked, "Why would she lie if she was all about protecting her rep and staying out of trouble?"

"Exactly." Brit frowned. "I mean, it doesn't make sense,

but then, what does?" She checked her watch again. "I really gotta go. I told you this was a busy day." She climbed off her chair and, using both hands, tightened her ponytail. "I don't know anything else."

Before Nikki could ask another question or thank her, she was off, running, starting at a trot until she reached the street, then as the pedestrian light changed, she sprinted away across the street, her ponytail swinging side to side with her strides as she sped around a woman walking a dog and a cluster of teenagers vaping and talking, all the while scanning their cell phone screens.

Nikki texted Millie, asking for Ryan and Ashley Jefferson's address on Tybee Island, then bought an iced coffee inside the shop before walking home.

She thought about calling her husband.

And tell him what? that naggy little voice in her head demanded.

Is that what you want, to always be reporting in?

To be one of those women on an oh-so-short leash?

Scowling, she reentered the park, deep in thought, hurrying past a woman pushing a stroller, looking at the baby swaddled beneath pink blankets, and her heart twisted a bit.

Someday, she thought, someday.

She wasn't giving up. She had an appointment later in the day with Dr. Kasey and then she'd find out when they could try again. The sooner the better. She walked, moving quickly, rounding the fountain, when she caught a movement out of the corner of her eye. Sensing someone was watching, she glanced over her shoulder and saw a few people in the park. Was anyone following her? Someone suspicious?

No.

It was a warm day under clear skies, a breath of wind whispering through the trees in the park.

So why did the back of her arms still have goose pimples?

Why did the muscles in her chest tighten?

She picked up her pace and told herself she was being a ninny, a "'fraidy cat," as they said in grade school. But she did understand about Reed's concerns. Who wouldn't be after the other night when a stranger had entered their home unannounced and uninvited?

She made her way out of the park, crossed the street and once on the steps of her home, glanced over her shoulder.

Nothing out of the ordinary.

Whatever she'd seen or thought she'd seen was gone.

But the uneasy feeling remained.

Reed was on his way out of the office when his cell phone rang and he took the call, settling back into his chair. "Detective Reed."

"Hey. Yeah. You been callin' me and, um, I decided if I didn't call ya back, you might come knockin' and I don't need any of that kind of trouble." The voice was male and rough.

"I'm sorry. You're—?"

"Oh, uh. Reggie Scott. You've been phonin', leavin' messages."

Owen Duval's biological father. "That's right. I didn't recognize the number." He sat on his desk and hit the record button on his phone. "You're in Atlanta."

"Yeah, got me a job at the mill and I don't want no one messin' it up for me. Don't need any cops comin' to the mill or nothin', but I ain't got nothin' to say anyway."

"I'm calling about the bodies that were found at the Beaumont estate."

"The Duval girls, yeah, I know. I put two and two together. Look, I don't know nothin' about that."

"What about your son?"

"Owen. He ain't my son. Gave him up way back when. Figured he'd be better off with Margaret." He snorted. "I was back on the booze then, y'know, had my share of troubles and so I guess I can't blame her for lookin' for somethin' better, but still it was a pisser, y'know."

"What was?"

"You know. To find out your wife is bangin' someone else? Sheeit. Doesn't do much for a man's ego, if y'know what I mean."

"She was involved with another man?"

"Well, hell yeah. Harvey. She and he were gettin' it on while I was doin' a little time and when I get out, she tells me she's takin' my boy and to leave her and her new family alone. She offered me some money and I'm not ashamed to say I took it, and Harvey adopted Owen and she had her perfect little family." The sarcasm in his voice was palpable. "Guess it didn't turn out all that perfect after all."

"Where were you the day the girls went missing?"

He laughed. "That's a good one. Never met 'em. That was twenty years ago or so? How the hell would I know?"

"Seems like something you would remember."

"Oh, for the love of Christ. If I remember correctly a friend of mine—Bill Seymore—and I were shootin' dice, but he's dead now. Can't confirm. So just leave me the hell alone. I had nothin', not one damn thing to do with those girls. Hell, I wouldn't have recognized 'em if I ran over 'em. As I just told ya, I never met 'em. When Margaret and I split, that was it. Never saw her again and as for Owen, just a time or two. It just wasn't worth it. I borrowed money from him a couple of times, but that was it. We didn't have what you'd call a normal father/son relationship, if you know what I mean."

"He loaned you money."

Reggie snorted. "Had to pry it out of him. I figured he owed me. He *did* owe me. Look, man, now you know, so leave me the hell alone."

He ended the call, and Reed went back to the records but saw no mention of Reggie Scott in the reports other than a mention that he was the biological father of Owen Duval.

Nothing else.

Somehow Reggie had fallen through the cracks.

Reed made a couple of quick notes and headed out to grab some lunch. He'd just stepped outside and was crossing the parking lot when the phone rang again. "Detective Reed?" a sharp female voice inquired.

"Yeah." Using his remote, he unlocked the driver's door.

"This is Deputy Tina Rounds." He remembered her. Tall, by-the-book, with mocha-colored skin, near-black eyes and a no-nonsense attitude. "Hey, I got a call from emergency. A fisherman found a body. He came up here to Black Bear Lake and found the remains. Freaked, called 911, and I caught the call. I'm here now and all I can tell you is that it's definitely human cuz the skull is still there, though other body parts are missing, and it's small. A kid."

"Rose Duval," he whispered under his breath, his heart sinking. Damn. He'd hoped she had somehow survived.

"Don't know yet."

Jesus. He started jogging to his vehicle. "I'm on the way. Text me the address."

She did and he typed it into his GPS, then drove out of the lot, the Jeep's interior already warm, the windshield dusty. He hit the wipers and wash, then hit speed dial on his phone.

Delacroix picked up before the phone rang twice. "Yeah."

"Looks like we may have found Rose Duval."

A pause. "Really?" Disbelief.

He filled her in.

"Holy shit," she whispered. "That's about what . . . less than a mile upriver from the Beaumont place?"

"Yeah." He checked the map as he drove away from the heart of the city, centuries-old buildings giving way to strip malls. "Closer to the old Marianne Inn."

"Don't know the place."

He pushed the speed limit, cutting around an old diesel truck pulling a dirty, time-worn boat filled with crab pots and fishing nets.

"The Marianne's been closed for years but used to be kind of a resort or fishing lodge."

"You really think it's Rose Duval?" Again, he heard the skepticism in her voice.

"No idea," he admitted. "Only one way to find out."

Delacroix said, "I can be there in fifteen."

"I'll meet you there." His pulse kicked up and he

pushed the speed limit, driving out of town, through suburbia to the road that wound along the river.

The thought of finding the third Duval girl bothered him, and he was surprised at his disappointment. At a gut level he'd hoped to find her alive, living under an alias, perhaps not even knowing she was the missing Rose Duval, that the memory of her youngest years had been erased or blurred with the passage of time. But why would she be located away from the crypt, where it seemed the killer had created a space for her.

His fingers clenched more tightly over the wheel as he turned off the main road to a lane where the asphalt had buckled and finally turned to gravel. Dry weeds scraped the undercarriage while the Jeep's tires bumped through potholes. Around a scraggly pine he found the deputy's cruiser and a dirty white pickup with a canopy, fishing poles propped against its side.

Tina Rounds was as daunting and by-the-book as ever. The man beside her, Frank Mentos, was no more than five-six, a little round in the middle, his eyes huge in their sockets. His hair was gray beneath a baseball cap, and he was wearing hip waders and a fisherman's vest.

The story was simple: Mentos had been fishing around the lake, started back to his truck, when he noticed something half covered in brush and dirt. Upon closer examination, he'd realized he was looking at a denim jacket, beneath which he thought he saw bones. He'd freaked, called 911, and Rounds was the first on the scene. She'd phoned Reed.

"Damnedest thing I ever seen," Mentos said, swallowing hard as he stared at the partial skeleton.

Reed bent down on one knee, careful not to disturb anything, and looked at the bones and tattered clothing:

the raggedy jacket and once-red shirt. If there had been pants, they had either disintegrated or been dragged off by animals, along with several obviously missing bones.

His heart nose-dived. The skeleton was, indeed, small.

"Hey!" A shout behind him caught his attention and he turned, still kneeling, to find Delacroix, her expression serious, sunglasses over her eyes as she hurried down the path. "What've we got? Oh, geez." She nodded at Rounds and Mentos, and Reed filled her in as she, too, crouched for a better look at the body. "This all there is?" she said. "Missing leg bones and an arm?"

"All we've found so far," Rounds said as the sun beat down, and Reed felt himself sweating.

"It's not Rose Duval," Delacroix said, rocking back on her heels and shaking her head. "But some other kid."

Rounds asked, "How do you know?"

"Size," she said, and Reed agreed. The skeleton would be too large for a five-year-old. "And she was too young to have lost her baby teeth. This one has adult-size incisors."

"Unless she was brought here later," Reed hypothesized. "The killer could have kept her a few years, then returned her here."

"Unlikely." Delacroix straightened and kept her voice low. "He already had a spot picked out for her," she said, reminding him of the space for a third body at the Beaumont estate. "Why leave her here?"

Mentos's Adam's apple wobbled. "You think there were more?"

"Victims?" Delacroix asked.

"Yeah." Mentos nodded and licked his lips. "Like more than those poor girls?"

"Unknown," Reed said.

"Could be unrelated," Delacroix said. "Why don't you come down to the station and make a full statement?"

"I thought I just did." Mentos looked from one cop to the other.

Delacroix offered a hard grin. "I know. Thank you. But there's some red tape involved. Not much, but you know, this way it's official."

Mentos turned his eyes on Reed, as if looking for confirmation.

Reed backed up his partner. "You heard the detective," he said. "Best way to wrap up your part."

Mentos gave a short nod, as if he'd just won an argument with himself. "Okay, then. I will." He glanced down at the bones now exposed to the harsh afternoon light. "I just hope this was an accident of some kind. That there ain't some psycho out there pickin' on kids."

"You and me both," Reed agreed. "You and me both."

CHAPTER 18

It was after three when Nikki finally hit the road to drive to Tybee Island. Since her meeting with Brit Sully, she'd attended back-to-back appointments with her physicians. The first had been with an orthopedic surgeon, who had been satisfied with her shoulder.

"Healing nicely," he'd said, and when she'd asked if she could ditch her sling, he'd told her she didn't have to wear it twenty-four/seven, but not to overdo it and start by easing out of it a couple of hours a day.

She had. It was now on the passenger seat next to her.

She rotated her shoulder as she drove through the city. It felt fine. A little tight maybe, but no real pain. Nothing serious.

She guided her Honda into the thin stream of traffic

heading across the Talmadge Memorial Bridge to the island.

Her second doctor's appointment, with her OB/GYN, had been good news as well. Dr. Kasey had informed her that physically she was fine, that everything checked out normally after an exam.

"I know it's hard and there is bound to be a lingering sadness and sense of loss. You've been down this road before and there are support groups you can join," she advised.

"I have." The truth was she was still part of an online group of families who had survived miscarriage and early child loss and she would reach out to them again. She'd even made a couple of friends through the connection, but Reed hadn't. Wouldn't. Preferred to bury his loss deep in his soul and not discuss it.

"Good, so when you and your husband are ready, there's no physical reason you can't try again," the doctor had said once Nikki had dressed and was seated across the cluttered desk in the small office tucked inside the clinic. "It's the emotional and mental part that concerns me."

"I'll be okay," Nikki had said, meeting her doctor's gaze. "Been here before."

Her doctor's eyes had been kind and understanding and she'd offered Nikki a small smile. "Good. But it doesn't hurt to talk to someone if you need to. A counselor. Someone who deals in loss and grief."

"Got it." She nodded. "If I do, I will." And she meant it.

"Okay, then. If you decide to go for it and do get pregnant again, we'll monitor you very closely."

She hadn't said "again," but it was there.

"You're in the high-risk category because of the multiple miscarriages, but that doesn't mean there's any reason you can't have a healthy baby."

As always, Dr. Kasey had been encouraging and comforting, though Nikki had heard the words before.

Now, as Nikki drove onto the wider part of Tybee, she decided she was ready. She wanted a baby. Reed wanted a baby. They could afford a child and though she'd considered the idea of going throughout life without becoming a parent, it wasn't for her. She had friends who had happily made that decision and were very happy, but Nikki couldn't see herself without a growing family. So, she saw no need to wait, and her biological clock was already ticking loudly in her ears.

But Reed? He might need some convincing.

She didn't know if he was ready to jump back on the pregnancy train so soon. The losses just tore him up inside.

She turned her thoughts to the interview ahead.

Ashley Jefferson hadn't returned any of her calls and probably wouldn't be thrilled to see Nikki on her doorstep. Well, too damned bad. The woman was Owen Duval's alibi, so Nikki needed to talk to her.

Tybee Island had been in the hurricane's path and was still recovering, utilities still iffy in some places, the road clean but buckled in spots where trees had been uprooted. She caught glimpses of the Atlantic, peaceful now, the tide lapping at the wide, sandy beaches, the rage of the hurricane now a memory.

Traffic clogged near the center of the island, where a construction crew was still working. She inched her Honda around a series of orange cones only to be stopped by a huge white truck parked near an open manhole cover with two workers peering into the depths. She checked her rearview, making certain the white Cadillac that had been on her bumper stopped. It did. Inches from her own bumper, a small, elderly woman peering over the steering wheel. Behind the Caddy a gray pickup with darkened windows idled and behind the truck, a motorcycle revved, its rider obviously impatient.

The driver of the Caddy honked.

Nikki threw up a hand. "Nothing I can do," she said into the mirror, as if the drivers behind her could hear.

Finally, a flagger waved her through, the small caravan following. A few blocks later she found the address listed for Ryan and Ashley Jefferson. Their house wasn't in a "gated community," as Brit Sully had told her, but had its own set of private wrought iron gates and a tall stucco wall that blocked it from the street. Now the gates were propped open and Nikki seized her opportunity, turning into a wide drive that circled an area where palm trees surrounded a dry fountain, no water spraying upward or pouring over the sides of the tiered basins. Instead a pool of sludge had collected in the reservoir, and across the yard, palm fronds and shingles that had been torn from the roof littered the ground. A Georgian mansion, built of stucco and painted the same pale pink as the walls surrounding it, dominated the landscape. Tall black shutters framed the door and windows, and one door of three to the garage was open. Nikki spied a Range Rover and a Bentley SUV, parked side by side, a golf cart, bikes and various sporting equipment filling the third bay. A second two-storied building with more garage space beneath was positioned on the other side of the circle, a beat-up van parked near the covered entrance.

She assumed that was Ryan Jefferson's vehicle and workspace.

Nikki eased her Honda behind the van, parked and walked to the front door of the main house, where the salty air of the ocean was carried on the breeze. She peered inside through the windows flanking the door. The foyer was grand, a huge chandelier hanging from a ceiling two stories high. A sweeping staircase descended from the second balcony to a marble floor, where a circular table with a pot of vibrant flowers filled the space.

Nikki tried the bell, heard nothing and knocked on the wide glass doors. Seconds later she spied movement inside, a barefooted blonde in a sundress walking briskly from the back of the house.

Here we go.

She recognized Ashley McDonnell from pictures she'd seen browsing the Internet. Ashley was older now, blonder, her hair sun-streaked. Not quite as slim as she'd been in high school, she was still fit, her complexion flawless, a gold chain at her neck and irritation etched firmly across her face. After peering at Nikki through the sidelight, she opened the door just a crack.

Nikki spoke first. "Ashley McDonnell?"

"Jefferson," she corrected, her eyes narrowing. "It's Ashley Jefferson now. Has been for a long time."

Nikki had known that, of course, had just wanted to see the reaction it evoked.

"Who're you?"

"My mistake. Sorry. I'm Nikki Gillette. I'm with the *Savannah Sentinel.*"

"The *Sentinel*? You're a reporter? For the love of God." Her lips twisted into a deeper frown.

"Yes, and I'd just like to ask you a few questions and clear up any—"

Crash!

Both women jumped at the sound.

Ashley's sour expression changed to one of distress. "Oh, God!" She looked over her shoulder. "Zeke!" And then she was running toward the back of the house, hurrying down a short hall, bare feet slapping on the tile as she disappeared through an archway.

Nikki stepped inside and followed as a child's wail echoed through the house. "Oh, honey, are you okay?" Ashley said.

Rounding a corner, Nikki found herself in a huge living space with a wall of windows that opened to a pool area. Beyond the decking was a boardwalk that extended through a marsh to the beach, sunlight glinting off the ocean.

Ashley had landed in the kitchen, where she was picking up a shaggy-haired boy of about three who had toppled off a kitchen chair. "You're all right," she told the boy, while righting the chair with one hand and propping him onto her hip with the other. On the tile beneath the table, a ceramic bowl had cracked, a puddle of milk and soggy Cheerios spreading over the tile; a cocker spaniel hurriedly lapped up the mess.

"Cleo, stop that! Ick!"

Nikki bent down and retrieved the bowl before it splintered.

Ashley ranted, "I can't believe this! And of course Valentina has the week off because of the damned storm. And my blog—I haven't been able to even log on! Shit!" She stomped a bare foot in frustration, then took a deep breath and said to her son, "You didn't hear that, honey. Mommy didn't really say a naughty word."

"Valentina?" Nikki asked.

"Yes, the maid and nursemaid, the woman who usually works for us and . . . oh, what does it matter?"

As Zeke reduced his wails to sniffling, Ashley snagged a handful of paper towels from a dispenser near the sink, then bent down and, still holding the child, swabbed up the mess as she shooed the dog out of the way.

Nikki set the bowl on the counter next to the sink, where a pile of dishes overflowed.

A little girl appeared in the archway. "What happened?" she asked, then smiled. "I get it. Zeke made a mess," she said, obviously delighted, her eyes bright at the prospect of Zeke getting into trouble.

"It was an accident," Ashley clipped out.

"Ack-ident," the boy repeated, and gave his sister a churlish stare.

She narrowed her eyes in a perfect imitation of her mother. "He has a lot of those."

Ashley set the boy on the floor and tossed the wet paper towels in a garbage can under the sink. "Kelsey, take your brother to the playroom for a minute, would you?"

"Why?" Kelsey asked.

"Just do it," Ashley ordered, and though Kelsey obviously wanted to argue, she threw her mother a just-remember-I'm-the-victim-here look instead before flouncing out.

"Always a battle," Ashley said, and wiped the floor again, this time with a wet paper towel. "You have kids?"

Nikki shook her head despite the stab of pain in her heart. "Not yet."

"Well, I suggest you think twice about it." She let out a long breath. "It's a lot of work and it just doesn't get any easier." Then, as if hearing herself, added quickly, "But, of course I wouldn't change anything. I love them both beyond words."

"Of course."

"So, now I know you're here about the Duval girls and what you think I know about their disappearance."

"It's more than that, it's murder now."

"I know. I heard that." She glanced at the doorway where the kids had disappeared and lowered her voice. "It's all disturbing. *Really* disturbing. And I don't want to come off as a heartless bitch or anything, but I don't know anything more than I've already said. I already talked to the police about it. On the phone and in person. I don't have anything else to add. I just wish . . . I just wish this disaster would end!"

"I'm not with the police."

"I know, I know. But I can't tell you anything else. I don't *know* anything else." And then something clicked in her brain, her expression changed and her eyes thinned. "Wait a sec. I know you." She pointed at Nikki. "You're that reporter who nearly drowned the other day out there where they found the bodies. You write those crime books. Is that what this is all about? A book?" Her lips twisted downward in contempt.

"I'm just trying to find out what happened."

"For a book?"

"For an article." What did it matter?

"And you're married to that cop who was here." Her expression turned dark. "What is this?"

"You said you were with Owen Duval that night."

"Yes! God, how many times do I have to say it?" She rolled her eyes as her daughter appeared in the doorway.

"Zeke's hitting!" Kelsey announced, obviously affronted.

"I'll be right there."

"It hurts! He's being mean."

"He's just acting out."

"He's not supposed to hit!"

"I know." In a louder voice, Ashley reprimanded, "Zeke, you be nice!" Then back to her daughter, "I said I'll be there in a second!" before adding in a lower voice, "Geez! I could use a drink." She glanced up at Nikki. "A double margarita, ASAP!"

The girl whined, cast Nikki a dark look, then stomped back into the hallway.

"This isn't a good time," Ashley admitted, having lost some of her irritation. "But, really, there isn't a good time. What you're talking about happened a long, long time ago. I'm sorry, really sorry that those girls were found . . . you know," she whispered sadly, "dead. How awful! But there's nothing, not one single thing I can do about it. I've told the police what I know and I've suffered through Margaret Duval's . . . persecution."

"Persecution?"

"I know what she's said about me and it really doesn't make any sense as I gave her son his alibi, right? Why should she be mad at me? As if I could have stopped what happened." She opened up a little. "I wish I could have, but . . . sometimes things happen. It's all been a nightmare. A horrible, unending nightmare." She gazed out the bank of windows to the deck with its bright umbrella over a shaded table and a chaise lounge angled toward the ocean, visible in the distance, darkening as the sun lowered behind the house. A cigarette had been left burning in the ashtray on a small glass-topped table, a pair of strappy gold sandals tucked beneath the chaise. Ashley had been occupying that spot, near the pool, when Nikki had arrived. Now, she seemed lost in thought, miles or more probably years away.

Nikki brought her back to the here and now. "So, to be clear, you were with Owen Duval from the second he dropped off the girls until he went back to the theater and found them missing."

"Yes! I told the police, over and over again, about the time when he showed up and when he left. That hasn't changed in twenty years." She fingered the small gold cross that hung from a gold chain around her neck. "I'm sorry for the Duval girls and their family, really, but I can't let what happened to them define me, now can I?"

"You were dating Owen Duval?"

"What? No, he was just a friend."

"He said you were his girlfriend."

"Well, he was wrong." She rubbed her temples as if she were developing a headache. "We were friends, sorta, I guess, but we didn't have a thing going, not even a secret one. Sorry to disappoint. He was kind of an outcast and I liked that about him. He was different. Smart. And he had a dark, almost sick sense of humor. That was it, I guess, he wasn't Goth, but he was . . . deep? Really into Edgar Allan Poe and watched, like, old black and white movies. Like *Psycho*. The original one." She paused, biting her lip. "He was just too out there, you know. One time he asked me if I ever listened to the voices in my head. I thought he was joking, but maybe he wasn't."

"What did you say?"

" 'What voices?' And he kind of laughed, but he was serious, I think. Anyway, he didn't have a lot of friends, so I was nice to him. I guess he thought because of it we were an item." She shook her head. "We weren't."

"Who did you date?"

"What does that have to do with anything?" she asked crossly. "A lot of guys, I guess? No one special."

"Beaumont?"

"What? Yeah." Her lips tightened. "It wasn't a big deal. Tyson dated . . . so many. I was just one in the crowd."

And obviously she didn't like it.

"What about Jacob Channing?"

She stopped cold. Just stared at Nikki. "Old news," she said. "Who cares who I dated in high school?"

"But you and he were involved?"

"*Not* involved." She looked away, then squared her shoulders. "It was nothing. Not a big deal at all. Okay? Again, he dated a lot of girls and I dated a lot of boys. It was high school. That's what you do!"

Nikki pressed on. "He's still around, right?"

"I guess . . . I don't really keep up with him. Or with any of them. No one from high school."

"But Jacob Channing inherited Channing Vineyards."

"Yeah, sure. I guess. Look, I don't really know. I heard that he and his sister inherited the business, and that he bought her out. Low-balled her, the rumor goes. I guess she needed the money. It sounds like Jacob, but really, it's all just gossip and I don't really pay attention. Like I said, ancient history. Who cares?"

Nikki wasn't going to be derailed. "So no one thought you and Owen Duval were a couple?"

"Other than Owen? Of course not. And if they did, they were wrong." She shook her head.

"So what about Owen's friends? Guys who hung out with him. You said he didn't have a lot. But there had to be some."

"I don't know!" she snapped, then seemed to collect herself. "I-I can't come up with anybody. He's still around, right? I heard he came back to Savannah, though God knows why. Maybe you should ask him."

"Mom!" Kelsey's voice echoed through the house, and Ashley closed her eyes for a second, as if she were fighting a headache as little footsteps pounded down the hallway. "Zeke's sticking his tongue out at me."

"Just a sec!" Ashley yelled back. "See what I have to deal with?"

"But he's also spitting!" Kelsey burst into the room, Zeke a step behind.

"School can't come fast enough," Ashley admitted. Then said to Nikki, "We're done here," and ushered her out the front door, as if glad for any excuse to get rid of the reporter and her prying questions.

Something wasn't right there.

Didn't make sense.

She paused at the second building and thought about checking with Ashley's husband, but the van was no longer parked where it had been and when Nikki rapped on the entrance to the building, she got no response. Instead she saw Ashley stepping out onto the back patio.

"Do I have to call the police?" she yelled. "That would be a little awkward, don't you think, you being married to a cop and all?" She'd lit a fresh cigarette and dropped a pair of reflective sunglasses over the bridge of her nose.

No reason to push it, Nikki thought.

At least not yet.

But she definitely wanted to talk to Owen Duval, now more than ever.

She climbed into her Honda and checked the messages on her phone. One from Reed saying he'd be late and a second from Millie, which said only: **Call me!**

Nikki did, through the hands-free device in her car. "Hey, it's Nikki," she said, driving away from the house, the smell of the sea still lingering.

"Have you heard?" Millie asked in a rush. "They found another body."

"What? Another body?" Her mind raced but before she could ask a question, Millie went on.

"Just this afternoon. A small one, a kid, up at Black Bear Lake. A fisherman came across it."

"Is it Rose Duval?" Nikki asked, her mind racing. Was it possible the third Duval girl had been found? She drove past the construction site, this time flagged through without having to stop.

"No one knows yet. I just heard this through my source at the department. I thought Reed might have told you."

"I told you, he's tight-lipped," she said, irritated that he couldn't confide in her. A dozen questions came to mind.

"Where on Black Bear Lake? Who found it? They were fishing up there? Was the body in the water?"

"Whoa. Slow down. I don't know much. My source just gave me the quick info and I thought you'd want to know. Metzger's already on it."

"That's a surprise," she said sarcastically as she turned toward the bridge.

"I know. I think he feels you breathing down his neck."

He should, Nikki thought, but kept it to herself. "What else?"

"That's it. Until I hear more."

"Keep me posted."

"Will do."

Nikki clicked off, her mind swirling with ideas and questions. If the body was that of little Rose, why wasn't she in the crypt with her sisters? Had she escaped? Was she murdered, or had it been an accident? Why at the lake? How far was that from the Beaumont mansion? Why was she up there?

"You're getting ahead of yourself." But she couldn't tamp down the sense of excitement she felt, a mixture of fear that Rose Duval was truly dead and a feeling that finally the case might be going somewhere.

Pushing the speed limit, driving by rote, she barely noticed the herons and egrets skimming the water. Instead she let her thoughts spin ahead. Someway, somehow, she had to find a way to get more into the story, to get the green light from her editor so that not only would Fink have her back, but she would have the legitimacy to keep investigating for her job, something Reed couldn't very well argue against. So, Metzger or no Metzger, she had to get Fink's approval.

She dictated a quick text to Reed again through her hands-free device. She asked him for confirmation even though she knew he'd be pissed that she was working. Well, too bad. This was her job, damn it.

So into her own thoughts she didn't notice the gray pickup with the darkened windows that was lying back, ever on her tail, keeping at least two cars between them for cover as she drove into the city.

CHAPTER 19

"Fuck!"

Turning onto the street where he rented a studio apartment in an older home, Owen saw the news vans—two of them, both white but emblazoned with competing call signs, their satellites angled toward the hazy sky. One reporter was already on the front porch, speaking through the screen door to someone on the other side. His landlady, no doubt, probably glibly chatting about her quiet tenant with the horrible reputation. Helen Davis, a devout Christian, would talk to the devil himself if it meant a chance to share a little gossip. He'd figured that out only after he'd signed a year-long lease and moved into one of the only places he could afford in the area.

No way was he going to deal with the press.

He did a quick turn into a neighbor's driveway, surprising a woman walking to her mailbox, then backed up and, throwing the truck into drive again, headed back the way he'd come. At the end of the street, he turned onto the main drag and drove three miles to the parking lot of a convenience store and, with the engine idling, pulled his Atlanta Falcons cap down low and slipped on a pair of sunglasses to cover his eyes. Then he called Austin Wells's private cell phone.

His attorney answered on the third ring. "Owen?"

"Yeah, yeah, it's me. Can't you do something? The goddamned press is hounding me, the police are following me—I'm sure of it—and I get calls at work! This is harassment."

"Refuse to take the phone calls."

"I do, but there are reporters at my place right now. Two fuckin' news vans. One reporter is talking to my landlady right now!"

"Calm down, Owen—"

"No! I'm not calming down. I can't go any damned where without being dogged. I feel like I'm goin' out of my fuckin' mind!"

"Whoa—slow down. It'll be all right."

"How do you know that?"

"Because you didn't do it. Right?"

"Right!"

"So just get through this. It'll all be worth it."

"I don't know, man, I'm . . ." His throat clogged and he looked through the bug-spattered windshield to spy a cruiser for the county drive slowly past. "Oh, Jesus, there's nowhere I can go." He closed his eyes for a second, tried not to give in to the paranoia, the worries that plagued him every damn night. He wanted to remember his sisters as they were, remembering how sweet and innocent they'd been and then . . . then the unthinkable. And when he did finally go to sleep, the nightmares would come and he'd see them, all three as skeletons with rotting flesh, blond tufts of hair and jaws that opened and closed jaggedly as they forever repeated:

It's your fault, Owen. All your fault.

Over and over again.

"I just don't know how much of this I can take," he said to the lawyer. "They found another body, you know. They think it could be Rose."

"No one knows that for sure. If you need to, go to a hotel."

"Won't matter. They'll camp out at the dealership." He closed his eyes. Thought of the unending days of being pursued. Why had he ever thought he should come back here? To be closer to a mother who was now married to a pious, self-serving prick?

But she's the only one who believes in you. The cops don't trust you, the press has already tried, convicted, tarred and feathered you. Even this attorney on the other end of the phone call is just using you. For publicity. To parade you out to the public, to grandstand. For his own purposes.

Fleetingly he thought of Ashley. How completely he'd loved her. Trusted her. Had faith in her.

And she had dropped him to marry some rich dude she'd met in college. He'd half expected it, of course. It wasn't as if she was all that true to him. She'd dated a ton of guys in high school, but he'd thought, no, probably fantasized that she'd see that he was a true heart and they'd end up together.

Happily ever after.

"Fuckin' moron," he said aloud.

"What?" Wells asked.

Oh, shit. He'd done it again. Lost track of where he was. "Sorry. Someone almost backed into me."

"So take my advice. Take a few days off work. Hole up in a hotel. Go to Atlanta. Get lost. Clear your head."

"That takes money."

"I'll advance it to you."

"It also takes a pretty damned understanding boss." He thought of Marv Thompson, the bulky ex special ops guy he worked for, a muscular black dude with a shaved head and thick moustache. Big and smart. Suffered no fools. Herb might understand, then again he might not, and the owner of the dealership wasn't quite so lenient.

"Just hang tough," Wells was saying, but Owen wasn't listening as he saw the news van pull into the lot. Of all the dumbass luck! What were the chances? He slammed his hat lower on his head, made sure his wrap-around sunglasses covered as much of his face as possible.

He would back out and ease into traffic because he was pretty damned sure the press had the make and model of his truck along with the license plate.

It would never end.

Hang tough, Wells had said. Oh, yeah, sure. That would solve the problem.

His cell phone buzzed and he checked the text:

**Murderer.
You're going to fry.**

His stomach knotted. He'd already deleted his social media accounts, but somehow they'd found him, gotten his cell phone number.

He swallowed hard and shoved the gearshift into reverse.

The voice in his head that had gotten louder by the day reminded him that all the "hanging tough" in the world wouldn't be enough.

They're gonna find you.

They're gonna hunt you down like a pack of wolves on a wounded stag and then, no matter what you do, they're gonna pounce.

Face it, Duval. You're doomed.

"I'm guessing preteen, maybe eleven or twelve," the assistant medical examiner told Reed and Delacroix hours after the bones had been discovered by Mentos.

They were standing in the morgue, looking at the remains of the body discovered at Black Bear Lake, the sterile room with its gleaming saws and knives and hanging scales surrounding them. On the metal table, the skeleton was incomplete, but the bones were laid out meticulously as Dr. Hancott studied them.

"But this," he was saying, indicating the partial skeleton lying upon the table, "is definitely not the remains of a five-year-old girl." A rotund man, with a fringe of hair around a tanned, freckled pate, he looked over the tops of a pair of half-glasses perched upon a short nose. "The teeth are the first clue," he admitted, examining the jaw. "Bicuspids and second molars have erupted, which, of course, wouldn't show in a five-year-old. And then there's the measurements to the skull and sole femur that was found at the scene, which suggest a prepubescent youth. If I were a betting man, and I'm not, mind you, I would guess a male due to the narrow hips, though that's not assured. At least at this point. We'll send out DNA samples and check dental records against any missing children."

"Do that and keep us posted," Reed said as he and Delacroix left the building, feeling the warmth of the Georgia sun as they stepped outside. Though the body didn't belong to Rose Duval, it would prove to be the son or daughter of some other set of parents who were still holding out a thread of hope that their child would return unharmed.

"It's a pisser," Delacroix said as they crossed the parking area to Reed's Jeep. "What the hell happened to that kid?"

"I think we'll have to find out. Most eleven- or twelve-year-olds don't drop dead due to natural causes."

"Amen to that," she said as he unlocked the car. "Did you see the left ulna? Broken. At least once. Radius, too."

He slid behind the wheel and started the engine. "Could have been anything. Biking accident, skateboarding, horseback riding, falling out of a tree—"

"Or it could be a defensive wound. Result of being hit with a baseball bat, or crowbar, or poker or—"

"I get it," he said, and caught her glowering through the windshield. He wondered about what she'd gone through in her own growing-up years. She was tough and there was a reason for it, but he didn't know why. Just a tomboy by nature, inherently strong, or was it because of how she'd been raised, the toughness really layer upon layer of calluses to hide her own vulnerability?

She caught his glance and seemed to read his mind. "I worked in New Orleans. Saw a lot of abuse I didn't want to. Runaways. Child trafficking. Domestic violence." Her jaw tightened. "The trouble was I can't erase it from my mind."

"So you took a job here in Homicide?"

"Mainly adults," she said with a shrug.

"You could have gotten out."

She snorted. "Shit, no. How the hell could I make a difference then?"

"That's what your job is all about? Making a difference?"

"Hell, no. I want to catch the bad guys, Reed. Catch 'em and send 'em up the river for good." Her eyes behind those oversize glasses stared at him. "What about you?"

"Same, I guess."

"Thought so." One side of her mouth lifted. "So let's do it, Reed. Let's go get the bad guys!"

Nikki found a parking space across from the centuries-old redbrick building housing the newspaper offices. The three-storied edifice had survived several wars, multiple storms, good times and bad, and hadn't crumbled. However, Hurricane Jules had made its mark. The first floor of the building had been damaged, a waterline visible on the exterior, the hair salon and spa on the street level still closed as repairs were ongoing, but the *Sentinel* was located on the third floor and since the elevators were still not operational, she hoped to find Fink at his desk.

A quick glance at the parking lot and she saw Fink's vintage Corvette gleaming in his premier parking space in the small lot.

Good. Now to plead her case.

She locked her car with her remote, jaywalked across

the street, then showed her ID to the security guard and climbed two flights to the newspaper's offices.

At her desk near the entrance, Millie cradled a phone between her ear and shoulder but managed to wave Nikki to her desk.

"You find out anything else?"

As she hung up, Millie said in a hushed voice, "No. You?"

Bob Swan, the sports editor, passed nearby on his way to the front door.

"Nothing, but I haven't been near a TV or computer."

"I have and the info is just filtering out. But Reed might—"

"Don't even say it," Nikki cautioned. "I haven't talked to him yet."

"He would be your best source."

"I know, but it's difficult." Millie was right. She had to find a way to work with her husband, not against him. "I need to talk to Fink. Keep me posted."

"You got it."

Nikki headed toward the back of the vast room through a maze of mostly empty cubicles, Norm Metzger's included. Even she had a desk here, though it was seldom used and too close to the digital side of the paper, where televisions and monitors glowed, several reporters and techs sat on stools, each wearing earphones and focused on computer monitors.

Fink was at his desk in his glassed-in office.

In his usual khakis and a polo shirt, he sat, nose-deep into a computer on his neat desk, the only objects on it his phone, a signed baseball in a porcelain mitt and a coffee cup proudly displaying the Starbucks logo. Three flat-screen TVs were bolted to the wall behind him, a rowing machine peeking out from beneath an oversize credenza. Today, as ever, the TVs were muted and tuned to different news stations, chyrons for the latest headlines running along the lower portion of the screens.

She tapped on the partially open door.

"Yeah?" he said, still staring at the screen.

"Got a minute?"

"What?" He looked up, his tanned brow beetling beneath silvering hair that was thinning as he recognized her. "Hey." Rolling his chair backward, he said, "Aren't you supposed to be staying at home, 'taking it easy' or something?"

"Or something," she agreed. "But it's been over a week and I've been to see the doctor today. I'm good to go."

"A hundred percent?" he asked, obviously doubtful.

"Pretty much." That was stretching the truth a bit, but she plowed on. "I got the green light to get back to it and I have another idea I thought I'd run by you before I dive in."

Now the truth was paper thin. She'd already started work on the story, even mentioned it to Reed this morning, just to cover her bases. While she'd sipped coffee and mentioned her idea, Reed, seated at the island with the newspaper spread in front of him, had glanced up. "You're doing what?"

"A story on the history of the Beaumont estate."

"The history?" he repeated, and finished off a final bite of his scone.

"Um-hmm." She'd buried her nose in her coffee cup but held his gaze above the brim.

He'd lifted one skeptical eyebrow. But he hadn't challenged her, just said, "Be careful," then placed his plate on the floor, allowing Mikado to lick up any remaining crumbs before leaving.

Now, Fink waved her into a side chair and listened as she pitched the idea. His eyes narrowed and he tented his fingers under his chin as she explained about the human interest side of the story, about not only the buildings but the family and history that was a part of the local culture. "I think people whose families have been here for generations would love the culture and even nostalgia of the series, and newcomers would like a little deeper knowledge of the area," she said as Fink listened.

He was nodding to himself, but he said, "So why do I think this is your way of working around me and digging into the crime?"

"Because I would be. I mean the recent crime involving the Duval girls, of course, would be a part of the story, but there's more to it than that. Another girl died there years ago. Nell Beaumont."

"The ghost girl?" he asked, unconvinced, but picking up the baseball and tossing it as he considered.

"Right. And there may have been more over the course of the estate's history. At one time before it was broken into pieces, it was one of the largest parcels in the Savannah area. Right now, everyone in town, well, in the whole state for that matter is interested in the Beaumont estate and family and history. I know it's because of the bodies being found there, of course, but with that interest comes a curiosity about the place where it happened. Who knows what other secrets are hidden out there?"

He caught the ball and stared at her. "Okay." He was nodding. "But be careful, okay? I heard about that break-in at your house."

"I will."

"And don't go stepping on Metzger's toes."

"Why would I do that?"

He scratched his jaw. "Because you're you and can't leave well enough alone, Gillette. So don't bullshit me."

She stood, wanting to leave before he changed his mind. "Wouldn't dream of it."

He slid her a disbelieving look, tossed his baseball into the air one more time, caught it and set it back into the ceramic mitt on his desk. "Yeah, right."

CHAPTER 20

Nikki drove straight home and took Mikado for a short run through the park, the first since her miscarriage. The afternoon was sliding into evening and it felt good to sweat, to get her blood pumping. As she ran down the wide walkways, around the other pedestrians, skateboarders and dog walkers, she thought about the mystery. What if the body found up at Black Bear Lake was Rose Duval? What if it wasn't? Reed still hadn't returned her calls, just texted saying he was working late and making certain she was okay.

So frustrating.

But their normal routine.

She remembered feeling that she was being followed the last time she'd passed by the large fountain, but now, as there were so many people crossing beneath the large live oak trees, she saw no one who seemed to be focused on her, no dark figure lurking behind the trunk of one of the trees.

Don't forget: Someone broke into your house just a few nights ago.

That thought brought goose pimples to the back of her arms. Out of the corner of her eye she caught a glimpse of a man in black and her heart clutched before she noticed the slash of white at his neck: his clerical collar.

A priest or preacher, for God's sake!

Nikki, get hold of yourself!

"Come on," she said to the dog, and took off toward home.

Once in the house, she threw a frozen pizza in the toaster oven and while it baked, filled a glass with ice and Diet Dr Pepper. Sipping the drink, she climbed the stairs to her office and opened her laptop to start researching the Beaumont family. What did she know about them? Tyson, her brother's age, was the current owner and manager of the property, a real-estate developer like his father, Baxter. Tyson was the only living child of Baxter and Connie-Sue, who lived in an expensive adults-only center on a golf course just out of town. Tyson's sister, Nell, had died at a young age, drowning in the river near the old house where they had all resided with Beulah, Tyson's step-grandmother and matriarch of the clan, and Connie-Sue had insisted they move from the estate as it was too painful for her to live so close to the spot her daughter had died.

The timer on the toaster oven dinged. Downstairs, where the kitchen smelled of sizzling pepperoni, oregano and mozzarella, Nikki retrieved two slices of hot pizza and a couple of paper towels, then returned to her attic office and pored over tons of information about the Beaumont estate. She sorted through deeds of sale, news clippings, articles and pictures, searched the Internet for historical records, joined a group dedicated to the history of the area, read for hours, immersed in all things Beaumont. As she picked at her dinner, she took notes and gave up around eleven.

In a nutshell, the Beaumont estate had once been massive, spreading across the shores of the river, and had been cut up over the years, the most interesting pieces being the Marianne Inn, near Black Bear Lake, where the recent body had been discovered, the abutting acres of Channing Vineyards, which was owned and run by Jacob Channing, and a much smaller parcel near the Marianne Inn purchased by Wynn Cravens and now home to Bronco.

She eyed the records for the Marianne Inn. After the Second World War, over a hundred acres had been developed into the Marianne Inn property, once a flourishing hunting and camping resort in the middle part of the last century. It had been built and run by Baxter Beaumont's father, Arthur, who had dedicated it to his first wife, Marianne, who had died when Baxter had been less than two. Arthur had married Beulah soon thereafter.

Nikki glanced out the window and saw her own watery reflection. The night was closing in and her neck starting to ache.

She stood and rotated her shoulder while looking down at the notes, pictures and copies of deeds of sale scattered on her desk.

Her gaze landed on a picture of the lodge at the Marianne Inn, which looked like an original black and white photo that had been tinted.

So maybe that's why the color was off.

Her pulse ticked up.

The sign for the inn had been tinted a deep crimson and the lettering a distinctive script in white.

"Oh, God," she whispered as she remembered the boat hidden in the shadowy branches of the willow tree at the Beaumont estate the day the bodies were discovered. It, too, was red but faded, and she hadn't been able to read the graying lettering, had only caught a glimpse, but now, staring at the sign for the Marianne Inn, she was certain it was the same.

"Let's see," she said to herself as she sat down at her computer and googled the old inn once more, searching through the images, which were an array of photographs of the inn in its heyday. Shots of the pine-paneled interior with its massive staircase and rock fireplace that climbed two floors, the waitstaff in the dining area, smiling cooks in crisp white dresses, pristine aprons and hairnets working over a massive stove. There were shots of guests lounging outside the French doors that opened to the river, women in swimming suits from the fifties and sixties sunbathing. Other shots of men decked in fishing gear while proudly displaying strings of catfish, bass and sunfish, the scales of their catches glinting in the sunlight.

She found several pictures of the back of the lodge and the private pier jutting into the river. Rowboats and motorboats were tied, each with the distinctive white on deep red logo of the Marianne Inn.

"Bingo," she whispered.

The color was off as the boat she'd thought she'd spied lurking under the drooping branches of the willow tree had been more of a faded orange than deep red, but the flowing script had been identical. The boat had once been part of the old lodge's small fleet.

And Nikki Gillette thought she was the only one who knew about it. She bit her lip and wondered who had been at the helm of the small craft. And more importantly, why had he or she been at the Beaumont estate on the day the two decomposing bodies of the Duval girls had been discovered?

It was after ten at night when Bronco cracked open another bottle of SweetWater, then flipped the cap of the pale ale into the overflowing trash. Only one bottle left in the fridge, along with half a hamburger and the usual bottles of catsup, mayo and mustard.

Not much else.

He'd become a hermit.

Ever since finding those damned bodies, he'd holed up in his house, only getting out for that meeting with the attorney and cops and a couple of runs to the closest convenience store, a mini-mart, where he also filled up his truck.

He'd lost his job a few weeks earlier and his unemployment hadn't kicked in and, the real problem, he hadn't found anything of value at the Beaumont estate. Just those dead girls. Their thin skeletons dressed in fraying girls' clothes from an earlier decade still haunted his dreams. The locket, the tennis shoes, the ring and hairband.

His insides went cold and he took a long swallow.

He thought about driving to his regular haunt, down to the Red Knuckle, where he would drink a few more beers and watch the Braves play.

But he didn't.

He was too spooked.

And the word had gotten out that he'd found the bodies.

More than one reporter had called.

He walked to the living room and peered through the window to the night beyond. The TV was tuned into the station that had aired the Braves game but right now there was a newscaster on the screen with yet another "breaking story." Of course it was about the Duval girls. He watched. As he always did. As the nightmare continued. The police were looking for people who might know something about the crime of course, and the report focused on two teenagers who'd never come forward at the time, boys captured on tape. He squinted at the grainy image of kids at the refreshment stand in the theater. Two guys who looked like every other teenager twenty years ago. No one he remembered. He frowned, took a pull from his longneck.

The next shot was of two men, computer-enhanced images of what those teenagers from two decades ago might look like, and he paused the screen shot. Had he seen either of them? He didn't think so, but . . . maybe?

Even if he did know them, he was out of it. He'd done enough, discovering the bodies and calling the damned cops, reporting what he'd stumbled upon. And now his name was being leaked.

Shit.

So far no one had shown up on his doorstep, not that the NO TRESPASSING and TRESPASSERS WILL BE PROSECUTED signs he'd nailed to the fence posts at the end of the lane would stop any member of the press.

Fender was whining at the back door, so Bronco made his way through the kitchen again and opened the door before unlatching the screen. "Go on now. Git out there and do yer business," he said, as the heeler shot out of the house and into the night, where crickets were singing and frogs croaking. Bronco stepped onto the porch and stared at the line of trees separating the house from the river and from the old Beaumont place. This whole area had been owned by the Beaumonts. All the way up the river to the Marianne Inn, which had been named for Arthur Beaumont's first wife, Marianne, the one before crazy Beulah, and then the land on both sides of the river, including this place, which his grandfather had managed to buy from the old lady before she died, before Arthur's son, Baxter, had inherited it and made it into another one of his damned subdivisions.

Another swallow of beer as a gust of wind rattled some of the new-fallen leaves, scattering them across the dirt and patchy grass of the yard.

He lit a cigarette and wondered where the hell the damned jewels and money and whatever the hell else Beulah Beaumont had hidden were. Had he missed them, not seen a hiding spot because he got the shit scared out of him? What was it his grandfather had said? What were the old man's words?

"I tell ya, boy, I've never seen the likes of it. Never in all my born days. A fortune, right there in that velvet bag of hers."

That was it. Talk of a velvet bag.

Bronco took a long drag from his Winston, the tip glowing red.

He was certain Gramps had said he'd helped Beulah hide it in the basement, in a niche of some kind. Could he have missed it? Maybe. When he was scared out of his mind, he could have run away before finding the treasure, but the cops, with all their man power and technology, they would have located anything of value. They wouldn't have missed it.

Would they?

Could it have been found?

Moved?

But by whom?

And when?

His eyes narrowed through the cloud of smoke he exhaled. That was his big chance and he'd blown it. He whistled to the dog, his thoughts returning to the basement of that huge monster of a house. Damn it all to hell. Gazing up at the stars, he cursed his luck—all of it bad.

He heard a rustle to the side of the house.

Fender.

Nosing around for a raccoon or possum or squirrel. "Come on in, then," he said, and dropped the butt of his cigarette and stubbed it out, grinding it beneath the heel of his boot.

But the dog didn't appear.

"Fender?" he yelled, a little louder, with more authority. "Come!" Peering into the darkness, he saw nothing. And the rustling at the corner of the house had silenced. The wind had died. Even the frogs and crickets had stilled.

The hairs on the back of his neck prickled.

It wasn't like the dog not to obey.

From inside the house, he heard a sound. The soft scrape of a boot on the old linoleum.

Or was it the TV that he'd left on in the living room, the volume low, the bluish light flickering behind him?

He strained to listen.

A floorboard creaked.

But he was alone.

All the spit in his mouth dried.

He licked his lips.

Just inside the door was his hunting rifle. A Winchester .30-30 lever action that Gramps had left him.

The screen door scraped open and he reached for the gun.

But he came up empty. His fingers brushing the kitchen wall near the doorjamb.

What the hell?

The rifle was always there.

Loaded.

Ready.

Just in case.

His heart began to knock and he peeked inside. Heard nothing, but saw in the flickering half-light that the gun was definitely gone. Had he put it in his truck? Or . . . ?

Or what? You know you left it there. It's always there unless you go hunting. And someone's in the fuckin' house. With your damned weapon. What the fuck are you gonna do?

His keys were by the front door, which he realized belatedly he'd left open. His insides turned to jelly as he remembered his phone and his other gun, the pistol, were in a drawer by his bed.

Shit, shit, shit!

At that moment the dog bounded onto the back porch and yipped to go inside.

"Shh!" he hissed.

Maybe whoever it was would just leave, take whatever he wanted and . . . but why was he here? Bronco didn't have anything of any value.

He took one step off the porch.

Click!

The distinctive sound of the Winchester being cocked.

The dog growled.

Oh, shit.

Glancing over his shoulder, he saw a figure in the doorway, behind the screen, backlit by the eerie light of the TV.

"No!" he yelled as the dog leapt forward.

The gun blasted, flashing white, splintering the screen door.

Hot pain seared through his back.

He stumbled.

Fell to the ground.

His head hitting the dirt.

Tried to get away.

Panic surged through him.

Who? Why? Oh, God, help me . . .

He crawled, muscles quivering, bleeding, his fingernails clawing through tufts of grass, the smell of the marsh and cordite and blood heavy in his nostrils.

Bronco wanted to plead for his life, but no words came and he tasted salt—blood on his tongue.

Oh, God, he was gonna die.

Right here in his own damned backyard.

The assailant stepped through the door.

Slowly.

With measured and evil determination.

Oh, God. Please, no!

"Don't," Bronco croaked, spitting blood, sneaking another glance over his shoulder, the words stalling in his throat. His entire life, all those whom he'd harmed, the names and faces of those he'd cheated who would want revenge spun through his mind. "Help me."

He couldn't see the person's face, but his body, backlit by the gray light of the doorway, was visible, and Bronco watched as the would-be killer cocked Bronco's own damned Winchester.

Again.

"No . . . please . . ." Bronco tried vainly to scurry away, but his movements were sluggish, his legs unresponsive no matter how loud his brain screamed. He tried to push himself to his feet. His arm gave way, his hand sticky with blood and dirt.

It was too late. From the corner of his eye he saw the monster level the stock of the rifle against a shoulder, then carefully take aim.

Jesus, please have mercy. No, no, no . . .

Blam!

A light flashed.

His body jerked.

He thought he heard a dog barking, but it was far in the distance and grew fainter as Bronco drew his last, wheezing breath.

Time is slipping steadily through the hour glass, I feel it, like the rapid-fire beating of my heart. After so long, so many years, now the seconds, hours and days are moving so fast. Too fast. Am I ready? I have to be.

I slow my breathing, try to find an inner strength.

I don't think about the sisters. Don't want to focus on the killing.

Not yet.

Not when there are so many pitfalls. So many who want to unmask me.

The worst: Nikki Gillette. But I will deal with her. The camera I bought used, the GPS tracking device now af-

fixed to the undercarriage of her Honda, will tell me where she is. Still, it may not be enough.

With each passing day, every hour that goes by, every minute that I breathe, they are closing in. I have to find a way to slow it all down so that I can finish. All too soon the sand will have drained away, my time up and I'll be exposed.

Naked to the world.

CHAPTER 21

"You found another body!" Nikki charged when Reed took a quiet step into the bedroom. He'd hoped she would be fast asleep when he sneaked into the darkened room, but he didn't get lucky.

She slapped on the bedside lamp and he noticed the books and papers and notes and iPad that were strung out on his side of the duvet. "Is it Rose Duval?"

"No, we're sure not," he admitted, sloughing off his jacket and draping it over the back of a chair. "But a kid. Possibly preteen, most likely a boy, though there are more tests that have to be run."

"Who?"

"Don't know."

"Murder?"

"Again, that's unclear." He sank down on the mattress beside her.

"You didn't call me!" she charged.

When he didn't answer she had the good grace to seem a little chagrined.

"Nikki—"

"Yeah, I know. What about the computer image of Rose? Has anyone come forward?"

When he took her hand, she rolled her eyes. "I can't help it. You know how I am. And you have since we first met." She leaned forward on the bed, pressing her face close to his. "Can't we work on this together? I'm going to be doing a lot of research on the Beaumont family and estate and I think I can help."

"You're not on the force."

"We've worked together before," she reminded him.

"And you nearly lost your life."

She flopped back on the pillows. "I'll be careful."

He thought about that and shook his head. "No, you won't. You don't know how to be. And, really, I think there's been enough damage done already." He held her gaze and didn't mention the lost baby or the fact that Sylvie Morrisette had given up her life. He didn't have to. She got the message. Her expression changed from hopeful to sad in an instant.

"Low blow, Pierce," she whispered, shrinking away from him. "Really low."

And she was right. But she had to be reminded. He couldn't take a chance on losing her, too.

Margaret Duval's voice was thin and quavering over the connection, almost inaudible over the rumbling of the air-conditioner as it blasted cold air through the vents at the police station. "Did you, Detective Reed? Did you find my Rosie? I heard about a body being discovered up at Black Bear Lake." She sounded so frail, her voice clogged with repressed tears. "Dear God. I prayed, you know. I prayed and prayed and prayed that she would be spared," she sniffed.

Seated at his desk, the phone pressed to his ear, Reed silently swore at the idiot who had leaked the bad information to the press. If someone was going to talk, they could, at the very least, get their facts correct.

"No, Mrs. Le Roy, we didn't find your daughter," he said, glancing over at Delacroix, who was also on her desk phone but had turned her head to listen to him as he continued. "We did discover a youth's body near Black Bear Lake, that's true," he said. "But it's not Rose."

"Thank God," she said, now sobbing, her voice broken. "Things are so bad. Do you know that Owen is getting death threats?" She sniffed. "Death threats! For something he didn't do. And he won't go to the police. Nuh-uh. Not after the way he's been treated. He's my only son, you know. The only one I can still talk to. Sometimes . . . sometimes I think God is punishing me."

"Mrs. Le Roy—" he tried to cut in, but she was on a roll.

"Ezra seems to think I can find solace in the Bible and I try, I really try. My husband, he's such a good man, a God-fearing man, so willing to forgive sins. Anyone's. Even mine. Just like our Lord Jesus." Her voice was thin again, the sobbing having given way to a steady whisper. "I don't deserve him."

"I'm sure that's not what he thinks," Reed said, though he had no idea what was in the reverend's mind.

"Rosie can't be dead," she said suddenly, her conviction renewed. "She just can't be! I can't lose them all."

He didn't want to give her any false hope. "Mrs. Le Roy—"

"You find my daughter!" she demanded, not allowing him to placate her. "Find her before something happens!"

"I assure you, Mrs. Le Roy—"

"Just do it, Detective. It's your damned job!"

Click!

The connection was severed. He shook his head and caught Delacroix watching him. "Guess she told you."

"Guess so."

She was still holding the phone to her ear.

"Aren't you . . . ?" He motioned to her cell.

"On hold." She rolled her eyes. "Checking with Missing Persons about the new body. Hoping for an ID—something that matches."

So far the body was still unidentified, though dental records were being checked. DNA would take longer.

He asked, "Did you hear that Owen Duval is getting death threats?"

She shook her head, took off her glasses and rubbed her eyes. "No."

"According to his mother, he's being harassed by the press and tried and convicted by the public."

"Great." Again she shook her head and glanced out the window. "I bet he wishes he never moved back here."

"Probably. You still on hold?" When she nodded, he asked, "Anything come in on the unknown teenagers who were in the lobby of the theater the last time anyone saw the Duval girls?"

"Nope, not yet. A copy of the tape of the lobby and with the teenagers went out to news stations. So far no one's biting. But it's still early."

"Twenty years doesn't seem so early to me."

"You know what I mean."

He turned back to the statement from one of the neighbors who had lived in the house next to the Duvals at the time of the girls' disappearance. The paper had yellowed and smelled of dust, but he read the typed report about an interview with George Adams. He'd been seventy-nine at the time of his statement and had died in the intervening years. George had admitted to not having noticed anything out of the ordinary on the day that the girls went missing, but had claimed fiercely that there were "all sorts of shenanigans going on over there at the Duval place! Harvey, he's an insurance salesman, but I sure as hell wouldn't have him for my agent, and that wife of his? Margie or whatever she calls herself, she's a nurse, but she got fired from the hospital, the way I hear it. To become a private nurse to the damned Beaumonts. Who does that? Something's not right there, let me tell you. I heard, well, it's just gossip really, but the missus and I, we don't go for that swingin'."

"Swinging?"

"You know. That exchanging partners in the bedroom if you know what I mean."

"The Duvals are 'swingers'?"

"Well, don't quote me on that, but it's pretty much common knowledge."

"You mean Harvey had an affair."

"Humph. One? Get real. I don't want to spread rumors, but trust me, Harvey has a wandering eye. And his wife? Same goes for her."

"Do you have any idea who they had affairs with?"

"Well, no, I can't say."

"But you're certain?"

"No, no. I mean I got no proof. It's just what we heard, the wife and I. And those girls they have? Allowed to run loose while their older son—Owen, I think his name is?—there's something about him I don't trust. Kind of sulks around, you know, won't meet you in the eyes. And I saw him once, late at night, leave the house. I was getting a drink of water at the kitchen sink, hadn't turned on the light as I didn't want to wake the missus, she don't sleep so good, and he comes right out of the upper window, clear as day and down the roof he goes, then hops to the ground. Just after one in the morning. And you know I always say, 'There ain't nothin' good happens after midnight.'"

Amen.

Reed had been a cop too long to not agree with the old man's observation. He would have loved to interview him, but George was now deceased and his wife, as of the last time anyone checked, was in an elder care facility. The lead investigator who had signed the report, Detective Charles Easterling, had retired at sixty-five two years after the Duval girls had been reported missing. He, too, had died, just last year. Heart failure.

There was only one cop still remaining on the force who had worked the case twenty years earlier, a deputy at the time and now a sergeant. Reed had spoken with her and learned nothing that he hadn't already read in the files that were now piled on a corner of his desk.

They had offered him no insight in the mystery.

He turned to his monitor and pulled up the computer-generated sketch of what Rose Duval would look like if she'd survived—a pixie of a young woman with blond, curly hair, bright blue eyes, short little nose and a dimple in her chin.

"Yeah, okay. Let me know when you find a match," Delacroix said into the phone before clicking off.

"Nothing yet?" he guessed.

"Too early. I told you." She leaned back in her chair and stretched her arms over her head, then caught sight of the image on his computer. "How about you?"

He frowned and shook his head as he stared at the computer model of what Rose Duval might look like. "It's too generic, I think. And who knows if she's still blond, or had her teeth straightened, plastic surgery or whatever."

"Yeah," she said, "could be anyone."

Or she could be dead.

Reed considered that option, didn't like it, but had to admit that it was the most likely scenario.

He sighed through his nose. The investigation wasn't gaining any traction, his home life wasn't exactly on track, someone had come into his house uninvited, and in a few days . . .

Oh, Lord.

In a few days, Sylvie Morrisette would be laid to rest.

* * *

Two hours later, Reed pulled up to Peaceful Glen, the adult care facility, and parked in one of the few shady spots available. The cement block building was long and low, built, it looked like, in the sixties with a flat roof and rows of big windows with individual air-conditioning units in the walls. Shadows from a row of shade trees stretched across the walkways, the afternoon sun warm as it slowly lowered in the west.

He stepped through a glass door into a large reception area separated from a dining space by a floor-to-ceiling rock fireplace with an oversize picture of Jesus above the mantel.

It was quiet inside, almost hushed, a few carts rattling, some muted voices in the hallways and a feeling of forced cheer in the colorful wall art that was at odds with the in-stitutional green walls and the tan indoor/outdoor carpet of the corridor and common spaces.

His badge gained him access, and he was told by a pert receptionist that Mrs. Adams "was resting" and that her daughter was with her in room 114.

Reed circumvented an elderly man pushing a walker and ignored the scent of disinfectant over the underlying odor of urine. He tapped softly on the door to room 114 and stepped inside as a woman called, "Come in." She was seated in a floral recliner by the window, the only chair in the studio apartment. A TV was muted to some decorating show and upon the twin bed was an emaciated woman with her eyes closed.

"I'm Julia," the sixtyish woman said, and quickly folded the newspaper she'd been reading. She was short and heavyset with narrow reading glasses set upon a small nose, and thick gray hair that was layered around a square face with a quizzical expression. "Ona's daughter."

"Detective Pierce Reed." He showed his ID and explained why he was at Peaceful Glen.

"Well, I don't know what I can tell you, and Mom . . ." She lifted a hand, gesturing toward the bed, where a blue comforter was tucked under the older woman's narrow chin. She was thin and frail looking, her cheekbones prominent, her eye sockets deep.

"She's in and out. Sometimes clear as a bell, especially about things in the past, but she couldn't tell you the day of the week, and sometimes I'm not sure she even remembers me, then the strangest thing, she'll pop up with something that's spot-on."

She sighed and went on. "I've been reading about the Duval girls in the papers and watching on television. It's awful. And it just goes on and on. Those poor parents, what they've been through."

The woman on the bed snorted, her eyes, beneath her papery eyelids, fluttering.

"Mom?" Julia asked, getting up and moving to the bed. She touched her mother on a bony, flannel-draped shoulder. "Mom. There's a policeman here. He wants to talk to you about Harvey and Margaret Duval and their daughters."

Nothing.

"Mom." She gave Ona's shoulder a gentle shake. "Mom? Can you wake up now? Talk to Detective . . ."

"Reed," he supplied.

"Detective Reed would like to talk to you. About the Duvals." Again there was no response.

Julia straightened and let out her breath. "See what I mean?"

"Maybe you can help me," he suggested as she perched on the edge of the bed.

"I don't know how. I barely knew those girls. I was out of the house before they were born. So I only saw them when I visited Mom and Dad."

"What about the brother? Owen?"

"No, I mean, I recognized him by sight, but that was about it." She began plucking at the pilling on the comforter. "He was just a neighbor kid, and I don't think Mom and Dad really knew him all that well. It's not like the families hung out or anything. Mom and Dad were already retired, I think, and the Duvals were raising four kids and balancing jobs, so . . . not a lot in common."

"And you?"

"We were living in Charlotte at the time. I was working and have a husband and kids of my own. Three of them. All in elementary school, so I barely had time to breathe, couldn't come down here all that often what with everyone's schedule." She offered a tentative smile. "So I really can't tell you anything and if you're hoping to get some information from Mom . . . well . . ." Julia sighed, her head wagging sadly. "As I said, sometimes clear as a bell, other times, well . . ."

Reed had told himself the trip to Peaceful Glen was probably a waste of time, but he still felt a sliver of disappointment.

"What do you know about Harvey and Margaret?" he asked.

"Not much. He was in insurance, an agent or a broker

or something, and she was a nurse. I do know that. She worked at the hospital when I was a kid. I remember because I went into the ER when I broke my arm from falling off my bike and she was the nurse who attended to me."

This much he knew. Everything Julia was saying checked out. "Your father said in his statement to the police that there was trouble at the Duval house. That things weren't . . . stable." He was pushing it as he found no reports of police being called to the home. It was all just hearsay. From a dead man.

Julia's eyebrows drew together. "I . . . I don't know about that."

"He seemed to think there was some marital strife."

"Well, probably. They divorced, didn't they?"

"He thought there were affairs."

"Oh. Again, I don't know."

"You didn't hear that Harvey had a girlfriend?"

She was shaking her head. "No, I never—"

"Margaret!" the woman in the bed croaked. "It was Margaret." Ona's eyes blinked open for a second and she focused on Reed. "She was a hot pants!"

"Mom!" Julia said, shocked.

Ona added, "You ask George! She came on to him."

Julia was shaking her head. "Oh, no. I don't think that's true."

"Common slut! With all those kids. Those girls probably weren't all her husband's." She snorted her disgust. "Hot pants!"

Julia gasped.

Her mother's eyes shut.

Reed asked, "Mrs. Adams?"

Nothing.

"Mom?" Julia, obviously distressed, glanced at Reed but touched her mother's shoulder again. "The detective has more questions." She waited and then raised her hands, palms up. "This is how it happens. A few quick words as if she's been a part of the conversation all along or at least listening in, and then she blurts something out and it's as if it takes everything out of her. She probably won't speak again for a couple of days." Then leaning down to her mother's ear, she said, "Can you hear me? Detective Reed is trying to find out what happened to the Duval girls. Margaret and Harvey's kids, you know."

There was a movement behind the older woman's eyes again and her face twisted into an expression of disgust, but she remained silent.

After ten minutes, Reed handed Julia his card. "If she wakes up or you can think of anything else, please give me a call."

"I will," Julia promised. "But I wouldn't hold my breath."

No, he thought now. He'd left after waiting for Ona to wake up and say anything clear or helpful. As he drove through the city, his thoughts turned over in his mind. How much of what the old woman remembered was true? How much of it was just gossip? How much of it had no basis in fact at all?

He was almost to the station when his cell phone buzzed and the call was connected to his Bluetooth, his display showing Delacroix's name and number.

"You're not going to believe this," his new partner said when he answered. "Guess who just walked into the police station?"

"I couldn't." Squinting, he flipped down his visor as he passed into the heart of the city.

"Rose Duval," she said, her voice heavy with skepticism.

"What?"

"I'm telling you, a woman saying she's Rose Duval. We've got her in an interview room. Thought you'd want to know."

"On my way," he said. "I'll be there in five."

CHAPTER 22

"If Muhammad won't come to the mountain," Nikki told Jennings as she grabbed her keys, "then the mountain is just going to have to go to the Red Knuckle." She patted the cat on his striped head, then drove into town. She intended to visit Bronco at his home, but she'd remembered what Morrisette had said on that final phone call Nikki had overheard:

". . . the Red Knuckle. He's a regular there. Hangs out there every damned evening, the way I hear it. They probably have a stool with his name on it . . ."

Nikki's heart clenched as that joke was the last Reed's partner had ever uttered. And it was her fault the woman was dead. Guilt, forever nearby, caught up with her and settled firmly on her shoulder. Close enough to keep whispering in her ear: *It's your fault, Nikki. Your fault that Morrisette jumped into the river to try to save you.*

Setting her jaw, she pushed that horrid voice away and concentrated on the here and now. Why the hell had Bronco Cravens been at the Beaumont estate that day? How had he discovered the bodies in the basement? What had he been doing? It was time to find out. If Bronco wasn't at the bar, then she'd go to his house and after that, she hoped to find a way to avoid Tyson Beaumont's cameras and visit the Beaumont mansion, the scene of the crime.

First things first: talking to Bronco, finding out what he knew, why he was at the house in the basement that day.

Nikki had learned that until recently, Bronco had worked at La-mont Construction, but she'd checked with the company and found he'd been let go; though, of course, she didn't know why. Not that it mattered, probably. Since she had to drive through town anyway, she headed toward campus, parked a block away from the Red Knuckle, and made her way inside the crowded bar.

The darkened interior was noisy, a din of conversation, clinking glasses, rattling ice cubes and click of billiard balls over the throb of some crossover country and pop song she couldn't identify. Most of the crowd was on the younger side, college students who were just starting a new semester.

All of the stools at the bar were filled, people laughing and talking, drinking and flirting, some watching the televisions mounted on the wall, all tuned to various sporting events. Currently, the Braves were down two runs to the Red Sox on one screen, a golf match on another and three husky suited men at a desk discussing college football on a third.

Bronco wasn't seated at the bar.

Nikki scanned the tables scattered over the darkened floorboards in the center of the room, then skirting two pool tables, slowly checked out the occupied booths. No Bronco. She nearly ran into a waitress balancing a tray of drinks as she headed to a screen door that opened to a back patio, where some of the patrons nursed drinks and smoked at umbrella tables.

But Bronco hadn't landed outside, either.

Maybe it was too early for him to show up. Or too late.

Back inside, she made her way to the bar. "Hey," she said to the bartender, and offered a smile.

"What can I get you?" He couldn't have been more than twenty-five with buzz-cut hair, freckles and an easy grin.

"Nothing . . . not now. I just wondered if Bronco's been in?"

"Cravens?" he repeated, and shook his head. "Not lately. Not for a few days, at least not on my shift and this is about the time he usually shows up." He glanced to his right, where a guy of about sixty, his gray hair braided into a long ponytail, a Braves cap mashed on his head, was seated. In jeans and a plaid shirt, his beer bottle and dish of Chex Mix in front of him, he watched the baseball action, his gaze glued to the TV mounted over shelves of liquors. "Hey, Joe," the bartender yelled.

The client turned toward him, one graying eyebrow cocked.

"You seen Bronco lately?"

"Nah." A gruff shake of his head.

"Know where he is?"

"Why would I?" Joe demanded, glancing from the bartender to Nikki in irritation.

"You two usually watch together."

"Yeah, well, he's been AWOL."

"Do you know why?" Nikki asked, breaking into the conversation.

"Who're you?" Joe wanted to know.

"Nikki Gillette. With the *Sentinel*."

"A reporter? Oh, geez." He scowled as the crowd at the bar let out a whoop, and Joe turned quickly to the screen to see a Braves runner slide into home. He shot to his feet. "What happened?" he asked just as the play was shown again. He waited until the next batter was up, then said, "I don't know nothin' 'bout Bronco. But he was spooked about what he found over at that big place, the old Beaumont house. Spooked him good. He used to play over there as a kid. His old man or grandpa or someone worked for that crazy old bat who used to live there."

"He tell you anything about that?"

"He had stories." Joe was nodding. "Wild stories about what went on over there."

"Such as?"

He thought for a second. "Well, he said something about the crazy lady having some kind of secret stash—valuables, y'know, but that might've been a lie. Bronco, he does stretch the truth now and again and especially when he's had a few." He scratched the back of his head. "And he used to talk about the old days, y'know. When he was a kid. He swore he saw his friend's old man getting it on with the nurse out in the stable." He snorted at the thought.

"His friend?" she said.

"Yeah, Bronco's friend. The rich kid. Tyler, no—Tyson. Yeah, Tyson. Anyway, Tyson's dad and the nurse had a thing."

"What nurse?" she asked, but she felt her pulse quicken at the information.

"The one who took care of the old lady who lived there."

What had Tyson said about Margaret Duval when Nikki had found him fixing the gate at the estate?

"She was Nana Beulah's nurse, so she was there a lot, even spent some nights at the house, I think."

Margaret Duval and Baxter Beaumont?

Joe studied his glass for a second. "Again, don't quote me. I'm just passin' on info that Bronco told me. Is it true?" He rocked his thick hand in a maybe, maybe not gesture. "But as I said, Bronco's tales tend to be pretty damned tall when he's into his cups, so I never gave any of 'em much thought."

Baxter Beaumont, Tyson's father, and Margaret Duval were having an affair?

"When was the last time he was in?" she asked, and the bartender shrugged, shaking his head.

"A week ago?" Joe was thoughtful. "Yeah, whatever night it was that the Braves were playing the Marlins. I remember cuz they had a no-hitter going until the bottom of the eighth. That's the last time I seen him. But I talked to him once on the phone and he was pretty jittery about those bodies been found up there."

"And you've been here every night since?"

"Sure. Well, except when the hurricane hit. I missed a few nights then."

The bartender swiped a white towel over the bar's

Lisa Jackson

glossy surface. "He was in one other time and was all pissed off that the coverage was about the hurricane. Interrupting the sports on TV. Hell, I thought we were lucky to even be open, avoid being hit hard, y'know. No flooding except the back lot." He tossed his towel into a bin of other wet rags.

Joe half turned on his stool and said to Nikki, "Hey, if you're lookin' fer him and find him, tell him he owes me a ten-spot for the Marlins game. Cheap ass is probably layin' low to avoid payin'." His attention back on the television, he said, "I could use another," to the bartender.

Nikki walked back to her Honda and saw she was hemmed in, a blue Ford Escape backed in tight, its back end nearly touching the nose of her CR-V.

Irritating.

She'd have to jockey her way out of the tight space.

"Great," she muttered, slipping into the warm interior. She started the engine and rolled down the windows to cool things off. Then, before trying to pull away from the curb, she slid her phone from her pocket to google the Braves' schedule.

Sure enough, the Atlanta team had played the Miami Marlins at home on the night before the discovery of the bodies at the Beaumont estate.

Not really a surprise.

Bronco had been freaked.

And it was time to pay him a visit and find out what the hell he was doing in that basement and what he knew about Baxter Beaumont and Margaret Duval. Had they had an affair? Did it matter? Was it a reason for Harvey and Margaret divorcing? What had Andrea Clancy said? She dropped her phone into a cup holder.

She put her Honda into gear and inched backward,

then forward, cranking the steering wheel, hoping to ease out of the space. Each time her back wheels hit the curb, she tried again, gaining inches and beginning to sweat. What kind of a jerk would pin her in like that? Backward. Forward. Backward again.

Finally, she thought she would clear the Escape.

Checking her side-view mirror before hitting the gas, she noticed someone lingering at the doorway of the bar, partially hidden by a lamppost. A man? A woman? She couldn't tell as the sun was in her eyes.

So what if someone was looking?

Probably getting off on watching her frustration as she tried to maneuver into traffic.

Or maybe someone had overheard her talking to the bartender. She cranked on the steering wheel to get out of the tight space and hit the gas.

An angry honk blasted.

She hit the brakes, her car rocking to a stop as a BMW roared past her, the middle-aged driver raising an angry fist as the car, tires screeching, fishtailed into the oncoming lane, nearly swiping a minivan heading the opposite direction.

"Stupid bitch!" the driver yelled, speeding off.

Nikki's heart jackhammered.

Several people smoking outside the bar were staring at her, and the figure hiding behind the lamppost?

Gone.

"It was nothing," she told herself as she eased into the flow of traffic, her pulse still in the stratosphere, but she couldn't shake the image of the person behind the lamppost surreptitiously watching her, and the memory of the intruder inside her home skittered through her brain.

"You're being an idiot," she said, and saw her worried

eyes in her reflection in the rearview mirror. "Get over yourself."

Traffic thinned as she eased out of the city and into farmland, where she spotted cattle grazing in lush fields, a tractor pulling a trailer toward a red barn, a few hazy clouds in a blue, blue sky. She told herself to calm down, to not let little things get to her, let the warmth of a lazy Georgia day settle over her. As she slowed to turn onto Settler's Road, another vehicle, a delivery van, caught up to her and rather than slow, moved into the oncoming lane as she turned. Behind the van, a gray pickup with tinted windows, too, gave her a wide berth and sped past.

Odd, she thought, but really not. Everyone was in a hurry.

As was she.

She hit the gas as the road wound along the banks of the river and using her GPS located the lane where several NO TRESPASSING signs had been posted.

"Too bad." She ignored the warnings, her Honda bouncing a little on the rutted lane where little gravel had been spread. She drove through a thick stand of pine and maple trees that gave way to a small clearing and Bronco Cravens's weathered cabin. A beat-up Ford Ranger was parked near a dilapidated garage.

He was home!

Good!

She pulled in behind the pickup and parked.

Bronco wouldn't be thrilled to see her. She knew that. Obviously, he was avoiding her, not wanting to discuss his reasons for being at the Beaumont estate, but it was now or never.

Grabbing her phone and iPad, hoping Bronco would

open up to her, she slid out of her Honda and headed to the front door.

It was open.

The screen door was unlatched and moving slightly in the slight breeze, the front door open wide.

She knocked and peered inside, where a television was tuned to the news, a lamp burning, nothing stirring, no noise from within. "Bronco?" she called through the screen. "Bronco?" She stepped inside and felt a little uneasy. "Hey, it's Nikki Gillette. We met years ago. I'm a reporter for the *Sentinel.*" She stepped through the living room, noting the empty dog bed, sagging couch, full ashtray and a couple of empty beer bottles left on the coffee table. A rifle, too, had been left on the kitchen floor. Odd. Or was it? What did she really know about Bronco Cravens?

Not nearly enough.

"Bronco?" she yelled again, a little louder, her nerves beginning to tighten, the smell of stale smoke hanging in the air.

She sensed he wasn't inside, that the house seemed devoid of life. Silent. Almost eerily so. Walking through his home seemed wrong.

"In for a penny . . ." she said under her breath as she stepped into the kitchen, where more empties littered the counter by the remains of a microwave meal near the sink, a fly buzzing near it. A dog's water dish was half-full on the dirty floor near the open back door.

Maybe he just stepped outside for a second.

She heard the crunch of tires on gravel and glanced through a grimy kitchen window but couldn't see the drive. It could be that Bronco and his dog had gone with a friend somewhere. And here she was basically trespassing *inside* his house. Locked door or no locked door, it would be hard to explain what she was doing poking around.

The engine died and a car door slammed.

Just one.

She started back to the living room, then thought better of it.

Maybe she should just step onto the back porch and act as if she hadn't been in the house and—

She saw the blood.

Thick red stains on the weed-choked grass and . . . Oh, God!

Her eyes landed on a body lying facedown in the backyard. A dark red stain had spread over the back of his T-shirt.

"No!" she screamed, racing outside, flying off the porch, whipping out her phone and already dialing 911. "No, no, no!" She slid on the bloody grass as she reached the man and knew before she tried to find a pulse.

Her stomach heaved and she had to fight the urge to throw up. She wanted to turn him over. To look at his face, but she knew better than to mess with the crime scene, so she stepped away as the operator answered, and said, "This is Nikki Gillette and I want to report a murder." Her voice was strained, her insides shaking. "It's Bronco—Bruno Cravens. I'm at his house out on Settler's Road. Send someone. Send my husband! Pierce Reed!" She was yelling now, unable to hear the woman on the other end of the line. "Get someone out here!"

And then she heard the footsteps.

Heavy and moving through the house.

Getting closer.

Who?

She didn't care. "Help!" she yelled over her shoulder. "I need help out here!" From the corner of her eye she saw a man appear in the door, a huge man, dressed in black, his expression hard, his gaze boring into her.

And he was carrying a long gun.

CHAPTER 23

"I don't think she's the real deal," Delacroix told Reed when he reached the office. She was seated in what was now her chair and desk, in what he assumed was her usual attire: black on black, jacket, T-shirt and slacks. No jewelry. No frills.

"Why?"

"Too old, too . . . I don't know. There's a resemblance, of course, but I just have a feeling that she's a fame whore."

"Wow. At least you're not biased," he said, surprised at her reaction. "She's in the interview room?"

"Yeah."

"And you've already met her."

"Briefly. A deputy took them into the room, but I

caught a glimpse of her. She's with an older dude, her husband."

"But based on that meet and greet, you think she's a 'fame whore'?"

She slid him a glance. "You'll see. Okay, I know it sounds a little harsh, but there's a reason for it. It's frustrating, you know, and I'm not getting my hopes up on this one. There are too many charlatans in the world and I'm just tired of us spinning our wheels." She was scooping up her phone and iPad from her newly claimed desk.

"We're making progress."

"Are we?" she countered, heading for the door and the outer hallway, where there was a buzz of conversation. Already the news had spread in the department that the long-lost Duval sister might have been located. As soon as the information leaked to members of the press, including his wife, the phones would be ringing like mad, reporters wanting interviews, questions hurled at anyone associated with the case.

They were in the hallway outside the door. "Don't you think it's a little too convenient that after all these years, a woman comes forward? I mean, why wait? Why now?"

"Maybe she didn't know what had happened to her sisters. She wasn't quite five at the time and it's been two decades. Maybe she was afraid to talk. Could be a lot of reasons."

Delacroix shot him a disbelieving stance. "Sure," she said, nodding her head, her voice filled with sarcasm. "That's it."

Fleetingly he wondered why she was so cynical at such a young age, but he didn't have time to dwell on her attitude as they stepped into the interview room where a petite blond woman was waiting. Her hair was flaxen and long, one side clipped away from her face with a sparkly barrette. Her eyes a clear sky blue, her skin pale, her smile fragile. She looked to be around thirty, he'd guess, but could buy twenty-five. As Delacroix had mentioned, next to her was a man whose expression was stern, his skin swarthy, his short military-cut hair nearly silver. Fit and dressed in a trim navy-blue suit and tie, a Rolex watch or pretty good knockoff glinting beneath his left cuff, he stood and held out his hand.

"You're Detective Reed," he said. "I've seen you on TV. Herman Kemp."

Reed took his hand and felt the guy's firm grip. Strong to the point of punishing, a shake meant to state his authority, the alpha male in action. "Good to meet you," Reed said by rote, all the while wondering what was going on. "My partner, Detective Jade Delacroix."

Delacroix nodded, her expression thankfully noncommittal.

"We've met," the woman said quietly. Dressed in a frothy pastel dress, she stood hesitantly and with a nod from the man next to her extended her hand. "Rose Duval." Her tone was breathless, her handshake weak. But there was a resemblance to the computer-generated photo of what the missing twenty-five-year-old girl might look like. And there was something else about her. It was almost as if she were scared, or maybe just nervous.

"You're Rose Duval?" Delacroix clarified.

"That's right." Her tone was pleasant and they all sat down with the Kemps on the far side of the table, where a recorder, as well as a box of tissues and several water bottles, rested. Delacroix reminded them that the interview was being recorded, then got right to it. "What's your legal name?"

"Mrs. Herman Kemp," the man answered for her. "Rose, here, is my wife."

"Rose Kemp," Delacroix clarified.

Kemp's thin smile was a little patronizing, Reed thought.

Herman pinned her with his icy glare. "Rose Duval Kemp."

"I was actually asking her," Delacroix said, indicating the blonde.

"It's all right." Rose laid a hand on her husband's arm, but her expression remained wary.

Reed suggested, "I think it would be best if we talked to Rose alone." He stared at Herman.

"Oh. No!" Rose seemed flustered.

"The deputy who brought you in," Delacroix cut in, "took your IDs. Both of them. Herman Ray Kemp and Greta May Smith Kemp. Nothing here about Rose Duval." She was scanning information on her iPad.

"That's before she realized who she was!" Herman insisted.

"Yes," she agreed emphatically. "Before my memory came back."

Reed held up a hand. "Okay. Mr. Kemp, if you'd step outside, a deputy will lead you to another room where you can wait for your turn."

"No." He was shaking his head, his color rising. "My wife is fragile. I need to be with her."

"What you need to do is wait outside," Reed insisted. "Detective Delacroix will escort you."

"Oh, please." Greta was shaking her head so emphatically her hair clip slid down the strands of hair it was supposed to contain. "I need my husband with me."

Delacroix was on her feet. "Mr. Kemp, if you'll come with me." Then to Reed, "I'll pick up a swab for a DNA sample."

"A what?" Greta said, looking frantic.

"Honey, they can't take one without your permission," Herman insisted, not budging.

"Or a court order." Delacroix was by the door. "Mr. Kemp. If you would come with me."

"No!" Greta was on her feet in an instant. "No, he has to stay. I need him."

Delacroix said, "If you really are Rose Duval, DNA will prove it."

Greta looked about to faint. "Herman . . . ?"

"Don't worry, honey. You have rights." Glowering at Delacroix, he added, "We both have rights. I'm calling my attorney."

"You do that," Delacroix said. "Good idea."

"And I've set up an interview with Kimberly Mason."

Reed remembered the reporter who'd shown up at Margaret Le Roy's house, the same one who had been leaving him messages. "Kimberly wants the story," Herman said. "She's with WKAM."

"We've met," Delacroix said dryly as she ushered him out of the room.

Greta sank back into her chair. She glanced at the recorder on the table, then the cameras mounted high in the corners of the room. "I don't like this," she muttered.

"Duly noted." Reed suggested, "Why don't you start at the beginning? Tell me what you remember or know about the Duval family and how you came to believe that you're Rose."

"I don't know." She looked at him skeptically and bit her lip. "I don't feel comfortable without Herman here."

"He'll be back. In the meantime, can I get you anything?"

"No." She wrapped her arms around her middle and elevated her chin.

"All right, then." But he made a quick call on his cell. "Yeah, this is Reed in the interview room. Would you mind, I could use a cold drink? No, not coffee or sweet tea. Diet Pepsi? Sure." He glanced at Greta, lifting his eyebrows. "So far just one . . ."

She didn't take the bait.

"Make it two. Yeah, thanks."

Clicking off, he leaned back in his chair.

"Now, your address is listed in Tampa and six months ago you were in Miami and the year before that—"

"I know where I lived!" she cut in. Then gathered herself and said a little more calmly, "What does where I lived have anything to do with this?"

"Just establishing some facts. But why don't you just tell me why you think you're Rose Duval. Start from the beginning and then tell me why you're coming forward now."

"No, I'll start with that," she said, her color rising. "I came because I read about it in the papers and it triggered something in my mind." She touched her temple. "I started remembering things from before."

"Before?"

"Before the 'accident,' that's what my mother called it. Car accident. I wasn't in the car seat the right way and my mother rear-ended the car in front and I fell forward and hit my head. I-I was unconscious for a couple of days and then when I woke up I didn't remember anything.

And so my mom, she thought maybe that was for the best."

"She told you that? What's her name?"

Delacroix slid into the room. She was carrying three sodas.

"Where's Herman?" Greta asked, obviously panicked.

"With another deputy." She placed a can in front of Greta and one in front of Reed, then popped open the third and settled back into her seat.

"I said I don't want this," Greta said, pointing at the diet soda.

"Sorry." Delacroix looked at Reed. "Just assumed."

He said, "It's okay."

"It's *not* okay," Greta said, her anger flaring a bit. "I don't like this. I want Herman here, with me." From the other side of the table Greta looked from Delacroix to the now-closed door. "This isn't right."

"You were telling me your mother's name," Reed reminded her.

"I've got that," Delacroix said. "Beth Morgan Smith, she's your mother, and your father is Ronald Smith. Right?" she asked.

Greta, appearing dumbstruck, nodded.

Apparently she didn't realize how quickly the department could look up documents, court records or any violations anywhere in the country via the Internet.

"Yes," she said, playing with her hair a bit. "Yes, that's right. Ronald's my dad."

"So did they adopt you?" Delacroix asked.

"What?"

"Well, you call them 'Mom' and 'Dad,' but if you're really Rose Duval, they would have to be your adoptive parents, right? Because Margaret and Harvey Duval would be your biological mother and father."

"I don't know. Well . . . yes. Of course."

"No paperwork?" Delacroix pushed. "What about a birth certificate?" She took a swallow from her drink, but her gaze never left Greta's.

Greta blinked, started fiddling with her hair, her composure slipping. "I-I think they used my sister's. I think she died and they just had me take over her information."

Nodding, Delacroix said, "But there should be some record of that. Of her death."

"I-I don't know." More flustered than ever, she shook her head, the shiny barrette sliding farther down, her recently pinned back hair falling into her eyes. "Herman needs to be here with me. He knows all this. Where's my husband? I want him here with me or . . . or I want my attorney!"

"I think he said he was already calling a lawyer, and you came to us," Reed reminded her. "Of your own volition."

"Because I saw on the news that you were looking for me! That woman who talks for the police, she was on the air telling people to call in with tips or come in here. Marlow, I think her name was, and she had this image that she showed, a computer thing, and it looks just like me!"

Delacroix leaned forward. "So you saw the image and thought, what? Wow! There I am?"

"It was Herman. He saw the news and . . . and since, well, you know, I have this weird childhood, he asked me about how I came to be with Mom and Dad."

"And what did you tell him?"

"That I didn't really remember, but he showed me a clip of the news where you all were looking for Rose Duval and suddenly it all clicked. I remember going to the theater with my sisters and . . . and my brother let us off and we went into the show after we bought some candy."

"And then?" Reed said, not buying her story for a second. Delacroix was right, the woman was a fraud, either intentional or because she was a nut. He wasn't sure which.

"And then it gets kind of blurry. I, um, remember being separated from my sisters; they went back to the refreshment stand or the bathroom or whatever and I started looking for them and I must've wandered outside but . . . I can't remember after that."

"We have tapes from the theater that day," Delacroix said. "Neither Holly nor Poppy Duval ever went back to the refreshment counter."

"There weren't cameras in the bathrooms. That's illegal."

Reed said, "The cameras covered the entire lobby, including the entrance to both the men's and women's restrooms."

"But that's what I remember!" Greta was agitated and on her feet.

"That's what you read and you added your own story to it."

"I want my husband and I want him now!" she said, and before Reed could say another word, she grabbed her purse and headed for the door. "I told him this was a big mistake. That you wouldn't believe me." With a toss of her head she was out of the room and into the hallway.

"I'll go get her," Delacroix said, but Reed shook his head. "We've got it all on tape. Too bad we can't prove it. I was hoping she'd drink from the soda, leave her DNA."

"We might not need it," Delacroix said, and snagged a tissue, then kicked back her chair and walked to the door, where she bent down and picked up a shimmery object. The hair clip, tossed off when Greta had flounced out. Delacroix examined it and grinned. "And there's a couple of hairs still lodged in it. Hopefully with a root ball." Her smile widened. "We might have our DNA sample whether she knows it or not."

"Oh, my God!" The face of the man looming in the doorway of Bronco's cabin contorted in horror. "Bruno! Bruno! Oh, God, no, Bruno!"

Nikki, nearly hyperventilating, tried to scramble to her feet but slipped in the blood.

The man dropped the shotgun.

He jumped off the porch and fell to his knees next to Nikki before she realized he was Reverend Jasper Cravens, Bronco's father. "Bruno!" he cried brokenly, grabbing hold of his son's shoulders and holding the stiff, bloody body close. "No, no, no!!!" His eyes bright with tears, he stared at Nikki. "What happened?"

"I don't know," she said as relief washed over her despite the frantic beating of her heart. "I came here to ask him some questions and I found him out here."

"Who did this to my boy!" Tears streamed down the man's tortured face. "Who did this?"

"I-I don't know. I just got here and I found him and—"

From the surrounding trees came the sound of a dog

whimpering. Jasper's head snapped up. "Fender?" he called over the distant wail of a siren. "Fender?"

"I called 911," she said, still wary. Jasper had come with a weapon even though it was lying abandoned on the porch.

A dog with a dirty mottled coat appeared from the shadows.

"Fender. Come here, boy," Jasper said brokenly, then openly sobbed as he petted the dog and sat next to the body of his son while flies buzzed around them and the gentle rush of the river as it slowly moved downstream was audible.

"Sir, this is a crime scene," she reminded him gently, and dialed Reed's cell.

"But my boy. My boy is dead." Jasper sat on the blood-soaked grass next to the body of Bronco Cravens. Jasper's big shoulders were shaking as he stroked the dog. "Why?" he whispered, blinking, and again, "Why?" He glanced up at the sky where a few tufts of clouds moved slowly. "Oh, Father," he cried. "How could you let this happen? Why Bruno? Why my boy?" His voice cracked and he closed his eyes. Almost in prayer, he whispered, "Why have you forsaken me?"

CHAPTER 24

"Who did this to my boy?" Jasper Cravens demanded hoarsely as he stood and smoked a cigarette next to Reed's Jeep.

"We don't know yet, but we'll find out," Reed assured him. He was still agitated, his stomach in knots, but calming down. Nikki was safe. After receiving her panicked call, he'd feared the worst. He'd driven here and found Nikki with Bronco's body and Jasper Cravens and two deputies who had received the dispatch from her 911 call. She'd thrown herself into his arms when he'd shown up, but otherwise held it together. She was tough and had been through a lot in her life, but he was still relieved to find her uninjured. He'd held her a long moment, then suggested she wait in her Honda, close enough that they could see each other, while waiting to give her statement to someone on the force other than her husband.

He should've been surprised to find her here, still nosing around the case after their last conversation.

He wasn't.

He knew his wife too well.

He glanced her way now, seeing her huddled behind the steering wheel, Bronco's dog on the passenger seat beside her.

"I just can't believe he's gone." Jasper took another long drag and expelled smoke through his nose. He was a big man with a rotund belly, dark eyes and a receding hairline, dressed in black, only his white clerical collar giving any indication that he was the pastor of a local church. He watched as two EMTs carried a body bag to the back of an ambulance parked between the Jeep and a cruiser from the department.

He studied the tip of his cigarette and watched the smoke curl toward a sky starting to turn lavender with the coming dusk. "You have to find out who did this. Bring him to justice."

"We will." It was a promise Reed intended to keep.

"You said you came by because you hadn't heard from Bronco—er, Bruno, for a few days. Was that unusual?"

"Not really. I mean, we talked once a week or so, but I just had this feeling. I'd texted and called and he hadn't returned them, so I came out to see what's what. I saw this other car in the driveway"—he motioned to Nikki's Honda—"along with Bruno's, and my first thought was that he had company and maybe I should just leave him be, but I noticed the front door was open, so I changed my mind. No one was in the house, but I found his rifle,

my dad's old Winchester, on the kitchen floor like someone dropped it in a panic. So I picked it up and walked
through the house and found . . . Well, you know." He
dropped his cigarette onto the gravel and crushed the butt
with the heel of his shoe. "Haven't had one of those in
thirty-three years."

"Did Bruno have any enemies?" Reed asked.

"God knows," Jasper said. "Probably. He had his
share of troubles, but if you mean who are they?" He
frowned, squinting upward where the tree tops met the
lavender sky. "I couldn't tell you."

"Girlfriends?"

"None recently. Last one was Daria, no, that's not
right." He rubbed his jaw, where a five-o'clock shadow
had developed, as he thought. "Darla. That's it. Darla
something or other. Don't know if I ever heard her last
name. She's the one who gave him the dog. Fender."

"Right." The dog was with Nikki in her car. Dirty, but
apparently unhurt.

The ambulance drove off and Jasper's shoulders visibly tightened and he blinked hard as if fighting tears.
"Bruno was a good boy," he said. "But he lost his ma
when he was eleven. Cancer. Never got over it, I think.
And maybe I wasn't all that good at being a single dad."
He rubbed his head and sighed. From their vantage point
they could see the photographer in the house, taking digital images that might have been missed in the video that
had already been filmed.

"Bruno was the one who discovered the bodies at the
Beaumont estate."

"What?" Jasper said. "I hadn't heard. He never told me."

"Do you know why he would be over there? We
talked to him about it, but he was pretty evasive."

"The treasure," he said, his eyebrows drawing together. "Oh, man, I bet he was over there looking for the jewels or cash or whatever the hell old Beulah stashed there."

"What?"

Jasper snorted. "It's something my dad used to talk about. The Beaumont treasure. I think it was just talk that Beulah Beaumont hid valuables in her basement. My dad swore he helped her stuff a bag into a hiding spot in the basement and Bruno ate it up. I thought it was all folklore, you know, a grandpa amusing his grandson, and he made Bruno swear not to ever go looking for it. But Dad died a few weeks back and he had a set of keys to the place. I'm betting Bruno went looking. He was always broke. And was always looking for that big score, you know. He didn't put a lot of stock in working and saving for a rainy day, nope. He always talked about hitting it big, and Dad always fed him a line of bull about the Beaumont fortune." He closed his eyes and shook his head. "That's got to be it."

"We searched that place top to bottom," Reed said, "looking for other victims. Found no treasure."

"My guess, it was stolen long ago, or more likely never existed in the first place. If it did exist, I think there was a good chance that someone else in the family found it."

"You do?"

"If my father knew it was there, then you'd think Baxter would have found out."

"Baxter is Beulah's son?"

"Adopted. But yeah. Beulah was Arthur Beaumont's second wife. His first was Marianne, as in the Marianne

Inn just up the road on this side of the river. Named it after her and I'm thinking that didn't set well with Beulah. She was a bit of a . . . let's just say she was a colorful character." He gazed through the trees where the river was visible between the trunks. "You know, there was a time when the Beaumont house was always bustling. They all were. When the whole family lived there and when Beulah threw those massive parties of hers. They had a whole staff then—maids, gardeners, cooks, even a nurse, and Dad, of course. My dad worked over there and he'd tell us about what went on. Not just about the hidden treasure."

"Like what?"

Jasper frowned. "Don't like to gossip."

"This is a murder investigation."

"I know."

"Your son," Reed reminded him.

The preacher's face crumpled. "Man. The trouble with the Beaumont men is that they all had wandering eyes. Started out with Arthur and, according to my dad, went right down the line. Grandfather, father and son."

"Meaning Arthur, Baxter and Tyson."

"According to my dad and he wasn't one to talk idly. But it came out. He was disgusted by it, y'know. He'd lost my mother early on and missed her every day of his life, so he didn't understand how some men could . . . stray, if you know what I mean."

A deputy walked by and Jasper asked to bum another cigarette.

"Sure." The deputy pulled a pack from his pocket and they both lit up.

"Thanks. I'm gonna quit again tomorrow."

"Right," the deputy said as if he didn't believe the preacher as he walked toward the house and Jasper drew deep, the tip of his cigarette glowing red in the gloaming. He asked Reed, "You think that's why my boy was killed? Over some supposed pie-in-the-sky treasure?"

"I don't know," Reed said, "yet." But it was a place to start.

Jasper watched a bat skim by as the first of the stars began to wink in the darkening sky and the lights in Bronco Cravens's home glowed through the windows, two members of the crime scene team still working, one pushing a vacuum cleaner, the rumble audible through the open front door. "This is a test, you know," he finally said. "The Father, He's testing me."

"How?"

"By taking my son from me just a few weeks after Wynn, my dad." His lips compressed. "A test of my faith."

"You think God would have your son murdered just to see how devout you are?" Reed couldn't hide his skepticism.

"Everything in life is a test," the reverend said, and Reed bit his tongue. People believed what they believed and even if you argued with them, they rarely changed their minds, only got angry, and the man had just lost his son to a violent end. "Can I go now? I'll take the dog." Again, he blinked against tears.

"Sure. If you think of anything else, give me a call."

Jasper cleared his throat. "I will."

Nikki listened through the open window of her Honda and though she couldn't hear all of the conversation, she caught bits and pieces that drifted on the air with the acrid scent of burning tobacco. She had her iPhone set to her best recording app and hoped that it could pick up the conversation. With her free hand, she petted the dog who sat shivering in the front seat, but she was tuned in to what Jasper Cravens was telling Reed about his son and the Beaumont family.

The parts she did hear agreed with what she'd already learned and also melded with what she remembered from her own childhood.

She saw Delacroix approaching and slid her phone into the side pocket of the door as Delacroix opened the passenger-side door. "I didn't know you were here," she said to the dog as Jasper approached.

"I'll get him," the preacher said, then whistled sharply. "Come on, Fender, guess you're my dog now."

The heeler hopped onto the ground, following the older man as Delacroix brushed off the seat and slid inside. "Detective Jade Delacroix," she said. "Don't think we've formally met."

"Nikki Gillette."

"Right." She nodded, pulled out her phone and a notepad from a jacket pocket. "Detective Reed thought it best if I take your statement, so as there's no hint of conflict of interest or . . . well, whatever. Since he's your husband."

"Got it." Headlights flashed into the interior as a car engine started, and she caught a glimpse of Reverend Cravens backing around one of the county SUVs and driving away, taillights winking a bright red.

Jade pulled the door closed and sat with her back pressed between the passenger seat and door so she could get a good look at Nikki even though the interior of the car was dark. "Let's start with why you're here and how you found Bruno."

"I'm a reporter, doing a piece on the history of the Beaumont estate and I knew Bronco—er, Bruno—had been over there recently, that he discovered the bodies of the girls who were hidden there, the Duval sisters. I thought he could give me some insight about the property as his family is tied into the Beaumonts. His property, this cabin and the acres surrounding, originally belonged to the Beaumonts, and his grandfather worked for the family for decades." She went on to explain about driving to the Red Knuckle, then out here and walking through the house to find Bronco's body.

Delacroix listened in silence, dark eyes observing Nikki closely, as if studying a bug under a microscope, searching for cracks. Lies. As if something in Nikki's expression, some little idiosyncrasy like a tic near her eye or a vein throbbing in her temple or her tongue licking her lips nervously would give Nikki's lies away.

Or was it because she found it fascinating and unlikely that Nikki was married to Reed?

Whatever the reason, Nikki felt uncomfortable in the tight confines of the SUV but tried her best not to show it. Obviously Delacroix didn't trust her, or probably didn't like her, but that was just too bad.

"So you're telling me you just happened to be out here on the night Bruno Cravens was killed."

"I didn't just happen to be here. I came to interview him."

"But he didn't know it. Isn't that what you said?"

"I said that he never returned any of my calls or texts."

Delacroix was nodding in the darkness. "So you just walked into his house."

"The door was open."

"And you saw the gun, the rifle, but just ignored it."

"I didn't want to disturb anything."

"Because you knew it was a crime scene?"

"No, because it was Bronco's home, his stuff."

"And you weren't invited? He didn't know you were there?"

"We've been over this."

"Just clarifying," Delacroix said.

"And badgering."

There was a tense silence where Nikki held the younger woman's gaze, or thought she did, who could tell since night had fallen, but Delacroix finally said, "I think that does it. If I have any more questions, I'll call." She opened the car door and the interior light snapped on.

"Do that." Nikki didn't bother to hide the irritation in her voice.

Delacroix didn't smile, just said, "Thanks," as Reed showed up and stuck his head inside. "Done here?"

"Got everything I need, I think," Delacroix said, and walked off.

"How're you doing?" he asked, his gaze finding Nikki's.

"I'll live."

One side of his mouth lifted. "I'm kinda counting on that."

"You?"

"Fine. It'll be a little while yet. Meet you at home?"

"Sure." She wanted to ask him a dozen questions that

were flitting through her mind, all about the Cravens family and the Beaumonts, but they would have to wait. Reed had his game face on, deep into the investigation.

"Don't wait up," he said, and at least offered her a wink that caught her off guard and caused her heart to trip a little.

"I won't," she said as she started the ignition, but they both knew she was lying.

CHAPTER 25

"Do you have any new leads?" Nikki asked her husband as he walked through the back door and tossed his keys into the dish on the edge of the counter. She'd been working in the kitchen, waiting for him, reading Ashley Jefferson's blog about the pitfalls of being the mother of two rambunctious kids.

"And I'm glad to see you, too," Reed said before brushing his lips across her cheek.

"I am, of course I am." She wrapped her arms around his neck, felt his arms slide under her robe to encircle her waist. "You know that." She sighed, then kissed him full on the lips.

"That's better," he teased, and patted her on her rump.

"Chauvinist."

"I've just missed you." His eyes sparkled.

"It's just that—"

"That your curiosity got the better of your manners."

"Okay, fine," she said, rolling her eyes. "Of course I missed you. I'm glad you're home. But I still want to know what's going on."

Reed disentangled himself and bent down to pet the dog who was wiggling at his feet. "I'm glad to see you, too," he told Mikado, and then when the dog raced to the slider, Reed opened it for him and the dog shot outside. "You've been watching the news."

She nodded. "Do you know anything else? Is Bronco's death related to the Duval girls' homicide?"

"Don't know yet." He slid out of his jacket and shoved a hand through his hair.

"But he found the bodies. And the land was owned by the Beaumont family. And he probably used his grand-father's key and—"

"You heard the interview," he said, shaking his head. "I wondered."

Not only had she heard parts of it, but she'd recorded it and gone over it bit by bit, using what she'd learned from Jasper Cravens to do some more research.

"Couldn't help it."

He sent her a sharp look and she held up a hand.

"Okay, so I eavesdropped. The car window was open."

"And you didn't bother to shut it."

She wanted to argue but couldn't. "No, I didn't."

"Sit down," he said, and took a seat at the table, waving at the chair opposite him. "Look, before we get into the investigation, don't you think we should talk about the fact that you found a dead body, that you were at

Bronco's house, obviously looking into the Duval girls' murders and—"

"Pierce, I—"

"And all that talk about doing research on the Beaumont history was a cover. I figured so at the time, but I didn't want to hear any more lies." She didn't argue and he grabbed one of her hands. "We can't go on like this."

"What?"

"You know it and I know it."

"No, you've got it all wrong."

"I haven't, so just hear me out." He took one of her hands. "We've been through a rough patch. More than a rough patch. And a lot's been going on. Maybe I've been a little testy, but you've pushed me."

"I didn't mean to—"

"Just hear me out. Okay?"

"Fine."

"I've thought things over and I decided that yes, I'll give you an exclusive on the story when the time is right."

"So we can work together."

"Absolutely not, but if you just don't get in the way and don't do anything that could potentially screw up my case, then when we've got whoever is behind this, the story is yours. I talked to Okano today and the higher-ups. Everyone's in agreement."

Katherine Okano was an assistant D.A., a smart no-nonsense woman who had worked her way up in the department and given Reed a chance when he was looking for a job. She, looking over the tops of rimless glasses, had listened to him and frowned, thinking everything over before giving him the okay.

"And I have to stop looking into things? My story on the history of the Beaumont estate?"

"That wasn't just BS to get close to the investigation?"

"Approved by Fink. You know that."

He stared at her long and hard, then squeezed her hand. "As long as you don't get in my way and stay out of trouble and, Nikki, whatever you do, don't do anything where you could get hurt."

"Okay." She nodded and said honestly, "I'll do my best."

He cocked a disbelieving eyebrow, which she found ridiculously sexy.

"I think I should tell you what I pieced together."

"While researching your story on the history of the place."

"Mmm." She nodded. "I found out that Margaret Duval had an affair with Baxter Beaumont way back when."

"I'm listening," he said, but got up to let Mikado inside.

"You don't seem surprised."

"I heard something of the sort. Though I hadn't heard Baxter's name."

The dog came over to Nikki and placed his head on her thigh. She ruffled his neck and scratched behind his ears.

"I'm just trying to piece it together myself, but Tyson told me about it." She explained about her run-in with Baxter's son and what Tyson had explained about his grandmother's nurse. Then she added the gossip she'd overheard at the Red Knuckle. "And then I did some calculations. Look, I know this is a little far-fetched. I have no source on this, no reliability. Just maybe a feeling."

"I deal in facts."

"Fine, I know. But I think it could be possible that Rose Duval might be Baxter Beaumont's daughter."

"What?" He was walking to the refrigerator and stopped dead in his tracks. "That's a pretty big leap."

"Maybe. But a possibility."

He opened the fridge and pulled out a beer, then twisted off the top. "And she's the daughter who escaped . . . well, maybe escaped. We've already had someone claiming to be the missing Rose."

She was out of her chair. "Really?" This was news she hadn't heard, her pulse ticked up. "And?"

"A fraud," he said. "We've got her DNA and are already processing it, but her story didn't hold any water."

"Tell me."

"She came in with her husband, claimed she had a memory loss." He sketched out the meeting with Herman and Greta Kemp. "Delacroix called her a fake from the get-go and it was obvious that they were hoping to cash in on the fame."

"Why?"

"You tell me." He took a long drink from his bottle. "We live in a whacked-out world. Fame. Money. Power. That's what everyone's looking for these days." He winked at her. "I know that's why you hunted me down."

"Hunted you—?" He was teasing. Despite how serious the conversation had gotten. "I guess you know me," she said. "A gold digger through and through."

Owen Duval was sweating, his nerves strung to the breaking point, his thoughts ragged and he didn't need any reporter begging for a story to tell "his side" of what had happened to his sisters. "No," Owen said into the phone, pacing around the small confines of his apartment. "No interview." He cut the connection with the pushy reporter and walked to the window to peer through the shades. The street was empty and dark, the cars parked along the curb all those he recognized as belonging to neighbors. Good! More importantly, there were no news vans that he could see. Double good. Those vultures must've found some other piece of carrion to pick at.

His head throbbed and he picked up his drink, his third—or was it his fourth?—of the night, then tossed back the last three sleeping pills in the bottle.

Thankfully that old busybody Helen Davis who rented to him was gone for the next couple of days, visiting her grandkids or whatever. She'd told him exactly where she'd be going—maybe somewhere in Florida? Orlando? Tampa? Who knew and who the fuck cared? She'd asked him to check on her cat, but he'd barely been paying attention. He really couldn't be bothered with the damned cat seeing as he was the primary suspect in the murder of his sisters.

God, what a mess.

Then again, his whole life was a waste.

The voices . . . they kept reminding him of what a loser he was. If they would just shut up, but oh, no. They only went quiet for a while after teasing him. Then they would suddenly start whispering again, always waiting for just the right moment to remind him of how he'd screwed up.

And they were coming back tonight. Starting to scatter around his brain, scraping and scratching, making him think he might be going out of his mind. He topped off his glass with whiskey, turned on the TV and turned off the lights. Then he sat down in his favorite chair and watched.

Of course the news was on.

This time the story was about the murder of Bruno Cravens.

"Jesus," he whispered. He'd known Bronco. They'd run in different circles in high school and were in different classes, but they were acquaintances. He took another swallow and grabbed his remote to increase the volume.

Details were sketchy, but Bronco's body had been found at his home, the victim of a homicide. Well, there was no surprise there. Bronco had been a two-bit criminal, had been in and out of the slammer, probably owed someone money for drugs or a gambling debt.

The news reporters were trying to link his murder with the discovery of the bodies of Holly and Poppy. At the thought of his sisters the old pain resurfaced, a heaviness that he felt in his heart. God, would it never end?

No. It will never *cease. It will chase after you until your last dying breath. You know what you should do.*

He ignored the voices. Knew they were evidence that he was crazy. He opened the drawer of the table next to his chair and retrieved his gun, a pistol he'd had for years, a pistol Harvey had given him when he was a teenager. God, that was a lifetime ago. For now he set it next to a box of tissues on the small side table and took another drink. Then he switched stations, found a talk show host whose jokes were as old as he was.

He glanced at the gun as he sipped. Picked it up. Felt its weight in his free hand.

Do it, the voices said, as they always did, *just end it all. You don't need this pain, this guilt. How many years are you going to put up with running and hiding and*

*knowing that everyone you meet thinks you're a mur-
derer. Wasn't it bad enough when they just thought you'd
hidden the girls, done something horrible to them? Now
they know about Holly. About Poppy.*

Their faces came to him.

Innocent and bright, all big, toothy smiles, freckled
noses and near-white curls. Holly had just become sarcastic, interested in boys and getting into trouble, starting to
give Mom and Harvey fits. Owen had even caught her
trying to sneak out a time or two. Poppy, still all legs and
arms and coltish, her beauty just starting to peek through
her gawky preadolescence. And Rose—little Rose, still a
little imp. Too young to have gone to the movies with her
older siblings and now . . . oh, Lord.

*The world will be a better place without you. If you
end it all, your secrets and Rose will be safe. Maybe. How
will you ever know? You have no idea what became of her
and probably never will. She might not be alive. You'll
never know and that understanding will eat you alive, is
eating you alive.*

"God help me."

God. Jesus. All the Bible stories he'd heard and memorized as a child under his mother's watchful eye.

*How many pieces of silver did it take to betray Christ?
Thirty? Does it matter?*

A soft, pervasive voice came to him, the most seductive of the lot: *End it all, Owen. End it now. Things will
be better. For your mother. For everyone. You could find
peace at last . . .*

His throat clogged. He would never be forgiven.

You won't be anyway. It was true. The rest of his life
would be filled with this torment.

Tell them. Leave a note. Let the truth out . . .

He couldn't. He rotated the gun in his hand, put the barrel to his chin, finger on the trigger. As he'd done a thousand times before. Rehearsed.

Squeeeak.

The sound caught him off guard, caused his heart to stop for a second.

He turned down the volume and looked around but saw no one. The old house was just settling again. He'd heard that same squeak or one similar to it a million times when he was alone.

Heartbeat slowing, he turned his attention back to the TV.

Still holding the gun, he reached across to the table for his drink and downed it in one final draught. He was feeling the alcohol racing through his blood, mixing with the downers—over-the-counter stuff—he'd taken to help him sleep. He'd tripled the dose, just to make certain he would sleep, and now his lips were numb, his tongue thick, his fingers wobbly as they held the weapon.

Owen's dead now.

He can't feel the pain any longer.

He doesn't have to live with his demons.

He's at peace.

Just do it.

The gun was heavy. So heavy. And awkward. It nearly slipped from his hand. He leaned his head back against the chair for support and his hand dropped to his side, his grip slipping, his finger still on the trigger.

You'll be asleep forever.

And they'll all feel bad about it.

It will be their turn to be tortured, to experience guilt.

His eyes drifted shut and he felt drool on the corner of his mouth. He reached up to wipe it away, but the gun in his hand was too heavy and he couldn't—

"Just do it," the voice said, and it was a soothing whisper, unlike the other mice-like squeaks still yabbering in the echo chamber of his mind. "Let me help."

"Whaaa?"

He felt strong fingers wrap over his and help him raise the gun.

"No . . . I . . . dun . . . I dunno . . ."

The barrel, cold metal, touched his temple.

"Do it, do it, do it." A raspy, determined whisper in his ear.

"I . . . I . . . wait . . ." This was wrong!

Too late.

The grip over his fingers tightened.

Owen's eyes flew open.

Was this a dream?

Fuck, no!

Adrenaline poured through his blood. He started to struggle.

The finger—was it his?—Oh, God! Pressured, it clenched over the trigger.

Blam!

The pistol fired.

Lights flashed behind Owen's eyes for one millisecond.

Then Owen's world died with him.

CHAPTER 26

The sky was gray and ominous, promising rain.

Not a perfect day to go snooping at the old Beaumont house, but Nikki was running out of time. With one eye on the darkening sky, she drove past the main gates to the spot where she'd parked on the day the Duval girls' bodies had been found. From her conversation with Tyson Beaumont the other day, she knew that security cameras and alarms would be placed around the old mansion and estate in the coming week, and she didn't want anyone to see what she was doing. So, she figured, it was basically now or never.

A beat-up old pickup with a camper was already parked near the trailhead, no one around, and she assumed the driver was a fisherman who'd made his way to the river. She pulled her Honda to a spot nearby, got out and hurried to the path leading through the woods.

The air was thick and muggy enough that she began to sweat as she jogged along the deer trail and through the thickets, the gloom of the day permeating the woods. This time she avoided the river and took a fork in the path that would lead directly to the clearing and the outbuildings near the old house.

Rain began to fall, droplets falling through the trees to the forest floor, the wind causing leaves to shiver. She threw up the hood of her light jacket and kept walking. The questions that had been swirling in her mind propelled her onward. Why were the Duval girls taken from the theater? To kill them? Why bury them here at the Beaumont estate? What's the connection? Or was this place chosen randomly? Who would know about the secret hiding spot? Margaret Duval? Nurse to Beulah? Mother of the sisters who were killed? And why or how did Rose escape? Was that all part of the plan? *Whose* plan?

Who the hell had access to the house? The Beaumonts? Baxter or Connie-Sue, his wife, or his son, Tyson? Margaret Duval, who had once been the nurse here—mother of the victims? Or any of the Cravenses? Wynn or Jasper or Bronco? They had access and their cabin had once belonged to the Beaumonts.

Or someone connected to the Marianne Inn? That old lodge kept coming up, and the boat that she thought she'd seen beneath the drooping branches of the willow tree. Who was in that boat?

The rain kept falling ever faster, the path growing muddy, leaves dripping. Nikki felt that she was getting closer to finding out the truth but was missing something vital, the damned link that brought it all together.

She kept moving, pushing wet branches aside, her thoughts a jumble. As she reached the edge of the thicket, she stopped and surveyed the place. Even though Tyson had indicated there weren't any cameras inside the fence line yet, she couldn't be certain. The house stood as she remembered from her last visit, but instead of the beehive of activity of a newly discovered crime scene with police officers and EMTs on the scene, the area was empty, devoid of life. Not even a bird in the dismal sky. The huge house was dingy and sad, the roof collapsed in one section, bricks crumbling in the chimneys as it loomed on the hill. Traces of crime scene tape flapped in the wind, while draping Spanish moss danced eerily, turning and floating, like wispy ghosts. The sky was somber and dark, the grass tall and shimmering in the breeze. All of the outbuildings were dark and empty.

The whole area seeming abandoned and sinister.

She turned her attention to the river, past the spot where the pier had been to the willow tree with its drooping branches, leaves turning with the breeze, the end of the limbs floating on the dark ominous water.

Shake it off, Nikki told herself and squinted, searching for any shadow of a boat hidden within the willow's shroud. *Don't freak yourself out. It's just a gloomy, depressing day. Get a move on.*

Cautiously she picked her way around the edges of the sheds and barn, then stayed near the surrounding trees, all the while snapping pictures. She eyed the contents of the machine shed, and pump house, barn and stable, all rotting, all empty aside from whatever equipment had been left to rust in the weather.

She passed by the old garden, now overgrown with tangled, out-of-control rose bushes and tall weeds, then walked beneath the drape of branches and leaves that turned in the wind. There was no boat tied to the gnarled trunk, but she saw a deep indent in the muddy bank where the prow of a boat could have rested if the craft had been tied to a thick branch or the trunk.

Who was here that day?

Someone who was curious?

Or someone nefarious?

Why hide in these protective limbs?

She thought about the accident that took Morrisette's life, the other boat with the red and white prow that had scraped against Nikki but dealt Sylvie Morrisette a deathly blow.

Could someone have been steering the craft? It was so crazy that day, so confusing, but surely someone would have seen someone in the boat.

But as far as she knew, it had never been retrieved.

"Odd," she said aloud, and peered from the shelter of the willow to the house, so dark and imposing. She took another couple of pictures with her iPhone, then stuffed it into the back of her jeans and walked through the rain to the back porch.

The rain had picked up.

A skitter of fear slid down her spine, but she ignored it and stopped long enough to take some pictures of the back of the estate, gloomy and dark and unkempt, the siding gray and rotting, the chimneys crumbling at complete odds with the way she remembered the house as a child. How grand it had been, how polished and proud with its gleaming windows reflecting the setting sun, the clap-board painted white, the tall shutters black and gleaming on that hillock with its groomed and terraced lawns.

No longer.

And never again, she thought, pocketing her phone.

She kept on, close to the woods, and once she was close to the house, crossed the knee-high grass, bent now with the wind and rain. She, too, was wet, her hair drip-ping, her shoulders damp. Quickly she hurried across the dirty floorboards of the porch. The doors to the back liv-ing area, French doors now boarded over, were locked and she wasn't surprised. She suspected that Tyson had secured the building the day she'd seen him at the front gate, but she also figured that old locks and windows would probably give way with a little pressure.

Walking along the wide wraparound porch, she eyed every possible way in. She checked a second door, a side entrance that she knew from her own exploration of the house as a child had been the servants' entrance and led to the basement. It, along with the front door with its arched transom, was locked tight.

No surprise there.

This wasn't going to be easy.

She tried several windows that weren't boarded over. All were locked tight. "Terrific," she muttered under her breath as she made her way to the back of the house again. Walking on the wraparound porch, she tried two kitchen windows that were secure and considered how hard it would be to remove the plywood over one near the corner.

Was she that desperate?

There has to be a way in.

She tried every window and door again, pushing harder.

The only one that gave at all was a smaller one over the sink in the kitchen that hadn't been boarded over. It was high and she had to find an old bucket to turn over and stand on, but when she reached up and pushed, she felt the window give a little.

Maybe she could get in here.

The window wasn't sealed as it was a bit crooked in its casing. But still. What did she have to lose?

Balancing on the overturned bucket, she jimmied the window, pushing up from the bottom, feeling it wiggle and give a bit.

Maybe?

Sweating, she pushed, getting her arms and weight into it. Slowly, with a noisy screech, it started to give. She pushed upward, straining, a jab of pain in her left shoulder reminding her she hadn't completely healed from her last visit to this place. "Come on, come on," she whispered, replanting her feet and pushing hard. Sweat beaded her brow and ran down her nose while rain pummeled the roof, water running in the old rusted gutters and seeping through rotting shingles.

Her fingers were beginning to ache, her back and shoulders straining.

The window budged again.

Another shove.

Bits of the old, swollen casing suddenly gave.

The window slipped upward a few more inches, just enough to allow her to wriggle through.

She didn't think twice.

Disregarding the pain in her shoulder, she pushed herself through the opening and crawled into the sink, where dust and rust were visible on the ancient chipped porcelain and a brown spider scurried down the drain. She dragged her body through, her shoulder starting to throb. Once inside, she left the window open for her exit.

The interior was dim, only bits of light from the dark day slipping through the few grimy windows that hadn't been boarded over. She walked carefully through the rooms, her ears straining. Using the camera on her cell phone, she took pictures of the interior, focusing on the tattered draperies, dusty tiles on the fireplace, and cobwebs draping the corners and balusters of the staircase. She climbed to the third floor, taking photos, shoving aside the feeling that she was walking on someone's grave. Most of the rooms were bare and empty, but she caught images of peeling wallpaper, old, rusted bedsprings and a broken treadle sewing machine, all objects of a different era, all deteriorating. She caught several images of the crumbling ceiling tiles, broken chandelier and even an abandoned bird's nest under the exposed eaves.

The house had a feeling of abandonment and with no air circulating, cobwebs and dust everywhere, it seemed dead inside.

Ridiculous, she told herself but couldn't help feeling goose bumps rise as she finally took a few shots of the narrow back staircase to the basement.

The scent of rot filtered upward as she, bolstering her courage, descended. So what if bodies had been found down here? Using the flashlight's beam, she stepped into what had so recently been a crime scene. Evidence of the police having been there was visible though the basement was still packed with old furniture and boxes and old clothes.

The floor was covered in mud, drying in some spots,

wet and gooey in others, the sound of dripping water breaking the silence. With a quick look around, she discovered the area that had been cleared away from an outer brick wall and the dark, gaping hole with its hiding place.

The Duval girls' tomb.

Her throat went dry at the thought of what had happened here, how the girls may have suffered, how they'd been laid to rest and hidden from their family and the world. She shined her light in the cavern, now clean, whatever evidence had been inside meticulously extracted by the police.

She took pictures, best as she could, the flash on her camera flaring like lightning in this basement with its low ceiling and dark secrets. She stepped closer to the wall and then stopped at the sound of a voice.

That was crazy. No one was here. But . . .

Was that a female voice? For a second she thought of Nell, the girl who had drowned here, Baxter's sister, the rumored ghost. The hairs at her neck lifted and she froze.

It couldn't be.

The voice was getting louder.

Seriously?

She couldn't be found here.

No one could suspect she'd been on the estate or in the house. She thought of the open window over the kitchen sink and the overturned bucket on the porch. Oh, crap, oh, crap, oh, crap! She backed up slowly, toward the stairs. If she could sneak out before anyone came down here—

Clunk!

The back of her legs hit something—God knew what—as she inched her way backward, the voice louder.

"I know, okay? I'll check it out. But we can only rush things through as fast as we can . . ."

Nikki recognized the voice.

Definitely not a ghost. She slid around what felt like a chest of drawers and hid behind it as she heard a key in a lock.

That stopped her cold.

Who had a key?

The person who killed Bronco Cravens? Had he . . . no, *she* found a duplicate? But why come here? Why in the middle of a rainstorm—

The door opened and footsteps sounded in the staircase.

Nikki's heart was hammering fast, her throat dry as she tried to make herself as small as possible. She peered around the edge of the bureau.

"Yeah, I know. I'll be back soon . . . okay. Talk to you then."

Who is the woman?

The footsteps started descending.

Oh. God.

A flashlight's beam swept into the basement, moving swiftly, startling a rat that scurried out of its path.

She bit back a scream.

Don't panic.

But she was already silently freaking out and wondering why the hell she hadn't brought a weapon of any kind.

Because you thought you'd be alone. You thought Tyson's cameras and NO TRESPASSING *signs would be enough to keep anyone from coming.*

Shrinking back into the cavity beneath the stairs, she hardly dared breathe while watching the bluish glare of the flashlight's beam as it swept over boxes and crates, stacks of bags and broken furniture.

The beam arched over the ceiling near her, exposing cobwebs and tools hanging on the crossbeam.

A hammer!

Not much of a weapon, but something. If she could just get to it.

The beam moved through the piles of trash, away from the stairs to the wall where the bodies had been buried.

Nikki thought about the hammer. Should she go for it?

It was risky and little help against a gun—

You don't know if this person, whoever it is, has a weapon.

Still . . .

The beam slid into the cavern.

Nerves strung to the breaking point, she silently stepped away from her hiding space and reached up, her hands swiping the air wildly. Shit! She tried again, touched the hammer and it slipped off its nail, sliding through Nikki's sweating palms. Her heart nearly stopped as her fingers tightened over the claw, feeling it slice her skin just before the hammer hit the ground.

But there was movement in the still air.

"What the hell?" The flashlight's beam swung toward the stairs.

Oh, God.

Nikki, like a frightened snail, withdrew as far as she could into the dark alcove. She shifted the hammer, holding on to the smooth wood of the handle, wondering if she'd have to use it.

"Is someone there?" the woman demanded, harshly.

Nikki's heart knocked crazily in her chest.

Her slick fingers held the hammer in a death grip.

Whoever was holding the flashlight started walking toward the stairs. "I know you're here," she said.

Nikki hardly dared breathe.

The beam swept closer, skating across the floor.

Slowly, Nikki raised her weapon and felt the spit dry in her mouth.

Closer.

The beam swept inches from Nikki's feet.

Oh. Lord.

She braced herself.

"What the—?" the woman said as a rat scurried across the swath of light. It darted from its hiding spot beneath the lowest step across the muddy floor to disappear into a crevice between two stacks of boxes.

"You little shit!"

In that second, Nikki placed the voice: Jade Delacroix.

Reed's partner.

What the hell was Delacroix doing down here?

She's a cop; she has every right to be here. It's you who shouldn't be down in this godforsaken basement.

Lowering the hammer, Nikki watched from the shadows as Delacroix turned and walked back to the tomb, snapped the flashlight onto her belt, and then placed her hands on the bricks above the dark cavern. Over the drip, drip, drip of water, Delacroix whispered what sounded like a prayer.

Nikki strained to hear the words.

"I'll find him. I swear," Delacroix said, before making a quick sign of the cross over her chest. With that she abruptly turned, grabbed the flashlight and headed for the stairs. Once again, Nikki shrank into the shadows as the policewoman mounted the steps quickly, almost running, the floorboards creaking overhead, a door opening and closing.

A lock clicked into place.

And then it was quiet again aside from the incessant dripping.

Nikki didn't move. She barely dared slip her phone from her pocket to check the time. Then she waited. For a full ten minutes while the cavernous basement with its makeshift graves seemed to close around her. She told herself she did *not* feel spiders on the back of her neck, that the rat she spied earlier was long gone, that everything was just fine.

Slowly, Nikki emerged, turning on the light from her phone, half expecting to hear Delacroix's voice say, "I knew you were down there. What the hell are you doing here, Nikki Gillette?"

But the basement remained silent. Ominously so.

She managed to take a few more pictures, then cautiously mount the stairs. Since the door was dead-bolted and she didn't want anyone to know she'd been inside, she left the way she came in, tiptoeing into the kitchen and hoisting herself over the sink. Once she'd wriggled outside, tumbling onto the porch and nearly losing her phone in the process, she lowered the window to within an inch of the sill, righted the bucket and observed the grounds again.

Delacroix or someone else could have arrived while she was inside. Her gaze skimmed the tall grass and dilapidated outbuildings, even sweeping over the weeping willow, but she saw no one, so she followed the path that had led her here, skirting the outbuildings before turning into the woods.

What had she just witnessed?

Was this some kind of weird ritual with Delacroix? Something she did with all her cases? Or was this specific to this case? Questions assailed her as she hurried through the rain, the path now muddy.

By the time she reached her car she noticed that the fisherman's camper and pickup were gone. Her CR-V was parked alone on the mashed grass and weeds and sparse gravel. She climbed inside, swiped her face with her sleeve, then switched on the ignition.

The windows steamed and she cracked the passenger side and cranked on the defrost by rote. She even fiddled with the radio, settling on a station that played music from the nineties, but she barely noticed as she thought about the case and the people involved. She drove past the gates of the Beaumont estate, firmly shut, then the acres of grapevines of the Channing Vineyards. Tyson Beaumont, Jacob Channing, Owen Duval, Bronco Cravens. How were they involved with the disappearance and murder of Holly and Poppy Duval? And what about Rose? Once over the bridge she glanced at the road leading to Bronco Cravens's home, where he had been so brutally murdered. Gunned down. Shot in the back? Because of the Duval girls' homicides? Or some other reason? It wasn't as if he was exactly an upstanding citizen. He could have owed the wrong people money or double-crossed a cohort in some crime.

But to murder him?

Beyond the Cravenses' cabin, just upriver was the Marianne Inn. The spot where Chandra Johnson caught Holly Duval crying. Holly—the tough, rebellious daughter of Margaret and Harvey.

Nikki nearly turned around and drove to the old inn, but glancing at the clock she knew she didn't have time.

Today was Sylvie Morrisette's funeral.

As difficult as it would be, Nikki would have to attend and somehow deal with the guilt that would surely settle on her. She would have to endure the silent accusations in the eyes of Morrisette's coworkers and family.

For Reed.

Nikki made a note to drive back to the Marianne Inn.

Once Detective Sylvie Morrisette was laid to rest.

I tell myself not to panic. I should be able to handle this. Haven't I always? Haven't I been able to keep my secrets and hide the truth for twenty years? It's not the cops that worry me. I can handle them—they'll never even suspect. But that damned Nikki Gillette. She's a problem. A wild card. And she won't back off. She might be the one who exposes me and I have to keep track of her. The tracking device will help. Now, I just need to keep track of her until I finish my job.

Then I'll deal with her.

CHAPTER 27

The funeral was tough.

Reed, with Nikki at his side, sat on a hard pew in the church and avoided staring at the black coffin, atop of which was a blanket of white and blue flowers, along with Morrisette's official department picture, a head shot of her in uniform. She would have hated this, Reed thought, avoiding looking at the posed picture, preferring to remember her as she was, alive and sassy, all grit and determination, her hair spiked, her ears studded, her language salty and her heart, always, in the right damned place. Now gone. Grief grabbed hold of Reed's soul. He tried to listen as the minister, a bald-headed man, his clerical collar stretched tight around his fleshy neck, gave a brief account of Sylvie Morrisette's life, but Reed's mind filled with images of the mercurial partner he'd once doubted but had come to trust.

From his pulpit, the preacher kept his remarks short, thankfully, but stumbled when speaking about Sylvie's early life and her career. Obviously, he'd never met Sylvie Morrisette. Reed guessed she'd never stepped one snake-skin-booted foot into this nave with its soaring ceilings, stained-glass windows and slow-moving fans moving the air around in the nave. Minister Linley glossed over Morrisette's marriages and concentrated on the fact that Sylvie was a dedicated cop and devoted mother.

No doubt Minister Linley had received his information from either Bart Yelkis and the Internet or possibly someone at the department.

Reed knew far more about his partner than the man leading the service.

Throughout it all, Nikki, dressed in black and seated next to him, had been respectful and solemn, bowing her head during prayer while, during the rest of the service, she'd kept her eyes on the preacher, avoiding the accusing gazes of Morrisette's friends—mainly cops—or family. Though Reed and Nikki had chosen to sit near the back, more than once Bart Yelkis had looked over his shoulder from a front pew, where he'd sat wedged between his children, both dressed somberly, both quietly weeping. When Yelkis caught sight of Nikki he'd sent her a hateful glare that Nikki either didn't see or ignored.

Reed didn't. His jaw tightened and he reached into his pocket to rub his new talisman, Morrisette's key chain with its star fob. It had been a rough day already as he'd had to explain to Margaret Duval that the woman who'd posed as Rose was a complete fraud. "I should have been there," she'd said over the weak phone connection. "I would have known immediately if that woman was my little girl."

"She wasn't," he'd said as gently as possible. "It was a scam, I'm afraid." He would have proof soon, when the DNA came through.

"Then find my daughter," Margaret had said brokenly.

And then there was Nikki's wild theory that Rose Duval could be the love child of Margaret Duval and Baxter Beaumont when they hadn't yet established the two had been involved in an affair. He'd posed the idea to his new partner early this morning while they were both sipping coffee and going over the reports that had come in overnight.

Delacroix had looked at him as if he'd lost his mind. "Are you serious?" she'd asked.

"Anything's possible."

"But is it probable? More importantly, is it a fact?" She reminded him, "We deal in facts."

"And theories that are supported by facts. So we need to find out the truth and before we go asking Margaret Duval or Baxter Beaumont if they had a child together, we'd better make certain they were really involved and this isn't just local gossip that's been embellished over the years."

"I guess it's worth looking into," she'd said reluctantly. "But you should really tell your wife to back off. Doesn't she have a history of screwing up your cases?"

"No, never screwed them up," Reed said, which was a bit of a lie. How many times had Nikki put herself in danger, all for chasing down a story, and yeah, getting involved with his work. "It's her job."

Delacroix didn't have to say any more, just shot him a knowing look, reminding him of the thin line he was walking between his marriage to a pushy reporter and doing his by-the-book investigations.

"If Rose isn't Harvey's daughter, it might explain why we didn't find her in the tomb with her sisters."

"How?"

"Don't know yet."

Delacroix hadn't been convinced. "You know, your wife has some real out-there ideas. Look, if we go down this rabbit hole and you think it's valid, you can be the one to ask the woman married to the preacher if she was fooling around on her husband and, oh, by the way, had a baby that she passed off as his." Delacroix had taken a final sip from her takeout cup and tossed it into the trash. "That's on you."

"Thanks." He wasn't looking forward to the prospect, but if it seemed like it was important, he'd deal with what would probably be an even more emotional Mrs. Le Roy.

He glanced around the church and saw Delacroix, four rows up, sitting near a couple of officers in full uniform.

They stood for a final prayer and Reed sent up his own private message to his once-upon-a-time partner.

Hey, Morrisette. Help me out, would ya? I'm running this case and I could use a little of the Texas attitude and smarts right now.

He rubbed the star and almost heard her say, *You've got a new partner now. A cute one. Not as cute as me, of course, and not nearly as smart, that's for damned sure, but you gotta trust her, man. And, for God's sake, quit with the stealing. The key chain? Really?* She laughed

that deep raspy laugh. *Now, leave me alone, would ya?*
I'm up here trying to rest in damned peace! Whatever the
hell that means.

He almost smiled. God, he wished he could really
hear one of her smartass comebacks one last time.

"Amen," Linley said aloud, breaking into his thoughts.

In hushed tones, the congregation echoed discor-
dantly, "Amen."

Reed opened his eyes.

Found Yelkis staring again.

Reed took his wife's hand as they walked out of the
stuffy church and down the front steps to the gray day beyond. The sun was trying valiantly to shine through a
shroud of clouds, and the air outside the reach of the
church's air conditioning was cloying and heavy, threatening yet another summer storm. "Let's get out of here,"
he said.

"Amen," she whispered.

Outside, cops, family and a few friends were gathering on the lawn beneath a canopy of the surrounding
trees. Reed wasn't in the mood for small talk. Nor was he
interested in drinking some kind of weak punch and nib-
bling on cake or sandwiches that were going to be offered
in the church's rec hall. Nor would he put Nikki through
it. And the graveside service was for members of Morrisette's family, which was just fine with him. Reed didn't
need to see the casket lowered into the earth.

Time to leave.

Still holding hands, they headed for his Jeep, when he
heard a woman's voice say, "Nikki Gillette?"

He glanced up and found a blonde with a microphone
thrust forward. Behind her stood a hefty man in his twenties, a shoulder cam aimed at Reed and Nikki.

"I'm Kimberly Mason with WKAM, and I'd like to ask you a few questions," she said, then her eyes found Reed. "And you, as well, Detective Reed. We've spoken before."

He remembered her. As a reporter he actually liked. "This isn't a good time," he said, noticing the red light on the camera.

Shit.

Nikki shook her head. "Not now."

Kimberly's smile tightened. "Oh, come on. Just a few words." And to Reed, "Maybe I can help with your investigation. Get the word out. Someone in our viewership might know something about what happened to those poor victims or even locate the missing Duval girl."

"This isn't a good time," he said.

"It's been reported that you," the reporter said to Nikki, "found Bruno Cravens's body at his home. Is that true? You were there? And his father, too? Were you two togeth—"

"Reed!" a deep voice yelled.

From the corner of his eye he spied Bart Yelkis barreling toward them. Bart was jerking at his tie, his face flushed, anger palpitating off of him. His kids started to follow, but he waved them aside, motioning Priscilla and Toby to stay in a group of mourners who had clustered near the foot of the church steps. While Toby glowered, his sister hid her face behind the veil of her own hair.

"What the fuck are you trying to pull?" Yelkis demanded, reaching into his inner jacket pocket.

Jesus Christ, the man was pulling a gun!

Reed reacted, pushing Nikki behind him, reaching for his sidearm only to remember his service weapon was locked in the Jeep.

"Don't move!" Jade Delacroix stepped into the parking lot, her own pistol drawn and pointed directly at Yelkis.

A woman screamed.

"Gun! She's got a gun!" another woman yelled, and she ran toward the church and the crowd reacted.

"Get down!" a man ordered sharply, while others shepherded people up the stairs and into the church. Others started cars and began wheeling out of the lot, tires screeching, a startled flock of pigeons taking flight.

"Dad! Don't!" Priscilla was running forward, her ashen face twisted in horror. "Please don't!"

Delacroix said, "Stop!" to the girl. But she kept her pistol trained on Yelkis.

Both of Morrisette's kids skidded to a stop.

Delacroix shouted at Yelkis, "Police! Drop your weapon."

"What? No weapon!" Yelkis's hands went straight up in the air. In his right fist he clenched a packet of white papers. "I don't have a gun!" he said. "For fuck's sake, I'm unarmed." The papers started floating to the ground.

The preacher was approaching. "What's going on here?" he demanded.

"Stand back, sir!" Delacroix warned, and slipped a pair of cuffs from her belt. Linley stopped dead in his tracks.

"This is a house of God," he reminded Reed's partner.

"Sir, stand back," she said, eyes trained on Yelkis.

The reporter, who had been frozen to the spot, said to her cameraman, "I hope you're getting all this."

"On the ground," Delacroix ordered.

Several other cops approached, weapons drawn.

Yelkis, some of his anger depleted, dropped to his knees. "What's wrong with you? Are you all nuts?" he said to Delacroix. "It's just legal stuff. Sylvie's will!" He turned his gaze back to Reed, his eyes filled with a hate so intense Reed felt cold inside. "This son of a bitch is supposed to become the guardian of my kids! According to my ex-wife, I'm not a fit father, but fuckin' Pierce Reed is."

"What?" Nikki whispered. "What's he talking about?" Reed shook his head. "I don't know."

"Like hell, you don't know. You were probably in on it. Maybe you and Sylvie had a little something going on the side. It wouldn't have been the first time."

"This is insane," Reed said.

Yelkis's hands were still held sky high, and he was on his knees on the asphalt as he glared up at Reed. "But it will never happen. Got it? Your little plan won't work. The kids are mine and whatever my wife had in her retirement, her accounts, it all goes to me and my kids!"

"Jesus," Reed whispered, then seeing that the camera for the news station was still rolling, turned on the reporter. "Enough, Ms. Mason. We're done here." He grabbed Nikki's hand.

"What is he talking about? What about Sylvie's kids?" she said, and he watched Priscilla marching to Yelkis's truck, her brother limping slightly before running to catch up.

"I really have no idea. None." His phone jangled. He checked the screen and answered. "This is Reed."

"Yeah, Deputy Tina Rounds. I was called over to the scene of a possible suicide." He listened to the officer, but his gaze was fastened on the scene unfolding. Obviously deciding that Yelkis posed no immediate danger, Delacroix slid her gun into the holster at her waist, then pocketed the cuffs while another officer tried to help Yelkis to his feet, just as the first drops of rain from another storm began to fall. Yelkis shook off the policeman's hand, stood and straightened his jacket. Squared his shoulders and narrowed his eyes at Reed. "I'm not done," he warned, then followed his kids to his pickup. All the while Nikki was picking up the scattered papers, a legal document from the looks of the neatly typed pages.

His stomach dropped.

Was Yelkis actually telling the truth?

"You got that?" Rounds was saying, bringing him back to the phone call. "Possible suicide. Gunshot."

"Where are you?"

She reeled off the address. "Male. In his thirties. Woman who called it in says the victim is Owen Duval."

"What?" In the moment everything changed. Nikki, who had come up to stand next to him, her gaze skimming the documents, glanced up suddenly, meeting his gaze.

"I said it sure as hell looks like Duval offed himself."

"You're sure about his ID?"

"That's right. Wallet is still on him and the woman who found him is Helen Davis, Duval's landlord. Positive ID." Reed's heart sank. "I'm on my way." He clicked off. "Son of a . . ." Why the hell would Owen Duval off himself now? Pressure? Guilt?

"What?" Nikki demanded. "Did she say suicide?"

"Possible. Look, I have to check this out." He was already fishing in his pocket for his keys. "Take the Jeep and I'll ride to the scene with Delacroix."

Nikki argued, "I can go with you and—"

"No." He was already motioning to Delacroix, holding up a finger, silently asking her to wait.

"I overheard the victim's name," Nikki admitted.

"Great. Then you know why I have to leave."

"I could come and—"

"No! This is police business, Nikki. I thought we were clear on that."

"Yes, but there's something I want to tell you." The way she said it gave him pause. "Something I did today." She inched her chin up and he knew he wasn't going to like whatever it was she was going to say. He glanced up and saw that the cameraman was still filming, Kimberly Mason at his side.

"Can it wait?" he said to his wife under his breath. Then at the reporter, "This is over. Now."

"It's news." Kimberly Mason's smile had all the sincerity of the Cheshire cat. "You understand." She glanced at Nikki.

"I'll come home directly," he said to his wife.

She wanted to argue, he saw it in her eyes, but she said, "Okay. But it's important."

Isn't everything? He handed her his key ring and noted that Kimberly Mason was still watching intently.

"Reed. You coming or what?" Delacroix shouted.

"It'll have to wait," he said into Nikki's ear. He again held up a finger to Delacroix, silently asking her to wait. "When we're alone."

"Fine, but don't say I didn't try to tell you."

That gave him pause, but he didn't have time to deal

with it now. He handed her his keys. "I'll be home as soon as I can and we'll talk then."

"Remember, we have a deal."

"A deal?"

"Exclusive?"

"Right." He gave a quick nod. "Exclusive," though his stomach tightened when he said it.

CHAPTER 28

Owen Duval?
Dead?
By suicide?
Before she even got to interview him?

Nikki tapped her fingers on the steering wheel and glanced in the rearview mirror. What the hell had just happened? In the few minutes since the funeral service, Morrisette's ex-husband had insisted that she'd left this world naming Reed as the guardian for her children, despite the fact that they had a father. And then Reed had gotten a phone call about another potential homicide that had caused him to leave her with his car and a promise that he'd be home soon.

She knew better than that.

Especially since she thought she'd heard the name Owen Duval from whomever he'd been talking to.

And what was with his keys? He got a new ring with a star on it? Why? Not that it was a big deal, but it was odd.

What isn't?

She put his Jeep into gear and drove home, but in her mind's eye she was at Owen Duval's home, at the crime scene watching the police investigate the suicide. Had the pressure gotten to Owen after all these years? Had the spotlight burned a hole into his soul and he couldn't go on? Had guilt eaten him alive?

With thoughts rattling through her mind, she parked the Jeep in Reed's space in the garage and sat for a second.

Aside from the death of Owen Duval there was the news that Sylvie Morrisette had named Reed as guardian for her kids should she die.

Of course that was only if their father, Bart Yelkis, was dead or incapacitated. Or unfit. That last thought bothered her. Was he able to care for a couple of teenagers? Oh, God, was she?

She went into the house and went through the motions of her life. Greeting Mikado and Jennings, letting the dog out, even throwing a frisbee in the backyard while the cat stalked through the wet foliage, hoping to catch an unsuspecting bird, but her thoughts were miles away, to the idea that she could, under the right circumstances, become the instant mother of grieving teenagers, to Owen Duval and his sudden death. She thought about the apartment that Owen Duval had rented. She knew where it was. Had planned on going there and interviewing him.

So why didn't you? When you had the chance, why

didn't you? Was it because you were healing from the accident in the river, or was it because you were being a good girl and doing exactly what your husband and the cops wanted?

She flung the frisbee past the fountain, skimming the air near a row of azaleas, and Mikado bounded after it, snagging it airborne before it hit the ground. "Good boy," she said, patting him on the head when he retrieved the plastic disk and brought it back. "We'll go out to Mom's place in a few days and you can stretch your legs there." The backyard here was a little cramped, but Mikado didn't seem to mind.

At the mention of her mother, she felt a little guilty. She'd avoided Charlene and told herself she'd visit. Maybe tomorrow. And wasn't there something she wanted to talk to her mother about? Oh, right—the Savannah gossip about the Beaumont family. "Come on," she said to the dog, and spying the tabby in a crouch, tail twitching as Jennings eyed a squirrel running along the top of the fence, she scooped him up and was rewarded with a growl. "You'll live," she told her cat, and carried him inside.

She checked her phone.

No text from Reed.

Nothing yet on the local news feed.

She dialed Millie.

"I figured you'd be calling," Millie said. "Owen Duval."

"You know anything?"

"Just that Metzger hightailed it out of the office around four."

Nikki eyed the digital clock on the stove. 5:17.

"Why was that?"

"I'm not sure. He got a call on his cell phone. Didn't come in through the office, but he's got a source in the police department. I overheard him mention the name. That's all I know. Oh, wait." She paused. "Yep, digital's got it. I just saw it go up on the screen. Looks like next of kin has been notified."

"Got it," Nikki said as her own phone pinged with an update on local news. The feed read: *Owen Duval found dead in his home. Police on the scene. Possible suicide.* "Keep me posted," she said, and cut the connection. "Damn it all to hell."

What was she supposed to do?

Wait here for Reed?

Hope that he would give her inside information on her "exclusive"?

"Fat chance," she muttered just as her phone pinged and a text came in. From her husband:

Don't hold dinner.

Hung up at the scene.

I'll call later.

"Swell, Reed," she said into the phone. "Just swell."

Another text came in. Again from Reed:

You okay?

"No, by the way, I'm not," she said aloud but didn't type the words. "Thanks for asking, but I'm not all that great. Not only am I shut out of this investigation, but you and I, dear husband, are one heartbeat away from inheriting Sylvie Morrisette's children." She sent him an emoji, a thumbs-up.

He responded:

Good.

Lock up.

She sent another checkmark emoji.

"You bet," she muttered. Then to Mikado, who was lying on the ottoman in the family area and staring at her, "Just call me the dutiful little wife. Maybe I should go 'freshen up' for my man, have a drink waiting when he gets home, ask him how his day is going? Seduce him while a pot roast is roasting in the oven?"

She heard herself and rolled her eyes as she realized she was mocking her own mother and Charlene's marriage, which had been far from perfect, but then was there such a thing as perfect wedded bliss? Of course not. And her parents had made it work despite their differences.

She punched out her mother's number and Charlene picked up on the second ring. "Nicole!" she said with a smile in her voice, and Nikki cringed inside, silently promised she wouldn't be so distant. "How're you doing?"

"Fine, Mom. I was just throwing a frisbee in the yard and thought I might bring Mikado out to stretch his legs soon—" Nikki felt even more guilty when she thought of her niece. How long since she'd seen Phee, Lily's daughter? It had been weeks, if not months, and soon she would be starting school again. She was seven now, had lost several teeth and was growing like a weed. "Not today, Mom, but soon. I promise," she said, then sat at the table, where the crumpled pages of Sylvie Morrisette's will and trust agreement spelling out her wishes were scattered. She changed the subject. "So, Mom, can you tell me a little more about the Beaumonts?"

"So this isn't a social call? You didn't just want to catch up," Charlene said, obviously a tad miffed.

"I am working on a story."

"Oh, Nicole. You're married. Want to become a

mother and . . . well, there's no talking to you about this.
I know. I've tried."

Nikki didn't argue. Her mother was right. It wouldn't
do either of them any favors. "You told me once that you
thought Baxter Beaumont was involved with Margaret
Duval."

"They were." She said it as if it were fact.

Okay, time to plunge on. "So was it possible that Margaret's youngest daughter, Rose, was Baxter's kid?"

A pause.

Nikki's pulse ticked up.

"There was talk," Charlene said evenly, "but it was
primarily conjecture."

"Because of Rose's age?"

"Yes, and because she didn't look like her sisters. The
first two were dead ringers, two years apart, but nearly
identical except for size, and Rose wasn't. Now that
could be just a case of genetics. Siblings sometimes don't
look a thing like each other. Look at you and Lily, for example, but the fact that she was a little different, facial
shape, hair not quite as fair as the others, gave the gossip-
mongers more grist for their mill."

Okay, so that told her a little more.

"What do you know about the Channings?" Nikki
asked. "The neighbors of the Beaumonts who have the
vineyards."

"Not much."

"I never saw them at any of the parties we went to at
the Beaumonts'," Nikki said.

"Well . . . that was because of Nell, I suppose. Elea-
nor, her name was."

"Baxter and Connie-Sue's daughter?" The dead girl

who had drowned in the river, the one whose spirit still walked through the woods according to local legend.

Charlene was thoughtful. "It was a long time ago and I wasn't there, mind you, but the way I heard it, the little girl was playing unattended, well, except that her brother was there. He was with the Channing boy, what's his name?"

"Jacob."

"Yes, that's it. They were roughhousing or playing some game in the river, which is dangerous enough, and little Nell tried to join them and somehow unfortunately drowned. Connie-Sue blamed the Channing boy, though according to the police reports, it was just a horrible, horrible accident. A tragedy. Connie-Sue never got over it. Eventually she made Baxter move, and the boys weren't allowed to see each other, at least not that their parents knew."

"You think that Jacob was involved in Nell's death?"

"No, no, I think it was a tragedy. Horrible. And sometimes when a child dies, it's natural for the parents to want to blame someone."

"In this case Jacob Channing."

"Yes."

"What about Tyson? He was there, too."

"But he was their son. Their only son."

They talked a little longer and as she ended the call, Nikki vowed she would visit Charlene this coming weekend. Come hell or high water.

She eyed the clock, read over Sylvie Morrisette's last wishes for the second time and then searched through accounts of Nell Beaumont's death. All the articles came to the same sad conclusion: accidental drowning.

Reed wouldn't be home for hours, probably.

She bit her lip and considered her options.

There was no way she could sit here idle. She remembered the gleam in Kimberly Mason's eye as she, while on her cell phone, climbed into the news van and the big white van took off out of the church parking lot, hot on Reed and Delacroix's tail. That burned her. Then Nikki thought of Norm Metzger at the crime scene trying to interview Reed.

That did it!

She knew what she had to do and it wasn't sit around here and mix martinis or sweep the kitchen floor. She headed to the garage and climbed into her Honda, leaving the Jeep parked in Reed's space. Backing out, she planned her evening. Since she couldn't interview Owen Duval, his story about the night that his sisters disappeared would never change, so she decided to follow up on what her mother had told her and decided to talk to Jacob Channing.

Jacob had been Tyson's friend.

He'd been at the river the day Nell had drowned.

He'd been blamed for Nell's death by Connie-Sue Beaumont.

He lived next door to the Beaumont estate.

And he'd been rich enough to date Ashley McDonnell.

She couldn't wait to talk to him.

"I'm not sure it's suicide," Delacroix said to Reed as they stood over Owen Duval's body. "Check out the back of his hand. GSR's not right."

The victim was slumped in his chair, his right arm hung over the arm rest, a pistol, the obvious weapon that ended his life, on the carpet beneath his fingers. He was dressed in jeans and a T-shirt, his eyes fixed and glassy, his color gray, his mouth open and the round dark hole at his temple encrusted with blood visible.

Reed eyed the back of Duval's right hand—presumably his gun hand.

"There would be more," she said, nodding. "Wait 'til the tests come back."

When he glanced at her, she said, "I took classes about gunshot residue and blood spatter while I was in New Orleans. This is all wrong." Her eyes narrowed on the victim. "Staged. I'd bet my badge on it. And get this. According to the landlady, Owen Duval was left-handed. Like me. Helen Davis said she'd watch him write out checks and saw him hold a hammer or screwdriver when he was fixing stuff for her, like a broken shelf."

Reed looked at the scene. Owen's drink and pill bottles were at the left side of the chair, on a table with the television remote. On the right little table, only a box of Kleenex.

"So you're saying homicide."

"Definitely."

She had a point, he saw it as well.

"Did we find out about forced entry?"

"None noted according to the first cop on the scene."

"Tina Rounds?"

"Yeah."

When they'd first arrived, Delacroix had zeroed in on Rounds, while Reed talked to a couple of cops outside, helping them set up barriers as a crowd of neighbors had already started to gather.

"Rounds checked everything out when she got here. The door wasn't forced, locks not broken, but the window in the bathroom was cracked, and then there's the door between the units; and Mrs. Davis, the widow who owns the place, said she did notice that her side door was unlocked and she can't remember if she left it that way by mistake or not. Originally she thought Owen, here, had left it unlatched."

Reed eyed the surroundings.

Cops were crawling all over the place, taking pictures, searching for trace evidence, going through the place, while the landlady, Helen Davis, holding a one-eyed cat, was just on the other side of the open door that connected this studio apartment to the main house where she lived.

Obviously upset, she walked back and forth from her kitchen to her living area and kept watching what was happening. She'd already given her statement to the first officer on the scene, and the story was simply that she'd returned home a day early from a trip out of town, discovered her cat hungry and without water, so she'd gone to Duval's outside door to ask him about it. He didn't answer, but she'd known his car was parked outside, so she'd gone back through the house, through the usually locked connecting doors and found him as he was. Dead. She'd called 911.

Reed walked through the doorway and introduced himself.

"I told the other officer all I know," she said. A small, round woman with tight gray curls and laugh lines cut into mocha-colored skin, she surveyed Reed as if he might be the devil himself. "I found Owen just as he is now. Dead. The gun there on the floor. I went over to ask him why he hadn't taken care of Romeo here like he promised and, well, really, I was going to give him a piece of my mind. That's no way to treat an animal, don't you know, and there he was." She bit her lip. "He wasn't a bad man, not like everyone says. He was decent, don't you know, went to work every day, paid his rent on time, even helped me out when I needed someone to move the refrigerator when it leaked or change a lightbulb I couldn't reach. He gave me no trouble, not one bit, and so I was surprised when I got home and found Romeo cryin' for his dinner!" She let out a breath and stroked the mottled gray cat in her arms. "Anyway, that's all I know."

Jacob Channing was just locking up the tasting room of Channing Vineyards, which was part of a compound of Italianate buildings with wide eaves and cornices supporting flat tile roofs and spread around a central parking area composed of pavers.

She parked next to his sleek BMW. He looked up and smiled, still a hint of a boyish dimple showing in a square jaw that sported three days' growth of beard. In a tight T-shirt and shorts, he was tall and lean, with deep-set eyes and blond hair that appeared a little unkempt. He had that whole casual, I-look-good-and-don't-have-to-work-at-it vibe going. "I know you," he said. "Nikki Gillette, right?"

"Right."

"And let me guess, you're here because they found the bodies of the Duval girls next door."

"Basically."

"I figured." He unlocked the door of the tasting room. "Come on in." Checking his watch, he added, "You've got twenty minutes. Then I have an appointment with my trainer."

Inside, he walked behind a dark wood bar and found a bottle, two glasses and, without asking, poured. "Sit," he said, pointing to a stool and handing her a glass. Then he pressed a button and classical music began to drift from speakers hidden high overhead. "You may as well have the full experience."

"You drink before working out?"

"I *taste* before working out sometimes." He held out a glass and she took it, sipping the cool white as she slid onto the proffered stool while Jacob remained behind the bar, polished wood separating them. The room had high ceilings, open beams and French doors that opened to terraced grounds, umbrella tables and views of the rows of vines stretching across the slight hill.

Jacob took a swallow, then said, "Look, I don't know what happened to those girls, have no idea. I was surprised as anyone that their bodies were found at the Beaumonts'—actually, I was blown away that they were there and dead. I kinda had this idea that they'd show up sometime, y'know, not that I thought about it all that often. I didn't even know them. They were a lot younger than me."

"Their mother worked over at the Beaumont house. As a nurse."

"A nurse? Oh. For the old lady?"

"Yes, Beulah."

Jacob screwed up his face. "Did she? I don't remember. But then that was probably after I was persona non grata over there. Connie-Sue, she made the edict." His expression darkened. "Blamed me for what happened to Nell."

Here we go, Nikki thought. "Because you were there the day she drowned."

"Yeah, we were all just screwing around in the water and it just happened. She got in over her head, couldn't swim and Tyson saw her, but it was too late."

"So why did Connie-Sue blame you?"

"She had to blame someone, didn't she? Couldn't be her son's fault, or God forbid, hers for not keeping an eye on the kid." He finished his glass in one swallow. "Anyway, the upshot was that I was banned from the property. And eventually they moved and let the damned house fall into ruin." He shook his head. "Who does that?"

"No one else was ever there?"

"After they moved out?" He shrugged. "I wouldn't know. As I said, I was ordered off the grounds and I stayed away." He eyed her and poured himself another half glass. "And if you want to know if I saw anyone carrying any dead bodies up there, the answer is no. And I sure as hell didn't hear anyone screaming or anything. There's acres separating these places, so I guess I can't help you." He took another swallow and glanced at his watch.

She didn't take the hint. "And you knew Bronco Cravens?"

"Yeah, he lives just—lived just across the river." He studied the contents of his glass as he twirled the stem in his fingers. "Shame about him. He wasn't really a bad guy, you know."

"And what about Owen Duval?" she asked, assuming he'd not heard about Owen's death. Nikki decided in this case, and to keep her husband from going ballistic, that discretion was the better part of valor. Jacob Channing wouldn't hear about the alleged suicide from her.

"Owen?" Jacob repeated. "What can I say? Weird dude."

"You think he killed his sisters?"

"What? Hell, no." Jacob shook his head, his pale hair shivering. "He wasn't weird that way, wasn't perverted or anything, at least not that I ever saw, just out of step. Different."

"So did you and Tyson stay friends after his sister died?"

"Kinda. It was never the same, though, but yeah, we hung out sometimes."

"You both dated Ashley McDonnell."

Involuntarily, his jaw tightened. "In high school? Yeah. What does that have to do with anything?"

"Just curious. And she's Owen Duval's alibi."

"I know. Strange, huh?" He seemed genuinely perplexed. "I didn't get it then, but now I think she might have connected with him on more of an intellectual level."

"So you all dated her. You and Owen and Tyson."

"If that's what you want to call it. Ashley and I went out, yeah. Had a thing for a while, or at least I did, but it would never have worked out." Once more he finished his glass.

"Why not?"

"Because she was hung up on Tyson. That's why the Owen Duval thing didn't make a lot of sense to me."

"Because she was hung up on Tyson Beaumont."

"Yeah, I mean, I expected that they'd end up getting married one day. But then I hear that she's marrying some guy she met in college or something. A computer software guy worth a fortune. Kind of blew me out of the water, you know. I didn't even know she and Tyson weren't a thing."

"How did Tyson take it?"

He shrugged. "How does he take anything? How would I know?"

"You were friends."

"Past tense. Remember?"

"But he got over it?"

"Sure. I mean, I guess." He glanced at his watch again. "Hey, I've really got to go." He finished his drink. "I guess you didn't like yours?" he accused, and swiped her glass from the bar.

"No, no. I just don't drink much of anything when I'm driving."

He gave her the oh-sure look but didn't ask if she was pregnant, though she saw the question in his eyes. She didn't explain and hiked her purse strap a little higher over her shoulder.

"He's never married," she observed as she climbed off her stool.

"Who? Tyson?"

"Yeah."

"It's not exactly a crime," he said. "Look at me. I got close a couple of times, but it didn't work out."

"What about Tyson? Has he ever gotten close?"

"Again, you're asking the wrong guy. But I've never heard that he has. As I said, I thought Ashley was the one he'd end up with." He ushered her out and locked the door. "Good thing I'm not a betting man."

He jogged to his sports car and she climbed into her Honda. She wasn't certain he was telling her the truth, or at least not all of it.

Thoughts of their conversation still lingering, she drove down the long lane and out the gates, noting that the BMW was right behind her. She turned toward town and right before the bridge, Jacob blew by her, the sports car roaring past and practically flying over the river.

"Idiot," she said, though of course he couldn't hear her. He was flashy. Flashier than Owen Duval or Tyson Beaumont.

But they'd all dated Ashley McDonnell.

And now one of them was dead. The one for whom Ashley had given an alibi.

She wondered about that and headed to Tybee Island again.

Maybe, now that Owen was dead, Ashley McDonnell Jefferson's story might change.

Owen Duval no longer needed her as an alibi.

There was a chance she could finally tell the truth.

If Nikki could find a way to pry it out of her glossy, tight lips.

CHAPTER 29

The crowd had grown in the two hours since Reed and Delacroix had arrived at Owen Duval's place. Reporters and neighbors clogged the street, making it nearly impossible for the crime scene unit and the ambulance to lumber through. Night was less than an hour away, dusk threatening, the sky showing a few stars as the rain clouds earlier had disappeared. Already the strobing of red and blue emergency lights reflected on the windows of the neighboring houses and pulsed on the boles of the trees lining the street. Reed, standing on the lawn and surveying the front yard where the hastily constructed barricade and several uniformed officers kept the crowd at bay, checked his phone. Three voice mails from Margaret Duval.

"Great." He slid the phone into his pocket. From the tone of her messages, she was nearly hysterical.

"My son?" she'd screamed. "My son is dead? You didn't protect him? I thought you were investigating the case and now he's dead?" She'd begun sobbing and Reed had heard the soft, placating voice of her husband asking her to hang up and go to bed.

Reed raked his hand through his hair. He needed to see Margaret face-to-face to ask her about a possible affair and Nikki's wild assumption that Rose, who was still missing and most likely already deceased, was Baxter Beaumont's child. He agreed the timeline worked, he'd double-checked Margaret's work records against Rose's birth date, but still, it was quite a leap. The thought of accusing her of having a child from an affair, then passing that kid off as her husband's, then losing all of her daughters, the child in question still missing while her son just appeared to have taken his own life seemed like it would be awkward and tasteless and extremely painful.

Then again, this was his job: finding out the truth and serving justice, no matter what.

But right now, he was stuck at the crime scene as Nikki had driven his Jeep home. Delacroix wasn't an option. She was already on her way to interview Duval's attorney, Austin Wells. Not only could Wells speak to Owen Duval's mental state but also to who would benefit financially, if anyone, so they agreed to meet at the station later tonight or early in the morning.

He bummed a ride with Tina Rounds, the deputy who'd been first on the scene, and she drove him to the station, where he'd either grab a department vehicle or have Nikki swing by the station and pick him up. That was definitely option number two as his wife would like nothing more than to show up at the department and nose around.

Nikki and he definitely needed to sit down and talk. Not only about the case and the fact that he had to remind her that he could not be her source, but also that the exclusivity of her story was only good once the case was wrapped up. That could be months and if a trial was involved, possibly years.

What a headache.

And then there was the added pressure of Bart Yelkis and his ludicrous claims that Reed wanted to take his kids away from him. "What the hell did you do?" he whispered, as if Morrisette could hear him.

"Pardon me? You say somethin'?" Rounds asked as they drove into the heart of the city, streetlamps already glowing, traffic moving easily.

"Just to myself."

"Out loud? You know what they say about that?"

"That I'm speaking with an intellectually acute audience?"

She actually smiled. "I was gonna say, the first sign of dementia." But she was kidding, her dark eyes glinting.

"Actually, I think the first sign is giving your wife the car keys and leaving yourself stranded," he said, and Tina Rounds, a tough, by-the-book, always-serious cop, actually cracked a smile and let out a little laugh. "That might be," she said as she wheeled into the station's lot.

Once in the office, he checked a few e-mails, signed out for a vehicle and hit the road. His stomach rumbled as

it had been hours since his takeout pimento cheese sand-
wich that he'd eaten at his desk before the funeral, but he
ignored the feeling and told himself to just get through
the interview with Margaret Duval Le Roy. It would be
tough, but he might just learn something.

Owen Duval's death was a tragedy and, he felt, had
struck a blow to the case, but he couldn't help that it also
tied it together. As he drove the department-issued,
stripped-down SUV to the Le Roys' home, he thought
about the violent deaths related to the investigation:
Holly and Poppy Duval, Bronco Cravens, and now Owen
Duval. Coincidence? He didn't think so.

"Help me out here," he said, and glanced at the empty
passenger seat, imagining Morrisette slumped in it, fiddling with the windows, her eyes narrowed as she stared
out the windshield to the coming night.

"You're on your own here, pardner," she said with
that cocky smile that was so Morrisette. "You're a smart
boy. You figure it out."

"Thanks a lot."

He parked in front of the Le Roy bungalow, lamps
lighting the windows of the little white house surrounded
by live oaks. He cut the engine and looked past the home
to the church, where, again, lamps were burning in the
lancet windows, the steeple, up-lit, a white sword slicing
into the dark heavens. He strode up the walk and pounded
a fist on the screen.

The door behind was opened in a second and Margaret Duval Le Roy stood behind the mesh, her chin
trembling, her eyes puffy and red. "Another one, Detective. Another one of my babies is dead, and . . . and . . ."

She didn't say it, but he read the unspoken accusation in her eyes.

. . . and I blame you.

Ashley McDonnell Jefferson was a hot mess.

Nikki found her sitting on her front porch, her makeup smeared, her face puffy, a barely smoked cigarette dangling between her fingers. When she spied Nikki driving through the still-open front gates she quickly dropped her cigarette into the pot of a hibiscus, burying it quickly, then waving away any lingering smoke as she stood and glared at Nikki as she climbed out of her car.

"What're you doing here?" she demanded, arms crossed over her chest.

"I came to talk about Owen."

"Not now. Not . . . maybe not ever." Ashley blinked and swiped away the tears that began streaming from her eyes. "He didn't . . . he didn't deserve this."

"So you heard."

"It's on the news. Just a few minutes ago. There weren't a lot of details, but from the sound of it . . . from the sound of it, he may have committed suicide." Her voice cracked and she put a hand over her mouth. "I just can't believe it. I mean, I never thought." Sniffing loudly, she pulled herself together. "I'm sorry. You're here why? To talk about him again? I told you everything I know."

"I don't think so."

"What?" she whispered. "But—"

"Your story doesn't make any sense."

"It's—"

"What really happened that night?" Nikki asked. "What happened to those girls?"

"I told you—"

The front door opened suddenly and Zeke, stark naked, his hair wet, grinned wildly. "Mommy!" He raced outside and flung his arms around Ashley's bare legs.

"What're you?" she cried as a man, presumably her husband, holding an orange towel in the shape of a crab, complete with claws and eyes, appeared. "Sorry," he said, looking from Ashley to Nikki. "One escaped."

Zeke squealed in delight as his father tried to scoop him up, but wriggled away. "No, Daddy," he cried, and took off, scampering through the yard, where twilight was descending.

"Gotcha!" Ryan wrapped the towel expertly around Zeke's slippery body and hauled the boy, laughing and flailing, back to the house. Pausing at the porch, he said, "Ryan Jefferson," and stuck out his hand from beneath his giggling son.

"Nikki Gillette." She shook his hand.

"Huh." He looked puzzled, his eyebrows drawing down to the tops of his glasses. "The name's familiar."

"Nikki's a reporter," Ashley said. "She was here before. About Owen."

"Oh. That. A tough one." His expression turned sober. "Well, nice to meet you. I'll leave you to it." He paused in the doorway when Kelsey bounced down the stairs. Her hair, too, was wet, but she was dressed, wearing a lacy lavender nightgown that looked like it belonged to a Disney princess. "Come on, Kels," Ryan said. "Mommy will be in soon."

Kelsey glanced up at Nikki and scowled but didn't say

anything, and Ryan closed the door. Ashley swallowed hard. Her lower lip quivered and she blinked against a new spate of tears.

"They're cute," Nikki said.

"Yeah. Yeah, they are. When they're not being horrible, they're wonderful." Tears filled her eyes again and she said under her breath, "I'm so lucky."

Nikki said, "So tell me what happened to the Duval sisters."

"I don't know," Ashley admitted. "I mean, I look at my kids and I think what Margaret and Harvey must've gone through with the loss of their daughters. I don't think I would survive. And now . . . and now Owen." Tears began to flow again and she looked up to the sky where an egret was soaring over the tops of the palm trees.

Nikki waited, her stomach knotting. She sensed a change in the atmosphere, an altering within Ashley the mother, as opposed to Ashley the teenager who liked to hang out with an outcast boy. Ashley was about to tell her something, but . . . she was still holding back.

"Tell me about Owen," Nikki said softly, and Ashley let out a sob. She put her fist to her mouth and her knees crumpled and she slid down the door. She reached into a pocket of her sundress and dragged out a pack of cigarettes and a lighter.

After lighting up, she sighed, breathing out a cloud of smoke. "It's what I said," Ashley said. "Just about. I did meet Owen that night. We did hang out at my house. My parents were gone. But we weren't together the whole time. I-I shouldn't have lied, but Owen begged me to."

Nikki could barely believe her ears and sat on the step next to her. "So you were with him? For how long?"

"I don't know, but at least a couple hours."

"And the rest of the time?" Nikki asked, her mind racing. What had he done? Where had he gone? What did it have to do with his sisters? The answer was plain as day:

Everything.

Those missing hours when he was not with Ashley were the key to what happened to those girls, why Holly and Poppy were murdered and why Rose was still missing. And probably dead as well. But what had Owen been doing? She wanted to drag the words out of Ashley. "So tell me what happened."

"That's it. He didn't stay as long as he said, and when he went to pick up his sisters they were gone. Missing. He came back to my house, freaked beyond freaked and swore he had nothing to do with it. He begged me to give him an alibi because he was certain the cops would say he was somehow involved."

"So where was he, in the time that he wasn't with you?"

"He never said and I didn't ask. I figured it was smarter not to know. So I didn't mess up my story." She thought for a second, took another puff. "And maybe I didn't want to know."

"Because?" Nikki prodded.

"Because . . . I . . . wasn't sure. I mean, he wouldn't hurt the girls, I knew that, but he might have been involved in something else."

"Like what?"

"I don't know. Something illegal. Maybe weed. He was into it. Anyway, then the police started looking at him, I mean looking at him seriously, and Owen was frantic. He begged me to keep quiet. So . . ." she trailed off.

"So you did. For twenty years."

She bit her lip. "'Til now." She lifted a shoulder. "Look, that's all I have to say. It's probably more than I should have." She put out her cigarette in the planter again, then stood. "Please don't come back here," she said, then walked through the door, and Nikki took the hint and climbed back into her CR-V.

Her heart was beating like a drum, her mind spinning, and she drove away from the house, out the drive and down three blocks to a parking lot for a park, and there she stopped and waited.

Because she didn't trust Ashley Jefferson.

Her confession, about providing Owen with a solid alibi and why she'd done it, came too easily. Was it possible she felt remorse for what she did, that her heart broke for Margaret and Harvey Duval because she, Ashley, was a mother herself? Could it be that Ashley was an emotional wreck and maybe Owen Duval's death had released her from the bonds of her lie about his whereabouts that night?

Even though Owen was now dead, it seemed a little quick to Nikki that suddenly, after twenty years, Ashley McDonnell Jefferson would open up.

There was a chance Nikki was being a little too jaded, that she was suspicious of everyone. But she waited and after twenty minutes turned on the ignition of her car just as she saw the nose of Ashley Jefferson's Bentley SUV appear in the driveway, Ashley at the wheel. She barely stopped as she turned onto the street, heading in the direction of the mainland.

"Bingo," Nikki said under her breath, her pulse ticking up. "Let's just see where you're going."

Perhaps just to the grocery store for a carton of milk or a pack of cigarettes or off to a Pilates class to keep herself in shape.

But Nikki doubted it. No, if she were right, Ashley Jefferson's destination had little to do with her suburban lifestyle or mommy blog and more to do with Owen Duval and the lies she'd spun for him.

CHAPTER 30

Nikki followed Ashley's Bentley through Savannah. She lagged behind the white SUV, maintaining her distance, keeping a couple of cars between her Honda and Ashley's luxury rig while wondering where the woman was going. Once they were outside the city limits, it seemed she was on a beeline to the Beaumont estate.

Of course.

Back to the scene of the crime where those small bodies had been discovered. She thought of Ashley's ex boyfriends, Jacob Channing and Tyson Beaumont, both of whom had lived in the area. Could either of them be involved? Or both? Or someone else?

Owen's death had to be the reason Ashley was on the move.

Right?

Surely—

Her thoughts were interrupted when she saw that the Bentley didn't cross the bridge and continue on toward the Beaumont estate. Instead, Ashley's SUV turned sharply right onto Settler's Road, the narrow country byway where Bronco Cravens's cabin rested on the bank of the river.

What?

Why—?

Bronco's cabin was empty, the man dead, the location of a crime scene, so why . . . ?

"Oh." Nikki understood.

Ashley wasn't heading to the Cravenses' cabin.

Her destination was beyond, past Bronco's home, to the Marianne Inn, which abutted the Cravenses' property on the river side of the road and where this road dead-ended. That had to be it!

But why?

Nikki didn't slow or turn onto Settler's Road for fear Ashley would notice headlights following her. Instead Nikki continued on the main road leading past the winery and the neighboring acres belonging to the Beaumont family. She crossed the bridge, then, on the other side, cut into a wide spot, the tires of her Honda slipping on the loose gravel as she cut a U-ey, turning back on her route and speeding over the bridge. On the far side, she cranked on the wheel and spun onto Settler's Road. "What're you doing, Ashley? Who are you meeting? Who, besides you, cares so much about Owen Duval's suicide?"

Chewing on her lip, her mind filled with questions, Nikki hit the gas over a rise near the Cravenses' cabin, then cut the headlights, using only her parking lights and the moon with its thin glow as her illumination. Scouring the area and squinting into the darkness, she searched for any sign that Ashley was ahead of her, but she saw no red glow of taillights winking through the trees.

Had she been mistaken?

Had Ashley figured out she had a tail and had turned onto this road only to turn around and head in another direction? Could Nikki have lost her already? "Damn," she muttered as she passed by the spur to the Cravenses' cabin and wondered how Bronco had been involved in all of this. What was it that had gotten him killed? Yes, he was a small-time crook, but had he been involved in something that would provoke murder? Nikki couldn't help but think he was dead because he'd been at the Beaumont estate and discovered the bodies. Had he met anyone there? Witnessed something? Been somehow involved? She thought back to the dark afternoon with the grim discovery of the bodies and again conjured the image of the person at the helm of the boat that had been tucked beneath the weeping branches of the willow tree, a boat with the Marianne Inn's distinct script on it.

Maybe tonight she'd finally get some answers.

Easing off the gas, she searched the darkness for a spot to ditch the car. No need to alert anyone that she was nearby. Her parking lights caught a glimmer of reflection. Eyes staring at her from behind a tree.

"Jesus." She stood on the brakes, her heart nearly stopping.

The eyes blinked and then, in a flurry of fur and dark mask, the raccoon scrambled up the tree to a higher branch in the pine.

"Idiot," she said, her pulse still pounding. "Get a grip, Gillette." If she was going to follow Ashley, she had to be calmer, her nerves steady, because who knew what she was about to discover?

Spying a wide spot in the road, she followed twin ruts
barely visible in the thick, dry weeds and rolled to a stop
behind a thicket of saplings and brush and killed the engine, the sounds of the night enveloping her. A chorus of
humming insects was punctuated with the throaty croak
of a frog hidden deep in the surrounding woods. She decided to come clean and sent a quick text to Reed, so he
wouldn't worry:

**Am out doing errands and research. Mikado and
Jennings need to be fed. Back home soon. Love you!**

Not a lie.

Not the truth.

Somewhere in between.

And she'd send him another missive once she knew
what she was getting herself into.

Rather than turn the phone off, she put it into silent
mode.

Maybe you should take a weapon.

*People are dying, being murdered. Remember: some-
one broke into your house just the other night.*

Quickly, she searched her car. No gun, of course. No
hunting knife. Not even a damned screwdriver. Nothing
that would help.

Think, Nikki, think. Find something. Anything!

Scrounging in the glove compartment beneath an
owner's manual and a wad of napkins, she located a
church key bottle opener. "Great," she muttered, pocketing it before spying a box cutter wedged near the small
light in the compartment, one Reed had left there years
before. Not perfect, but better than nothing. And she
hoped she wouldn't need it, prayed that she was over-
thinking the situation as she slid it into another pocket.

"Now or never," she told herself, leaving the car and

feeling that rush of adrenaline that always came with the feeling that she was getting close to the truth, the sense that she was about to cut through the lies, in this case, a web that had existed for over twenty years.

And Ashley Jefferson, Owen Duval's alibi, was the key.

Don't get ahead of yourself. You don't know what's going on. It could be perfectly innocent.

Yeah, right.

As she kept to the side of the road, her eyes ever searching the darkness, Nikki guessed that Ashley, freaked that Owen had died at his own hand, had contacted someone and they had decided to meet out here in the middle of nowhere.

So who?

She thought of Jacob Channing and Tyson Beaumont, both of whom had dated Ashley, and the friends who had made up her clique at school, an elite group who had allowed Holly Duval to be a part of it. Andrea Clancy, Maxie Kendall and Brit Sully. Were they involved?

What about Baxter or Connie-Sue Beaumont?

The names and people kept running through her mind. Who was so damned important she meet that Ashley dropped everything, tore out of her driveway and drove straight here?

Nikki couldn't wait to find out. Anticipation fired her blood.

Hey! Don't get ahead of yourself. This could be dangerous.

People have died, Nikki. Think of Bronco. Of Owen. Of the Duval sisters.

She didn't break stride. No matter what the danger, she had to know, and those who had died deserved, no, demanded justice. Twenty years had passed and in that time the murderer had run free. While two of the Duval sisters had been hidden away in a secret tomb.

But no longer.

She felt it in her bones.

Tonight, come hell or high water, Nikki was going to uncover the truth.

Reed knew the interview with Margaret Duval would be difficult, and he'd expected her to break down at the news of her son's death, but he hadn't expected her to blame him.

"How could you let this happen?" Margaret demanded. Against her better judgment, she'd allowed Reed into her home only at the urging of her husband, who now sat beside her on the couch, holding one of her hands in his. But she was far from comforted. Her lips trembled, her eyes red rimmed, her free hand fiddling with the tiny cross held on a fragile chain around her neck.

Reed, sitting in a chair opposite, said, "I'm sorry for your loss."

"Losses," she snapped, tears tracking down her face. "Losses. They're all gone now! Every last one of my children!" She was beginning to sob, her shoulders shaking. "Why am I being punished?"

Her husband tried to comfort her. "No, Margie, you know—"

"Don't say it was God's will," she warned. "Don't."

"We all have sorrow and—"

"No," she argued. "No, 'we' all don't!" Blinking, she stood suddenly, sniffing and scowling, her mind turned inward. "Was I so bad?"

"Of course not," the reverend said gently. "Oh, honey, you're not bad."

"But I sinned. You know it, Ezra." Margaret was nodding quickly, agreeing with herself as she fussed with the chain around her throat. "You and God."

"Honey, none of us is perfect," he said a little nervously.

"But God is punishing me." She stopped fidgeting to stare at her husband, her gaze locking with his. "That's what's happening. It wasn't enough to have the girls gone, oh, no. That horrible not knowing, the waiting and wondering, the long nights of despair and fear, that wasn't enough punishment for what I've done. Now He wants me to know that they died and how they died. Were murdered! And now . . . now Owen, as well." Her face twisted into a knot of pain, as if she were being physically tortured.

"No, Margie, that's not—"

"Don't placate me, Ezra," she ordered, tears springing from her eyes again. "Don't!" She sniffed loudly. "I'd thought that Rose was still alive, and I prayed that the woman who came forward, the one you, Detective, said was a fraud, was her. But now you're telling me that it was all false hope."

Reed nodded. "Her name is Greta Kemp. She and her husband are con artists."

"Who would be so cruel?" she asked. "And the body you found at Black Bear Lake? Thank God that wasn't my Rosie. Though it's someone's daughter."

"Probably a son," Reed said. "We think a runaway. Male." He didn't say any more than that, but the police were narrowing their search and were waiting to compare dental records to a teen who had run away from a foster home a few years back. How had the boy died? That had yet to be determined, but a drug overdose was likely. Tissue samples might be able to confirm the suspicions.

"You haven't found her, have you?" Margaret asked. "Rose. You still don't know where she is."

"No." Reed shook his head, hoping that his frustration didn't show through, that his expression remained calm, though he was frustrated and still had no idea what had happened to the third sister.

"Margaret, you're asking the detective things he doesn't know," the reverend said, trying to assuage her.

She was having none of it and folded her arms over her chest, stretching the sleeves of her blouse as she walked to the canary's cage and stared at the little bird swinging and twittering on its perch. "It's because of me that she's gone!" Margaret said softly. "Because I sinned. Unfaithful."

"Honey, ssshh. Not now," her husband warned, touching his wife on the arm, trying to quiet her while he said to Reed, "This isn't a good time, Detective. As you can see, Margaret's very upset."

She flung his arm off. "Yes, I'm upset, Ezra. Who wouldn't be? My son is gone. My only son!" She blinked hard and crossed back to the couch. From a side table she plucked several tissues from a decorative box. "Is it true what they're saying? That he . . . that he took his own life?" she asked, her lips trembling.

"We don't know that."

"He . . . he wouldn't!" She was shaking her head and dabbing at her eyes. "He just wouldn't. Not Owen. Nuh-uh. He's a God-fearing boy. He wouldn't have killed his sisters, and he wouldn't have taken his own life. He has— had—his problems, yes, but I know he didn't do this."

Her voice cracked and she closed her eyes, took in a shuddering breath. "It's not Owen who sinned," she admitted. "It's me."

"Oh, no." Her husband was shaking his head rapidly, but Margaret was undeterred.

She squared her shoulders. "I need to tell you something, Detective. Something I probably should have told you years ago about—"

"No, honey!" Ezra cut in, sending a worried look Reed's way. "This isn't the time and you're talking about a family matter. A personal matter. Just between you and the Father, but not . . . not the police."

"Rose was not Harvey's daughter!" Margaret inched her chin upward. "There. I've said it. After all these years."

Reed listened. Waited.

"He, um, Harvey, my husband at the time. He didn't know it." She looked away, out the window. Ashamed. "And Rose . . . she didn't know it, either. Was way too little." She flapped a hand, as if brushing aside any arguments her husband might be making. "But the truth is that Baxter Beaumont and I were . . . we were involved romantically, and I got pregnant and I know Baxter is Rose's father."

"You're certain?" Reed asked as Ezra's lips pursed tight.

"I'm a nurse. That's how it all started. The affair. When I was Beulah's nurse. And of course I had a paternity test done. DNA. There's no doubt about it. Rose is Baxter's child." She straightened her shoulders again, lifting her head almost defiantly as if she expected Reed to castigate her.

So Nikki's wild theory was correct. The room went silent, only the sound of the canary pecking at his little mirror and the hum of the air conditioning making any noise at all.

Margaret was tearing up again, sniffing and touching the corners of her eyes with a nearly shredded tissue. Reed finally asked, "Did your other children know?"

"About Rose's father? No, no one did. Well, except for Baxter, of course, but we . . . we decided it was best to keep it a secret, just between us, at least for the time being. We were both married and his wife, Connie-Sue, she suspected, I think, though it never came up and then time went by and we . . . we ended it, to save our marriages, and then . . . oh, and then . . ." Her voice was getting higher, tears flowing more rapidly. "And then the girls disappeared." She let out a long, unsteady breath. "It's just so hard to think they're all gone." Her face crumpled and her husband came to her, wrapped his arms around her.

"I think we're done here," Ezra said, looking over his wife's shaking shoulder to stare at Reed.

"Just a couple more things," Reed said. "Can you tell me, was Owen left-handed?"

"Yes, all my children inherited that from my side of the family. Even Rose. It was really too early to tell, but she favored her left, ate with it, colored with it, combed her hair with it. And Owen definitely. Like me. Not the least bit ambidextrous."

"Did he have any enemies?" Reed asked, and she turned in her husband's arms.

"Oh, yes," she said, angry again. "Too many to count, but they were all because of you cops and the press. He was your number one suspect when the girls disappeared and the press never let him forget it. The way I look at it, Detective, you've got my son's blood on your hands."

Nikki slipped through the darkness, the smell of the earth and river in her nostrils as she kept to the side of the road. Night had descended. Aside from the silvery glow of the moon reflecting on the river, the area was dark and thick, the noises of the night surrounded her. Crickets chirped, mosquitoes buzzed and a breath of wind whispered through the pines, all normal. All unsettling as she realized how alone she was. She thought about calling Reed but dismissed the thought until she was certain about what was going down. She wasn't going to call her detective husband because Ashley Jefferson had come to the lodge by herself as some sort of personal journey in dealing with her grief over the death of Owen Duval.

Though Nikki expected Ashley to be meeting someone and she believed that whoever it was had something to do with Owen's and possibly his sisters' deaths, she had to be certain. This could, possibly, end up being a wild-goose chase, though deep in her heart, she didn't believe it.

No, she thought, circumventing a branch protruding into the lane, this hastily made journey was about Owen and his siblings. She knew it. She could *feel* it. Whatever meeting was so hastily convened was to do with the Duval girls and what had happened to them.

But cops, her husband included, didn't run on instinct or intuition. They needed cold, hard facts. Evidence.

Well, tonight, if her gut feeling was right, Nikki planned

to serve that evidence, those cold, hard facts, up to them, on the proverbial silver platter!

She smiled to herself, her curiosity, ambition and need to uncover the truth propelling her on.

A bit of moonlight reflected on the puddles as she rounded a wide curve and suddenly the old inn came into view, a dark, looming structure rising two stories. A flat parking area stretched from the massive front door, a wide clearing rimmed by the woods. Nearby, visible through the stands of oak and pine was the river, a wide waterway glinting as moonlight danced over its surface. The roof and chimney were intact, the siding weathered, a wraparound porch encircling the lower level.

Nikki paused, hiding behind the bole of a huge live oak and peering beyond the drape of Spanish moss shifting with the breeze. Though the windows on the upper story were dark, an eerie glow emanated from those on the first floor, and in the unnatural light she spied two vehicles parked near the front door, their bumpers nearly touching the porch rail.

Ashley's white Bentley gleamed with the silvery moonlight and next to it, a large gray pickup with darkened windows.

Nikki's heart dropped.

She'd seen that vehicle before, remembered spying it following her upon occasion. It crossed her mind that she should leave now and text Reed, tell him to come out here, but still, nothing illegal had happened.

Yet.

But they have to be in cahoots. This has to be because of Owen's death.

She still needed more evidence. *So get it. What're you waiting for?*

Pushing all her doubts aside, she inched around the tree, and avoiding the patches of light cast from the windows, she, crouching, made her way quickly to the far side of the inn. Anticipation fired her blood. Who was Ashley meeting?

She considered trying to sneak inside but decided it was too risky. At least at this point.

Maybe she should leave now. Call Reed. Admit to what she'd done. Tell him her suspicions.

Of what?

That Ashley Jefferson after hearing the news about Owen Duval had gone to meet someone at the old lodge? So what?

First, she needed proof that Ashley and whomever she'd come to meet knew far more than they'd admitted.

Finally, Nikki felt, she would have some answers.

You're not going to thwart me any longer, Nikki Gillette.

My thoughts are with the damned reporter as I drive through the night, my nerves tight as bow strings, my breath uneven. There is little traffic, which is a good thing, because I pay little attention to it, don't see the oncoming headlights, brake by rote, the countryside fleeting by, my heart a drum.

I'm not letting you get in my way. I'm coming for you now.

With my foot on the accelerator I glance down at the GPS tracker's screen and smile to myself. "I see you," I say out loud, "and I know where you're going. To the

Beaumont estate. How fitting. Where it all started and now, it will end."

I try to calm myself as I'm itching for this confrontation. I've waited far too long. All of my life seems to have led to this one decisive moment. I lick my lips in anticipation and don't let my mind wander to the aftermath of what I'm about to do. Whatever comes of it, whatever I have to face, I'll deal with it.

Haven't I always?

I glance down at the tracking screen again and I nearly stand on the brakes as I see I've nearly lost her, the blinking dot that represents her car on the screen has turned off the main road. She's not headed to the Beaumont estate? To the scene of the crime? To the tomb in the basement of that decrepit old manor?

I recalculate, thinking there must be something wrong with the tracking device, but I follow anyway, turning abruptly into a lane and spraying gravel, winning the exasperated honk of the van that had been following me. The beams of its headlights catch in the rearview, and for a split second I see my reflection, a fake image because of the colored contacts I wear, the hair dye that casts my hair in a darker hue, the makeup that always covers my freckles and covers the tiny scar near my temple. I probably never needed to take all the precautions. Probably no one would have ever recognized me, but I needed to be certain. I need the anonymity so that I can fulfill my destiny. I can seek retribution.

Me.

For myself.

For the others.

For justice.

And to wash away the guilt I've borne for so long.

In a second, I'm back on the road again, flying over the bridge.

To Settler's Road.

Why here?

I leave the question in my dust and turn onto the narrow country lane and conjure up Nikki Gillette, that nosy reporter's face again, and I speak to her.

"It doesn't matter where you're going. It doesn't matter where you're hiding. I'll find you. I'll track you down like a damned bloodhound and I'll run you to the ground. You won't get away from me." The words calm me and I feel the anticipation coursing through my veins.

Soon, there will be a reckoning.

After all this time, all the years and all the pain, it's about to go down.

My fingers tighten over the steering wheel.

I can't wait!

CHAPTER 31

Streetlights were glowing, the evening warm, a few pedestrians out for evening strolls as Reed turned into his drive, parked and cut the engine of the department-issued vehicle in front of his garage door. He was tired, his muscles weary, even if his mind was still in overdrive.

It had been a long day and was going to be an even longer night. Though he hadn't admitted as much to Margaret Le Roy earlier, he believed that her son's suicide had been staged. If so, Owen Duval had been murdered.

According to statements from the neighbors, they had heard the gunshot and, like so many others Reed had interviewed over the years, Conrad Bell had thought the noise was a firecracker or a car backfiring. He'd been watching TV, had heard the shot, gotten up and looked out his window and seen nothing, heard nothing more.

Too bad. Reed was convinced that Duval had been helped along in his death. But by whom? And why?

Reed rubbed the back of his neck.

Owen's homicide was linked to the discovery of his sisters' remains. Reed was sure of it; he just couldn't prove it yet.

But it wasn't a coincidence that Owen had been killed—silenced?—after the bodies had been located and identified.

There had been no sign of forced entry at Owen's apartment, but Mrs. Davis had admitted to having a spare key "hidden" on the back porch, which made it possible that anyone who had been watching or had some knowledge of the key could have snagged it, let himself in and helped Owen along on his journey to death. There was no doubt that Owen had been drinking, and probably taking a few pills, possibly to bolster his confidence as he may well have been suicidal. Toxicology tests would prove if any drugs had been in his system. As to his mental state? That was something that would be tough to prove. So far no one had indicated that he was depressed enough to have taken his own life.

Reed climbed out of the car.

Margaret Le Roy was right. All of her children with the worrisome exception of Rose were now dead, all victims of homicide. And who knew about the youngest? Whatever Owen Duval had known about Rose's whereabouts had died with him.

"Son of a bitch," he muttered, walking up a short path to the back door, hearing excited barks emanating from the kitchen. He punched the code to the keyless entry to get into the house as his house key was on his key chain, which he hoped Nikki had left inside.

The dog and cat greeted him, Mikado's tail wagging wildly even as he pranced to be let outside. "Been a long time?" Reed asked, dropping his keys onto the table before bending down to scratch the dog behind his ears, then picking up Jennings. "How about you?" he asked the cat, who immediately struggled to get down. "Okay, okay. Yeah, I love you, too." He let both the animals into the backyard, watching as Mikado streaked to a magnolia tree while Jennings slunk through the chairs surrounding the small table where he and Nikki sometimes drank coffee in the mornings or shared a bottle of wine with friends on an evening like this.

So where was she?

As he closed the glass door, he read his wife's text again, texted her back that he was home, then did the same with Delacroix. His partner, too, wasn't responding, and Reed only hoped it was because she'd gotten some new information from Owen Duval's attorney.

Upstairs, he shed himself of jacket, slacks and dress shirt, opting for jeans and a faded T from a rock concert he'd attended twenty years earlier.

Still no response.

Which wasn't all that unusual.

Yet.

Once downstairs in the kitchen again, he opened the French doors. Mikado bounded inside, his tail still whipping back and forth at warp speed while Reed found the animals' bowls and food. Although he was practically tripping over Mikado, the cat was taking his sweet time about returning. "Come on, Jennings," Reed yelled through the open door. "Dinnertime." He opened a can of wet food, mixing it with dry and feeding a ravenous Mikado just as the tabby deigned to stroll inside and sniff before daintily eating.

Reed turned on the TV and checked his phone, rereading Nikki's last communication once more:

Am out doing errands and research. Mikado and Jennings need to be fed. Back home soon. Love you!

And then the heart emoji. That was odd. She wasn't one for gushy notes or hearts and flowers and oftentimes just responded with a checkmark or a thumbs-up emoji.

Don't overthink it. She sent you a text. Heart emoji or no, it's not a big deal.

But he did. He couldn't rein in his thoughts now that they were careening down that dangerous path. He knew his wife too well; had been in too many situations where she and her damned curiosity, her need to write the next crime article in the *Sentinel* had gotten her into trouble. Serious, life-threatening trouble.

"Damn it, Nik," he said as if she were in the room with him. In an instant he realized she wasn't doing errands and research. Not the kind she wanted him to think about. He looked through the windows to the night beyond, where the ambient light of the city permeated the backyard and cast a sheen up into a night where a full moon was rising.

Where the hell could she be?

Had she been going to let him know earlier when she'd said she wanted to tell him something? He tried her number again, but, of course, she didn't pick up.

And then he noticed the voice mail. One that had somehow slipped through, maybe while he was texting. From a number he associated with the department. He hit speaker, set the phone on the counter and listened:

"Hey, this is Rivera in Evidence," the woman said. He knew her: petite, in her fifties with laugh lines near her dark eyes and a quick smile. "I'm lockin' up the case files on Duval and I can't get hold of Detective Delacroix. Been tryin' for a couple of hours. Since you all are her partner, would you pass it along that we need that locket back? I'd like to seal this up with all of the evidence intact, if ya know what I mean. Sheesh. I don't have to tell you this is highly irregular. Tell her to get in touch." With that she hung up.

Reed stared at the phone.

Delacroix had Holly Duval's locket?

That was news to him. Earlier in the investigation, he remembered that she'd gone down to see about the evidence in the Duval case, specifically about the locket. Right? And when she'd come back? He remembered her saying that the locket had been empty. Part of the conversation came back to him because she'd made a bit of a joke:

" . . it wasn't like some kind of Nancy Drew moment when the final and dangerous clue to the mystery is revealed within the clasp of a small piece of jewelry. So I just put it back with everything else."

She'd lied.

Intentionally.

His eyes narrowed. Why? Why would his partner lie to him?

Because she has something to hide? What the hell do you know about her? Only what you've been told. Only what she's told you.

A knot of fear began to tighten in his stomach. She was a recent hire, he did know that much, and the depart-

ment vetted all of their employees, of course. She'd transferred from New Orleans. That's where she'd learned
about blood spatter.

Or so she claimed.

And now both Nikki and Delacroix were missing?

"What the hell?"

Fear galvanized him. He swept his phone from the
counter and snagged the keys to the department's SUV
from the table. He reached for the door, but second-
guessed himself and hurried back upstairs, retrieving his
service weapon and holster. "Not this time," he told the
dog, who looked eagerly up at him. "Walk, later." Reed
had one foot out the door when his phone jangled. He
looked at the screen. Not Nikki. Not Delacroix. A number
with an out-of-state area code. He answered as he shot
out the door. "Pierce Reed."

"Uh. Yeah." A male voice he didn't recognize asked,
"You're the detective, right?"

Reed slowed. "Yes."

"Yeah. Good. I, um, I saw you on TV. You're in
charge of that missing girl case, aren't you? The one
where they found the girls."

Reed froze on the back walk, his toe hitting something
that had wedged between the bricks and the root of an
azalea bush. He bent down, still listening, and picked up
the object, expecting it to be a dog toy. "That's right.
Who're you?"

"Dennis. Dennis Kaminiski. And . . . and uh . . . y'know
twenty years ago, um, I was visiting my aunt in Savannah. I did that every other summer or so."

"Yeah?" Reed said, his interest piquing.

"Yeah. And well, my aunt still lives there, in the Savannah area, and she texted me a news clip where you were asking about a couple of teenagers who were in the movie theater that night. The night those girls disappeared?"

Reed couldn't believe his ears. "You know them?"

"Well, yeah, I am one of 'em. Me and Carl Jetkins, we were at the movies that night, but we weren't supposed to be. We, uh, we snuck in through a side door. Carl, he knew someone who worked there and knew that the security cameras weren't working and that this guy would let friends in the side for free. So we went to the flick and ducked out the same way we came in."

"You saw something."

Reed listened hard. Finally, a break!

"Yeah."

"And you didn't come forward?" He was listening hard.

"I was a kid. Doing a lot of things that I shouldn't. That day I was supposed to be with my grandma. She was out of it, didn't really know I wasn't there. She was in the bedroom, I was in the living room, had the TV on and snuck out. No one was the wiser."

Stunned, Reed listened, barely aware that the object he'd picked up wasn't a dog toy as expected but an e-cigarette.

"Anyway," Kaminiski continued. "I think maybe I saw what happened. A guy came in the same way I did, I think, and took the girls out early. I saw him with two of 'em."

"You mean three," Reed said, trying to reconstruct the events at the theater.

"No, man. Just two. Blond. Girls. Maybe like ten or twelve or so. I just caught a glimpse, you know?"

Reed's attention was laser focused on the conversation with the first witness to come forward in two decades.

"And I think maybe the little one, she was hiding. Carl, he said he saw a kid hiding under the row of seats, you know. He told me as we were leaving and he said he thought she maybe touched his ankle or something . . . I don't really remember, but he was pissed about it. Like, she knocked over his drink or something."

Rosie.

The reason she wasn't taken. Because she wasn't with the others.

"Would you recognize him, the guy who took the girls?"

A pause. Then, "I don't know. It was dark by then and I didn't really know anyone in Savannah. I lived in Cincinnati with my folks. Now, I'm closer. Just south of Charleston. Anyway, like I said, I was only there visiting. And really, I wasn't payin' much attention, just saw this dude slip out with the kids. Didn't think anything of it, y'know? Thought he was with them. It's not like they were struggling or seeming scared or anything. And, to tell the truth, I was just killin' time, avoiding babysitting my nana. Gettin' high." There was a long pause. "I think I heard something about it later, but again I was more into girls and weed and well, whatever. Truth is, I barely made it through high school and, at the time, I didn't really put two and two together. I mean, I didn't want to, right?"

Reed couldn't believe it. This could be the break in the case he'd been waiting for. But he had to keep moving. He glanced down at the Juul still clutched in his hand and, in the light from the fixture over the garage, saw it had lettering on it: TY.

Thank You?

Didn't matter. He jammed the e-cig into his pocket. He didn't have time to think about it. Right now, Nikki might be in trouble.

"Carl Jetkins can confirm this?" he asked, climbing into the department's vehicle.

A beat.

Reed was about to start the engine but paused. "Right?"

"Uh. No, man. Carl's dead."

"Dead?" That stopped Reed cold.

"Yeah, car accident. Like right after that summer."

All of a sudden Reed second-guessed the caller. Could this be a prank call? A phony? Someone just pulling his chain or looking for fame like Greta Kemp, the phony Rose Duval? He heard a baby crying and then a muffled, "Just a sec, honey." More loudly. "Look, I gotta go."

"No, wait."

The baby's cries intensified.

"I really have to go!"

Reed asked, "Are you willing to come to Savannah and give a statement?"

"Sure, yeah. I'm married, got myself a family now. A little daughter of my own. In fact, I'm babysitting her now. I called when the wife was out, didn't want to upset her if she overheard me cuz she doesn't know about any of this, but, yeah, I could probably drive up on Friday, probably, after work. I just don't want Sharon to find out. She'd be beyond pissed."

As if Reed could keep a lid on this. No way. But he didn't have time to warn Kaminiski that the cat was already out of the bag, and probably wouldn't have if he'd had the chance. He heard the baby crying again, screaming at the top of her lungs.

"I really gotta go. I'll come to Savannah. On Friday," Kaminiski promised, and then he was gone.

Reed's mind was whirling, he had a million questions to ask Kaminiski, the first witness who had seen what had happened to the Duval girls. Maybe, just maybe, they would finally be able to put this case to rest.

As he was backing out of the drive, another text came in from Nikki and he hit the brakes. For a second he felt relief, but it was short-lived as he skimmed the message:

At the Marianne Inn. Settler's Road. Get here fast. Be careful!

He pushed the button to speed dial her and held the phone to his ear. The call went directly to voice mail.

Crap. What did that mean?

Nothing good.

The Marianne Inn. What the hell was she doing out there?

The answer was pretty damned simple:

She was in trouble.

Serious trouble.

Possibly life-threatening trouble.

Again.

Delacroix's head was pounding.

Anticipation fired her blood, but she slowed her car as she eyed the screen on the GPS, the red dot on the GPS screen pulsing, but not moving.

It didn't take a Rhodes scholar to realize Nikki had ditched her car.

Damn that woman!

Delacroix had waited too long.

All the planning and all the finessing to get to this point. For what? So that Nikki Gillette could fuck it up?

No way.

This was her case. More importantly, it was her life. She pounded the steering wheel with her fist, then caught herself. *Pull yourself together. You can do this. You have weapons. You have training. More than that you have the need to free yourself of this, the pulse-pounding desire to see this through. You can handle it. Use what you know. Practice the patience the nuns forced upon you. Control yourself like your pious parents demanded of you. Focus the way your instructors explained to you. And examine the situation with the tools all those psychologists gave you. You can handle this. You know what you have to do.*

She touched the locket on the chain that encircled her neck. It gave her strength. Calm. Centered her. She concentrated on her breathing. Slowing it deliberately. Focusing.

Her cell phone beeped again.

On the small screen, she saw Pierce Reed's name.

Again.

Great. Just . . . effing great.

Delacroix didn't need to deal with him, either.

Not tonight. Not when everything was finally coming together.

He would only get in the way.

She ignored the call as she passed by the Cravenses' cabin.

A shame about Bronco. He shouldn't have died. But then, he got curious, snooped around and . . .

She thought about texting or calling Reed.

Lying again.

But then they'd get into it.

And then she might expose herself.

Not yet.

She held on to that mantra as hard as she gripped the steering wheel.

Not yet. Not yet. Not yet!

According to the indicator on her GPS screen, Nikki Gillette's car was parked nearby, so she drove into a spur that dead-ended not twenty yards from the country lane, parked at the base of a live oak, where scrub brush partially hid her vehicle, and climbed out. Snagging her backpack from the passenger seat, she felt the weight of her pistol at her waist, then set off along the side of the road at a brisk pace.

The night was quiet aside from the hum of insects and the lapping of the river.

Undisturbed.

Serene.

But it wouldn't be for long.

No one was answering!

Reed jammed his phone into the cup holder of the SUV.

He'd called his wife multiple times.

Something was wrong. Really wrong.

He knew it and tasted fear rising in the back of his throat.

What the hell was Nikki doing at the Marianne Inn?

He saw the turnoff for Settler's Road and hit the gas, cutting in front of a huge semi heading the opposite direction and getting a loud, angry honk from the driver.

Too bad.

The SUV slid a little, then held and he thought about hitting his lights and siren, then held off. If she was in trouble, he didn't want to warn anyone who might want to harm her that he was coming.

"Son of a—"

He rounded the corner and spied the spur leading to Bronco Cravens's cabin and whipped past. The Marianne Inn was less than a quarter of a mile ahead and he slowed. Nikki's last text came to mind:

Be careful!

This, from the most careless woman he knew. Oh, God, what had she done? His mind flashed to the other times he'd thought he'd lost her, how she'd barely escaped with her life. Too many times to consider and just recently in the river near the Beaumont manor where she'd nearly drowned, how he'd watched her sink below the surface, how Sylvie Morrisette had given up her life while trying to save Nikki. His jaw clenched and his heart was cold as ice. He recalled Nikki in the hospital and how relieved he'd been that she'd been saved, only to hear that his partner had died. Wasn't that enough?

And now? Now, dear God, he knew that Nikki was in danger again. He might lose her all because of her reckless need to ferret out the truth.

His phone rang and he snagged it from the seat. "Reed," he spat out irritably as the call hadn't come from Nikki.

"Yeah, this is Austin Wells." Owen Duval's attorney. "You called me."

"Right." He nodded as if the lawyer could somehow see him through the connection. "I'm looking for my partner. She's not answering her phone. Thought I could catch her through you if she's still at your place."

"Your partner?" Wells repeated.

"Detective Delacroix. I need to talk to her."

A beat.

In that instant Reed felt a new, unnamed dread.

"Detective Delacroix?" Austin said. "She was supposed to be here?"

"To discuss Owen Duval's will."

The attorney snorted. "I don't know what you're talking about. I haven't seen anyone from the police department."

The concerns Reed had been having about Delacroix congealed. Dear God.

"You're sure?"

"Of course I'm sure. Been here all evening. You all have got your wires crossed."

"Thanks," Reed said automatically, but his mind was racing, his jaw set, guts twisting. Where in God's name was his partner?

And more importantly, why the hell had she lied to him?

A floorboard on the old porch squeaked loudly as Nikki reached a window on the back side of the lodge's great room, a window that was open slightly, as if it didn't seal correctly. When she dared peek over the sill, she saw the cavernous great room of the Marianne Inn. The ceilings soared two full stories with a balcony visible on the second floor. A rock fireplace dominated one end of the room and faced a staircase at the far wall. She was able to see all this because of a lantern set on the mantel, over a firebox large enough for a small child to stand inside. The unnatural light cast the Georgia pine walls in an unnatural glow and displayed the remains of a couch, its stuffing tumbling from ripped arms, the pillows scattered haphazardly on the dusty floorboards near the hearth. In the pool of that weird light, Ashley Jefferson squared off with Tyson Beaumont.

So he was behind it all.

Ashley's boyfriend in high school.

Why was Nikki not surprised?

Tyson, the privileged only son of one of the most prestigious and wealthy families in the area. Tyson, born with a silver spoon delicately cemented in his mouth.

Now, they were obviously fighting and Ashley was even more disheveled than the last time Nikki had seen her on Tybee Island, her makeup nearly nonexistent, her hair mussed and falling into her eyes. While her dress was wrinkled, her eyes swollen, her face flushed, he, dressed in camo pants and a black T-shirt, looked military-sharp. He wore a belt, where a gun and what appeared to be a taser, flashlight and some kind of baton were anchored. A pair of night-vision goggles hung from a strap at his neck, and Tyson was as poised as Ashley was emotionally strung out.

Without making the slightest sound, Nikki hit the record button on her phone and gently placed it on the sill next to the open window while silently praying she would not only be able to hear their conversation but also record their every word.

"You crossed the line," Ashley charged, obviously upset, her voice cracking, her eyes shedding tears, an accusing finger jabbing at Tyson's chest. "Owen was off-limits," she said, glowering. "We talked about this over and over."

"And I made myself clear: No one is off-limits." He

eyed her harshly. "Admit it, Ash, you were always hung up on him."

"He didn't need to die!"

"Of course he did."

And there it was. Nearly a confession. Nikki couldn't believe it. Just like that.

"And you were always jealous," Ashley accused. "Which was just . . . ridiculous. You know I was always in love with you. Owen was a friend. A gentle, sweet person. He liked poetry, for God's sake! He didn't deserve this." She was advancing on Tyson, disbelief in her eyes.

"And you always had a thing for him," Tyson charged.

"No, babe, that was the problem. I always had a thing for you. Always. And now look what a mess . . . Oh, God. Can it just stop?"

"Not yet. And Owen was a liability."

"A *liability*?"

"Yes."

"Jesus, Tyson, you are so fucked up. Owen didn't have a mean bone in his body. He was a kind, gentle soul. Do you know how he beat himself up over his sisters? He blamed himself that they were gone!" She threw up her hands and turned her back on him. "And now he's dead. You fucking murdered him."

CHAPTER 32

Tyson's nerves were jangled, every muscle taut. This dark, decrepit lodge with all of its bad memories had been a bad choice to meet, but Ashley had caught him off guard when she'd called him, all freaked out about that damned Duval. And now she'd decided to be a bitch, second-guessing all he'd done. For her. For them. He couldn't believe she was fucking it up, again. He had to calm her down even as his own agitation was creeping up. "Look, babe. Chill. Okay? It had to be done," he pointed out, trying to stay calm, trying not to think that everything he'd worked for was unraveling.

"What? You *had* to kill Owen? Is that what you're saying? God, that's nuts!"

"Don't worry about it. I covered my tracks. The cops will think he killed himself."

Why was she turning on him? Why now? After all this time, all they'd been through together. Didn't she know that everything he'd done, including the murders, he'd done for her? Weren't they in this together? Her reaction to Duval's death was over the top. But then he shouldn't be surprised and he felt his old jealousy rise to the surface. The fact was, he didn't trust her. Not completely. She'd always had a weird fascination with Owen. The truth was that Tyson had only gone along with her idea of giving Owen Duval an alibi because it gave her one, too. It took the heat off her when she was in this up to her pretty neck. Sure, she hadn't known that he'd killed the girls, but so what?

"You don't know what the cops will think," she said, glaring at him, defending Duval even in death.

The muscles at the back of his neck tightened and he fought the rage he'd always battled when it came to Duval. "Face it, Ash. Owen was becoming dangerous. To us."

"Dangerous?" she spat out. "Are you serious?"

"The cops interviewed him."

"Of course they did. He was their number one suspect. Dangerous like Bronco? Jesus, Tyson, why?" Beneath her anger, she seemed genuinely perplexed. "Why kill them? Owen and *Bronco*?"

"He saw me."

"What?" She was staring at him as if she thought he was mad.

"That day that he discovered where we stashed the bodies, he saw me in the boat."

"Whoa—whoa. The day 'we' stashed the bodies? That wasn't my idea. You didn't need to kill those girls, Tyson.

The plan was that you were going to abduct Rose from the theater, just Rose, right?"

Oh. Fuck! She was really going off. Trying to absolve herself, just like she did way back when by marrying that loser Ryan Jefferson. Tyson should have put his foot down then, but at the time, they'd cooled it, trying not to look suspicious, letting people think they'd broken up, but she'd taken it too far.

"We've been over this, Ash. You knew what happened."

"Afterwards. After the mess-up at the theater. You were supposed to abduct Rose—that was the plan. You said you had someone who would take her and so while I was keeping Owen busy, you killed two innocent girls."

"Not so innocent," he reminded her, but he felt a well of satisfaction when he remembered the terror in Holly's eyes just before he choked the life from her, after he'd done the same to her sister.

"You're sick!" Ashley charged. "And besides that, Rose got away."

"Because of Owen Duval. He came back before he was supposed to and found the kid."

"No, Tyson. It wasn't because of Owen. He came back after the movie. We knew he'd do that. It all happened because you messed up. You messed up big-time. And I never agreed to any killing. That was all you."

That much was true. She was never supposed to have known what his true plans were. He'd taken the girls to the mansion, and there in the basement, choked them before placing their limp bodies together, lacing their fingers together in Beulah's old hiding spot, room for a third when he caught her. And only he knew about the secret latch as he'd watched his grandmother open the hidden door in the bricks on more than one occasion. It had been the perfect crypt. Except one of his victims—the important one—had gotten away.

Unfortunately, he'd admitted as much to Ashley years later when he'd had too much to drink at Ashley's fucking wedding reception, an event he'd attended as his family had been invited. It still galled him that she'd gone so far as to marry Jefferson and on the day she'd said her vows, Tyson had made a point of taking her hand at the reception and pulling her behind the vine-clad archway where she'd exchanged "I dos" less than an hour before.

"Just remember," he'd reminded her as he'd brushed a kiss across her cheeks. "You're mine. People have died so we can be together."

"What?" she'd gasped, her eyes rounding in horror as she'd backed away from him, her arm scraping the latticework laden with white roses. The June day had been bright, sun not yet setting, the sky an unreal shade of blue as he'd dropped that particular bomb on her. "No one died," she'd whispered, but the sudden horror in her gaze had told him she believed him.

He'd smiled then, knowing it was an evil, drunken leer, but not caring as he'd teased her. "Oh, come on, Ash. What do you think happened to those girls?" He hadn't explained anything more and avoided her during the rest of the reception, but he'd felt her appalled gaze on him as she'd stood with her new husband, a smile pasted onto her perfect pink-tinged lips. There had been horror beneath her supposed happiness, a darkness hidden deep behind her pure white dress and veil.

He'd loved it.

And he'd felt a greater sense of satisfaction when not

a month later, she'd called and demanded answers. Tanned from a honeymoon in the Bahamas, she'd feigned fury and outrage as they'd met in this very lodge, where he'd admitted that two of the Duval girls were dead, but Rose, their intended target, had somehow escaped, probably, he assumed, due to Owen fucking Duval, who had put it together that his youngest sister was still in danger.

Tyson didn't know for certain but believed somehow, probably inadvertently, Ashley had tipped Owen off.

In many ways, she was a liability.

As much as Holly and Poppy Duval had been.

And now she was acting all high and mighty. Noble. Well, it wasn't flying. Not with him.

"Well, you're in it now, aren't you?" He felt the old rage flare up and as she stared at him he couldn't help but wonder what it would be like if he just grabbed her, pulled her close and let his hands circle her throat, his thumbs pressing hard, cutting off her air, hearing the tiniest of snaps as he choked her like he'd done with that stupid spying Holly Duval and her sister.

Tyson felt a sudden rush of adrenaline in his bloodstream, the anticipation as tempting as sex. Maybe more so. He felt himself growing hard, itching for release of a different kind. He licked his lips and rubbed the tips of his fingers as he fantasized.

But a noise brought him up short. A loud creak that was more than the old lodge settling on its ancient foundation.

"You hear that?" he asked suddenly, his cock shrinking, his gaze narrowing on the window.

"Hear what?"

He strode to the French doors and peered out at the night, to the darkness and a faint ribbon of moonlight seeming to float on the restless water of the river. His eyes narrowed. His ears strained. He felt it then . . . unseen eyes. Boring into him. He held his pistol tight and strode to the window. "I'm telling you, Ash, someone's out there."

Nikki gasped.

She flattened herself to the old floorboards as she heard footsteps approaching the window. Biting her lip, she inched her body sideways and caught a glimpse of Tyson staring out into the night; she didn't dare breathe. She'd heard enough, she could leave now. If she risked retrieving her phone from the ledge.

That would be tricky.

Sweat from the heat of the day and her raw case of nerves trickled down her forehead and nose.

She felt the seconds of the night ticking away with each of her heartbeats, smelled the scent of cigarette smoke and dust flowing out of the small opening beneath the window. And something more. The musky scent of male sweat. Tyson was anxious, worried and now, she knew, had a hair-trigger temper and a lust for killing.

Her throat closed.

The realization that she had drawn her husband into danger struck a terrifying chord in her. What had she written him in her text?

At the Marianne Inn. Settler's Road. Get here fast. Be careful!

But she hadn't said anything about danger, that she was chasing down a psychopath. Reed would be careful, wouldn't he? He was a cop, a detective, and had been in tight places before. He'd know what to do. His instincts were razor sharp, his intuition spot-on.

Inadvertently she crossed her fingers. Despite trying to tell herself otherwise, she couldn't fight the overwhelming sense of dread that she'd lured her husband into desperate, fatal danger.

Tyson glared through the dirty glass to the sultry August night and saw nothing out of the ordinary. But there was someone out there. He was sure of it. He could *feel* the unseen eyes watching his every move. He swiped at the sweat beading on his forehead.

"You're paranoid," Ashley said from in front of the charred, oversize fireplace, where he'd seen his damned father and that whore fucking like damned rabbits so many years ago.

"What?"

"I said, 'You're paranoid.' No one followed me!"

He whipped around, his eyes focused on the woman he'd loved for so long, too long. "Don't," he warned, and he listened hard, still thinking someone was out there, someone intending to ruin all he'd worked for so damned hard for.

"You called me out here," he reminded her. "After that reporter bitch rattled your cage. You could have been followed."

"What? By whom?"

"Nikki Gillette. Face it, Ash. You were played."

"And you're paranoid. This is out of control!"

"We've been through worse."

"Have we?" she charged, and rubbed her arms as if

she'd felt a sudden chill when the interior of this old forgotten inn was sweltering. When she fumbled for a cigarette and shook one from her pack, her hands were trembling.

"Of course we have! Just calm down. I told you the cops are going to think Owen offed himself, so we're clear there." Tyson was thinking. Second-guessing himself. And he hated that. "Everyone knew Duval was nuts, and they'll take his suicide as a confession, that his guilt drove him to it."

"You're out of your mind. Do you think Margaret will let it go? No way." She lit up, took a long drag, then blew out a long stream of smoke. "Not that woman. Did she ever once think to thank me for supplying Owen with an alibi? Hell, no! She twisted it all around and blamed me." Another pull on the cigarette. Another cloud of smoke. "She made my life a living hell."

"A living hell? Out on Tybee? Tennis? Golf? Boating?" He snorted. "If that's hell, count me in!"

"Shut up! You know what I mean!"

"Hey, we're in this together."

"I don't think so. I never signed up for murder. You were supposed to kidnap Rose and find a place for her, a home . . . that was the idea." She squared her shoulders. "Holly and Poppy were never supposed to be a part of it."

"Things evolved." Tyson was calm for the moment, but he was sweating and he felt that small tell-tale tic developing beneath his left eye. He rubbed it with the back of his hand holding the gun, but it remained, a testament to his own tension. They needed to end this. *He* needed to end this. "If Gillette followed you . . . if she's on to us? I'll deal with her."

"Deal with her?" Ashley repeated, obviously distressed as she looked up at the ceiling as if searching for strength or divine intervention. "Oh, God, Tyson. You mean kill her. Jesus, Tyson, listen to yourself. That's always your answer, isn't it? But it has to stop!"

What was she not getting about this? "Ash, it has to be permanent. You know that."

"No! No more!" Ashley's voice was quavering. She took a final drag, then tossed the rest of her cigarette into the firebox, the cig's red ember glowing in the charred remains of a long-ago fire. "There's been too much killing." She was shaking her head, her blond hair shimmering in the lantern's light. "There's been too much." And she looked up at him with accusing eyes. "It all started with Nell, didn't it?"

"Nell? What's Nell got to do with any of this?"

"Didn't it?" she demanded.

What the hell did Ashley know about his sister and how he'd let her drown? It was true Nell had been the first to die because of him, but no one knew about that. Not Jacob, who'd been there, not his parents and certainly not Ashley. She was driving blind. Had to be.

"How dumb do you think I am?" she said, getting to her feet and challenging him. "If you were going to 'take care of Rose' because of your father's damned estate, then why wouldn't you start with Nell?"

"Nell drowned," he said simply, and silently kicked himself for explaining to Ashley years ago about his need to be Baxter's only heir, that he felt the estate, the grounds, the rights, and everything with the name Beaumont in Savannah belonged to him. Now, with Ashley in such an agitated state, her eyes blazing with accusations, there was no reason to confess.

"You were there, Ty." She walked closer, poked a finger at his chest.

"You're crazy."

"Am I?" She was only inches from him now, her face upturned, her lips tight, this woman he'd loved for decades, the girl he'd killed for so they could have a future together. And she was pissed as hell.

"I didn't *kill* my sister," he said, forcing a calm he didn't feel.

"Bullshit!"

She wasn't having it, so he lifted a shoulder. "Look, don't make more of it than it was, okay? I just didn't save her. And it happened years ago. So let it go, Ash. It's over."

He heard what sounded like a scrape outside. Fuck! He glared at the window. Was he going crazy? Or was there really someone out there? The hairs lifting on the back of his arms warned him of an unseen danger and he took a step toward the grimy panes only to spy a rat dart toward the fireplace, its tail slithering behind it as it scrambled into a crack in the mortar. He started for the window once more.

"You killed her," Ashley accused again, and he stopped dead in his tracks. "Your own sister."

"I already told you. I just didn't—"

"Save her. I know. But you could have," she charged, as if any of this was a surprise. "You were on the damned swim team!"

God, Ash was getting irritating, and this old lodge with its creaking beams and scurrying rodents was getting to him. "It's not like I held her head down in the water."

"Isn't it?"

He remembered Nell flailing in the river, struggling to keep her head up, her wet hair floating on the water's surface as she gasped. No one noticed but Tyson and he'd decided in a split instant of understanding about the rest of his life, and what it meant to be an only child, a single heir, what it would mean if he just let her lose her battle. "Like you care. It was a million years ago."

"Right." Ashley stared at the lantern as if it were a crystal ball, capable of predicting the future, while the lodge settled, ancient timbers creaking, the wind whistling through a partially open window. Somewhere far away he heard the hooting of a lonely owl. It all gave him a case of the creeps. How had he and Ashley, the only woman he'd ever loved, fallen so far from each other? And why didn't she understand they were in it together and it was good, was for the best.

When she finally spoke, it was with less venom. "Maybe I didn't care then. About Nell." She swallowed hard. "And maybe I didn't want to believe it. It was easier not to think about it. But that was a long time ago, before I had children of my own."

"Oh, Jesus. Don't go all Mother Teresa on me, babe. It's too late now."

But she was on a roll. "And then . . . then it was different with Holly and Poppy. You didn't just let them die, didn't let nature take its course like Nell and the river. Nuh-uh. You killed them, Tyson. You strangled those two little girls and hid them in the basement, like a dungeon, that's what the press is saying. When I didn't know . . . didn't want to know the details, I could pretend that it was all just a bad dream, that it hadn't really happened, but now . . ." Her voice cracked.

"It had to be done."

"They were just kids!"

"They knew, babe. Remember? I told you. Holly found out about the old man and Margaret. She was a snoop and she came here, following her mother to this very place." He gestured broadly to include this huge building with its warren of bedrooms surrounding this wide common area and stale, horrid memories. "This is where Dad and Margaret would sneak off to. They probably did it in every damned room and Holly knew. And if she knew, you can bet your sweet ass Poppy did, too. I'm just lucky I caught Holly up here that day, that I found out she'd seen them." He remembered that hot summer day. "It was like a fuckin' circus. That woman who rides the horses and gives lessons? Chandra Whatever?"

"Johnson. Maxie's mom."

"Yeah, right, right. She was here, too. Rode right on by like she was in a damned Fourth of July parade." Tyson felt the old anger and worry about being discovered that he had on that sweltering day. "I don't think Chandra saw anything. Well, except maybe Holly. But that was the problem, Holly was peering through the window and she watched her mother going at it with my dad and she, like, burst into tears." Tyson should have taken care of Holly right then and there, he thought, before she put two and two together and figured out why her youngest sister didn't look like Poppy or herself, but he hadn't been able to take a chance. As it was, he'd ducked quickly behind a jagged stump, hiding in the brush and stirring up a hornets' nest. He'd been stung twice and bitten his lip to keep from crying out before the damned horsewoman had ridden into the woods.

"You're a monster," Ashley whispered.

"And you?"

"I didn't plan anything like this, you know it."

"What I know is that if you hadn't tipped Owen off somehow, if he hadn't come back for Rose and taken her away, if he'd left her in the goddamned theater or let her go home, I might have had a chance to—"

"To kill her, too," she finished for him. "But I didn't—"

"You did! You knew, damn it. And you were a good girl, keeping your mouth shut, not even confiding in your husband."

"Don't bring Ryan into this," she warned.

"Oh, come on, babe. As if you care." He walked over to her, bent down and sat on his haunches so he could look her in the eye. "You only married him because you didn't want anyone to suspect we were together. Just in case this all came out." He touched the side of her face with the muzzle of his gun and she didn't even flinch because that was the thing about Ashley, one of the things he loved about her. She was drawn to danger, liked the adrenaline rush of it all, the reason she'd agreed to go along with his plan all those years ago. Well, that and the promise of a fortune once his old man kicked off. How lucky for her she'd found a husband, a cover, with enough money to keep her happy.

If not satisfied.

She, like Tyson, was a restless soul and that, more than anything else, had bound them together for more than two decades. He drew the pistol down her jawline and she just stared at him with those wide, curious eyes. God, he was getting hard just looking at her. "It didn't hurt that he had a buttload of money."

"Stop it!" She threw herself to her feet and, lighting another cigarette, walked to the window at the front of the house.

"We're in this together," he reminded her, following her to the window, hearing the floorboards groan against his weight, smelling the dust mingling with the acrid scent of burning tobacco. As he reached her, he wrapped his arms around her and pulled her tight, wedging her firm buttocks into his crotch, letting her feel his erection as it began to harden.

"Stop," she whispered, but didn't sound convincing.

He didn't. Instead he pressed his gun between her breasts, and she didn't push him away. Because she wanted him. Yeah, she was angry, but oftentimes over the years her anger had sparked to passion. Hot. Intense. Heating his blood. As it did now. That was the thing about Ashley. She always wanted him. He nuzzled the side of her neck and she moaned, tossing her head back.

"I hate you."

"You're a liar." He kissed her nape, touched his lips to the shell of an ear. "And a bad one."

"My lies saved your ass," she reminded him. She curled a finger over the barrel of the pistol and said, "Those girls did not need to die."

Who was she to get so uppity, so goddamned right-eous?

"Collateral damage," he said with a sneer, and walked away from her. God, didn't she get it?

"Because it was Rose you really wanted."

"She's Dad's only other heir. Right? We've discussed this about a million times." He threw her a disbelieving look. "Don't be so high and mighty, Ash. It's like you're trying to play the virgin after fucking the whole damned football team!"

"I'm telling you, all this killing's got to stop!"

"It will!" he snapped, then caught himself and softened his voice, made it a little more cajoling. "I promise, babe. Then when this is all over, you can get the divorce and we can be together."

"And my kids?" she asked, walking back to the fire-place.

"They'll be with us, of course." That was a lie and she probably knew it. Her bratty daughter and son were the problems. After having the first—the girl—that's really when Ashley had changed. When she'd become a mother and gotten all domestic, throwing herself into the role of rich suburban mother of two; she'd even started that stupid mommy blog. "So now," he said, "we have to track down Rose."

"You should have thought of that when you decided to kill Owen!"

"He never would have talked." Tyson knew that much. He closed the gap between them. "Not after keeping it a secret for twenty fuckin' years. And once he knew for sure what had happened to the other two, he would've kept his secret to the grave."

Ashley squashed her cigarette on the hearth. "So why do you care now?"

Was she really that stupid? "Because with all the media attention, someone, somewhere might figure it all out."

"The press?"

"Yeah!" Finally, she was getting it. "And it starts with that fuckin' Nikki Gillette! There was a reason she came to see you tonight, you know. I mean, she already interviewed you, right. And now, tonight she was back. You know she's like a dog with a bone when she goes after someone. And right now she's after you. She's danger-ous. To you. To me."

He looked around the huge, open room, up to the rafters and then again to the windows, outside where he sensed danger lurked. He'd been a hunter for years, had stalked prey in the predawn hours and deep into the twilight. He knew the feel of the forest, the woods, could almost sense another predator, and tonight he was itchy, felt something was off, something he had to right.

"No." Ashley was shaking her head, a new worry appearing in her gorgeous eyes as she understood what he was getting at. "Wait a second. Tyson, what are you saying?"

"Oh, for God's sake. It's pretty simple, Ash. Nikki Gillette needs to be stopped. Permanently."

Nikki bit back a gasp.

She'd stayed too long.

Intrigued by the conversation, by the confessions, she'd lingered on the porch, her phone recording the exchange as Tyson Beaumont had admitted to the murders of the Duval girls, his own sister, Nell, Bronco Cravens, and Owen Duval.

Nikki had what she came for. More than she'd expected. Now, though, it was time to leave.

"Gillette's onto us," Tyson was saying, his voice rising again as he straightened. "That's why she showed up at your place tonight."

"You don't know that." But Ashley's protests sounded weak.

"Yeah, I do."

Nikki reached for her phone and caught another glimpse of the couple inside. Ashley was trying to shake another cigarette from a pack and, finding it empty, had crushed the small box and tossed it into the cold grate. But where was Tyson? He wasn't visible in the room.

Oh, God.

She took a chance and straightened, surveying the interior.

Pistol in hand, Tyson was striding to the French doors leading to this very porch, less than six feet from where she was standing.

Crap!

Nikki's heart started beating double time. She didn't dare grab the phone for fear she would drop it. She stared at the window, saw his nose press to the glass. Oh. Dear. God. Swallowing hard, she shrank back against the wall, silently praying he couldn't see her.

"No one followed me," Ashley insisted, her voice floating through the crack beneath the panes. "Not Nikki fucking Gillette, not anybody."

A minute passed by. Stretched endlessly.

Nikki held her breath. Saw movement in the glass of the doors.

She nearly sprang from the old plank decking but knew he would see her. Would hunt her down.

Counting her heartbeats, ignoring the irritating buzz of a mosquito flying near her head, she waited.

After what seemed an eternity, he disappeared from her field of vision as he walked away from the French doors. Nikki chanced a look through the window again and saw Tyson striding closer to Ashley before he slowly turned, his eyes skimming over the cavernous room, as if he expected to see someone in the shadows. "How do you know you weren't followed?" he asked Ashley.

"I was careful!"

"Nikki Gillette's husband's a goddamned cop!"

Nikki's stomach dropped. He wasn't giving up on this.

"She could have called him. Texted him."

Oh. God. Time to go.

"No one followed me!" Ashley insisted.

"Let's hope to God you're right, but if you're not"—he reached into his pocket and retrieved a small black pistol—"use this."

"What the fuck? Are you crazy?" Ashley cried, recoiling. "You brought another gun."

"I thought we might need a couple of backups."

"A couple?"

"You can never be overarmed."

Ashley was shaking her head. "No . . . no, I do not need a gun."

"You don't know that."

"You're nuts," Ashley accused, but took the small weapon from his hand.

Nikki had to leave. Now! Could she sneak across the deck, let the dark forest swallow her? Race back to the car in the darkness?

No! Just get far enough away and text or call Reed. You have a phone! Just be careful!

"You know how to use it?"

"Do I know how to—are you nuts?" Ashley asked. "Let me think. Point and shoot," she mocked. "Have I got that right?"

Nikki felt a new fear. Now they were both armed. If they found her . . . Oh, Lord. She flattened herself to the weathered siding again.

"You really think I'm nuts?" Tyson demanded, an amused, evil smile in his voice.

Ashley didn't back down. "Paranoid for sure."

"Is that right?"

"Okay, then." Nikki heard the sharp, distinctive click of a clip being shoved into a gun's magazine. "Let's find out."

CHAPTER 33

"Just send backup," Reed ordered, his voice low as he jogged toward the abandoned inn, his cell pressed to his ear. He cut the connection to the department and slipped his cell into his pocket as the night closed around him. A full moon was on the rise, offering a shadowy silver light, and stars winked bright in the vast sky above the tree line, but dread filled his soul. What the hell had the Marianne Inn to do with anything?

Why wasn't Delacroix answering?

Why the hell had she lied to him about the locket, about visiting Austin Wells?

Because she's not the cop she wants you to think she is. He mentally kicked himself for not calling and checking on her himself. He knew a detective in New Orleans— Reuben Montoya. They'd worked together long ago and he could've given Reed the goods on Delacroix. But he hadn't. He'd trusted the department.

Dear God, why was his wife here?

He had a bad feeling about what was going down out here in the woods, a real bad feeling. As he approached the old lodge, he kept to the side of the lane using whatever brush he could find as cover, his eyes searching the surrounding darkness.

Hugging close to a row of live oaks, he rounded a wide bend to a weed-choked clearing where the Marianne Inn loomed on the shore of the river.

Windows on the lower floor of the huge, rambling structure glowed eerily, the upper story steeped in darkness. The inn, like its counterpart the Beaumont manor, was abandoned and falling into total disrepair, though tonight, it seemed, the Marianne was in slightly better shape, most of its windows intact, its chimney not yet crumbling, its wide porch still flanking the structure.

Was Nikki inside?

Dread pounded through him.

His jaw clenched so tight it ached.

He pulled his service weapon from his holster and focusing, trying to keep his emotions under control, hurried forward, surveying the grounds.

Two vehicles were parked near the front door: a dark pickup with smoked windows and a white SUV—a Bentley? With stickers of a family—man, woman, son, daughter, and dog—and a license plate holder announcing: LIFE IS BETTER AT THE BEACH scrawled across the top and TYBEE ISLAND written along the bottom.

The SUV had to belong to Ashley Jefferson.

So what was she doing here, and what did it have to do with Nikki?

His bad feeling was getting worse.

He had no idea who owned the pickup but was about to find out.

As for Nikki's Honda?

Nowhere in sight.

Was that a good sign?

Or an omen?

Her text replayed in his mind:

At the Marianne Inn. Settler's Road. Get here fast. Be careful!

His stomach churned. He had assumed she'd written the text herself. But what if someone else had her phone? What if she'd been coerced into sending it? No—she was clever enough to have added something that would cue him that she wasn't writing it of her own volition. But someone else could have her phone.

Dread propelled him forward as a hundred horrid scenarios of what may have happened to her screamed through his brain, but he couldn't concentrate on them now, couldn't give in to the fear. Not when there was a chance he could save her.

But if she was injured, if anyone had harmed her . . . He'd kill them.

Plain and simple.

You're getting ahead of yourself. Just keep focused.

Jaw set, with deadly intent prodding him forward, Reed eased forward, startling a possum that hissed, showing teeth, round eyes catching the moonlight. Reed stopped and the creature shuffled into the underbrush, disappearing behind a fallen log. Reed kept going, edging along the overgrown lane, his gun in hand, his gaze focused on the lodge.

Lamplight glowed through the dirty windows, figures appearing and disappearing. Two, he thought. A man and a woman. He squinted as he neared, closing in on the wide porch. The woman came into view again.

Ashley Jefferson. Smoking a cigarette. Owen Duval's alibi. What in God's name was she doing here? Who was she meeting? And where the hell was Nikki?

Ashley approached the window and peered through the panes, her nose nearly to the glass. And behind her? Coming up to wrap his arms around her waist and nuzzle the back of her neck?

Tyson Beaumont.

Clutching a gun in the hand he buried between Ashley's breasts. Was she captive? Reed started to step forward and then watched as she let her head fall back, her blond hair shimmering in the lamplight as she allowed him to kiss her exposed throat.

What the hell? They were a couple? From the looks of the way he was holding her, as if he owned her, Reed would guess so. And here they were together, so soon after Owen Duval's supposed suicide.

It smelled rotten.

From the corner of his eye, he caught a movement, something shifting in the umbra. His eyes narrowed and his pulse jumped.

Nikki! His heart tightened.

It had to be Nikki.

What the hell was she doing?

But no—the shape was all wrong. He knew his wife backward and forward, recognized how she walked, how she ran, how she carried herself. But this person? He squinted, his focus narrowing on the movement. The muscles in the back of his neck tightened. This person was definitely a woman, he could see that much, but a shorter, more petite woman than his wife.

A woman he recognized.

A small knot formed in his gut.

What the hell was Delacroix doing here?

And why didn't the sight of her give him a sense of relief?

Hardly daring to breathe, Nikki grabbed her phone from the sill and backed up.

A floorboard groaned against her weight.

"You hear that?" Tyson demanded sharply.

Ashley asked, "What?"

"Something." Through the window, Nikki saw him place a finger to his lips and appear to listen.

Nikki's lungs constricted. She shrank back from the grimy window. Pressed against the siding next to the panes, she heard Tyson's footsteps, thought she felt the ancient floor vibrate as he strode closer to the window.

She held her breath, *sensed* him behind the glass, a thin wall separating them.

She swallowed back her fear, but she knew he was squinting into the darkness, could almost feel the hatred palpitating from him.

As he, intent on taking her life, searched for her.

Her insides turned to jelly and she had to fight back the fear. If she could just noiselessly slide away, creep down the side of the building, toward the river and—

A text came in. Though silent, the phone screen lit.

"What the fuck?" Tyson said, staring out as she

pressed the phone to her body, smothering the screen. A pause. Obviously he didn't know what he'd seen out of the corner of his eye. He said, "Something's not right." She closed her eyes, hoping not to cause any reflection if he angled for a better view of the porch.

Please, God, don't let him see me. She willed herself into the wall and held her breath, not moving an inch as he continued to stare into the darkness.

Nikki's mind screamed: *Run! Run to the river! It's your only way out.*

But it wasn't much of a chance and against her screaming brain, she held back, her back flat against the siding. He had a gun, no, two guns, now Ashley had one, and other weapons and night-vision goggles. If she took off now, he'd find her in a second. He was still uncertain about what he'd seen. So she had to be careful, not tip him off.

"Let's get out of here," Ashley said, and there was movement inside, lighter footsteps.

"I'm not sure it's a good time. I think someone's out there. Waiting for us to make a move."

"Again: paranoid."

"Shut up!"

"Okay, fine," Ashley said angrily. "You stay, but I'm leaving."

Yes, just go. I have everything recorded!

Ashley added, "I can't stay any longer anyway. Ryan will get suspicious. He probably already is."

"Ash, c'mon. You can handle him. Just wait . . ." More footsteps. And the creak of a door opening. The French doors just ten feet away. The ones between her and her escape route to the river. Her throat went dry as sand. In a second he would step onto the porch and then it would be all over. He'd find her and put his damned gun to her head.

Without thinking, she crouched low, beneath the slightly open window, and started creeping along the side wall, moving away from the river and closer to the forest. If she could just vault over the rail.

She caught a glimpse of Tyson, backlit by the lantern as he stepped outside, only a thin panel of glass panes separating them. He snapped his night-vision goggles over his eyes with one hand, while in the other he clutched his pistol.

Oh. Dear. God.

She slipped silently along the wall, rounding the corner of the porch.

"Hey!"

Oh, shit!

Footsteps followed.

"Ash!" he ordered, yelling so loudly his voice echoed through the surrounding forest. "She's out here! Damn it! Cut her off! Go out the front!"

No! Oh, no!

She moved more quickly and then heard the front door moan as it opened.

No!

She was trapped!

She eyed the railing.

There was no time!

Tyson rounded the corner just as she tucked herself into the alcove on the far side of the chimney, the stones pressing hard against her back.

"Shit!" Tyson growled. Stopping. The footsteps no

longer clambering. He must think she propelled herself off the porch!

Nikki shrank inside, willing herself to be smaller.

"Tyson?" Ashley called from the front of the house. Oh, God, she was heading this way. When she turned the corner Nikki would be visible against the old stones!

Just leave, Ashley. For God's sake, get in your car and take off! Please, please, please!

"Shhhh!" he hissed back. Tyson was moving again, the floorboards creaking with each of his approaching footsteps. He was at the corner.

Close. He was so damned close. Nikki's heart thundered, nervous sweat slathered her body. She bit her lip and willed herself to remain still. Unmoving. Pressed tight to the rocks.

But she could hear his breath, could feel him nearby.

She was trapped!

Cowering against the stone wall, Nikki slid her phone into her pocket and reached for the box cutter, a pathetic weapon against a taser, night-vision goggles and a gun. *Two* guns, she reminded herself, two damned guns and two shooters!

Crap!

Think, Nikki, think!

You've been in tight places before!

With trembling fingers she reached into her pocket and withdrew the church key. No match for a gun. But . . .

She hefted the bottle opener's weight and then, hidden from Tyson's view by the chimney stack, flung it as she had Mikado's frisbee, skating the key through the air, whizzing it away from the lodge until it landed with a sharp thud on a tree in the surrounding forest.

"What the . . . ?" Tyson moved. The floorboards groaned.

Go! Go!

But he didn't take the bait. Didn't jump off the porch. Didn't race after the sound, was still only inches from Nikki. She heard his uneven breathing, sensed his indecision.

Go! Chase after it! Fetch, damn you!

"What the fuck?" he whispered under his breath.

Now what?

"Ty?" Ashley called.

"Shh!" he hissed.

Nikki didn't dare breathe. In just a second or two, Ashley would discover her and then she'd be a sitting duck. She had to risk leaping over the rail. It was the only way that she had the slimmest of chances! Oh, Lord. She looked across the railing to the forest not twenty yards beyond. Could she risk it? If she could spring over the rail, drop to the area beneath the deck, then if he was looking for her bolt across the open way into that border of—

As her eyes scanned the woods, she thought she saw something shift. Movement in the dense, dark foliage.

Her heart stilled.

Reed!

He was here! She felt a second's elation, then sudden, horrifying dread.

Tyson had night vision. With his goggles, he could detect not only movement but see images. Oh, God, no.

Reed would be an unwitting target!

That couldn't happen!

She wouldn't let her husband pay for her damned mistakes!

Tyson was shifting again.

Looking into the forest?

Spying Reed?

Even now, taking aim?

"Who the fuck are you?" Tyson whispered under his breath.

He'd seen Reed. Even now was probably locking Reed into his sights. In a nanosecond, Nikki reached into her pocket, her fingers clamping around the box cutter. Noiselessly, she slipped the cutter from her pocket and slid the blade from its sheath. A shallow, but razor-sharp weapon.

Used the right way?

Deadly.

Give me strength.

Pulse pounding in her ears, she dared peek around the corner of the chimney.

Tyson Beaumont was there. Inches from her.

Staring not into the forest, but straight at her!

His gun was level with her head, his night goggles a dark mask on his white face.

"I knew it!" he spat.

She couldn't get around him! Not with the building to her back and him blocking her path. Beneath his goggles, he gave her a dark, evil grin. Gloating. He'd won and he reveled in it. Fear curled her insides. He was going to kill her. Like he'd done with all the others. She knew it.

In that instant Nikki dropped and threw herself at his legs.

"Hey!" Tyson yelled, startled, backing up, juggling his gun.

A deep female voice ordered, "Police! Tyson Beaumont, drop your weapon!"

"What the fuck?" he cried, momentarily distracted as he looked sharply into the woods.

Nikki grabbed hold of one of his thick calves, nearly knocking him over. The gun flew out of his hand and skittered across the decking, dropping between the rails.

"You crazy bitch!"

She sliced upward.

Threw all of her weight into the jab that tore through his pants and buried deep in his groin.

Doubling over, flailing, he squealed in pain. "Eeeee-oooow!"

She let go. Fingers sticky with his warm blood, she threw herself away from him, scrambled to her feet and, placing two hands on the rail, vaulted to the ground. Landing, she swept the area for the gun.

"You bitch. You goddamned fuckin' bitch!" he roared from the decking. "Ash! Shoot her! Shoot her!"

The sound of a gunshot cracked, splitting the night.

Every muscle tense, every sense heightened, Reed sprinted across the parking lot. His gun was drawn, his eyes centered on the lodge, when the front door flew open.

Ashley Jefferson stood in the doorway, backlit by the eerie light from a lantern when a squeal erupted from the porch near the chimney stack. A male in agony, yelling and screaming, "Ash! Shoot her! Shoot her!"

Nikki!

He was too late! Though Reed hadn't noticed her vehicle. She was here. And in trouble.

Weapon drawn, he sprinted toward the lodge, running between the parked cars, and was about to announce himself when he heard Delacroix's voice ordering Tyson Beaumont to stand down.

So she was here?

A shot rang out.

His body jolted.

His gun flew from his hand.

Hot pain scorched his shoulder.

Thud! His head bounced off the passenger door of Ashley Jefferson's Bentley.

White light flashed behind his eyes.

Intense pain blasted through his brain.

He blinked. Trying to grasp on to consciousness. Aware of blood flowing from his arm and the stars in the night sky above him appearing to circle and spin.

A second later, the blackness prevailed.

Another shot.

A bullet zinged past Nikki's head.

Too close!

How?

Where had the blast come from?

Tyson? Ashley?

Or her husband?

God, where was Reed?

But a woman's voice had rung out, demanding Tyson drop his weapon. *Delacroix?* But why was she here? How did she know? Had Reed contacted her?

It doesn't matter. Just run!!!

Frantic, Nikki raced deep into the woods, trying to get some distance from the lodge. Despite being injured, Tyson was still equipped with night goggles, could follow her tracks. She ran wildly, dashing and darting, stubbing her toes, thrashing through the undergrowth that tried to trip her. She couldn't fall. Wouldn't make it easy for him!

"Ty?" Ashley screamed from somewhere near the lodge. "Where are you . . . Oh, Jesus!" She'd reached him, Nikki assumed, but she didn't look over her shoulder, just ran. Fast. Cobwebs and branches slapping her, brush tangling her legs.

Blam! Blam! Blam!

The blasts thundered as he shot wildly, bullets zipping all around Nikki, striking and splintering wood from saplings too close for comfort.

For a split second she wondered about Reed.

Hadn't she seen him? Somewhere out here in the forest?

"Shoot her!" Tyson yelled at Ashley, gasping. "That bitch . . . that . . . fuckin' bitch . . . she tried to cut off my balls!"

"I-I already . . . There was someone . . ."

"For God's sake, Ash! Just fuckin' blow her away!"

Blam!

Tyson yowled again.

"What the fuck?" Ashley screamed. "Who's that? Who the . . . ?"

Another blast. Tyson yowled again. "Run!" he yelled, not at Nikki, but she took off anyway, running headlong to the river.

Oh, God, oh, God, oh, God!

Nikki tripped over an exposed root and went down hard, her chin bouncing on the ground, hard. Jarring her.

Blam! Blam! Blam!

"Who the fuck is shooting?" Ashley screamed just as Nikki reached the river and the sagging pier. At the last moment, she thought of her phone. If she lost it or it became waterlogged it would prove useless. At the last second, she crammed it into the open hull of a canoe.

Something sharp sliced into her palm and she gasped.

God, what?

Too late she realized she'd sliced her hand on a gaff, a long pole that curved into a huge hook and was used to haul big fish into a boat. Obviously it had been forgotten and left to rust in the rotting canoe. Blood bloomed between her fingers. Pain burned in her palm.

Could she use it?

As a weapon?

If she needed to?

Shoot her!

Tyson would stop at nothing to kill her.

She grabbed hold of the hook, swinging it from the boat and deciding if she needed to, she could drop it at any second. But just in case . . .

Why the hell not? She plunged into the cool water, splashing loudly, finding deeper water, then diving.

The gaff wasn't much of a weapon, she thought, slipping into the current.

But it was something.

And all she had.

CHAPTER 34

Adrenaline burned through Delacroix.

Her finger was tight over the trigger as she took aim and fired off several quick shots.

From her hiding place behind a split trunk of a maple, she had watched the horrific tableau unfold, with that prick Tyson Beaumont with his night goggles, taser and gun. He'd come after Nikki Gillette and as Delacroix got her first shot off, he'd attacked. Somehow Gillette had gotten the upper hand, if just temporarily. The reporter had cut him with something, then vaulted over the rail to leave him bellowing like a stuck pig while firing wildly, bleeding and calling for his girlfriend to help him run Gillette to the ground.

But Ashley had hesitated, stopping on the front porch, turning and pointing to shoot at someone or something in the shadows. A man . . . Oh, God . . . it looked like Reed. Of course. His wife had contacted him.

Fuck, fuck, fuck!

Incensed, sick at the thought that Reed had given his life for this shit show, Delacroix had tried to put Tyson down, but her own shot had missed and now she was hiding in the shadows, knowing that he'd seen her in his night vision.

Too bad.

Come on, you son of a bitch, I'm ready.

He was the killer? Tyson Beaumont? Why?

She tried to remember, forcing the jagged memories that had propelled her back to Savannah, to this very spot, to make sense.

Tyson Beaumont. Son of Baxter.

For a split second she closed her eyes and ears, cutting off the harsh shouts, the distant wail of a siren, trying to force the distorted pictures in her mind into clarity. But there wasn't time, and the partial memories refused to meld into anything that made sense.

Move! There's no time for this. Not now. You can piece it together once you've settled the score.

Delacroix took a deep breath and, mind racing, darted through the underbrush. She'd figured that Nikki Gillette was onto something, and had thought by following the reporter, she'd get a new insight into the mystery, but she hadn't expected this. Not a showdown with the killers.

Blam! Blam! Blam!

She threw herself onto the forest floor. Tasted dirt. Felt the shudder of trees as bark splintered off from the shots. Tyson was on to her. She rolled quickly, settled behind a pile of rocks and chunks of rotting wood.

She felt more than a twinge of guilt that she'd gone

behind Reed's back, but she'd known he wouldn't approve of tracking his wife. Delacroix had intended on following her and facing off with her, forcing her to tell what she knew, but she hadn't been prepared for this shit show.

Damn that Gillette.

If she'd only backed off.

Delacroix had tried to run her to the ground first and deter the pushy journalist however she could. The idea had been to catch her trespassing, handcuff her, find out what she knew, then, if Gillette was onto something, she would be neutralized and Delacroix would take down the killer herself.

Because she had her own reasons for dealing with the maniac. Personal reasons.

But she hadn't known that Tyson Beaumont was the murderer.

If only she had.

Maybe they wouldn't be in this no-win, deadly situation.

And now Pierce Reed was down.

Possibly bleeding out.

No way.

Not on Delacroix's watch.

She got her feet beneath her and lifted her head to spy Ashley and Tyson moving to the front of the building. No doubt to finish Reed off. Well, it wasn't going to happen.

Delacroix aimed.

Tyson, backlit by the window, turned.

Too bad. Delacroix was ready to fire into the cocksucker's back, her finger on the trigger.

He twisted his head and looked over his shoulder.

His silhouette was thrown into relief and in that moment, Delacroix's heart nearly stopped. A ragged piece of memory rose to the surface. Nothing distinct. But . . . She blinked, remembered hiding under the seats of the theater, seeing sandals, and feet in flip-flops, purses and candy wrappers and popcorn everywhere. She could almost feel the sticky stuff on the floor as she'd slid beneath the rows only to lose track of her sisters.

As she'd inched along, she'd brushed against the back of someone's leg. "Hey!" he'd yelled sharply, and she'd knocked over his drink, the cola running down the sloped floor, toward the screen where the film, a fairy-tale monster story, was playing, the noise of the donkey's voice so loud. She'd peered around the aisle and seen both of her sisters hurrying to a side exit and a boy in a hoodie standing in the open doorway, the faint glow of a streetlamp at his back as he'd glanced over his shoulder, his youthful profile in relief.

She didn't know him then, didn't understand why they were leaving, but she recognized him now, in an instant.

Tyson Beaumont.

He'd been at the theater.

He'd lured her sisters away.

Her blood ran cold and bile rose up her throat.

Why had he done it? Even now when the repressed memory surfaced, she didn't know. Bits and pieces of that night, memories long abandoned, were teasing at her, and she felt her blood pumping, her heart beating out of control. It was as if she were on a razor-sharp ledge, balancing against falling into the abyss of never knowing, or climbing a sheer mountain to reach a pinnacle of truth that might destroy everything she'd believed, her whole existence.

If she killed Tyson now, she might never know the

truth, a truth she'd been chasing for as long as pieces of
her fragmented memory had erupted. First, just a bit here
and there, but as she'd grown, more and more, the pieces
never meshing with the story she'd been told by her
adoptive parents.

All because of Tyson Beaumont.

You murdering prick.

She aimed at his head, her finger steady on the trigger.

Go straight to hell.

Reed's eyes blinked open and for a nanosecond, he
was lost, aware that he was lying on the ground, gravel in
his hair, his head thundering and his shoulder throbbing.
He was staring up at the sky, a wide black expanse filled
with thousands of stars winking far away.

Where was he?

What was he doing outside in the warm summer night
. . . and then another thought: *Nikki.*

He was here for Nikki.

He heard voices and far away a siren and . . . in a
heart-stopping moment it all came crashing back. His
shoulder was burning because he'd been shot, his head
aching as he'd slammed it against the side of a white
SUV. He was at the long-forgotten Marianne Inn because
his wife was here.

His heart dropped.

Where was she?

And then: Was she still alive?

As his mind cleared, the question burned through his
brain, over and over.

His gun! He had a weapon. It was here somewhere.
He recalled it flying from his hand when he'd been hit. It

was so damned dark, but he thought the weapon had slid beneath the SUV—no, the truck. Pain wracking his body, he scooted under the large rig, his fingers outstretched in the dry weeds and a pool of his own blood. Tucked up against the inside of the front wheel, he found his gun. No doubt Tyson would eventually come to him, to double-check that he was down, to put a bullet through his brain. Well, not without a fight. And not before Reed found out what had happened to his wife. Dragging himself beneath the undercarriage to the side of the truck, Reed eyed the area, then rolled from beneath the rig and crouched beside the wheel, the truck being his cover. His bloody fingers held his pistol in a death grip as he tried to think. If Nikki was inside the house, he needed to free her, but if it was already too late, if that bastard Beaumont had harmed her? It was over.

Tyson Beaumont was a dead man.

Nikki let the river carry her. She held her breath for as long as she could, kept into the darkest of depths, clutching the damned gaff as if it were a lifeline, letting it drag her lower into the cool, calm depths.

Already panicked, she didn't let her mind wander to the creatures that inhabited the river. At this point, no alligator or water moccasin was as deadly or determined as Tyson Beaumont. To think that he'd killed the girls and that Ashley had known it, never divulging the truth and then Tyson had gone on a new, murderous rampage once the bodies were discovered.

Nikki moved quickly downstream, feeling her lungs tighten, then burn before she surfaced, fifty yards from the old pier. Her car would be farther and she was about to sink into the depths again, but her gaze was drawn to the lights of the lodge, winking through the reeds. Her eyes narrowed as she searched the shoreline, heard the water lapping against the pebbles and dirt of the riverbank. Where was Delacroix? Had she survived? Nikki couldn't just abandon her. Both vehicles—the Bentley and truck—were still parked as they had been, near the front doors, so that meant Tyson and Ashley were probably somewhere nearby.

And what about Reed?

You texted for him to come here?

Now, you're going to leave?

Why didn't you try to contact him again before leaving your phone in the canoe?

That had been a mistake. She knew it now. She had to retrieve it and to warn Reed—

Oh, no!

As if by thinking of him, she'd conjured him, she thought she saw him, a dark figure struggling to get to his feet between the Bentley and pickup. But no . . . of course it wasn't him . . . but . . .

Her heart stilled.

She knew her husband.

And what had she expected. She'd told him to come here.

Heart thudding, she moved closer to the shore. An owl sailed over her head, and she heard the faraway sound of a train on distant tracks. Beneath it all was the faint, but distinctive shriek of a siren. Was it getting nearer? She hardly dared hope and right now, she didn't have time to wait for it.

Not with Reed struggling to stand.

Oh, Lord, he was injured.

And it was her fault.

She thought of all the pain she'd put him through, of losing the baby, of Morrisette's death. Now Reed himself.

He'd come here.

Because she'd sent him a text to show up here.

And at the corner of the building, night goggles in place?

Tyson Beaumont, doubled over as if in pain but carefully taking aim.

"Reed! Look out!" she cried.

Bang!

Too late!

Nikki screamed.

Reed fell to the ground.

Oh. God. NOOOO!

Rage bored through her. She plunged through the cattails and reeds, making her way to the shore. On land again, she slunk through the trees, her heart pounding, dread pulsing through her. If Reed were dead . . . her entire world spun on its axis and fell off. She wasn't going to think like that. He had to be alive, she told herself. Had to.

And she had to get to him before Tyson, wounded though he might be, finished him off.

Her fingers curled over the long gaff.

A ridiculous weapon against two guns.

But it would have to work.

It was all she had.

Delacroix moved forward silently.

The pieces were beginning to fall together.

She'd heard about Margaret Duval's affair with Bax-

ter Beaumont and the supposition that Baxter had fa-
thered the youngest Duval child, that he was in fact
Rose's biological father, not Harvey Duval.

Daddy Dearest.

Delacroix thought about that. It made sense in a twisted,
sick way. And gave her own life a new meaning. She'd
spent so many years not knowing, not understanding, and
now it was all coming together—the fractured pictures in
her mind:

Owen shuttling her out of the theater and leaving her,
crying, with strangers.

A dark ride with two arguing strangers, the acrid smell
of cigarettes and beer and then, a few days later, being
left with new people. Kind people. Worried people who
insisted she call them Mama and Papa. Nervous people
who insisted she never talk about what happened in the
"before" time. It had been scary and upsetting and she'd
cried herself to sleep in a room all of her own and deco-
rated with pink bunnies and kitties . . .

Mama and Papa. Her throat closed as she thought of
them and how disappointed they were with her, unhappy
that she'd always wanted to know more, had never totally
forgotten . . .

Owen, her brother, had saved her. Not that she had
understood at the time.

Not that she'd completely put it together, only remembering small moments for years.

Now, though, as she stood in the forest, her splintered
life came together; her hand was rock steady as she pointed
her service weapon at the back of Tyson's head.

Tyson, the one who had taken her sisters.

Tyson, who had choked the life from those little, innocent girls.

Tyson, who had hidden them deep in the bowels of his home, placing their hands together and locking them away in his grandmother's secret crypt.

Tyson, who was her own half brother.

Tyson, the murdering bastard.

Now she knew.

She took a bead on Tyson and nearly squeezed the trigger, when he suddenly whipped around, staring into the darkness, as if he'd heard her. Sensed her presence. "Watch out," he said to Ashley.

He cocked his gun, his eyes, in his night-vision goggles, searching the darkness.

Good.

He'd see her.

Recognize her.

And then, by God, she'd blow him away . . .

"I killed him! I killed him!" Ashley was frantic. "Tyson. We have to go. Oh, God, you're hurt . . . we have to go. Do you hear that? Sirens. They're coming and I killed him."

"Killed who?" he demanded, concentrating on the wilderness surrounding the inn. He'd seen a woman out there, a woman with a gun. She'd fired at him, then disappeared, but the pain in his crotch. He could barely think.

"Go inside," he said.

"No, no! I'm going home. I need a lawyer. You need a lawyer. I killed him, Tyson. Did you hear me, I killed the cop!"

"The cop?" What was she talking about?

"Reed. Detective Reed. He was coming. Right there!"

She flailed wildly with her pistol, gesturing toward the parking area, to her Bentley. "He was out there. And I killed him."

"Just go inside." Tyson needed to think. Things were falling apart. Nikki Gillette had been here and she'd taken off, getting away after nearly neutering him, and then there was the cop in the woods. He'd recognized her. Delacroix, Reed's partner, and now the lead detective himself was here? Ashley was right. They needed to leave.

And go where?

"Tyson Beaumont. Ashley Jefferson. Drop your weapons. Put your hands over your head and—"

Tyson caught a glimpse of her and fired, then dropped to the floorboards. "Get inside," he yelled at Ashley. "Get the hell inside."

"Oh, God . . ." Ashley screamed.

From the corner of his eye he saw a flash of movement. And Nikki Gillette was there, swinging something over her head.

He turned just in time to see the gaffing hook, sharp and deadly, before it slammed into his face, crunching bone, cutting flesh, causing blood to spurt.

He tried to shoot.

Bam!

The blast was deafening and he reeled, feeling his face rip apart, the hook pulling out his cheek with pieces of jaw. Blood filled his eye socket as he stared up and saw Ashley standing over him.

"No more," she said as Nikki Gillette stumbled backward, and he caught a glimpse of Pierce Reed, his weapon leveled at Ashley as he shielded his wife with his bloodied body.

Tyson felt the blood oozing out of him as he lay on the porch, staring up at the rafters, the world growing dark. There was movement, and voices, and a siren so loud it pierced his brain.

His last image was of that younger detective, the one who had been skulking in the woods. "Go to hell, brother," she said to him, and kicked his gun off the porch, into the weeds. "Go straight to hell."

EPILOGUE

October, two months later

With Mikado curled at her feet and Jennings staring out the window to the bare branches of the tree outside, Nikki ignored her cooling coffee and stared at her computer screen. Her attic loft was cozy, a throw covering her legs, the chill of autumn held at bay as she worked on her next book. She'd already written a series of articles on the Beaumont estate, as she'd planned for the *Sentinel*, but the series had been expanded to include the Duval sisters' disappearance and homicides. As Reed had promised, Nikki had been given exclusive interviews and she felt she'd nailed them, enough so that Norm Metzger was talking of leaving Savannah for a sports job in some town south of Tampa, where he could fish and check out spring training.

"Go for it," she said as if Metzger could hear her. Jennings hopped onto her lap and she set her laptop aside to stroke the cat's head.

Some things had turned out surprising. She'd put together that Tyson Beaumont had followed her in his gray truck. He'd been worried that she'd been getting too close. The same had been true with Jade Delacroix, who had placed a GPS monitor on her car as Jade figured Nikki was onto more than she was letting the police department know, which was true enough, and because as irritated as Jade was that Nikki might mess up her own investigation and tracking down of her sisters' abductor, she'd used Nikki to help her uncover the truth.

Reed was still pissed about that.

At the newspaper, Fink was dangling the carrot of her taking over the crime writer's job at the paper, but she wasn't certain she still wanted it. She found working on the true-crime book less stressful and she had more time to delve deep into a story.

She was currently waiting for a call from the Houston police as Greta and Herman Kemp had been picked up for another scam after their attempt to pass Greta off as Rose Duval had failed. What had they been thinking? Didn't they know about DNA?

On a sadder note, the body of the boy found by Frank Mentos at Black Bear Lake had been ID'd as Billy Nichols, a runaway with a history of drug abuse. Toxicology reports had suggested that he'd overdosed, and though his death may well have been acccidental, and he hadn't been the victim of foul play, it was a sad commentary and happened far too often.

As Nikki was trying to piece together a longer, detailed story of the Duval girls and what had really happened for the book, she'd received some of her information from Ashley Jefferson before her attorney had insisted Ashley speak to no one, including Nikki. Ashley, who was currently out on bail, awaiting murder charges for the death of Tyson Beaumont, the man she loved and hated, while her husband, Ryan, was going through the motions of divorcing his wife and demanding sole custody of their children.

"So much for the mommy blog," Nikki said aloud, and Mikado swept the floor with his tail. Ashley was facing other charges as well, all stemming from aiding and abetting Tyson in his abduction and killing of the Duval sisters twenty years ago. And though how Ashley had pieced together that Tyson had killed Bronco Cravens and Owen Duval was still unclear, Nikki's recording of Tyson and Ashley's last conversation was part of the evidence against her. Along with Nikki's testimony.

Tyson's need to be Baxter's only heir had, ultimately, gotten him killed.

And then there was Rose Duval/Jade Delacroix, who, as it turned out, was now the single living progeny of Baxter Beaumont.

Fitting.

Though Jade, on leave from the department pending an investigation into her actions, seemed disinterested in the Beaumont fortune. And there was Connie-Sue, Baxter's wife, who had lost her only son and was dealing with a mental breakdown. She probably wouldn't be welcoming Rose into the family with open arms. But there were ways to cut an unhappy wife out of the lion's share of an estate. If that was Baxter's intent. He, too, had lost his son.

But Jade was an enigma. Two people. An innocent child, robbed of her rightful destiny, and a scheming adult who, Nikki imagined, would stop at nothing to make her way in the world, her own way.

In that respect, Jade/Rose and Nikki were alike. But Jade's actions bordered on the criminal, maybe not only bordered but stepped well over the line between right and wrong. Nikki only bent that line . . . and just a little.

Yeah, right? Who are you kidding? You'd step over just a bit to chase down a story—be honest.

She just wasn't certain how far Delacroix would go, how much of a risk she would take, how deep she would dive into the world of lies and deception.

Maybe it was all she knew.

Nikki glanced outside to the magnolia tree and wondered how long before Jade capitulated to accepting the mantle of being the Beaumont heir, if it were offered. Would she stand by her guns and dismiss a portion of the fortune, or would she give in? Wealth was just oh, so seductive. It would take an incredibly strong person to deny its pull.

But then, who was Nikki to say?

Time would tell.

The reverend's house wasn't home.

And Margaret Duval Le Roy wasn't Jade's mother.

For that matter, Jade was no longer Rose Duval, no matter what any DNA test proved. Yet here she was, sitting on a couch beneath a huge picture of *The Last Sup-*

per, a Bible laid open on the coffee table and a woman who studied every angle of Delacroix's face as if she were memorizing it. She probably was. And her husband, grim-faced but silent, his gnarled hands folded in his lap, sat in one of the chairs near the picture window.

"I just don't understand why you didn't look me up. When you started figuring things out . . ." Margaret took one of Jade's hands and laced her fingers through those of her daughter. "I spent years searching for you. I never let the police let your case go cold, so why?"

"Oh, come on. How could I? I was five," Delacroix heard herself explaining. "I had no way to contact you, I didn't know how, and my parents, they wouldn't even let me discuss it. And then, you know, the years rolled by and the people who adopted me, they didn't want me to think of anything before. It wasn't until I was in college that I decided I had to know. And I figured if I got into law enforcement that I might be able to find out the truth, that there would be ways I could search through records and investigate, so I changed my major, got a part-time job in New Orleans, then transferred here. I knew I was from Savannah and I read enough to realize who I probably was."

"Then you could have just looked me up!" Margaret said, as if it were that simple, as if all the years could be erased, as if she weren't afraid that she might be found out by whoever had stolen her sisters away.

"I was hoping to find Holly and Poppy." She thought of Holly's locket, the one thing she could steal from the evidence department, a bit of the sister she barely remembered. Of course, she'd had to return it and she was in trouble for that, too. Her days as a cop were numbered, but that would be okay. Being a cop and playing by the rules was way too restrictive.

At least for her.

She stared at the canary locked in its cage and pecking at its own reflection and figured the bird probably understood.

"So why the disguise?" the reverend asked.

"I didn't want to come forward until I had all the facts, until I knew what had happened. Until I was ready. And once the other girls were located, I couldn't change my appearance, could I? These days with all of the technology, the computer enhancements, the cameras, I thought it best to stay hidden. As I said, until I was ready for the media circus that was sure to erupt."

Which it had.

She hadn't had a moment's peace since the story had broken, but she'd promised an exclusive to Nikki Gillette, and Pierce Reed had helped her keep some sanity in her life.

Of course, it would never be the same.

"I've missed you, Rose," Margaret said. And she reached up and touched the smallest trace of a scar near Delacroix's temple, the one she now remembered she gave herself while trying to cut her own hair at four, the one she'd covered with makeup and the bow of those stupid clear lensed glasses she didn't need. All part of her disguise.

"I know. But you lied. About me." Jerking her head away, she stared at the woman who had borne her, straight in the eye. "From the beginning. You lied to Harvey. You lied to me. You lied to the world."

Tears glistened in Margaret's eyes. "But I never, not

for one moment, stopped loving you." She sniffed and lifted her trembling chin. "I've lost all of my children but you," she said. "I'm hoping that we . . . we can have some kind of relationship. Start over. I know you have other parents, but they lied, too." That much was true. In her investigation she'd talked to Reggie Scott, Owen Duval's biological father, the man who, along with his girlfriend at the time, had sold Rose. Through a friend of a friend, they'd learned of a couple desperate to adopt a child, by any means possible. Owen had enlisted his father's help and thereby had owed him, having to loan his old man money upon occasion, just to keep Reggie's lips sealed about Rose's whereabouts.

So yeah, Margaret was right, they, too, had kept the truth from her and from the world.

"I'll, um, see what I can do," Delacroix said, and stood. "Look, I gotta go." She'd had enough of the emotional trauma for the day.

"Please, honey." Margaret didn't try to stop her. "Come again. We'll . . . we'll start." She looked to her husband for approval, and the reverend said, "I think it's time we all mended fences."

Maybe so, Delacroix thought, but she wasn't certain as she drove out of town to the Beaumont estate. Ignoring the NO TRESPASSING signs and the flap of yellow tape that still remained wrapped around the trunk of a solitary pine, she hiked back to the old house, through an overgrown rose garden and past live oaks with Spanish moss draped and dancing in the breeze. The house was cold and dark, a crumbling behemoth from another era.

Delacroix broke in, picking a lock and using a flashlight for illumination as she made her way down the narrow stairs and across the moldy basement to the crypt where her sisters had been buried. She opened the concealed tomb with its secret latch and shined her beam over what had been the final resting place of Holly and Poppy Duval, her half sisters.

The truth was she barely remembered them. They'd been older and interested in boys and friends and Rose had probably been a pain to them, a little chattering person they had to babysit or occupy. Be that as it may, Rose was the reason they'd died and that still hurt.

"Sorry," she said, and placed a kiss on the old bricks over the gravesite. "I did the best I could."

They couldn't hear her, of course. They were no longer alive. Their bodies didn't even remain here, but she thought there just could be a piece of their souls left behind.

"I love you," she said to the dank, shadowy cavern, "and I'll always remember you." She felt a cold brush of an autumn breeze filtering through the cracked mortar and touching the back of her neck. She pretended it was her sisters, letting her know that they'd heard her, even if they couldn't forgive.

"I'll be back," she promised, and left, locking up and jogging through the knee-high dry grass and tumbling weeds to her car. She climbed inside, blinked back tears, silently cursed herself for being a sentimental idiot, then switched on the ignition.

The drive back to the city was by rote, her mind caught in a swirl of what-ifs.

What if she had gone with her sisters and Tyson that day?

What if Owen hadn't saved her?

What if Reggie Scott hadn't found someone to adopt her—someone with shady connections who could make the sudden arrival of a five-year-old daughter legal?

What if she hadn't landed the job in Savannah?

What if Wynn Cravens hadn't died and Bronco hadn't found the bodies?

What if, what if, what if?

She'd never know. And, really—it didn't matter. She'd felt a lot of hostility over the years and lately she'd targeted Nikki Gillette. The damned woman had kept getting in her way, so she'd had to use the nosy reporter to help track down the truth. She'd probably even allowed Nikki to get into serious danger, and at times she'd wanted to throttle the nosy reporter herself.

But, of course, she never would have let any real harm come to Gillette.

She thought about that, thought about how razor-focused she'd been to track her down. It had been to stop her, right? So that Nikki wouldn't intentionally or just plain stupidly get in her way.

And just how far would you have gone?

She glanced in her rearview, caught a glimpse of the doubts in her blue eyes and refused to dwell on it. Not now . . . not ever . . . not even if she ended up on a psychiatrist's couch.

She pulled into her parking space, surprised no reporter was camped out near her unit. But then other stories had broken over the past two months and so she was less interesting, thank God. She passed by the leafless trees along the path to her front door and felt lonelier than she had in months. A squirrel scrambled to the top of her roof and scolded her as she unlocked the door and sent him a withering glance.

Inside, Delacroix surveyed her few belongings—a sofa, bookcase, TV and side chair, along with three computers—her passion. The Internet was knowledge and knowledge had led her here.

To the tangled mess that was her life.

A mess that hopefully Austin Wells, her new attorney who had once represented Owen Duval, would help her out of. His fees were astronomical, but then, she really was a Beaumont, if she chose to go that route, and her story was worth a small fortune, one she alone could write despite what Nikki Gillette might think.

She shrugged off her jacket and tossed her keys on the table, then she reached into her freezer and brought out a bottle of vodka. After scooping ice cubes into a glass, she poured herself a shot and stared out the window to the common area, where a mother was watching two toddlers playing hide-and-seek in the shrubbery.

She took a long, cool swallow. Felt the alcohol slide down her throat to settle and warm her belly. She could be a rich woman if she gave a crap. She might be able to find another job as a cop, because she was a good one, but she had too much of a blemish on her career here to think that would happen.

But she could become a PI.

That sounded good.

She sucked in an ice cube and cracked it between her teeth. Then watched the mother gathering her two kids into a double stroller. Her eyes narrowed. She thought about a family of her own.

What if . . .

"Get real." She swallowed another long drink from her glass and looked at the door to her bedroom.

One step at a time, she reminded herself.

She'd start with a dog. She finished her drink and left the glass in the sink. A rescue dog. A big, unwanted mutt. Yeah, that's what she'd do. She'd get herself a dog.

Maybe they could rescue each other.

Reed climbed the stairs to Nikki's office. She looked up from her computer as he appeared and offered him the smile he'd found so intriguing all those years ago.

"Got an errand to run. I'll be back in an hour or so," he said.

"Want company?" she asked, but he knew she was neck-deep into plotting out her next story, that there was already interest in the Duval case from her publisher and she was trying to put the synopsis of the story line together.

"Not this time. I won't be gone long," he said, and didn't want to pique her ever-present curiosity. "I'll be back with takeout. What'd'ya want?"

"Ummm. Surprise me."

"Impossible." He'd been on medical leave since waking up in the hospital, his left arm pinned together by surgeons after his humerus had been shattered by Tyson Beaumont's bullet at the Marianne Inn in August. He was "healing nicely," the orthopedic surgeon had told him, and his physical therapist was putting him through his paces.

"What errand?" she pushed.

"I'll tell you about it later."

"Ooh, so mysterious."

"It's just that I'm late."

"Then, go. Go. I'll see you later," she said as he kissed

the top of her head. He started to walk away, but she grabbed his hand. "You okay?"

"Sure." He nodded. "You?"

She hesitated a beat, her green eyes catching his for a second, a shadow passing behind them. "Yeah, there's still time." She smiled and he believed her. This morning she'd suffered the disappointment of realizing she wasn't pregnant. Again. Each month it got harder and harder, but he told himself as he walked down the stairs, the dog following, Nikki was nothing if not resilient. "I'm letting Mikado out," he yelled up two flights.

"Okay. I'll get him in a few."

Patting his pockets to make certain he had the things he needed, he slid open the door and Mikado took off like a shot, bolting and barking at a squirrel that had the audacity to cross his yard. Hastily the offending rodent scrambled up the magnolia tree to sit and scold the dog, who whined at the tree's base.

Yeah, things were back to normal.

Almost.

He climbed into the Jeep and backed out, then headed across town. Currently he was not only not working yet, but still without a partner. It was his guess that Jade Delacroix, aka Rose Duval/Beaumont, would never regain her job. He wasn't even certain she wanted it.

It was complicated. Her biological parents, Margaret Le Roy and Baxter Beaumont, were still living, but they'd lost all of their other children, and Rose was a painful reminder of all that had been sacrificed.

The ironic twist was that while Tyson had worked so hard to ensure himself to be the sole heir to his family's fortune once his father and mother had died, the girl he'd tried to kill, the half sister who had eluded him, could end up inheriting it all.

"What goes around, comes around," he said, and looked over at the passenger seat as if Morrisette could hear him. He imagined her there, playing with the window buttons, glancing over at him.

"You got that right," she replied as he turned onto the street of the apartment building and parked at the curb under the branches of a pine tree. Checking his watch, he settled in to wait and in that time he thought about Jade Delacroix. Their conversations after the night at the Marianne Inn had been intense.

"You should have been straight with me," he'd charged, back at the station as they were wrapping things up and she was still seated at Morrisette's old desk.

"I couldn't drag you into it." She'd been defiant, nearly belligerent, staring at him with eyes as blue as a mountain lake since she'd ditched her contacts.

"You put my wife's life in danger."

"No, man," Delacroix had argued. "She did that herself. She didn't need any help in that department! I was just trying to piece together my life. And keep her from exposing me before I'd figured it all out. And I wouldn't have hurt her or let anyone else harm her."

"Good to know," Reed had said with more than a bit of sarcasm.

"You realize she's a pain in the butt, right? That *she* could have messed up the investigation."

He hadn't argued.

Delacroix had glared at him. "And it's a good thing I followed her to the lodge. I probably saved her butt."

Maybe.

Still, Reed had trouble understanding the woman who had lied about her identity, who had worked with, yet against him. Yeah, she'd had a vendetta against the person who had kidnapped her sisters and altered the path of her life, but she hadn't needed to dupe everyone else involved.

Or had she?

The jury was still out on that, and he was certain she'd never be a cop again. But she was out of the department and when he went back, he'd be assigned yet another partner. Hopefully one who was a little more forthcoming. Make that a partner who was *a lot more forthcoming and a lot less complicated.*

He tried to convince himself that her intentions had been good.

But he still wasn't certain.

Probably never would be.

He heard the rumble of a huge engine and looked up to spy the school bus lumbering down the street. It stopped in front of the apartment building, its doors opening with a screech. A handful of teenagers piled out, talking and laughing, one lone boy with a backpack, nose-deep in his cell phone, bringing up the rear.

Reed was out of the car and across the street in an instant. Toby Yelkis looked up from his phone.

"I think this belongs to you." Reed tossed the e-cigarette to Toby Yelkis and the kid snatched it out of the air, pocketing it quickly, as if his dad might appear at any second.

"It's not mine." He shifted his backpack from one shoulder to the other as the big bus lumbered noisily away.

"Really?" Reed sent him a look of disbelief. Reed had been waiting for Morrisette's kid and wanted to catch him alone, so he'd waited here, at the bus stop outside of the apartment building that Bart Yelkis called home. "It's got your initials on it." TY. After he'd gotten out of the hospital and found the Juul in his jeans pocket, he'd initially thought the e-cigarette was marked for Tyson Beaumont, but then he remembered Toby at his mother's funeral, that he'd been limping, perhaps because Mikado had tried to take a chunk out of his calf when he'd been in the house.

"I said, 'It's not mine!'" He tilted his chin up belligerently and Reed noticed the peach fuzz on his jawline, acne breaking out over his nose. An awkward age. On the precipice of manhood, where the mistakes you made could haunt you for the rest of your life. Reed remembered.

"I just don't understand why you broke into my house."

"I didn't."

Reed sighed. "I'm a cop, Toby. Don't bullshit me."

"Dad says you want to take me and Priscilla away."

"Nope." Reed shook his head. "Wouldn't do that unless I thought you were being harmed, you know. Or in some kind of trouble."

"We're fine!" More defiance.

"Good." Reed glanced up at the sky for a second, watched a crow land in a bare branch of the solitary pine. "So the next time you come over, knock."

Toby glowered up at him and seemed not sure about what to say. "Your wife killed Mom."

"No, Toby." He met the kid's angry eyes. "Your mother died in the line of duty. My wife wasn't making good choices that day, that's true, but your mom, she did what she was trained to do and it was a horrid accident. If you want to know the truth, I miss her. Every day. And you do, too, but that doesn't mean you break into someone's house, even if it's just to scare her, because you're mad or hurting."

"I . . . I . . ." Toby stared at the ground for a moment, dry leaves scattering with a gust of cool October air. "I never meant to hurt nobody."

"I know that," Reed said, his suspicions confirmed.

"So you're not going to take us away." He needed to hear it.

"As long as your dad is good to you."

"He is."

Reed reached into his pocket and withdrew his key chain. He unclipped his keys and handed the star to Toby. "This is for you," he said, and the kid looked up. "It was your mom's. I've had it for a while. Gave me a little pleasure, you know. Made me think she was nearby. I think she'd want you to have it."

Toby hesitated, bit his lip, snagged the key chain from Reed and rammed it into his pocket. "You mean you stole it."

"Borrowed it." But Reed smiled. "You've got my number, right?"

Toby shrugged.

"Well, you know where I live. We've established that. So, if you need anything or, just you know, want to shoot the shit?"

Toby's head snapped up and he almost smiled. Just not quite.

Reed invited, "Come on by."

"Your dog—?"

"Will be fine with it. Just ring the bell. Don't break in."

Toby didn't answer, his cell phone buzzed and he took off toward the front door of his father's unit as the crow cawed from its wobbly tree limb.

Reed climbed into his Jeep and glanced over at the empty passenger seat. "Don't worry," he said as he started the engine and hoped to hell the ghost of Sylvie Morrisette was still riding shotgun. "I've got their backs."

Dear Reader,

I hope you enjoyed THE THIRD GRAVE. Right now I'm in the thick of writing a new stand-alone novel. *The Girl Who Survived* is a story that I've been thinking about for years. I can't even remember when the idea first hit me.

I wondered what would happen to a very young girl who survives a massacre of her entire family at Christmas. What if she were locked away in a closet by a family member to ensure her safety. What if she could hear the horror going down, but couldn't do anything about it. How would she live through the horror and aftermath? What would the psychological scars be? What about her survivor's guilt? What if what she perceived to be true was actually a lie? Or worse yet, had the figments of her own wild imagination created a false narrative about that horrible Christmas Eve?

The Girl Who Survived took years in the creation. I thought about it off and on while writing other books. It was one of the stories that just wouldn't leave me and was always there, just below the surface, waiting to be told. But it was fragmented with so many different twists and turns in the plot over the years. I was worried that this years-in-the-making story wouldn't come together with the different thoughts I'd had over the years, but once I met Kara, the heroine, the story came together. Damaged and different from many of my heroines, she nonetheless grounded the story. The odd thing is that had I written this book when I first considered the idea I'm sure it would be a different novel than it is today. So, it was worth the wait! Anyway, I hope you pick up a copy and enjoy reading it as much as I love writing it.

As I mentioned earlier, once *The Girl Who Survived* is completed, I intend to jump right into the next New Orleans story with Detectives Bentz and Montoya! Yay! That story is another one where the idea came to me a few years ago, and I can't wait! It will be so much fun writing about my favorite detective team again!

As for the actual dates of publication for these next projects? I'm not sure at this point, but I'll keep everyone posted on my website, Facebook, Twitter and all the social platforms, so check in often.

In the meantime, stay safe and . . .

Keep Reading!

Lisa Jackson

Please turn the page for a sneak peek of
Lisa Jackson's newest novel
THE GIRL WHO SURVIVED
coming soon wherever print and e-books are sold!

CHAPTER 1

Mount Hood, Oregon
Twenty Years Earlier

*C*reeeaaak!

Kara's eyes flew open.

What was that?

She squinted into the darkness.

"Don't say a word."

She started to scream.

But a hand came down over her mouth.

Hard.

"Shhh!"

Marlie? Her sister was holding her down, forcing her head back against the pillows?

She started to struggle.

"Stop it! Just listen and don't say anything!" The

warning was whispered against her ear. Hot breath against her skin. "Listen to me." Her voice was urgent. This was no joke, not the kind of prank Kara had grown up with due to the antics of three older brothers. "Handfuls," her mother called them. "Delinquents," her father had said.

Now, though, it was just Marlie, and she was freaked. "Just do what I say," Marlie warned. "No questions. No arguments. This is serious, Kara-Bear, so don't make a sound."

Why?

As if she read Kara's mind, Marlie said, "I can't explain now, just trust me. You're a smart girl. That's what all the teachers say, right? That you're way ahead of kids your age? So just do as I say, okay? Now, come on."

Kara shook her head, her hair rustling against her pillow, her eyes adjusting to the thin light. Whatever had scared Marlie so much could be handled. Mama would know what to do.

"You can't make any noise, okay? Got that?"

Marlie lifted her hand and Kara couldn't help herself. "What's—?" she started to whisper and Marlie's hand returned. Firmer. Pressing Kara back against the sheets.

"Just listen to me!" Marlie insisted through clenched teeth. Her sharp, desperate plea stopped Kara cold. Though Mama, at times, had accused the older girl of being a "drama queen," this time was different. Marlie was different. Scared to death.

Kara sensed it. She laid still.

"You have to hide. Now."

Hide?

"Right now. Do you understand?"

Wide-eyed, Kara nodded.

"And it can't be here." Marlie started to take her hand away from Kara's face.

"Why? Where's Mama . . . ?" Kara said in a whispered rush. She couldn't help herself.

"Shit! Stop! Kara, *please!*" Marlie's hand was over her younger sister's mouth again. Harder. Forcing Kara's head back into her pillow. "No questions! They'll hear you!"

Who? Who would hear her?

Kara's heart was beating crazily. Fear curdled through her blood.

"Just come with me and don't say a word! I mean it, Kara. There are bad people here. They cannot find you. If they do, they will hurt you, do you understand?" Marlie's face pressed closer and even in their dark bedroom, Kara saw that Marlie's blue eyes were round with fear. She was dressed, in jeans and a sweatshirt, her blond hair pulled into a single braid.

Kara shook her head violently.

"Okay. Now, this is the last time," Marlie warned. "Got it?"

Kara nodded slowly. Scared out of her mind.

"Promise you'll be quiet."

Kara swallowed against the growing lump in her throat, but nodded again.

"I love you, Kara-Bear. . . . I'll come get you. I promise." Marlie hesitated just a second, then withdrew her hand.

Kara didn't speak.

"Okay." Marlie glanced out the window, where moonlight played on the thick blanket of snow, then grabbed

Kara's palm. "Come on!" She tugged, but Kara didn't need any more encouragement. She scrambled to get out of the tangle of bed clothes. They crept past Marlie's bed, where even in the darkness Kara could see several neatly stacked piles of clothes piled over the rumpled coverlet. Even Marlie's boots were on the bed. Now, though, she, like Kara, was barefoot.

So her footsteps wouldn't be heard.

Kara's blood turned to ice. This was wrong. So wrong. She stepped on a toy, probably a Barbie shoe, but held her tongue as Marlie cracked open the door to the hallway.

Along with the scent of wood smoke from the dying fire, the faint sounds of a Christmas carol filtered up from the floor below.

"Silent night . . ."

Marlie peered into the darkness.

"Holy night . . ."

Taking a deep breath, Marlie squeezed Kara's hand and whispered, "Let's go." She pulled her younger sister into the dark, narrow corridor, past the closed doors of the boys' rooms toward the far end of the hall, where the stairs curved down to the first floor, light curling eerily up from below, the massive doors to Mama and Daddy's bedroom just beyond the railing.

"All is calm . . ."

For a second, Kara's heart soared. Marlie was taking her to get Mama and—but no. She stopped at the last door before the staircase leading down, to the door that was always locked, the doorway leading upward to the attic and the warren of unused rooms above.

What?

NO!

"All is bright . . ."

Kara balked. She wasn't going up there! *No, no, no!*

She started to protest when Marlie caught her eye and sent her a look that could cut through steel.

Bong!

Kara jumped at the noise, her heart hammering.

But it was only the grandfather clock near the front door, striking off the hours, drowning out the music.

"Jesus," Marlie whispered under her breath and pulled Kara behind her as she slowly mounted the narrow wooden steps.

Bong!

"Marlie, no," Kara whispered, feeling the temperature drop with each step.

"We don't have a choice!" Marlie snapped, her voice still hushed as they reached the third floor.

Rather than snap on a light, she used the flashlight app on her cell phone, its thin beam sliding over draped furniture and boxes, forgotten lamps and stacks of books, open bags of unused clothes. Her family used the extra space for storage, though according to Mama it had once been servants' quarters. "I wish," Mama had added, lighting a cigarette as she warned all of her "patchwork family" that the area was forbidden, deemed unsafe. "Don't go up there, ever. You're asking for serious grounding if you do. Hear me? Serious."

Her threat hadn't stuck, of course.

Of course they'd all sneaked up here and explored.

Though the area was declared off-limits, her brothers were always climbing up here, and Kara had poked around the rabbit warren of connected rooms often enough to know her way around. But tonight, in the darkness, the frigid rooms appeared sinister and evil, the closed door standing like sentinels guarding the narrow corridor.

Bong!

"Where's Mama?" she asked again, fighting panic.

Marlie glanced at her and shook her head. She placed a finger to her lips, reminding Kara of the need for silence, then pulled her anxiously along the bare floor of the third story.

This was wrong.

Really wrong.

At the far end of the hallway was another staircase, much narrower and close. Cramped. It wound downward and ended up in the kitchen. For a fleeting second, Kara thought they were going down the back way, which seemed stupid since they'd just ascended, but Marlie had other plans. She stopped just before they reached the steps, at the small, cupboard-like entrance to the attic.

Kara's bad feeling got worse. "What are you do—?"

Marlie pulled a key from the front pocket of her jeans and slipped it into the lock. A second later, the attic door creaked open. "Come on."

Kara drew back and shook her head. "I don't want to." Marlie surely wouldn't—

"Don't care." Forcefully, Marlie pulled her through the tight doorway and yanked the door shut behind them.

"What the hell is this?"

"Don't swear."

"But—"

"Look. I'm saving you. Us." A loud click sounded as she flipped the old switch. Nothing happened.

"Shit," she muttered as they stood in the darkness.

"Don't swear," she threw back. "And saving us from what?"

"Shhh. Quiet. You don't want to know."

"Yes! Yes, I do! Tell me!"

"Look, it's . . . complicated." Marlie hesitated.

"And scary."

"Yes, and really scary." She pulled a small flashlight from her pocket and clicked it on so that they could see the stairs winding upward. The steps were steep and barely wide enough for Kara's foot, a rickety old staircase winding to the garret under the eaves. It was freezing in the tight space and dark as pitch.

"I'm not going up there."

"Of course you are. Come on."

This was bad.

Kara's skin crawled and though she wanted to argue, she didn't. The tone of Marlie's voice, so unlike her, made the ever-rebellious Kara obedient as she was prodded up the stairs. Marlie was holding the small flashlight, its weak beam illuminating the path.

At the top of the stairs, under the sloped ceilings where Kara was certain bats roosted, Marlie stopped, leaving Kara standing on the floorboards of the attic, while she hesitated on one step lower, so they were eye to eye, nose to nose. She shined the flashlight near her face, distorting her features in shadow, causing the small dimple on her chin to shadow and creating an eerie mask much like their brother Jonas's face when he held a flashlight beneath his face for a macabre effect as he told ghost stories.

But tonight was different.

Tonight wasn't a game. That much Kara knew.

"You need to stay here and wait for me to come back."

"No!"

"Just for a little while."

Kara shook her head. "I want Mama."

"I know, but I already told you that's not going to happen."

"Why?" Panic welled in her heart. "You're not leaving me here alone."

"Just for a little while."

"No!"

"Kara—"

"I'm not staying here. Why would you even say that?" Kara demanded.

"I just have to make sure it's safe, okay—?"

"No, it's not okay."

"Then I'll come get you. I promise."

"Safe from what?" Kara cried, freaking. Anytime her siblings added an "I promise," it was because they weren't telling the truth. "You said there were bad people here. Who?"

"I-I don't really know."

"What're they doing?"

"I'm not . . . I don't . . . I'm not sure, but I know this, there's something . . . something really bad, Kara."

"What . . . what's bad?"

"I don't know."

"And it's here."

"I . . . yes . . . please, just do as I say."

Kara suspected her sister was dodging the truth. "Where're Mama and Daddy?"

A beat. "Out."

"Liar." Why was Marlie lying to her?

"Kara—"

"What about Jonas and Sam and Donner?" Kara asked frantically. Her older half brothers. They'd all been here earlier. She'd seen them at dinner and after. Donner and Sam had been listening to music and playing video games, maybe even drinking, and Jonas, the loner, had been in his room practicing his ninja moves or whatever it was he always did. Sam had kidded him, calling him Jonas Joe-Judo. Which Jonas hated.

Marlie said, "Everyone's gone."

"Gone?" On Christmas Eve? That didn't seem right. "Then what're you afraid of?"

Marlie licked her nips nervously. Her voice was the merest of whispers. "As I said, there's someone here. Someone else. Someone bad."

"Who? How do you know?" This was crazy. "But you just said everyone was 'out' and now . . . You're scaring me."

"Good."

"I want Mama."

"I told you she's not here!" Marlie's voice was still a whisper, but there was an edge to it. Like Mama's when she got mad or frustrated with Kara's brothers. "Just listen to me, okay? You're going to stay here for a little while until it's safe, and then I'll come back and—"

"No!" Marlie was going to leave her here, in the middle of the night, all alone?

"Just for a while," Marlie was saying again, but Kara was violently shaking her head.

"No, no! You can't. Don't leave me!" Frantic, Kara clawed wildly at her sister. Why was Marlie doing this? Why? At seven, she didn't understand why she was being left. Alone. Here in this dark, horrid attic that smelled like mold and was covered in dust and probably home to spiders and rats and wasps and every other gross thing in the world. "I'm not staying up here alone, Mar—"

"Shh. Keep quiet!" Marlie's hands tightened over Kara's forearms.

"Please—"

"Listen!" Marlie's voice was sharp. A whisper like the warning hiss of a snake.

She gave Kara a shake. Her fingers dug through the long sleeves of Kara's pajamas.

"Ow!"

"Don't say a word, Kara-Bear. Keep quiet. You hear me? I'm serious."

"But you can't leave me here." Not in this cold, drafty space situated under the eaves of the cabin's peaked roof. "I'll freeze!"

"You won't."

This wasn't right. Kara might be almost eight years old, but she knew this was wrong. All wrong. "You're lying!"

Marlie gripped her forearm so hard Kara dropped the flashlight and it rolled down the steps. Marlie's fingernails dug through Kara's pajamas and pinched her flesh. "Damn it," she swore. "For once, Kara, just do as you're told." And then she was gone, nearly tripping over the flashlight as she fled down the stairs.

Kara took off after her but was a step behind and Marlie reached the door first, slid through and shut it.

Click.

Kara grabbed the door handle, but it wouldn't move.

Locked? The door is locked? Marlie has locked me in?

Fury and fear burned through her as she heard Marlie's swift footsteps as she hurried away.

No, no, no! "Marlie!" She rattled the door handle and pounded on the door, then as her rage eased a bit, thought better of it. This was no prank. Something was wrong. Seriously wrong. Something . . . evil. She swallowed back her fear and brushed aside the angry tears that had formed in her eyes. Her arms ached in the spots where her sister's fingers had clenched.

She wanted to scream, to yell, to beat her fists against the door so that someone would hear her, so that she could escape this sloped-ceilinged jail and breathe again.

But she didn't. Marlie's words, whispered like the sound of death, ran through her head. *I just want to make us safe . . .*

Shivering, she bit her lip and stared at the door, a dark barrier to the rest of the world. She couldn't just sit here and wait.

What if the whoever it was Marlie thought had come into the house came up the stairs and found her?

What if he hurt Marlie? What if he *killed* her? Kara's heart wrenched.

Again she wished for her mother and father. They would know what to do. But they were gone, according to Marlie, and she wouldn't lie. Not about that.

Or would she?

Teeth chattering, heart knocking erratically, Kara grabbed the flashlight and stared at the door, shivering and trying to hear something, anything over the wild beating of her heart. Her skin crawled.

She sat on the lowest step, clicking the tiny flashlight on, then off, watching its yellowish beam illuminate the back of the door for a second before she was swallowed in darkness again.

On.

Off.

On.

Click, click, click.

The light growing fainter each time she turned the flashlight on.

She couldn't just sit here and wait while the batteries in the flashlight died. What if Marlie never came back?

Kara wanted to rattle the door handle frantically, to scream and flail at the door. She reached for the handle again, her fingers curling over the cold lever. But she stopped herself. It would do no good. And probably cause unwanted attention. No, she had to be smart. She had to find another way to escape.

Determined, she climbed up the rickety steps again to the attic, where a single round window mounted high above and the faint moonlight cast the dimmest of light through the dusty, forgotten boxes piled everywhere, The boxes and crates were marked with words scribbled on them, some of them Kara could read: Books. Clothes. Office. Or marked with names: Sam Jr. Jonas. Donner. Marlie. Her sister and brothers. No box for her, the youngest, the only child of both mother and father. Not yet. She heard the rustle of something, something *alive* in the far corner. Tiny claws on the wood floor. A squirrel? Or a mouse . . . or a rat?

She shivered and was sorting through the box again when she heard it—a horrid, bloodcurdling scream rising up from a lower floor.

"AAAAHHHHHGGG!"

Kara jumped. Nearly peed herself. She sucked in her breath as the horrid wail echoed through the house.

What was that? *Who* was that?

Marlie?

Mama?

Or someone else?

Thud!

The house shook.

Something really big had fallen.

Kara's mouth turned to dust and she blinked against tears.

Was it a body?

Someone hurt and screaming, then falling?

Marlie?

"Mama," she mouthed around a sob.

Don't be a baby.

Pulse pounding, fear nearly paralyzing her, she forced herself to sweep the flashlight's thin beam over the boxes again and spied the one marked *Office*. It was closed, cardboard flaps folded but gaping. She shone the light inside and saw yellowed papers, an old stapler, envelopes, a tape dispenser and a pair of dusty scissors. She picked up the scissors and a paper clip that held some papers together, then silently made her way down the stairs to the door.

As she'd seen Jonas do at the locked bathroom door when she'd been spying on him, she took the paper clip, straightened it as best she could, and slid it into the small hole beneath the lever. She'd tried it once before on Sam Junior and Donner's room and it had worked and now . . . she wiggled the tiny wire, working it inside the lock as she strained to hear any other noise coming from the other side of the door.

Come on, come on, she silently said to herself, pulling the wire out once before sliding it back through the hole and twisting gently . . . feeling it move. With a soft *click* the lock gave way and fighting back her fear, she took a deep breath, held her scissors in one hand, and pushed the door open.

Visit us online at
KensingtonBooks.com
to read more from your favorite authors,
see books by series, view reading
group guides, and more!

Visit us online for sneak peeks, exclusive
giveaways, special discounts, author content,
and engaging discussions with your fellow readers.

Betweenthechapters.net

Sign up for our newsletters and be the first
to get exciting news and announcements about
your favorite authors!
Kensingtonbooks.com/newsletter